D1789375

AMALTHEAN QUESTS

ONE

JERI DION

STOCKWELL
PUBLISHERS SINCE 1898

First published in 2016
This edition published in 2022 by
A.H. Stockwell Ltd.
West Wing Studios, Unit 166
The Mall, Luton
ahstockwell.co.uk

Copyright © 2016, 2022 Jeri Dion

The right of Jeri Dion to be identified as the author
of this work has been asserted in accordance with
the Copyright, Designs and Patents Act 1988.

All rights reserved. No part of this publication may be
reproduced, stored in a retrieval system, or transmitted,
in any form or by any means without the prior written
permission of the publisher, nor be otherwise circulated in
any form of binding or cover other than that in which it is
published and without a similar condition being imposed on
the subsequent purchaser. Any person who does so may be
liable to criminal prosecution and civil claims for damages.

British Library Cataloguing-in-Publication Data: A catalogue
record for this book is available from the British Library.
ISBN 9780722352106

All characters appearing in this work are
fictitious. Any resemblance to real persons,
living or dead, is purely coincidental.

*Thanks to everyone who encouraged me
to go on and create this novel. Past and
present you know who you are.*

Contents

The Universe of Amalthean Quests

Units

1 Milon = 3 miles in distance

Milon is pronounced mile-on

Names and Their Meanings

Hourons [pronounced Hour-on]	1 Houron = 70 Minons
Minons [pronounced Min-on]	1 Minon = 70 Cencrons
Cencrons [pronounced Cen-crons]	Equivalent to our second
Dayon [pronounced Day-on]	1 Dayon = 25 Hourons
Weekon [pronounced Week-on]	1 Weekon = 8 Dayons
Tomorron [pronounced Tomorr-on]	Means next day
Mornet [pronounced Mor-net]	Mmeans morning

Level steps are the steps between Levels/decks

Drinks and Beverages

Plicetar = Water

Coffeen = Coffee

Vardox = Vodka with a strong alcohol content. Refreshing and enjoyable at bars, often drunk by criminals and pirates.

Stavern = Champagne-like drink which can be quite intoxicating.

Glassene – Glass (this has varied uses in a number of ways; one is for holding drinks.

Amalthea One Layout

Front Decks: Level One

Organisation Deck
Meeting Centre
Resources Centre
Slazer Emergency Cabinet
Cruiser Emergency Hatch (10 Crew Life Pods stored here)

Front Decks: Level Two

Life Deck
Life Ability Centre
Medical Ability Room
Laser Healing Unit
Isolation
Docking Bay Doors
Medical Supplies Stores
Vacant treatment Room

Front Decks: Level Three

Science & Agricultural Deck
Lab Gardens and Specimen Unit
Experimental Science Room
Saplings bringing on room (for seeds and plants)
Computer Study Centre

Front Decks: Level Four

Travelsport Centre / Transpot
Quarters for the Team Members on this level

Front Decks: Level Five

Combat & Training Practice Centre
Armed Combat Practice Centre
Robot and Technical Section
Gym and Sauna Rooms
Shower rooms
Recreational Rooms
Vacant Rooms (2)

Rear Decks: Level One

Escape Pods

Rear Decks: Level Two

Leisure Centre
Slazer Supply Stores
Stores for Blue Midges spare Components.
Male WC and Sanitary Room
Vacant Room

Rear Decks: Level Three

Flight Hanger Bay
Flight Maintenance Unit
Suiting Up Room
Cleansing Room
Decontamination Centre
Confinement Rooms

Rear Decks: Level Four

Engineering Deck
Engine Room
Electronics Centre
Engine Access Shaft
Main Weaponry Centre
Ladies WC and Sanitary Room

Rear Decks: Level Five

Interrogation Centre
Freight Hold
Main Food Supply stores

Amalthean Team Members

Tayce Traun
COLONEL TO THE TEAM
Daughter to Lydia

Tom Stavard
LIEUTENANT COLONEL
(Husband to Tayce, Brother to Treketa)

Marc Dayatso
COMPUTER ANALYSING TECHNICAL OFFICER
(True Rank Commander)

Treketa Stavard
NURSE
(Sister to Tom)

Lance Largon
QUEST RESEARCH & INFORMATION OFFICER
(Son of Jonathan Largon)

Duncan Leyres
NAVIGATIONALIST & CO-RELEASE PILOT

Midge
CRUISERS GUIDANCE AND MAIN OPERATION COMPUTER

Cargo
TOMS DRONE & ESCORT
(from his ship)

Donaldo Tysonne
MEDICAL OFFICER

Dean Addams
CAPTAIN OF DELTALINE 4

Questa Base Personnel

General Jonathan Largon
GENERAL IN CHARGE OF QUESTA
HEAD OF THE COUNCIL
(Father to Lance)

Lydia Traun
ASSISTANT TO JONATHAN LARGON AND COUNCILLOR
(Mother to Tayce)

Jan Barnford
SECURITY PATROL OFFICER
INVESTIGATION DIVISION

Adam Burnford
RESCUE MISSION PILOT
(from the Research Colony, where he was an Officer)

Craig Glenn
SECURITY MISSIONS OFFICER

Dr Paclan Sellecson
CHIEF DOCTOR & MEDICAL SURGEON
THE INTERGALACTIC MEDICAL COLONY
(Tayces Doctor)

Aidan Lord
GENERALS ASSISTANT
LYDIAS FIRST OFFICER
QUESTA

Empress Tricara
EX INHABITANT OF TRISTARCUS
HOLDER OF THE BLUE TELEPATHIAN CRYSTAL
COUNCIL MEMBER AT QUESTA
(Friend of Tayce and her Mother)

Cordec Parglen
CHIEF DESIGNER & ENGINEER
(of the Pollomoss Weapon)

Adam Carford
GENERALS FIRST ASSISTANT
QUESTA

Enemies

Countess Vargon
Enemy to all she destroyed

Sallen Vargon
Countesses Evil Daughter

Lord Dion
Notorious Leader of the Boglayon Tribe

Karcman
Sallen's guard from KARCLAX

Norgan
EVIL POWER SORCERER

The Arkarans
A GALACTIC RACE

Vargons Outlaws
CRIMINAL RACE
(Joined the Countess and her daughter Sallen to fight against Tayce)

Robanea
CONMAN & CRIMINAL

Paydargon & Seven Assisting Criminals

Planetary Information

Questa
Headquarters Base
Serving Earthon 2 and Spatial Travellers.
Constructed by Man Power and Machine.
Population 2,205 Men, Women and Children.
Diameter of Base 400,000km.

Micacer
Research,Search and Rescue Colony.
3000 milons across in diameter.
It has an Earthon 2 type breathable atmosphere.
It caters for every aspect of Research.
It also caters for all search and Rescue Operations.
Population + Personnel
Roughly 360.

Intergalactic Medical Colony

Caters for all Intergalactic Medical Emergencies.
Diameter of Colony.
Seven Square milons.
Personnel 860.

Intergalactic Criminal Court Colony

Most Intergalactic Criminal Court Cases are held here.
Constructed by Man Power and Machine.
Diameter of Colony five milons.
Law and Court Personnel 400.
Supported atmosphere environment.

Vargons Lair

Home to the Evil Countess.
Diameter 1 milon
Once a dead Asteroid

Greymaren Space Station

Originated Earthon 2 Questa Linked.
Purpose – Space Exploration.
Constructed by Man Power and Machine.
Crew Personnel 460.
Diameter four milons.
The station has a supported atmosphere environment.

Maldigri

A paradise world environment.
Weather conditions-Tropical .
Diameter 4000 milons across.
Atmosphere-Breathable.
Uninhabited

Tristarcus

Home to Empress Tricara.
Planetary diameter 4,900 milons across.
Population 8,000.
There is a city built on its surface.
Atmosphere-breathable.

Genuslan 2

The Countesses new hideout.

Atmosphere, breathable and tropical with hazardous conditions

Diameter roughly 1.519 across the surface.

Population-Countess Vargon, Sallen Vargon and 1 Vargon Warrior Army.

Trinot

Colony/World

Constructed by Man Power and Machine.

Population-5680 Personnel

Operating in the field of Hospitality .

It is roughly the same size in Diameter as Neptune.

AMALTHEAN QUESTS

ONE

Beginnings

Space could be a lonely and hostile place at the best of times. But especially if you were a lone female twenty-four yearons old and your only companion was the cruisers guidance and main operations computer, that was there to just protect you in any oncoming life threatening situation.

At the age of nineteen it had all started for Tayce Traun. Drastically, one night her home world, 'TRAUN' was plunged into a war that had been building for sometime. The peaceful existence of the 17,000 men, women and children of all ages, who lived their every dayon lives unaware they were going to be drawn into such a situation, began. It was a war of possession to the death. Life as a privileged Commodores daughter, was over. Suddenly she faced turmoil and shear dread.

Two yearons of unexpected galactic war passed and most of Traun had been destroyed. By this time Tayce had reached the age of twenty-one. Her parents had called for a private audience in their living quarters below ground. They informed her, they were secretly having an intergalactic cruiser constructed for her safe escape of their surroundings as Traun looked like it was near it's end. She would be classed as the sole survivor of Traun should she be the only one to escape the final moments of their world. Tayce was devastated at the news and felt like breaking down, but she knew she had to pretend to be brave, it had been instilled in her in her growing yearons to do so. Over the coming monthons it was vastly becoming obvious, that everyone of the home world was going to die in the agonising unsuspecting continuous bombardment, from the evil side in the war. Some had perished already. Two monthons after the cruiser called AMALTHEA ONE was completed, by coincidence the possessors in question trying to get their hands on the paradise beautiful world it once was, the evil Vargon Warriors, made their final devastating ambush of weapon fire at Traun. Buildings, parks, homes and many other special places to the Traunian inhabitants that were left after the previous attacks, took hit after hit and were destroyed in the mass of firepower.

1

The Vargon Warriors struck their final blow in the dead of night, sending the whole planet into total and utter chaos. People died in their bunks, some being burnt alive unable to escape the sudden attack. Tayce had less than an houron to make it to the Amalthea One, so that she could safely leave what was left of her home. She was dragged away under guard from her Mother and Father's mansion. The last she saw of her parents was in the falling debris of what was once the most beautifully designed structure on Traun. Marc Dayatso, Tayces Father's personal aide and Commander, had the final job of making sure Tayce made it safely to the cruiser. He was a tall strong looking man and could more than hold on to Tayce in ducking and diving their way through the turmoil of the falling debris, fires and dying inhabitants, around them. Upon arrival at the cruisers entrance Tayce tearfully begged Marc to go with her, as they had always been like a brother and sister to each other. But Marc ignored her pleas and pushed her aboard, he had his orders. She turned rushing back to give him a strong farewell hug, thanking him for everything, then ordered him to head for the nearest escape craft. Marc nodded in agreement, but he had obligations to the Commodore, Tayces Father, and once she was safe that was where he was heading back to. Marc raised his wrist communication device and ordered Midge, the cruisers main operations and guidance computer, once Tayce was inside the docking bay doors. To seal the cruiser and leave. Midge could be heard in his childlike male voice above the explosive din and humanoid cries, acknowledging. Marc stepped back and turned to walk away. He paused for a moment to turn and see the Amalthea One lift up off the surface of the bunker floor and head out into deep space. Once clear of the bunker the cruiser went into protection mode and took off into the deep depths of the Universe like a Slazer shot from a gun. Once Amalthea One was clear of what was left of Traun, Midge allowed Tayce to see what was left of the home world, that was once a place to call home. Tayce fought back the tears of anger and hurt at seeing the burning mass, that was once her birthplace, declaring that one dayon she would seek out the Vargon Warriors and the evil Countess and destroy them in a cruel agonizing death, the same way her people died.

In the dayons that passed after Traun was left behind Tayce grew familiar with her new surroundings. Amalthea One. Midge showed her what he was capable of, and the fact that she was on board an exploration cruiser. Also what their surroundings were capable of, the speed of Hyper thrust turbo. This was the equivalent of Mach 3. It was powered by nuclear fission quick reaction engines (four in all), she was a match for anyone or anything that strayed into her path. Amalthea One was not only all speed and protection she was more and one of a kind, she was graceful in flight and shaped like the letter 'A' from point to tip, bow to stern. Her capacity was a crew of ten, plus three on board guests if need be. Main operations of the cruiser and many of the weaponry and guidance functions, were care of Midge being main operations and guidance computer.

He had been designed by Marc Dayatso with a childlike male voice, with Tayces total welfare in mind. His childlike voice enabled him to communicate with Tayce on a humanoid level. He had also been given a very high IQ enabling him to take on the many on board functions and decisions, without the command of his new mistress, if she was unable to perform what was needed to protect the cruiser at short notice.

Three Yearons Later the Present Time

Traun's destruction was behind Tayce and she'd begun to live the life of an independent young female alone in the stars and perilous Universe. Midge had become like a second member of her crew and her only best friend. Together they had shared a lot of tricky moments, like buddies in times of turmoil. The space time was 00:800 hourons, mornet of yet another new dayon, travelling the stars. Down in Tayce's quarters, she lay asleep in her sumptuous designed bunk, luxurious quality was something standard aboard the Cruiser. Midge sounded the Repose Centre alarm to signal time to get up as he did every mornet since they'd left Traun. Three short soothing notes of tone sounded. Tayce woke stretching. She brushed her blonde hair from her face and slowly opened her eyes. They were a sapphire shade of blue.

"Mornet mistress, how are you feeling todayon?" enquired Midge trying to sound caring in his own way.

"Fine Midge, just give me an houron and I'll be in Organisation, we can go through what's been happening during the night hourons in our current orbit and anything that you think we need to take care of todayon," suggested Tayce sounding the true independent woman in charge that she'd become.

"Very well, I'll have it ready for you when you arrive mistress," he replied.

"Oh by the way Midge I've decided, that from now on you can call me Tayce, we've been together for the best part of three yearons and I'm fed up with being called mistress, even though it is polite to be addressed as such, you can call me Tayce, are you fine with this decision?" asked Tayce.

"Absolutely Tayce," replied Midge eagerly.

Tayce slid from the Repose Centre Bunk and headed across to the Cleansing Unit, for the first refreshing cleanse of the dayon. Her quarters were of a comfortable size and split into three sections, a living area, a repose centre and a cleansing unit. Furnishings in the quarters gave the impression of light, airiness and quality. In the living area there was a soft grey coloured soffette and two mouldable comfortable easy chairs. There was an occasional table and various other pieces of soft furnishing, scattered around to make the area comfortable away from duty. The floor was covered with heat reflective cushion carpetron tiles, in a navy blue. The lighting for the quarters was of natural level, which emitted from square tubes in the walls here and there. Which had high and low settings, depending on what the person required at the time.

A while later Tayce now cleansed and changed, elegantly walked out into the living area. She was of average height and slim build. She checked her appearance of her make-up in the Imager. She then picked up her Hairbrush and ran it through her straight shoulder length, blonde Hair. Once satisfied, she walked from the living area of the quarters. The doors opening and closing behind her. Once out in the corridor she began on the way to Organisation, to begin another dayons duty as Colonel of Amalthea One. A rank that her Father had left for her, in a computerized briefing the night she arrived on board.

Organisation Deck was situated at the top level of Amalthea, to the front of the cruiser. Here everything was organised, literally, from navigation to weaponry and deck by deck functions, throughout the cruiser. The deck was 450 metres in length, by 350 metres wide and lined from floor to almost ceiling with 245 metres of computers consoles, VDU screens and chairs of chrome and black Leatherex, for a hoped future team one dayon. The front of the Amaltheas Organisation Deck, had a large wide sight port, where the main Cruisers Universal Scanners were situated underneath. The biggest computer which filled one corner of the deck, was Midge. He covered an area of two metres, which included the large triangular blue screen and console, plus components underneath. Tayce felt the space filled by Midge was well worth it, as he had pulled her away from quite a few near misses, during the past three yearons, they'd been together. Also without him she would not be able to operate and guide the cruiser, throughout the Universe, she'd just drift. There were two main seats towards the front of Organisation, this was Tayces Command Chair and the Co-pilot seat. They were navy blue in colour and designed for comfort and for long flight duration. High back and shaped to support the spine, matching in with the rest of the modern design, which made Organisation a first class command deck. As Tayce entered, a sequence of small square red and blue lights flashed on the main console. This signified that Midge was handing over command to her. She walked across Organisation Deck and dropped herself into the seat next to the empty Co-pilot seat. She gathered her thoughts of what she was going to do for a minon trying to shake off the feeling of another lonely dayon ahead, before continuing. Midge picked up on her train of thoughts, and understood that she was still feeling the loss of her home and parents after all this time, it wasn't easy and it always hit her in the mornet.

"Are you feeling all right Tayce?" asked Midge casually breaking her thoughts and fixed expression.

"I'm fine honest, have you sorted anything out for us to look at todayon, what, happened as I slept, I should be made aware of out in the Universe last night?" said Tayce in questionable tone.

"Yes sorting as you ask, there will be a slight delay, as I sift through last nights occurrences and prioritise the most important issues," replied Midge.

"In the meantime open main sight port, lets see what's happening now," suggested Tayce wondering what the dayon would bring to their attention.

The main sight port in front of her opened it's outer force field shutters, turning the dark blue into a full blown spacial scape and a clear present one, at that, but was it truly clear? Just as Tayce settled back Midge informed her that there was a damaged craft drifting four milons ahead, it looked like it had been pounded from all sides by weapon fire of extreme magnitude, judging by the scorch marks on it's outer hull.

"Scan immediately for any signs of life, humanoid preferably," ordered Tayce watching the distant craft.

She was concerned at the fact if any decent traveller had been caught in this present perilous sector, they would be lucky to escape with their life. It was a sector notorious for pirates, as she herself found out a couple of dayons previous when she and Midge had managed to fight off a merry band, who quite fancied the look of Amalthea One. Tayce waited thinking of the best route to take, if life was found on the damaged craft. Midge soon returned from the scan and informed her there was one humanoid life form aboard. A male, roughly in his late 30's early 40's and he would need medical attention, judging by the readings he was presently receiving.

"Midge check if it's an elaborate pirate trap, or hostile, if not place Tractor Beam on and prepare to bring it aboard, land it safely in the Hanger Bay and activate the Life Ability Centre on Level 2," ordered Tayce in true tone of command.

Tayce upon Midge acknowledging stood to her feet and for a moment, stood watching the small bulbous looking craft being pulled towards Amalthea via Tractor Beam. She then continued across Organisation to the entrance in thought of who might be aboard. Upon reaching the entrance Tayce glanced back across Organisation, then continued on out, walking down the corridor, heading down to the Flight Hanger Bay on Level 3, rear of the cruiser. On the walk there she would get changed into a medical protection flight designed suit, from the Medical Stores.

The Flight Hanger Bay

Soon the small white scorched and red bulbous looking craft came within the Flight Bay open Hanger Bay doors. Midge brought it through various decontamination procedures to rid it of any harmful radiation and infectious space particles. Once through, via a beam of yellow energy, he placed the craft on a clear area away from the on board Shuttle/fighters. Here it remained in a silent and scorched state. Tayce soon entered carrying a Medical Emergency Kit.

Amaltheas Hanger Bay wasn't massive in size just average enough to withhold a fleet of fifteen Quest Shuttle/fighters ready for the hoped crew that would one day join Tayce.

"Is decontamination procedure completed Midge, do I have an all clear?" asked Tayce pausing, studying the craft.

"All clear is given," announced Midge confidently.

Tayce proceeded approaching the scorched entrance hatch. She paused and took a sonic pencil shaped de-locking device from her uniform pocket, which would search the right combination when aimed at the lock. Tayce aimed the device and in a few cencrons the entrance hatch gave. There seemed to be a click sound, followed by three blips, then the sound of compressed air as the hatch began to open. As the hatch slid back so Tayce stepped back raising her Slazer weapon, just in case there was any nasty surprises ready to spring out at her. Nothing! She walked up the three steps of the craft and entered the red emergency dimly lit atmosphere looking all the time for the injured humanoid. She ventured on into the pilot section that seemed large enough to withhold two people.

"Oh my God!" came Tayces sudden spoken words.

She was shocked to see that there were in fact two people in this crew, and Midge had not informed her of such. Whoever this was, she was female and extremely beautiful. Tayce wasted no time, she took the Heart and Pulse Counter out of the Medical Emergency Kit and placed it on the young females slim slightly tanned wrist. She waited in anticipation, but didn't hold out much hope, the young female was injured beyond recognition, she would be extremely lucky to have survived whatever had befallen her and Tayce could only think this craft had been the unlucky victims of pirates, of the worst kind. Tayces delicate blue sapphire eyes showed concern as she waited for the reading. The signal blipped. She removed it, and read the display much to her assumption that she had been right. The young female in her mid 20's had not been fortunate to survive the onslaught, and she felt sorry for the male beside her who was obviously her crew companion. It had Tayce wondering even though she felt she shouldn't jump to conclusion. Was this a couple, that had been caught stealing? She quickly stopped this thought rushing through her head, and considered the fact maybe this couple were in fact legally intimately joined, as the female wore a gold band on her joining finger as did the male. She moved onto the male pilot, as there was nothing she could do for the female. He was extremely handsome, despite his cuts and bruises, she thought. As she placed the Heart and Pulse Counter on his wrist waiting with hoped anticipation that he was alive. Tayce studied his handsome features, thinking he had the kind of look that would send any females heart racing. He had a brown Moustache and a well groomed one too. His hair was brown and slightly curly, swept away from his forehead to the nape of his neck. She wondered what this pilot did, what rank he held, and what was his name. Somehow he intrigued her. The counter gave a good signal and she removed it, studying the reading. He was alive, but unconscious, she had to go to work and save him, fast!

"Midge Travelsport this male to the Life Ability Centre and place him under emergency survival procedures, also place force field restraints on him, that's an order, now Midge, we have to save him," ordered Tayce in tone of urgency.

"Yes Tayce, facilities in the Life Ability Centre are activating as you request," informed Midge.

"Also there's a second person in here, she's female, she didn't survive the onslaught we need to arrange a space burial," informed Tayce, as she turned to head back to the entrance.

Turning for a moment she watched as the male pilot was Travelsported to the Life Ability Centre. She saw something fall from his uniform jacket and noticed it was a Wallet of some sort. Crossing back, she bent and picked it up, then continued on out of the craft, wondering what it contained. Once outside she looked over at the craft once more then walked away up to the Life Ability Centre. On route Tayce opened the small turquoise coloured wallet taking out the ID. Studying it, she saw in the top right corner, a colour image of the pilot. Reading down she found a name Tom Barry Stavard and a rank, Ace One Fighter Pilot, Age thirty-nine. Then it went on to his personal appearance. Most, she'd seen, but eye colour green, she hadn't. She glanced at the other side of the Wallet, there was a silver Disc Chip tucked inside. Later, she thought. Mr Stavard was her first priority and getting him back on his feet. She would study the details on the disc later.

The Life Ability Centre

Tom Stavard lay on the Exam Bunk, restrained by force field restraints. Tayce did not want him waking and deciding to walk around her cruiser if he felt he could, even though he was in no fit state to do so. Midge was watching him and monitoring him from overhead. Tom was a broad tall man, strong in build but his physique conveyed he looked after himself. Tayce soon entered the Life Ability Centre. She crossed to Tom, ordering Midge to begin scan for injuries. Midge did as requested. An orange band of pure energy surrounded Tom's head and slowly worked it's way down his body to his feet. Tayce thought to herself, it was times like this she was glad her parents and Marc Dayatso forced her to study for a yearon in space medicine. At this moment in time she was glad she did. Midge paused, once finished.

"Scan completed," announced Midge.

"Outcome and diagnosis please?" requested Tayce studying Tom.

"Apart from a few cuts and bruises and some fatigue Mr Stavard will return to normal health, in two dayons," replied Midge informatively.

"Very well, I will give him a pain easing sedative, and leave him in the restraints to rest," said Tayce.

She moved over to the trolley on the far side of the roomy sized Life Ability Centre, where she took an Inject Pen and pushed home a vile containing a pain relieving sedative. Crossing back, she leaned over the thought unconscious body of Tom. Suddenly without warning, Tom's right hand shot up and tightly grabbed Tayce around the throat. She struggled in the sudden onslaught of attack and dropped the Inject Pen on the floor. She fought hard to break free in the struggle of Tom's persisting grasp.

"Midge do something," gasped Tayce feeling the life drain out of her.

"Mr Stavard release my mistress, or I will be forced to use means to stop you this instance," warned Midge.

"How do I know you aren't going to kill me, that your not some female pirate, tell me, what were you going to give me, something to finish me off?" he demanded angry and mistrusting, he'd been through to much already, he was prepared to fight to the end if he had to.

"If you release me Mr Stavard, I will explain otherwise I will give Midge the word and you'll be in a lot more pain than you already are at present," warned Tayce, she didn't like this situation at all.

Tayce continued to tug at Tom's arm with both hands. He studied her coldly for a minon as if summoning her up, wondering whether to believe her or not. From above Midge fired a thin pencil shock beam at Tom's hand. He'd seen enough of his mistress suffering in this beings hands. The beam hit home and Tom yelled and let his grip loosen, releasing his hand from Tayces delicate neck. She stood and backed away rubbing her neck, trying to regain her composure and normal breathing.

"Is this the way you thank people who save your life Mr Stavard, I'm not impressed," began Tayce giving him a mistrusting look.

"How do I know, that you weren't a female pirate out to finish me off, with whatever you had in that thing you were about to use, I've been through hell travelling through this sector so far, what makes you think I could look at you any different than what I've been through already?" he retorted.

"If I was a pirate you wouldn't be here, you would be destroyed," retorted Tayce angrily.

Tom turned his head to study her. She didn't fit the criteria for some of the pirates, he'd been up against so far he had to admit nor did she fit the shape for one either, she was quite breathtakingly attractive, he thought. Slim curves in all the right places, but well proportioned, almost like a galactic beauty pageant contestant. She'd probably win, he thought. Maybe he'd just made the wrong move.

"Keep an eye on Mr Stavard, Midge," announced Tayce heading over to the entrance.

With that she walked from the Life Ability Centre leaving Midge to begin treatment with operating the many functions, that contributed to healing Tom's cuts and bruises. As long silver arms began to move around Tom, with points attached, he began to feel very uncomfortable, panicked even, wishing that he had allowed Tayce to treat him. Midge picked up on this and assured him there was nothing to fear and that he should lie perfectly still. Tom did as requested. But the feeling of nervousness did not ease.

A while later Tayce was back in Organisation. She sat thinking about Tom's actions towards her. Her neck still felt sore. But in a way she didn't blame him, in the way he had reacted, she guessed she would have done the same, if the roles had been reversed. Midge broke her silence of thought.

"Are you all right Tayce, is your neck all right?" he enquired in soft tone.

"Yes it will be okay, thanks for your help earlier," she replied rubbing it.

"Mr Stavard is resting in restraints, I have treated his injuries."

"He can stay there until I decide otherwise," ordered Tayce coldly.

"I took over his treatment for you as I could sense that you did not want to treat him after what happened and it was quite understandable," he said understanding.

"Can you blame me, I felt our on board guest would learn that not everyone was pirate trash and that is why I let you give him the cold hearted treatment, he wasn't worthy of my gentle touch," replied Tayce plainly.

Midge picked up the fact Tayce was not going to suffer Tom's behaviour gladly and he could understand where she was coming from. He said no more on the matter. Tayce studied the turquoise Wallet that she'd found aboard the craft. She removed the Disc Chip and studied it.

"What have you got there?" asked Midge scanning the Disc Chip in her hand.

"It's a Disc Chip I found it in Tom's Wallet, which I found aboard his craft," replied Tayce.

"Put it in the Chip Reader, lets have a look and see what makes Mr Stavard tick, I don't believe he is as bad, as he makes out, I deter that it's what he's been through lately, that made him react the way he did to you, after all three dayons ago, we ourselves encountered pirates who liked this cruiser, remember," pointed out Midge in a reminding tone.

"Okay point taken," replied Tayce.

She opened the small clear perspexon flap, then slid the Disc Chip into it's slot. Pressed a key. The flap closed, at the same time drawing the Disc in slowly ready to scan the information and transfer it to Small Vid Screen. The Vid Screen came to life and Tom's figure filled it, he began by saying if whoever was playing back this information, then he was either dead, or alive, and badly injured. Tayce thought to herself, Midge had been right, this was a man that was like any other

9

normal man, despite his earlier behaviour in time she could come to trust him. She relaxed back watching and listening on. Tom came from Earthon 2, a place called Americal (America). Midge picked out certain pieces of important facts and stored them away in his memory, for a later date retrieval. The Disc Chip stated to Tayce and Midge how good Tom was in certain aspects of space flight. Then it came to the female that had been in the craft beside Tom. He announced her as his wife 'Alenea' Tayce began to feel sorry for Tom, he was now in the same situation as she was, losing someone he cared for. For a moment her mind drifted back the three yearons, to that fateful night on Traun and wondering if Marc Dayatso had made it off their crumbling world, or even her parents? Midge brought her back to the present, as the Disc Chip concluded, he suggested she should go down to the craft and get all the useful information, that maybe helpful for storage and help Mr Stavard when he was back to normal health.

"Like what?" asked Tayce unsure what to collect.

"Star Charts, Disc Chips etc. anything that could be useful to us," he replied.

"But Tom might not be staying Midge and I feel like I'm prying," she replied casually.

"Believe me Tayce his craft is in no fit state for him to leave, for the foreseeable future, his engines are out of sync and many of his crafts components are fried, due to the assault," explained Midge.

"But there's a dead female on board, it's eerie, I'd feel she would be watching me rob her husband's craft," said Tayce far from easy at the fact.

"Leave it to me, I will Travelsport her body, to burial casket ready for the space burial, you're going to need the information that you may find and I can deal with Mr Stavard if I have to," said Midge.

Tayce stood up and walked away from her seat, she began across the Organisation Deck. Midge informed her that he would inform her of any change in Mr Stavard's condition on route. Tayce agreed. She walked on out, heading on the way back to the Flight Hanger Bay. On the way she would change back into her normal navy and white stripe Amalthean Uniform.

Once Tayce had changed back into her normal every dayon duty attire, she continued on down to the Cargo Section. Once there, she retrieved a holdall from the top storage space, she could just reach up, as she was only 1.65 metres high. Upon retrieving the holdall, she continued on along to the damaged craft.

In the Life Ability Centre Tom Stavard lay silently under restraints. Midge above monitored his heart and pulse rate, everything was returning to normality, Midge ran a new scan of Tom's healing injuries. Everything was going according to what it should be for returning to normal human body status of a normal male. Tom's eyes flickered open. He focussed on his sterile surroundings. It came back to him, where he was and how he had come to be there.

"Welcome back Mr Stavard, I'm Midge, the main computer for this cruiser, how are you feeling?" enquired Midge in a soothing tone.

"Where is this place, where's she gone?" asked Tom referring to Tayce.

"By she! I assume you mean Colonel Traun, she will be here soon enough, you are on Amalthea One, an exploration cruiser, you have nothing to fear Mr Stavard, we are peaceful here, travelling the stars in an exploration capacity," informed Midge.

"Is she always that hostile to people she rescues?" asked Tom casually.

"Not generally, but you did assault my mistress," expressed Midge.

Tom said no more, but awaited the arrival of Tayce. He reflected on his actions, as he lay where he was, maybe he had been wrong to react the way he had, but he bet she'd do the same, if the tables were reversed.

Tayce was alerted in Tom Stavards craft by Midge on Tom's current condition. She'd just finished retrieving Tom's close possessions, like small mementos, besides journals, records and other things that would be useful. She quickly walked back towards the entrance stepping back out into the light of the Hanger Bay clasping up the strip on the holdall. She headed across the Hanger Bay, going on out up to the Life Ability Centre. As she went, so she kept in mind, the last encounter with Tom, if he tried anything again this time she may think twice about keeping him on board altogether.

The doors to the Life Ability Centre opened. Tayce briskly entered, but stood her distance away from Tom. He glanced over at her, in an apologetic way.

"Colonel I apologise for my actions earlier towards you," he said half dazed.

"Apology accepted, though next time you should think twice before you strike out at a person, who saves your life, he or she may not be as understanding as I am," pointed out Tayce, she was not going to let Tom off the hook to soon.

"Where's my wife, where's Alenea?" he demanded looking around at the other bunks in the centre that were vacant.

"I'm afraid to tell you… your wife is… dead… she was when I examined her upon boarding your craft when we first brought you aboard," said Tayce in a gentle tone.

"Oh… are you the only crew on this vessel?" enquired Tom fighting back the tears of hurt for his wife.

"Yes for the moment, it's just Midge and me," she replied with a casual smile, she could see Tom's pain and understood where he was coming from at the loss of his partner.

"It must get pretty lonely out here on your own and dangerous too?" he asked showing some concern.

"I'm not out here by choice, I was cast away from my home in the middle of a war between the Vargon Warriors and my people, but I've got use to being alone, anyway I have Midge," expressed Tayce.

"Will you call me Tom, look, thank you for rescuing me, I guess I shouldn't of done what I did, sorry again," he said managing a handsome gentle smile to convey as much.

11

"Tom I will leave you to continue your recuperation, Midge you may remove the restraints, they are no longer needed," ordered Tayce feeling a lot more at ease where Tom was concerned.

"Restraints deactivated," replied Midge.

The restraints vanished. Tayce advised Tom to continue to rest, then left Midge to fill him in on what had been happening. She began back to the entrance, but paused, turning she informed Tom his craft was in no shape to travel anywhere in. It was damaged beyond repair, owing to the bombardment of weapon fire, obviously from the pirate attack. Tom didn't know what to say, he knew the situation had got out of hand out in the Universe, but he guessed he didn't really realise how bad. Tayce continued on out. Once outside she picked up the holdall with the contents inside and walked on back to Organisation. On the way she thought about the Disc Chips, that she'd found on Tom's craft and what they might contain. She would retrieve information that would be needed to compile a file on Tom and store anything else that may be needed for later retrieval. She would, then place the whole holdall in one of the quarters for Tom to find his personal belongings later to make his new quarters like home.

Three dayons lapsed. Amalthea One was now in another sector of the Universe. Tom Stavard was up on his feet and now in an Amalthean Quests uniform. Tayce had offered to do the honourable and decent thing in giving Alenea Stavard a space burial, so that Tom could say his proper goodbyes. The silver casket was set on runners to be jettisoned into the Universe. Tayce handed Tom a rose from the Lab Garden to place on the casket. It was red, aptly fitting for the occasion, Tom fought back the loving tears for Alenea, he had explained to Tayce they had only been officially linked to each other for two monthons. Tom placed the red rose on top of the casket, stood back and said a few silent words, then nodded to Tayce. She gave the command to Midge and the casket began down the runners of a blue light force field, until it reached the jettisonhatch. Tayce stood in silence waiting. The hatch opened. The casket headed on into space. Once Aleneas body had been sent into space, Tayce let Tom stand in thought for a few cencrons, then she took him on a guided tour of Amaltheas five decks and the various sections ending up back at what was to be his new quarters. Temporarily or permanent the choice was his. Here she left him to be alone and settle in. Returning to the Life Ability Centre, to clear away the various things that Midge had used to treat Tom. Half way there, her Wristlink bleeped. It was Midge, he informed her it was urgent, and she was to go to Organisation immediately. On this Tayce hurried to the Deck Travel. This was the lift between Levels. She entered as the doors opened, on approach. Once inside she selected the desired level, by depressing an inset maroon key. The Deck Travel began to ascend. It stopped abruptly, and all the lights went out. Lucky for Tayce she always carried with her, her Sonic Energy Pencil, so she was able to get out. She aimed it at the locking panel. A small thin beam emitted at the doors.

They moaned an electronic sound, then opened. Tayce found as the doors opened she was stuck half way off the level, she'd just left. But there was a gap big enough to climb out of. She quickly threw herself up and out into the corridor, landing face down on the deck floor. Standing to her feet in the dark, she began off. As she ran in the dark, she ran unknowing straight into Tom who was looking for her. They collided in full force.

"What the… Tayce is that you?" said Tom stepping back realising he'd probably winded her.

"Yes! We've got a circuit malfunction come on," she replied gaining her composure.

She raised her Wristlink as they began off and contacted Midge wondering if he was still operational. Much to her relief, he came back loud and clear. He informed her he was being drained of all energy by some strange force. It was affecting the cruisers on board power supply. Tayce ordered him to keep emergency power going for as long as he possibly could, in the meantime, to release any doors and functions that could be handed over to manual control. Midge agreed. Tayce and Tom were now sprinting and working their way to Level 1. They reached the Level Steps and halted for a minon, then ran up two at a time until they reached the desired level. Level 1. They soon ran into Organisation to see out the main sight port. Nothing! but dark space. So what was unusual about this thought Tayce? Midge addressed Tom instructing him which panel to remove and check behind, under his console, before finally crashing. Tom obeyed, getting down underneath. Removing the panel, he could see the system was straining by the minon. Just as Tom went to examine the component, sparks flew.

"Tom be careful, you've had one accident, I don't want to have to treat you again so soon, especially as Midge has crashed completely," said Tayce watching on.

"Don't panic, I know what I'm doing," he assured her.

"I hope you do, I don't want Midge inoperative forever, we'll be flying blind, come to think of it, we'll just drift," she said thinking the worst.

"Look will you relax! I studied ship wide electronics whilst in training, and in case you've forgot, I did own that heap that's in your Flight Hanger Bay," he replied.

"I wouldn't adopt that kind of attitude Tom, your still a guest on board this cruiser and I'm still in command and I can pull you out of there any time I want," she retorted not liking his smart aleck answer.

"Fine then you fix this problem," he said without further word, he turned his head looking up at her far from impressed she thought he couldn't do the job in hand.

"Your down there now, aren't you?" she replied knowing he'd won the point.

"Just let me get on with repairing this, and you can get under way," he replied coolly.

"Fine!" she replied having the last word, after all it was her cruiser.

She went to her seat at the front of Amalthea Ones Organisation. Sitting down she patiently waited while Tom repaired the problem in Midges functions. Eventually Tom gained emergency power, then informed Tayce she could continue on, whilst he continued to find the real problem and restore full operations mode. Just as soon as Midge came back online Tayce asked him for an update. Tom explained getting to his knees, that the repair would hold for a while, but they would have to look for a service and repair colony, or port. Tayce ordered Midge to chart a direct course to the nearest port or colony. He accepted his orders and began to commence the request. After a few cencrons, he came back to announce he had found a service and maintenance port in sector X5. Tayce suggested he head for it and the sooner the better. Tom climbed into the adjacent seat to Tayce. Midge once Tom was seated ordered him and Tayce to place seat restraints on, it was going to be a rough ride to cut time. They were going to travel at Hyper Thrust Turbo but because of his temporary repairs, it was not going to be the usual smooth journey it normally would be. Both Tayce and Tom did as asked preparing themselves for a rough ride ahead.

Amalthea One entered Hyper Thrust Turbo speed on it's journey to the Orge port which was were the maintenance port was situated. But it was a case of spasmodic travel. Even though the cruiser looked impressively sleek in design in a shade of white, with red line trim through the middle. She looked far from the splendid and impressive sight she normally was, as she spasmodically headed across the Universe to the destined port of call.

The speed of Amalthea One was from 186.000 milons a cencron (warp 1) to 3.360.000 a cencron which was Hyper Thrust Turbo. But with the quick reaction halting system, she could stop at a cencrons notice and all on board would not feel a thing. Amaltheas biggest problem was criminals at large. If they saw she was travelling in spasms across their path, they may feel the cruiser was easy pickings, for the taking. But what they didn't realise was, that even in her present state this cruiser was an equal match for them, in firepower. With Slazer Cannons placed throughout the cruiser, from bow to stern. Plus, she had energy disintegrating missiles that exploded on impact disintegrating the enemy. They emanated from the lower stern of the cruiser, dropping down and heading straight for the target.

Tom watched the horizon as they travelled. Tayce found, even with all the spasmodic travel, she drifted into a sudden sound sleep. Forty-eight straight hourons she'd been on duty, without a break. Tom asked Midge how long had Tayce been on duty, and was surprised by his answer. That she had not taken a break in all that time. Midge explained that most of those hourons had been taken looking after him. Tom shook his head, he had no idea she'd been that dedicated to her position. He looked at her, and smiled to himself, thinking she was one exceptional young woman. He was beginning to like her, admire her even, considering what she'd gone through alone in the Universe so far. He suggested maybe Tayce would be a lot more comfortable in her quarters, if he could steady the cruiser long enough for him to take her there for a rest. Midge agreed, he placed the Stabilizer System into operation for the time it would take Tom, to take Tayce down to her quarters and the Repose Centre. Tom on Midges word, undid both his and Tayces restraints. He lifted Tayce up and carried her across the Organisation Deck to the entrance. Walking on out down to Tayce's quarters. Midge while Tom was gone, took over control of the cruiser and continued across the last few milons of the journey towards the destined port of call. An Earthon 2 colony, especially for vessels needing repair and service.

Down in Tayce's quarters Tom gently placed her down on the Repose Centre bunk, then draped the thermal coverlet over her. She was totally unaware Tom was doing such a thing, because she was so exhausted. He smiled as she moaned and turned over, to carry on in her comfortable state, he also wondered how she would react, knowing he was in her quarters. She'd probably lose it with him. Tom studied her for a moment noticing how peaceful she looked, before he turned and walked on out to return to the Organisation Deck.

Upon his arrival back in Organisation, he briskly crossed back to Tayces seat, and sat down. Midge released control of the cruiser back to him in Tayces absence. Together they headed on across the last few milons to the to the service port for the new circuitry for Midges repairs, for his operations port.

"Tell me about Tayce, Midge," asked Tom waiting to hear, interested.

"I really shouldn't, but as it's you, I will divulge, she's a good person, always sees fair in most situations, I think she gets this from her Father, he was a good man and good teacher, he taught her a lot, but she will not be taken in by fools and time wasters," replied Midge in informing tone.

"How long has Tayce been out here?" continued Tom.

"Since the destruction of Traun our home world, when she lost her parents, and the people she loved, that was about three yearons ago now," continued Midge.

Tom continued asking questions, and Midge was quite happy to go on an answering as best he could. He was realising, as they communicated, there was more than a casual interest growing between his mistress and Tom Stavard. Time would tell whether there would be anything in it he thought. He hoped so.

Amalthea One came within a two milon orbit of Orge Midge began clearing communications for docking to repair the problem that had occurred. The head Flight Control Commander listened to the problem and soon granted the Amalthea permission to dock for a duration, to enable repairs. Tom asked Midge if the Travelsport system was operational? Midge went silent while checking. He confirmed it was operational. Tom informed him he was going over for the parts and to tell Tayce if she woke where he'd gone. Midge agreed. Tom walked from Organisation Deck, heading on down to the Travelsport Centre to journey across, via spot vaporization technique, removing him across to the port. Midge decided to watch Tom to make sure he was okay, the whole time from the cruisers scan.

Down in Tayce's quarters she was still in a deep peaceful sleep. Midge was monitoring her, as she slept, as he always did. As the time approached for the Repose Centre Alarm to sound, it had been five hourons since Tom had left. Midge had decided it was time to wake his mistress, as he was growing concerned. Tayce woke to the familiar soothing sound and stretched expecting to find herself still in the Control seat in Organisation Deck. As she focussed on her surrounding, she realised where she was and sat quickly bolt upright thinking and wondering what on earth had happened? How had she become where she was? Midge informed her he was concerned Tom had been gone five hourons, he'd promised he'd be back with new components, but as yet he hadn't returned. On this Tayce wasn't amused, how long did it take to get replacement parts? Also who did this Tom Stavard think he was taking her job and cruiser over. Once she had freshened up, she briskly began on the way up to Organisation Deck.

Tom returned, and walked into Organisation Deck a while later. He'd brought with him the replacement parts to repair Midge. He came to an abrupt halt, as he found Tayce standing waiting for him hands on hips in the middle of the deck looking far from pleased at his lateness to return.

"Enjoy your jaunt Mr Stavard I'm waiting for your explanation of why you thought you could take my place in going over to the port for the parts, and the time it's taken you," she said displeased.

"I'm sorry," he replied he could see she was angry.

"We have a policy aboard this cruiser, you should have let Midge know or me know, you were going to Orge in my place, you left this cruiser unattended, we could have been boarded by any unscrupulous being and his merry band, also with Midge working on temporary repaired operations, he could have failed and this cruiser and I would be prisoners of whoever, do you understand what I driving at?" pointed out Tayce plainly.

"For your information I did tell Midge I was going in your place, the supply vessel that had the repair parts had only just docked, so I had to wait for the cargo to clear, and book it out to you, I was in constant contact with Midge I guess he didn't pick it up," retorted Tom.

"I take it that's the right parts we need?" said Tayce glancing to the items in Tom's hands.

"Quite! Now I'll do the job and we can get up and running," replied Tom.

He said no more. He felt Tayce had said it all, he did not want to argue with her further, it would be pointless. Right now she was a typical overreacting female and this was her cruiser that no one else, not even him who had tried to help her must interfere with. Women he thought. But deep down he also could see her point, he probably would have acted the same way, maybe he did act irresponsibly, but he wasn't letting her know it. He got down under Midges console and removed the panel. Removing the broken makeshift repaired board he replaced the old one, for the new improved one. Once everything was running smoothly and in full power they could get under way. He soon stood up meeting Tayce. She suddenly caught his calm look at her, and it make her feel wrong. He didn't say anything, just passed her and climbed into the Co-pilot seat. Tayce awkwardly crossed to join him, in silence. Concentrating on the future and what it held.

Tayce was no longer the young woman alone travelling the Universe, and she realised it. It was taking time to adjust to. She now had a space partner and the first of a hoped new team, that's if he decided to stay.

Questa

Amalthea One was running a lot more smoothly with the newly installed components. Tayce was at the controls, under the usual assisted control of Midge. Tom Stavard had been on board almost two weekons and had decided to stay as part of the crew and possible proposed new team. This idea Tayce had discussed with him to form a crime fighting team. He liked it. But he wanted to think about it. The frosty reception between the two of them had gone, they were almost working as a mini team.

Tom was currently down in the on board Technical Centre. He managed to retrieve his dented and damaged small intelligent mobile robot named 'Cargo' so far he wasn't having much luck. He was beginning to wonder if he would ever get the little Robot to work again. The occasional blaspheme filled the air every time something failed, in trying to get the system to boot up. Midge was trying his best over head to advise Tom on what he should try next. So far both were being left speechless as to what to try.

Back in Organisation Deck Tayce was watching the Spacescape, for anything untoward, or unusual.

"Midge latest scan information of the immediate sector please," she requested.

"We have a port in this sector, and it's sending out a distress signal, do you want to investigate?" he put to her.

Tayce thought about it, as Midge considered the possibilities of a trap, or running into danger. Both were silent for a cencron. They'd been through so many near misses from set up distress calls before in the past, why should this one be any diverse, as any other.

"Proceed with precaution for diverting, in case it's another elaborate trap," ordered Tayce.

"Very well, will do," replied Midge.

"Let me know the moment everything checks out, and we come into orbit," suggested Tayce.

"Where will you be?" he asked.

"I've heard Tom's expletives long enough, I'm going down to the Technical Centre to see what he's trying to put together," she replied leaving her seat, she walked across to the entrance.

She began on the walk down the corridor in thought about the distress call. Suddenly from below decks there came an agonising cry from Tom in the Technical Centre. She froze for a cencron, then broke into a sprint. Upon reaching the Level Steps, she began down. But half way down she caught her high heel in the silver steps, and ripped it from her cream boot, which threw her head long down the steps. She tumbled all the way down coming to a halt on Level 5. She screamed, wondering where she'd stop. Finally she impacted with the wall on Level 5, and knocked herself out cold. Her slim form rested in an unconscious sprawl. Her head tilted on one side.

Tom alarmed at the commotion of Tayce falling down the steps, put down the silver slim probing instrument and broke into a sprint, running out of the Technical Centre, into the corridor. He paused looking down the corridor towards the Level Steps to see the lifeless form of Tayce laying silent. He quickly ran along the corridor in urgency and alarm, wondering what the hell had happened. He knelt down upon reaching her, not knowing quite what to do for the best. Which bit to move first, in case she'd broken anything. A cold shiver rushed through him at the sudden thought, maybe she was dead even! No! he thought.

"Midge, can you scan Tayce here, is it safe to move her?" he asked extremely concerned via his Wristlink.

"Everything's in hand Tom, scanning now stand clear," informed Midge calmly.

Out of nowhere an orange energy glow materialised around Tayce. It hummed whilst it scanned her where she lay. Once done Midge suggested Tayce be moved to the Life Ability Centre. Tom carefully slipped his hands under Tayce in a supporting manner and climbed to his feet, picking her up in his strong arms. Once up he headed straight along to the Deck Travel. The doors opened on him pausing just before them. He slipped inside and managed to push the button for the required level, with Tayce cradled in his strong arms out cold. The Deck Travel ascended to Level 2. No sooner had the doors drew open, Tom hurried out and along and into the Life Ability Centre. The doors opening on his approach.

"Okay. Midge take care of her," said Tom crossing to the Exam Bunk placing Tayce down gently.

He then stood back, while Midge did another more thorough body scan, for internal injuries.

"It's all right Tom, she's only got what we term, impact bruising and she'll have a headache from hitting her head tumbling," assured Midge seeing Tom's concern.

"Thank God for that," expressed Tom much relieved.

"What happened?" asked Tayce beginning to regain consciousness.

"Take it easy, you fell down the steps hit your head, Midge said you'll have a headache, but you've no broken bones," he assured her softly.

Tayce lay looking up at Tom, listening to what he was saying. She felt her head still spinning. Midge overhead advised she should remain in the Life Ability Centre for at least forty-eight hourons, just as a precaution. He ordered Tom to administer a 'Select' pain relieving injection, it was especially for the kind of pain Tayce was enduring owing to her injuries and it incorporated a sedative for her to sleep and to restore her health back to normal levels, ridding her bloodstream of the shock. Midge showed him how to administer the Inject Pen. It hit Tayces bloodstream quickly and painlessly. She soon closed her eyes, and drifted back into deep sleep. Tom left her in Midges care. He did however, before walking out, fetched a Coverlet to drape over Tayce. He then turned, leaving. On the way he began to wonder if he was a jinx, as everything that happened lately had occurred since his arrival on board, maybe it would have been better if Tayce had left him in space.

Tom returned to the Technical Centre. But just as he entered, Midges voice stopped him, mid way back to the Tech Bench and 'Cargo'. Midge began that enemy fighters were closing in fast. Firing as they came, Tom spun on his heels and ran back on out heading up to Organisation Deck. As he ran up the steps Tayce had fallen down earlier in an uncontrollable fashion. Fire power from his surroundings was already being unleashed upon the oncoming enemy fighters. Upon his arrival on deck, Midge briefed him on what was happening.

"They appeared from, the 2nd North sector, and they mean business, believe me," announced Midge sending back retaliating Slazer bursts.

"Who are they Midge?" said Tom, crossing, dropping into Tayces seat, as he reached it.

"Our worst enemy, the race that destroyed Tayces home world, the Vargon Warriors, Tayce has encountered them before, they never give up, last time we outran and out fired them," pointed out Midge.

"Looks like they won't take no for an answer, would you like me to take control?" asked Tom helpfully.

"No, I have everything in hand, these guys make their own rules and so do we in retaliation," replied Midge.

Tom raised his eyes in surprise at the character of this Midge computer, he was certainly something else, he'd like to shake the hand of the man who designed him. He was impressed at how Midge retaliated in weapon fire on the oncoming enemy fighters. The cruiser seemed to manoeuvre this way, and that, just to stay ahead of the game, so to speak.

"Midge this is getting too dangerous, hand controls over to me now!" ordered Tom.

"Handing over now Tom, give them hell!" said Midge releasing the controls to continue firing.

A Slazer burst flew from one of the front cannons of Amalthea in the control of Tom. It hit home on the nose of one of the enemy fighters, blowing it into an array of debris and sparks. Amalthea suddenly jolted as another passing fighter unleashed a shot, which bounced off the cruisers protection shield. Tom quickly retaliated, returning a quick succession of firepower, blowing it to smithereens. Tom waited till the group of enemy fighters were in formation, then released an Energy Disintegrating Missile. There was one massive explosion of immense magnitude. Then nothing, but clear calm dark space. Tom sat in silence.

"We won again! Your quiet Tom, are you all right?" asked Midge not hearing any comments from him as to what had just happened.

"I'm fine Midge, it's just I've never seen firepower like that before, it was awesome!" replied Tom thinking about what he'd just witnessed.

Out of nowhere came a lone enemy fighter. The caterpillar shaped black fighter hovered, then thought better and turned tail and flew off out of sight. Midge had the idea he had gone back to report to his chief what had occurred and informed Tom so. He sat poised ready.

In the Life Ability Centre, Tayce had been jolted from the sedative induced sleep. She opened her eyes to a sight she thought she would never have to endure again. On the far side of the centre, stood the illusion of none other than the woman who she hated in all the Universe, the woman leader who headed the attack and destruction on her world. 'Countess Vargon! Upon seeing the illusion, Tayce sat up in alarm. Something was wrong. Badly wrong! This illusion of the Countess laughing in all her black dressed evilness conveyed one thing, she was back once more to take the cruiser. She forgot all about her aches and pains from the fall and slid from the bunk. She ran for the entrance, the pain still hitting her occasionally as she went. She began thinking to herself, the bitch was not going to get her hands on her cruiser, not now or ever, if she could help it. As she ran from the Life Ability Centre, she realised that she was still wearing her broken heeled boot. Pausing she pulled both boots off and discarded them against the corridor wall, going on. Tayce pushed her aches and pains to the back of her mind, as they quickly continued to remind her of her sustained injuries. Pausing at the Slazer Emergency Cabinet and tapping in her master code, the door slid open and she retrieved a handgun, checking it was at full charge, she let the door slid shut. Heading on cautiously to Organisation.

Up in Organisation Deck, Tom was having trouble with an on board uninvited guest, in the form of one of the Countesses men, a Vargon Warrior Pilot. Who had returned to carry out his mistresses wishes, to take the Amalthea. Midge had control of the cruiser, while Tom was beating the hell out of the intruder. But he was finding he was more than an equal match for him, in brute strength. Eventually Tom managed to grab hold of the Green Platex (plastic) shielded Warrior and hurtle him across the deck. Where he sailed up against the wall with a thud. One that was not occupied luckily by computer functioning panels. Tom didn't let up, as the Warrior looked like he was coming back for more, he went straight for him. He forced him back against the wall and held him there with an angry glare in his eyes. He was angry beyond control now.

"What's your business here, tell me before I take you out permanently?" demanded Tom holding the Warrior by a broken piece of his armour

"I have orders to destroy this cruiser," replied the Warrior full of resisting anger and hatred for Tom.

"Oh really, you've got orders, well you Green armoured jerk I'm giving you one, get off this cruiser before I tear you apart and send you back to your leader in a sealed container, gift wrapped," said Tom getting fed up with this big built barbarian.

The Warrior managed to reach for his hand weapon. He drew it aiming it in Tom's midriff. Tom looked down. For a moment he saw his whole life flash before his eyes. Then he heard a welcome sound behind him. Tayce stepped into Organisation. Her Slazer set to kill and she was prepared to use it to save Tom and Amalthea.

"Drop it, don't think for a moment that I won't use this because I will," said Tayce coldly behind the warrior.

"A female! Me afraid of you, you forget where the guns aimed woman," retorted the Warrior over his right shoulder.

"You should be, I never miss, ask your Countess, now get off my cruiser and go back and tell your leader she better start praying because this little girl from Traun, is ready to take her on," said Tayce continuing her hostile tone.

"And," replied the Warrior not moving.

"When we meet, it will be her last meeting with me, forever!" said Tayce aiming the Slazer more precisely.

He was not prepared to back down. Tayce pushed the Slazer in a armour vacant space in his midriff and fired. Midge travelsported him off the Amalthea at the same time. The last Tom and Tayce saw of him was his agonizing look of pain. As he vaporized away, leaving Tayce and Tom to look on in relief.

"Thanks for a moment I thought I'd had it," expressed Tom gladly.

"Are you hurt, another cencron and you would have been in eternity," replied Tayce casually.

"Where did you learn to shoot like that, nice aim?" he said with a warm smile.

"My Father taught me once, you wound someone enough to send them home with a cold reminder to who ever sent them in the first place do this again and there will be repercussions for you, you have been warned and if you can't send them back to where they came from, you just kill them, watch them disintegrate or jettison them into space," she replied recalling her Father's words.

Both she and Tom stood for a moment, then Tom reached out and gently pulled her in towards him for the first time. He hugged her in a warm embrace thankful for her actions to save his life. Tayce for some strange reason felt she didn't want to resist him in doing so. He asked her if she felt better. She answered with a slow nod against his warm chest. They released each other. Tayce advised him to go and get cleaned up. He did as suggested and began over to the entrance. He paused in the doorway. She looked at him questioningly wondering what was wrong. He winked at her in an affectionate way, then carried on out the entrance. Tayce walked over to her chair and sat down in thought about how she and Tom were becoming real good mates.

"He likes you," said Midge in teasing tone.

"Stop it Midge, what's our next port of call?" Tayce enquired seriously changing the subject.

"Well, that distress call we received earlier was answered by another passing vessel, but do you remember your Father talking about a headquarters base called Questa, the Earthon 2 space link colony and General Jonathan Largon, well that's our next port of call," said Midge informatively.

"Why there in particular, do they need our help for some reason?" asked Tayce curious.

"No, it would appear the General, when he heard that your Father had built this cruiser and Traun was destroyed yearons ago, has been putting out a space wide communication to try and track us, I've just picked up that communication, and replied to it, and now he wants to see us," replied Midge.

"Really, I remember General Largon, Father and him were the best of friends, always holding discussions on the troubles of the Universe, he came to Traun a couple of times," recalled Tayce.

Tayce raised her eyebrows in surprise at the thought that General Largon had been seeking to meet her so long. Midge continued that a course for Questa had been set. Tayce strapped herself in. Amalthea One now known just as Amalthea, headed on to Questa Headquarters Base to meet an old family friend.

On the Earthon 2 link up Headquarters Base Questa, the General was studying the VDU portable screen in front of him about the message update that Midge had sent him on what had been happening in the last yearons since Trauns destruction. He was looking forward to meeting Darius Trauns now grown up daughter and putting what Darius had asked him into action in the event of his death. The Generals young male aide stood by like an obedient servant, ready to answer any questions he may have, over their proposed visitors.

"Tom Stavard, where does he fit into Tayces life?" asked Jonathan looking to his aide questioningly.

"Midge, Amaltheas computer informed me, he was someone that Colonel Traun rescued, from the aftermath of a pirate ambush," replied the young slim tall dark haired aide.

Both men continued on in discussion over many of the points of the update type of message that had been sent in from Midge over Aircom. The General at his ornate mahoganex desk with his young aide by his side, continued to pick out points and discuss matters that needed to be addressed on arrival of his prospective guests.

Questa was 400.000 km from Earthon 2. It was situated on the surface and underground of the man made colony. Life was a living breathing environment of a population of 2,205 men, women and children. Children that had been born on Questa. The population varied, because of the many people that came and went to Earthon 2. Some worked on the colony, some lived full-time. It was a thriving community, massive in size almost covering half the planetary dimensions. There was a City Mall and Square, where children would play safely. To a Hospital Complex, that catered for every ailment or injury. A large Flight Travel Area that would fit six full sized football pitches on Earth One. A Crime Division Building for all aspects of crime, planetary or Universal. Plus many other facilities over it's vast sized complex of Dome and Skyscraper type constructed existence.

General Jonathan Largon was overall leader of a Planetary Council, of which Darius Traun, Tayce's Father was once a member. He had promised Darius that he would take care of Tayce, in the event of his untimely death. He stood now looking out of the sight pane, down on what was called, Questa Square, thinking about Tayce in general. He was a tall man in his late 50's, early 60's and of medium build. His hair, was short sleek, to the nape of the neck, in a silvery platinum shade. His features were the calm authoritative type, but pleasant. His eyes were a dark brown shade with a hint of Spanish about them. Jonathan fitted his uniform with perfect fit and pride. The uniform was navy in colour. Navy trousers in a tough wearing material. A navy jacket completed the suit, with a smart thin white trim running all the way down the sleeve of the jacket, then all the way down the trousers. The General turned, beckoning to his aide, he began towards the entrance. The young aide followed. Together they began on their way out through the opening doors, to the Space Port Lounge, to wait the arrival of Tayce and Tom.

On Amalthea Tom soon returned to Organisation Deck in a clean uniform. Upon entering the deck he saw the first sight of the impressive Questa Headquarters Base in all it's glory. He crossed and sat in the seat beside Tayce. He found her and Midge going through final arrival procedures, with Questa Flight Control and could see they were about to go into final docking.

"It's impressive isn't it?" said Tom studying the large planetary type colony, which almost looked like a city from the air, with it's tall skyscrapers of stealex and glassene and Dome shaped covered areas with lights shinning from within.

"Wait until you see the rest, this colony, it's just like my world, but we had an atmosphere and daylight/night rota," informed Tayce thinking about it.

"Midge, keep on alert while we are over on Questa, we can't take any chances now, considering Countess Vargons even more determined to take this cruiser, she could be waiting for the first chance we are away from here, to board," said Tayce standing to her feet.

"Enjoy your time on Questa, I will contact you via Wristlink should you be needed in an emergency," replied Midge.

"Let's hope there isn't one," said Tom standing to join Tayce.

Both he and Tayce walked across the Organisation Deck on out through the entrance and off down to the Docking Bay doors on Level 2. Tayce shared her apprehension to leave the cruiser in Midges hands with Tom because of the growing threat from Countess Vargon to get her hands on their surroundings. He assured her that usually when a vessel was in port, criminals didn't like to venture where they knew they could be caught easily, and a colony like Questa seemed the place that was pretty tight on security. Tayce felt a little easier, knowing this, but it would still hang in the back of her mind during this visit. Eventually they made it to the Docking Bay doors, on Level 2. They paused while Midge made sure that Amalthea was secured with Questa. Suddenly the doors drew apart in front of both of them. Tom gestured for her to go first, which she did. They began to walk down the walkway. Tayces high heeled replaced boots made an echoing sound each time they met the walkway surface. After walking along for a while they both walked out into the main Space Port Lounge. The General stood with Adam Carford his aide, patiently waiting. He smiled kindly, when he saw Tayce coming towards him. He knew that Darius would have been proud to see what she had become, a truly independent grown up young women.

"Tayce it's good to see you, welcome to Questa, it's good to know that your safe and sound after all this long time," he said giving her a fatherly hug, as she came to a stop before him

"It's good to see you too after all these yearons, I had no idea that you've been looking for us until Midge picked you up," replied Tayce hugging Jonathan back.

"You must be Tom Stavard welcome to Questa," said Jonathan releasing Tayce and turning his attentions to Tom.

"It's an honour to be here Sir! May I say this place is impressive to say the least," said Tom impressed glancing around.

"We take great pride in making Questa a good place to stay, at all times shall we proceed to my Officette?" gestured Jonathan then began walking off ahead.

They all walked off together in a small group heading to Jonathan's Officette. Tom walked along talking with Adam, whilst Tayce talked with Jonathan, as they walked away from Amalthea towards a thirteen storey building in cream colour and shaped like a triangle. The square and walkways symbolized a busy colony. People came and went, some talking and carrying equipment etc. Children, ducked and dived, laughing as they went. It made Tayce think about happier times back on her world, it had been just the same environment then. She was somewhat saddened to know that she would never see it again. They soon came to a clear glassene travelling lift, that was round in shape, and rose and fell at a gentle slow speed, with people on board. Some leaving, some boarding on different Levels. This thought Tom must be a means, to get to other Levels. The doors opened on a vacant one, on their approach. The four of them walked aboard. The doors gently slid shut and it began to ascend the required level. The lift was termed as a 'Vacuum Lift'.

"As we go up Tom, you can see the rest of our base from here," announced Jonathan, he knew Tayce wouldn't be that interested, she'd seen it numerous times before when she'd visited with her Father.

Tom looked out. There was a grand panorama, buildings, fields, modern living habitats, as far as the eye could see. Vehicles flew through the air, hovering this way and that.

"That's our Recreational Complex over there, it caters for all kinds of sports, you name it, it's covered from the less strenuous, to the real competitive, we have our own team you know," announced Jonathan pointed out to his left with pride that they had.

"What's that over there?" asked Tom pointing to a burnt out two storey building on his right.

"That I'm afraid happened two monthons ago the cause of the fire is still under investigation by the council," replied Jonathan sad in thought.

The Vacuum Lift soon stopped. The doors drew apart and the small party walked forth, the glassene doors drew shut behind them and the lift returned to a requested level. They walked up a corridor with shiny floor, towards doors in brown, that went from floor to almost ceiling in height. These drew inwards as Jonathan and Adam approached. Inside the Officette were first class furnishings in a mahoganex finish conveying a high ranked standard. A large desk with two mouldable Leatherex chairs before it. The command high back brown Leatherex chair belonging to Jonathan behind it. Pictures of various vessels and places lined the walls. Whilst trophy's lined the chrome and mahoganex shelves. The floor was brown carpetron tiles. Lighting was natural through the large sight pane. Jonathan sat down at his desk. He enquired if anyone would like refreshment before they commenced business? Both declined.

"Right let's get down to the reason I've been trying to trace you for the best part of three yearons, your Father Tayce had me make sure you came here when we managed to find you," began Jonathan.

Tayce sat down first, then Tom followed. He listened wondering what was meant by Jonathan's words. He stayed silent listening, he felt this was totally Tayces business. Jonathan continued on explaining she knew that her Father had great wealth and he was one of the main sitters on the Intergalactic Planetary Council for Intergalactic Matters. His seat was now sadly left vacant, as a mark of respect. Tayce thanked him and to pass on the appreciation to the other members for this. Jonathan reached across his loaded desk, and retrieved a Platex thin file.

"Your Father filed this with me in case anything untoward happened to him or your Mother and Traun," said Jonathan in a gentle kind tone, as delicately as he could.

Tayce silently took the Platex black thin file. She fought back the sad feelings that were trying to engulf her, thoughts that her Father had been the last person to see her apart from Marc and hold what she had in her hands. She slowly opened it, asking Jonathan what was it? Jonathan then handed her a cream coloured Platex Wallet with the name in goldex across the middle 'TAYCE AMANDA TRAUN' in bold. Tayce accepted it. Setting the file down, she opened the Wallet, taking out the contents. A document which had a hand written letter by her Father. Tayce focused between the tears, that were surfacing. It felt like yesteron, that the terrible tragedy had befallen her and the people of her home world, she could still hear the screams. A letter was attached to a trust document. There was a list of things that had been suggested by her Father to attend to. She read it down, subject by subject, at the end there was a paragraph which Tayce felt amused by, even though she knew she shouldn't. It read:

I know your a strong willed young woman, even though you are my loving daughter, now that I have gone, all I ask is that you remember your Mother and I with love and pride, that we made you who you are good luck for your future my darling, your Father

Commodore Darius Traun

Tayce couldn't hold back the tears any longer, they went into full flow, uncontrollably. Tom reached over and took hold of her hand for a few minons, as she let the emotion go that had got the better of her. He soothed her softly. Jonathan felt her pain. He waited patiently for her to continue. He understood that it had been hard for her all alone in space, all those past yearons. She'd been a Commodores daughter and lead a life of doing what she wanted, when she wanted, to a certain degree. Then she was thrust into a dangerous Universe on her own, it couldn't have been easy to get use to. Tayce managed to bring herself under control.

"General I had no idea, I don't know what to say," she began with tear stained eyes.

"Your Father maybe right, you maybe strong willed, but it was a good thing that you were, otherwise you wouldn't have survived in our Universe as it is, he was very proud of you and often conveyed as much," said Jonathan in a sincere way.

Darius Traun had left Tayce the sum of 66,000,000. In the matter of cencrons she'd gone from an average to a very rich young woman and Colonel. She handed the document to Tom. He nodded congratulating her saying how glad he was for her considering all that she'd gone through. In his eyes she was worthy of such a trust. Tayce stood up and walked over to the sight pane. She stood in thought for a minon. Both Jonathan and Tom glanced over silently. Tayce turned after a few cencrons.

"General, I know my Father has given me a list of ideas to undertake, but there's something I would like to put forth as an idea," she began.

"Go ahead I'm listening," said Jonathan giving her his full attention, as did Adam nearby.

"I with Tom here have been considering the idea of forming a crime fighting team to combat some of the criminals there are out in the Universe, I would head it, Tom would be my first member, others would join the team along the way?" explained Tayce carefully.

"I think it's a very excellent idea, we'll give you any assistance you need, and I would be pleased, if you could call Questa your new home and carry our emblem on the outside of your cruiser, also on your hoped team uniforms," agreed Jonathan with total enthusiasm.

"When you say use Questa as my home, what way?" asked Tayce curious she didn't want to be on the base full time. Amalthea had and always would be considered her only home.

"You just use this base as your headquarters, also take on our crime assignments as they materialise, plus other assignments as they arise," explained Jonathan hoping she would agree.

"Yes I would be honoured," said Tayce proudly.

"That goes for you too Mr Stavard, we'd like to offer you the same," said Jonathan.

"Whatever Tayce decides, is fine by me, I think it's a good idea," replied Tom.

"Your Father would be proud Tayce to know you have come up with such a good idea, welcome officially to Questa," said Jonathan standing up, outstretching his hand, to shake both Tom's and Tayces.

Both shook hands making it official. The General turned to Tayce, requesting she remain on Questa for a couple of hourons at least, so this would allow the sign techs to affix the Questa emblem to Amalthea One. Tayce agreed. Tom suggested that they go for refreshment, take in a bit of their new headquarters base. Jonathan agreed, exclaiming it was a good idea. Adam suggested he call them on Wristlink when everything was finalised. Tayce nodded, with this, both she and Tom turned leaving the documents, that had been given to her earlier with Jonathan, until they returned later. General Largon began immediately getting in touch with the Graphics Complex, he knew that if he ordered the job on Amalthea One to be done there and then, it would be done, at that moment without further word. Adam suggested he get on preparing the official documentation for Tom and Tayce to both sign later. Jonathan nodded. Adam walked on out of the Officette to take care of the request straight away.

A while later, Tom found the Refreshments Hall. It was occupied by travellers and workers from Questa. It was quite busy. A celebration of some kind was taking place in one area whilst in another there were, others sitting quietly, reflecting on the dayons events that occupied their lives. Tom had found a quiet table in a corner slot, near a sight pane, that looked out on the passing people, in the square. The atmosphere was filled with vocal loudness at times especially from the ongoing celebration. Some kind of strange music played in the background. Out of the dark area of the hall, he walked towards Tom and Tayces table. Tall of medium build, and good looks. His dark brown short curly hair, shone in the reflection of the overhead lights. He didn't look at any other table, or person in the hall other than where Tayce and Tom were seated, he just headed with hoped anticipation that who he was seeing, was, who he thought it was. He squinted to make out Tayces features, if this was who he thought it was, she had grown into a beautiful young woman. Yet, she looked somewhat tired. Her hair was as he remembered it, long and blonde about her shoulders in a bob. He paused nervously hoping he hadn't got the wrong person, and that this woman was not a twin of who he thought it was.

"Excuse me ma'am, Tayce!" said the male softly and politely.

"Yes!" said Tayce turning at the sound of this males voice.

"Is it really you?" he said overwhelmed with relief and joyousness.

"Marc Dayatso! I can't believe it, your alive!" said Tayce standing, ecstatic at the thought he was present and very much alive ignoring Tom's wonderment of who this dark haired stranger was.

"Yes Taycey! How about a hug?" he said affectionately, giving her a warm affectionate hug.

Tayce stayed in his warm embrace for a few minons, it felt good to know she was now no longer the only Traunian alive. Marc released her, seeing the male over her shoulder looking concerned, wondering who this Marc Dayatso was. Tayce studied him, he was just as she remembered him warm, friendly, a big protector, good looking and above all else a good friend. He was just three yearons older that was all.

"How come your here on Questa, are you passing through?" Tayce asked curious.

"Would you believe, looking for employment," he replied.

"Your looking for a position, well look no further, I'm looking for team members for Amalthea, I'm starting to gather together what is hoped to be a crime fighting team, I know it will be a come down for you, but would you be my Navigationalist, if you want the position?" she asked hoping that he would accept.

Marc stood in silent thought teasing Tayce as he often use to. He stood keeping her in suspense, then when he figured he'd kept her in suspense long enough, he wholeheartedly agreed, exclaiming that he couldn't think of a better person to work alongside of. Tom welcomed him to the team. Marc then continued.

"I'm going to need time to gather my stuff together, is that okay?" he put to Tayce.

"Of course, but before you go I'd like you to officially meet Tom Stavard, Tom this is Marc Dayatso my good friend and Father's aide from my old world Traun that I was telling you about," introduced Tayce.

"Hello so your the person behind Midge, he's quite a computer, there isn't anything he can't take care of," said Tom outstretching his hand for Marc to shake, impressed over Midge.

"Tom! Pleased to meet you, yes we made sure Midge was Tayce friendly and could do almost everything that was thrown at him, when we designed him, he is quite extraordinary I must admit," replied Marc.

Marc excused his presence, exclaiming he'd catch them later, just as soon as he'd gathered his belongings together. Tayce agreed. With this Marc walked away off to collect his gear from his accommodation. Tayce watched him go, still not believing that he was alive after all this time, but glad he was back in her life again. Tom sat down, as did she, continuing on with the meal, that they were half way through. They sat talking whilst eating, discussing on the future of the new Amalthean Team, and what they might undertake during the future of the crime fighting in the Universe. When finished they left the Refreshments Hall heading across the square to wait for Marc by a cascading fountain, that flowed through the centre of a chrome and stealex letter 'Q'. Both watched the various sorts of people go back and forth including some strange looking aliens, which made Tom and Tayce exchange wondrous glances.

Marc Dayatso entered the sparsely furnished room, he called home for a while. It was nothing to write home about, nothing luxurious. Bare just the plain essentials, in a cold grey shade. A bunk, Cleanse Centre that was almost like a cubbyhole. An eating surface with one old shabby stool underneath. It had been all he had been able to afford. He'd escaped Traun almost penniless. He soon packed his holdall and silver Attaché case. Once finished, he picked up the holdall by the strap, placed it over his shoulder, picked up the Attaché case, gave one last look at the hovel he'd called home for the last time and walked out the entrance. He realised it may have been a hovel, but when he arrived he was just glad to get any kind of shelter. Passing people he often exchanged a few words with in the past, seeing he was packed to leave, wished him luck. Marc acknowledged them with a nod and thanks. He paused to hand in his de-locking device at the main desk and signed out for the last time gladly in silence, with the serious looking Desk Attendant. Marc continued on out of the Complex, walking to the Vacuum Lift. He followed some other people inside as the doors drew apart and stood silent as the doors closed. The lift descended to the square ground level. Marc had a swarthy face, but the kind that would make any female fall for him. His eyes were the kind of warm and inviting eyes, in a shade of bluey grey. His complexion was flawless. He was the ideal man for any women who admired him, but he was no Romeo. Sure enough he liked women, but no more than the next man did. His nature was the kind easy to get along with type but he could be protective at times. He could turn mean however, if the situation arose. He had no secrets to be ashamed of left in his past. Marc was as clean living and proud as he always had been, this is what had made Commodore Traun, Tayces Father take him on as his aide. He exited the Vacuum Lift behind the others and walked away to meet up with Tayce and Tom. In no time they were all walking on back to Jonathan Largons Officette.

"Tayce you said the Amalthea, you still haven't got the same cruiser?" asked Marc in surprise, he thought she would have lost it in battle, or had it stolen by pirates.

"Yes it's still as good as the dayon it left Traun," replied Tayce, wondering what he was getting at.

"I would have expected for all the pirates there are out in the Universe, Amalthea One would be fit for scrap by now," he said surprised at Tayces reply.

"I'll tell Midge what you just said, he'll be quite interested," replied Tayce giving as good as she was getting, she could see Marc was trying to wind her up in a teasing way like he use to.

"I think you've just hit a raw nerve," whispered Tom to Marc.

Marc smiled amused, he knew Tayce too well and he would be surprised if she took his words seriously.

All paperwork was ready when they arrived at Jonathan's Officette. Jonathan was somewhat surprised to see Marc, but glad he was all right. When Marc informed him he'd been living on the base, Jonathan reprimanded him, demanding to know why on earth he hadn't gone to see him sooner, as he could have helped him. Tayce signed the voyage documents, collected the items her Father had left her. She listened as Jonathan explained that the emblem of Questa was on the outside hull of Amalthea One. Uniforms were at this moment, already being loaded on board. All that remained was for him to ask her, to be ready to work for Questa in the new future capacity of Questas first crime fighting team, under the new title of. 'The Amalthean Quests Team'. Upon this all three shook hands with Jonathan and Adam, then walked from the Officette. The doors opening and closing behind them. Jonathan looked on. He felt this proposed new venture was going to be a good one, and much needed, in the kind of galaxy they lived, in the present.

Later once at the walkway the three new Amalthean Quests team members took one last look for the present time at the impressive sight of Questa, then walked on board, as the Docking Bay doors opened. The familiar warm interior atmosphere rushed out to meet them. Once on board Marc started feeling a feeling of deja vu. It all came back to him, the fateful night he'd helped launch

Tayce in their present surroundings and for a few moments it felt hard to comprehend. Tayce could see it and fully understood.

"Tom will you get us under way, I'll show Marc to his quarters," ordered Tayce she could see Marc recalling the past and she could see that it hurt him, just as much as it did her at times she wanted to help.

"Yeah sure! You go ahead, see you in a while," he replied walking off.

Both Tayce and Marc walked along down to the Quarters Level. Marc enquired how did she come to meet Tom? Also how did she know, she could trust him considering all the vagabonds there were in the Universe? Tayce began explaining that Tom had been the victim of pirates himself. He and his wife Alenea and their craft had been used for a pirate target practice. His wife sadly had died through her injuries. Marc raised his eyebrows not surprised by what she was saying.

"What's he like to work with?" he asked, so he would have an idea how to handle him.

"He's a good man, he single handedly took on one of Vargons Warriors, when they boarded, yes, don't look so surprised, she's still out here," said Tayce.

They came to what were to be Marc's quarters. He entered seeing the vast difference to his last residence. He crossed dropping his things on the soffette. Turning saying it was good to be back in space and with a good friend and almost like sister. Tayce walked to meet him and hugged him, glad he was back in her life also. She handed him his quarters de-locking key, then suggested he see her up in Organisation. Marc agreed beginning to unpack. Tayce walked from the quarters which were a shade of navy blue floor carpetron tiles and grey smooth furnishings.

On the walk back to Organisation Tayce Wristlinked to Midge, to inform him that Marc was back and had taken up quarters '3' on the Quarters Level. Midge accepted the fact, exclaiming he would materialise him a Wristlink and talk with him. Tayce agreed lowering her Wristlink, she continued up the steps.

Tom was busy in conversation with Jonathan Largon, when Tayce returned to the Organisation Deck. She walked across to her seat. Just in time for Jonathan to order Tom to take good care of Tayce. She silently sat down hearing Tom assure him he would.

Amalthea One began to manoeuvre out from the Docking Port, with Questa. Once free, it turned to position itself ready to take off into the Universe slowly. Once in position, it travelled forward. Questa disappeared into the distant past minons by minons.

On board Tom was keying away on the console, running constant checks. Tayce stood up as Marc came into Organisation, a while later. He'd brought a bottle of Stavern, (champagne), and three disposable glassenes, glasses. Marc opened the bottle. Midge took control. Tom stood up and walked around the Co-pilot seat to join both Tayce and Marc. Even though he liked this Marc, he had a feeling he was going to be in contest with him for Tayces affections. Marc poured the drinks, handing one to Tom and one to Tayce. He set the bottle down after he'd poured his own.

"I propose a toast, to all of us coming together and more team members joining us and the successful future of the Amalthean Quests crime fighting team," said Marc.

All three held their glassenes in the air, and chinked to mark the start of the new life of the Amalthea One Cruiser and the hoped Team.

Amalthea One travelled on into the Universe.

Exhaustion

It was night hourons on board Amalthea One. One weekon later to be exact. The three team members were in their quarters in what was suppose to be contented sleep. But, all was not what it should be. Marc Dayatso for some strange reason woke in his quarters in alarm, why he had no idea, he sat bolt up right. Something was telling him, something was wrong. He sat in his bunk listening and looking around his immediate surroundings. Nothing was present and all that could be heard was the distant sound of the cruisers fission engines gently running. Midge who was monitoring everyone's vital signs, picked up Marc's agitated state, he came online enquiring what was the problem? Marc began that something was bothering him, though what he couldn't put a finger on. Something was giving him strong uneasy feelings, that something was happening to someone he knew close by somewhere on the cruiser. Then if by some strange coincidence he found himself asking if Tayce was okay. Midge offered to run an immediate scan on his mistress. Marc waited ready to spring into action. Midge came back with urgency. This didn't surprise him.

"Hurry Marc, it's Tayce, she's having trouble breathing, she's laying on the living area floor of her quarters, hurry!" said Midge getting desperately worried.

Marc threw back the coverlet of his bunk and reached for his black silkene 'D' gown, slipping it on, sliding from the bunk in urgency he ran across the quarters tying up the tie belt as he went. He soon reached the entrance doors and they opened before him on approach, with the sound of gentle compressed air. Slipping out into the corridor of Level 4 he headed along to Tayce's quarters. The doors were locked on night security mode.

"Midge bypass night security system immediately, let me in," said Marc in urgency.

Without further word, Midge put into operation the releasing of the locking system on the quarters doors. As they slid back, the sight that greeted Marc was of Tayce laying on the floor, on her side, half propped up. Her right hand to her throat and her left reaching out to him in a pleading gesture, gasping for breath.

She was also wheezing. Something was not right thought Marc, but he'd seen this before many yearons ago on Traun and he'd helped her Mother the last time. So he knew what to do. He immediately crossed and crouched down, carefully, picking her up in his strong arms.

"It's all right baby, I've got you, your going to be fine," he reassured her softly.

"Marc why now?" she asked in strained tone still trying to breath.

"It's just one of those things, we'll get you help, don't worry," he promised

He had a feeling though, that she had been pushing herself to the limit, and this had been the consequence of her actions of doing what she use to do, push herself beyond endurance without any rest. He recalled the last time this had happened, she had to been flown to the Intergalactic Medical Colony. This would have to happen again and he had a feeling she was not going to like it, but it had to be done, so that she could see her specialist Dr Paclan Sellecson. A man Marc knew, she didn't much care for. He was bossy and straight with her. Marc raised the alarm immediately ordering Midge to put in an emergency course for the Intergalactic Medical Colony. Midge agreed.

Upon hearing the on board emergency alarm. Tom in his quarters fell out of his bunk, literally, at the sudden sound that meant something dangerous was unfolding on board. He unravelled himself from his coverlet on the floor and was soon on his feet heading towards the entrance. Upon reaching the doors and them opening before him, he focussed in the brightness of the corridor and tried to shake the feeling of grogginess and focus on what might be in hand before him. He looked both ways up and down the corridor. Nothing! He was far from impressed, if this was Midges idea of 'ALERT' practice, he'd picked one hell of a time to hold it. Then he heard strange noises as if someone was trying hard to get their breath somewhere. He listened intently and it seemed to be coming from the direction of Tayce's quarters. He ran up the corridor coming to an open doorway, where the sight of Marc comforting Tayce on the soffette greeted him.

"Midge thought he'd get your attention," said Marc trying not to laugh at the half asleep Tom leaning on the wall, trying to make himself fully coherent, as to what was unfolding.

"What is it, what's happening to her?" asked Tom in true concern, looking at Tayce trying to breath.

"It's all in hand, I'll remain with her, you go and get dressed, then get up to Organisation were on course to the Intergalactic Medical Colony, I want you dressed to take command when we arrive," said Marc taking charge of the situation.

"Sure, right, okay," replied Tom seeing the urgency to take Marc's orders.

Without further word, he raced away to get cleansed and changed. Marc stayed comforting Tayce reassuring her that everything was in hand. She looked up trying to manage a small weak smile at him. He rested her carefully back against the soffette high back. Standing to his feet, he crossed to retrieve her coverlet from the Repose Centre Bunk. He hurried back and draped it over her, to keep her warm. Then remembered the last time she'd been in this state, her Mother had placed an air mask over her mouth with portable breathing container of oxygen to help her breath a bit easier. Crossing to the Emergency Med Store, that withheld some emergency items, he took out the mask and portable oxygen container. Putting it altogether he walked back to where Tayce lay. He sat on the soffette, placing the mask over Tayces mouth, turning it on enough so that she could breath a bit more comfortably. After a few cencrons Tayce looked up at him thankful. Marc smiled kindly.

"Take it easy, you'll be all right," he assured softly.

"Thank you," said Tayce struggling a little easier, as she breathed in the oxygen.

There was little more Marc could do until they arrived at the Intergalactic Medical Colony. He sat down beside her, figuring that him being present was a help to her in itself, just knowing he was there. He studied her knowing this wasn't easy for her, but if she'd taken breaks, it needn't have happened.

Two hourons had lapsed Tom was dressed and on duty on Level 1 in Organisation. They were nearing the Intergalactic Medical Colony. Midge contacted the head Emergency Control Centre. Tom explained what the problem was to the operator and that Dr Paclan Sellecson was needed. After a few minons, it was confirmed Dr Sellecson and his team would be standing by, ready to board, when they docked at the colony. They did however request that Colonel Traun be ready on a Hover Trolley, for immediate transfer. Tom agreed wholeheartedly. Midge took back control. Tom glanced at his Wristlink time display, it read 00:300 in the mornet, he hadn't planned his nights sleep being interrupted like this, he thought. Standing he headed back across Organisation, hurrying on out down, to get a Hover Trolley from the on board Life Ability Centre, to take along to Tayce's quarters, to prepare her for transfer to the team, that would be waiting for her on arrival at the colony.

In Tayce's quarters she had managed to drift off into a deep natural sleep. Midge was monitoring her vital signs, whilst she did so. Marc sat wondering what had brought on the latest attack, besides her not taking a break. Was it the fact of what had happened all those yearons ago, on that fateful night on Traun? Had she kept it bottled up and seeing him had brought it all back to her, hence the attack. He also noticed that since he had been on board, she hadn't taken many duty breaks. Tom soon entered the quarters, bringing with him the Hover Trolley. Marc gestured for the fact Tayce was sleeping, as he stood to his feet.

"The emergency controller on the Intergalactic Colony has advised that we prepare Tayce for transfer into their hands," explained Tom.

"Right let's do it," agreed Marc eagerly.

Marc stood to his feet and started to spread the Heat Sealant Blanket over the Hover Trolley. Then both he and Tom lightly lifted Tayce up onto the surface, Tom at her feet. Marc lifting her under the arms. She moaned, as they lowered her gently down. They worked quickly to seal the Heat Sealant Blanket up to her neck, to keep her warm and comfortable.

"I'll stay with her, if you want to go and get cleansed and changed?" said Tom.

"Yeah, I don't think meeting Dr Sellecson dressed like this is going to give a good impression, he'll think I'm the patient not Tayce," joked Marc.

He hurried away to his quarters to cleanse and change. Tom was left in silence studying Tayce. Wondering why hadn't he seen what was happening, coming. Tayce slept on unaware of what had happened since she'd fallen asleep. Wheezily breathing under the mask.

Outside and drawing near was the Intergalactic Medical Colony. It looked like half a Christmas glassene ornamental star, on a flat white base. It covered a vast area of seven square milons. Ships all shapes and sizes were arriving and departing. Some where even collecting or dropping off patients and emergencies. The colony was open twenty-five hourons around the Time Display, for anything and anyone that needed medical facilities urgently, or not. On board Dr Sellecson stood with his specialist team, all waiting to take Tayce as an emergency. He was of medium height and medium build, with a strong indication of Mexican in his ancestry. His skin was tanned which confirmed as much. His eyes were Mexican dark brown, but conveyed warmth and the true meaning of who he was, a caring no nonsense medical man in his field. His features were handsome yet distinguished with a well groomed moustache. Even though he was a man who believed in principals and rules, off duty he was quite the ladies man and every nurse loved him, because off duty he was a totally different person. Some said it was as if he put his doctors coat on with the job, and adopted the manner that went with it.

On board Amalthea, Tom and Marc heard from Midge, that final docking procedures were under way to dock at the Intergalactic Medical Colony. They both began out the quarters with Tayce on the Hover Trolley down the corridor towards the Deck Travel, to take her to the Docking Bay doors on Level 2. Both walked in an urgent manner and silent, occasionally looking down at Tayce, to make sure she was all right. Amalthea slightly bumped as it locked home with the colony to signify docking had been completed. Midge made sure as usual that the cruiser was secure before opening Docking Bay doors. Upon arrival Marc controlled the Hover Trolley as they came to a stand still. The medical team from the colony walked aboard Amalthea and quickly took over moving Marc and Tom back out the way. They had been briefed by Dr Sellecson what was required of them. Soon Tayce was taken off the cruiser and into the sharp sterile bright lights of the medical interior colony, on the way for treatment. She was soon gone from sight into one of the off side treatment centres.

"Which one of you is with the patient?" asked a pretty ginger haired female nurse, coming forth, in an all in one white suit.

"I'm Commander Dayatso, how can I help?" replied Marc turning to face the young nurse.

"You can follow me Commander to give some details on the young woman you've just brought to us," said the young nurse slightly blushing at Marc's good looks and charm.

She began away in a forth right manner, heading towards her desk ahead. Marc and Tom followed her across the wide open waiting area. On the way Tom's Wristlink sounded on his right wrist with a quick succession of musical notes. He raised his right wrist, depressing the small 'Commun button'. Midge came through loud and clear. Tom turned away taking the message discretely from Midge, while Marc continued on upon reaching the main desk talking to the young nurse, to give her the requested details about Tayce. He rested on the shiny white desk top waiting for her to complete the keying in of the information, that he was giving her. Halfway through, Tom approached wanting to talk to him.

"That was Midge, you'd better finish quickly, he wants us back on board, and it sounds urgent!" exclaimed Tom discretely.

"I'm nearly through, did he say what the urgent matter was?" asked Marc curious.

"No! Just that we should return to the cruiser as soon as possible, like now!" said Tom eager to get going.

"Whatever it is Midge has got lousy timing, with Tayce stuck in here," replied Marc in discrete reply.

"Excuse me sir, if I may cut in, your Colonel may be here for a couple of dayons, so if there is something urgent you need to take care of we can contact your vessel should we require you sooner," announced the desk clerk.

"She will be okay here, until we return for her?" asked Marc, he didn't like the thought of just up and running away leaving Tayce as if he didn't care.

"Very, our security is the best," assured the young female nurse, with the name Lacey on her badge.

Upon this, Marc asked if there was anything further he needed to answer? Lacey shook her head. Marc turned and with Tom headed away in urgency, back to the cruiser across the open planned waiting area. He commented that whoever wanted them, they had picked one hell of a moment to ask for help with Tayce under medical care. Just as Marc and Tom were about to exit the waiting area and walk on back to the cruiser, Dr Sellecson stepped from the Emergency Centre.

"Commander Dayatso!" he called after Marc.

"Dr Sellecson, is it what we expected?" asked Marc coming to a pause walking back to him.

"I'm afraid so, it's her usual problem Astral Exhaustion, she never learns, it's probably a combination of things, the turmoil of what happened to her on

Traun, it was quite traumatic from what I've heard, plus she obviously hasn't been taking any regular duty breaks, but she'll be fine," he explained.

"How long will she need to be here?" spoke up Tom, just behind Marc.

"For a weekon to ten dayons considering what we've discovered, I'll leave you to continue on," replied Dr Sellecson walking away back to Tayce.

Tom and Marc continued on back to Amalthea. Marc thought to himself, he had no idea Tayce had been heading for this latest exhaustive attack, she'd hidden it well. Why hadn't Midge picked this up sooner? He would have to give Midge a proper check over and install new programming information, so that anything like this arose again, he would detect it straight away. The Docking Bay doors soon came into view and opened on both Marc's and Tom's approach. They both walked on board, heading straight up to Organisation, letting the doors seal shut behind them.

A while later when they arrived on deck, Midge began announcing that an urgent message had come in from General Largon. Tom ordered Midge to playback the message.

"Message coming through now," announced Midge, as he activated the frontal Sight Screen.

The message was suddenly cut short, by Midge, who announced that Jonathan Largon was live on Satlelink from Questa. Midge transferred him to the main Sight Screen, cancelling the Message to be played.

"General what's the problem?" asked Marc pretending nothing was out of the ordinary.

"Is Tayce there Marc?" asked Jonathan.

"No Sir, she isn't," began Marc thinking to himself, his pretending everything was fine, looked like it was not going to last more than five minons judging by the General's change in expression.

"Where are you, my information states here, your docked at the Intergalactic Medical Colony, is this true, what's happened? Whose ill?" asked Jonathan in disbelief and true concern.

"Well Tayce was suddenly taken ill just after we left Questa, I found her in the dead of night hourons on her quarters floor, it's her health problem, too much duty, not enough breaks, plus the turmoil of what happened on Traun, quite simply, it's exhaustion, we had to bring her here to the Intergalactic Medical Colony to her specialist Dr Sellecson, but we've seen him and he assures us she'll be fine in about a weekon," assured Marc in a sincere tone.

"Good, that's good news, I thought for a moment you were going to tell me she had been badly injured," said Jonathan with great relief.

"No Sir nothing like that, now how can we help you, is there a Quest you want us to take care of?" asked Tom.

"I have some exceptionally good news, well I hope it is, a Questaline exploration search, research and rescue colony announced, would you believe, they have picked up a life escape craft containing, none other than, Lydia Traun, Tayces Mother!" expressed Jonathan sounding both optimistic and open minded whether they had or had not. After all it had been three yearons.

"Tayces Mother, but I thought she was dead?" asked Tom in somewhat surprise.

"It's a possibility, we did have single person jet propulsion escape craft, she could have made it off of the surface and suffered amnesia considering what she went through, she was somewhat of a good pilot in her own right, hence this is where Tayce got her aptitude to fly this cruiser," announced Marc knowing so.

"I was gentlemen hoping that Tayce would be able to identify if this was in fact Lydia Traun, but Marc I guess you will have to do it, would you?" asked Jonathan.

"Yes of course I will," replied Marc positively.

"I'll have the bearings sent to you, good luck gentlemen," replied Jonathan signing off.

Midge suddenly announced that the bearings were being received from Questa and he was feeding them in right away and preparing to activate the course. Tom contacted the Intergalactic Medical Colony to leave a message for Dr Sellecson to tell Tayce what had materialised and that they would be back as soon as time would allow. Amalthea once locked in for the trip to the destined port of call, 'Micacer' took off at great neck speed leaving the Intergalactic Medical Colony Docking Port behind and Tayce.

Micacer was a colony that was situated on a planet of sandy soil, no bigger than Mercury, roughly 3000 milons in diameter. Most of it's surface was covered completely with the many buildings depicting the aspects towards research and exploration Domes, buildings, enclosures and special separated specialised restricted covered areas. Vehicles landed back from research missions, some departed on long haul missions. Some towed in other galactic vessels, that had been rescued, stranded out in the Universe. Earthon 2 had built the colony type base, as a means of Central Universal Research, into the many situations that occurred out in the Universe. It was funded by Earthon 2's Council for Interplanetary scope. There was a personnel population of roughly 360 + men, women and upper aged teenagers all skilled in their specialised areas of the many angles of the Universal matters or learning in related to search and planetary research.

In one of the two storey octagonal shaped buildings, a Rescue Mission Pilot, who had been responsible for discovering Lydia Trauns Life Escape Craft, was making his way along a cream shiny floored corridor to temporary quarters, where Lydia or the person thought to be Lydia Traun had been taken. He was a young slim dark haired man, in his late 20's. He paused at the entrance doors and depressed the Intercom/arrival panel, to signify his presence.

Inside she sat looking out over the complex area, watching vessels come and go. A group of teenagers passed walking on the picturesque grounds dressed in training attire all laughing and mucking around. She smiled to herself, thinking of past memories of someone that meant a great deal to her, something that had happened in her past. Why did she feel that the people of this colony even though they were being kind helping her through her amnesia, were unsure as to the fact she was Lydia Traun even though her identity stated as much? Where was Tayce she thought? Had the evil Countess won and destroyed her cruiser? Was she like Darius dead? She fought back the tears, thinking about it. Lydia turned as the doors opened behind her. Her shoulder length blonde bob, moving on her slim shoulders, as she did so, Mother and daughter were alike in their true breathtaking beauty. Their eyes were the same shade of sapphire blue. Lydia's hair even though blonde, was a slightly whiter shade. There was a kind of regal supremacy about her. But she had a soft understanding side that had somewhat been battered of late, because of what she had been through. The young male pilot paused and studied her, thinking that she still looked somewhat tired after her ordeal and treatment. But for an older woman, she was breathtakingly beautiful, and quite appealing to the eye. Adam Burnford was the young pilots name. He introduced himself to her in a polite way as such.

"I hear your the young pilot who found me out in the Universe, I want to thank you I was near to giving up hope," said Lydia softly, standing and walking across to him in an elegant way, in her oyster coloured long length outfit.

"It was my pleasure, you were lucky, the planet I found you on was caught in a time trap what might have seemed for you as arriving monthons ago, was actually three yearons ago to the dayon, your life support was beginning to fail," he expressed in a sincere recalling educated way.

"Gosh I guess I was extremely lucky that it hadn't begun to fail before, thank you," replied Lydia.

She studied Adams features, they were pleasing to the eye, but in a boyish sort of way, it made her think that if Tayce were alive, she no doubt would fancy him. She could tell he had a face for duty and rules and one that when he relaxed, would be quite appealing to any free young woman. She thought he was the kind that no doubt had plenty of friends.

"Can I call you Adam?" she asked softly.

"Yes Ma'am?" he replied looking down at her gently.

Lydia gestured for him to sit opposite her in the mouldable chair. Adam crossed and sat down, as Lydia walked back and sat on the long seat by the sight pane.

"Tell me, how did you find me, I know that you were out on patrol duty?" said Lydia getting ready to listen.

"I came across your craft on a planetary scan, it's a planet that's well known for trapping vessels etc., in time, I was killing time in returning from a far off research patrol, at first I wondered if it was an elaborate trap, you'd be surprised at the great lengths criminals go to get their hands on our research vessels, but it was the emblem on the side of your craft, that once I'd checked it with our computer, told me what I had to do, and here you are," explained Adam.

"They say I was in a deep sleep, when you found me?" asked Lydia.

"Yes that's correct," he replied.

"What yearon is this Adam, only no one has told me yet?" asked Lydia preparing for a shock.

"It's 2417... does that concern you?" he asked quietly, concerned at the surprised look on her beautiful face.

Lydia was startled to say the least, that she'd been in the Universe for the best part of three yearons and didn't know it. All this time she'd wasted. It was hard to swallow that she'd lost this precious time, all because of an evil bitch and her greedy army. Adam quickly enquired would she like to look around the Micacer Colony? Lydia looked at him gently, in thought for a minon wondering if she could. She could see he was trying to make her feel at ease, in getting her back to a normal way of life.

"Are you sure you don't have some duty that you would rather take care of, I wouldn't want you getting in trouble with your superiors, I'd be interested to see what goes on around here though, it all looks interesting from what I've seen so far," she said lightly.

"It would be an honour to have a member of the Traun family in my company," he said in a reassuring polite light-hearted way.

"You know Adam, you should meet my daughter, that's if she is still alive," said Lydia with a hint of sadness in her voice knowing that a lot could happen in three yearons and she might not have a daughter.

"You have a daughter?" asked Adam gently interested.

"Yes, her name is Tayce, she like me was cast out into space on her own in a cruiser yearons ago, when Traun was destroyed, I don't know whether she's alive or dead now," explained Lydia in a sad way thinking about it.

Adam knew this was something he knew he could find out for Lydia, but would not tell her just yet, until he found some solid evidence, that Tayce was in fact alive. He stood to his feet, as did Lydia. They both began over to the entrance. Lydia adjusted the silkene oyster coloured suit in the imager at the entrance, making sure she looked her best. The doors opened, they both stepped out into the corridor. Adam straightened his dark brown jacket in suedex. Checking his matching trousers, were dust free. They began up the corridor to the Research Complex, which Adam figured would be the most interesting for her to see. On the way Lydia explained that Traun had done it's fair share of research, so where they were going would be interesting to see.

***

42

Meantime back on the Intergalactic Medical Colony, Tayce was in the designated room for her recuperation. She focused on the sight before her, laying in the uncomfortable medical bunk, bored to say the least! Looking about she was suddenly thrust into the bright light from none other than a Medical Light pencil torch, shining in her eyes which was held by none other than the medical man she loathed in all the Universe, Dr Paclan Sellecson.

"Do you have to," protested Tayce loudly.

She tried to flinch away from the sharpness and brightness of the light. Dr Sellecson looked down at her, not saying a word, but he was far from impressed with her and she could tell by the way he seemed to treat her impatiently, every time she tried to move away, he moved the light. Once he'd deactivated the torch she smiled sarcastically at him. She could see he was about to give her another lecture on how she hadn't been looking after herself. She refused to be treated no better than a child and turned away from him.

"Turning away young woman is not going to change the fact that you've put yourself where you are by not listening to what I suggested the last time I saw you," expressed Paclan in a no nonsense tone.

"Fine, then you try flying single handed around this perilous Universe after surviving the destruction of your home, losing the only family and friends you knew and loved, all in one night, the word is 'survival' Dr Sellecson and you sometimes need to forgo sleep, just to stay alive in some sectors I've been through, when your a lone female it's a matter of life or death, so shoot me for choosing life if you have to with your words, it won't bother me, if it means I have to do it all again," retorted Tayce.

"Maybe so, but your going to be here for a weekon at least, because of your actions, or until I feel your well enough to leave," he replied dismissing her attitude, he could see she was becoming worked up.

Tayce looked away, she was too angry to continue, and went back to staring at the other side of the room. Hoping that Paclan Sellecson would simply leave her alone, but she could hear him talking to another Medical aide over her treatment. Before leaving, he suggested she rest. An amused look crossed his features, she certainly was a young woman with a lot of spirit he thought.

"Nurse keep an eye on Colonel Traun in case she tries to escape," he said light-heartedly exchanging amused smiles with the young nurse.

"You wish," said Tayce under her breath.

"Yes Dr Sellecson," replied the young brunette female nurse, amused by the situation in hand.

Paclan Sellecson walked from the room much to Tayces relief. The nurse crossed and made sure that Tayce was comfortable. She relaxed into the pillet, wondering where Marc and Tom were, she heard they had to leave her there. Wherever they were, she bet they were having more fun than she was and a lot more action to boot!

43

On board Amalthea, Marc was in silent thought, in the Co-pilot seat. Tom was in the seat adjacent to his. Midge noticed that they were both in silence. Had they fallen out, or was Tayce on their minds, wondering if this woman that had been found, was Tayces Mother, Lydia Traun. Tom was tossing over in his mind what Lydia would be like and would she like him? Marc was thinking about the last time he'd seen her alive. Tom turned his head in Marc's direction, enquiring what was Lydia like? Marc without taking his sight from the sight port advised him to form his own opinion, when he saw Lydia, he would know how to take her. Tom agreed, he was right, he may not look at Lydia the way Marc did, he'd known her a lot of yearons. Both men travelled on the last hourons of the flight to the Micacer Colony. Marc hoped that the person who claimed to be Lydia Traun, was in fact who she said she was. He imagined how over ecstatic Tayce would be. It brought a smile to his face, at the thought of the Mother and daughter reunion.

***

Adam Burnford and Lydia on Micacer walked through a wide open doorway into a bustling and busy Centre where people were working away, some heading off for their next mission. Some sat at computer screens. Adam explained that the Centre was for research into planetary weather conditions, also it was where the weather pattern for Micacer, or for other colonies that needed weather programmes, were created. Lydia was amazed at the thought of such a thing happening. She glanced around the weather creating equipment, and other layout of hi-tech pieces of equipment, as they walked across. Adam explained that the dayon would be warm and sunny around the temperature of mid 70's, the equivalent of an Earth One summers dayon. She was impressed, Traun had done their own testing on weather procedures and conditions, but nothing nowhere near on a grand scale of what was being currently created. A man in his mid forties with short sandy blonde hair crossed. He wore a pastel green uniform.

"Councillor Traun, this is our Meteorologist for our planet and other planets weather conditions, Christopher Orkland," introduced Adam.

"Councillor, welcome officially to Micacer, it's an honour to have a member of the Traun family here with us," expressed Christopher outstretching his hand for Lydia to clasp and shake.

"Thank you, it's quite impressive, what you have here," replied Lydia shaking hands.

"Traun was quite an impressive world Councillor, it was a shame what that criminal army did to it, they deserve to pay for what they've done," expressed Christopher in a sincere understanding way.

"Thank you, we use to look at Traun the way you do too, impressive!" replied Lydia.

"Would you like to see what we have in store for Micacer this evening?" asked Christopher changing the subject and rubbing his hands together, as if he was about to form some amazing feat.

"Councillor are you feeling all right?" asked Adam noticing Lydia suddenly slightly waver and gently fight back a sudden moment of feeling weak.

"Forgive me gentlemen, I guess I'm not quite up to what you term full speed, do you mind if I return to my quarters, I suddenly feel quite exhausted, maybe next time Christopher," said Lydia in an apologetic tone walking away feeling awkward that she had to cut her visit short.

"Councillor if you get a chance to, look out of your quarters this evening, you won't be disappointed," called Christopher after her.

Adam took Lydia's arm gently, she felt a fool having to leave, but for some strange reason whilst standing with Adam and Christopher, she had a very alive startling image of Tayce flash into her mind, this combined with the way she still felt weakened by her ordeal on the time trapped planet, she realised she had to rest because it had given her an unsteady weak attack. But why had Tayce flashed into her mind? What could it mean? Adam silently and in a caring manner walked her slowly back to her quarters. On route a Hover Car came up behind them. Adam quickly stopped the on board courier, explaining the situation. He suggested they ride the rest of the way to conserve her strength she had left. Lydia nodded thanking the courier as she boarded. Both she and Adam travelled the rest of the journey in the open top buggy type vehicle, back to her quarters.

On board Amalthea Marc and Tom were watching, as they came within docking distance of Micacer. They left the final approach to Midge, going on out of Organisation to go down to the Docking Bay doors on Level 2. Tom, as they went was trying to sum up in his mind what Lydia was like, all Marc had said, was he should form his own opinion of her, but had further added, that she was one extremely intelligent high class lady, and no more. It certainly was hard, how he was going to treat her he thought? On the way Midge announced overhead, that final docking was near completion. They walked to the Docking Bay doors on Level 2 and stood waiting for final docking completion. Tom was finding he was getting more uneasy at the prospect of meeting Lydia by the minon. He was scared that he may say something that would be offensive when he wouldn't mean to. The doors soon opened, both walked through and onto Micacer. Adam Burnford had been told of their arrival and had been ordered to meet them on docking. He stepped forward as they both walked into sight, outstretching his hand and welcoming them with a smile.

"Welcome to Micacer, I'm Adam Burnford, please to meet you both," said Adam shaking hands with Marc and Tom in turn.

"We understand you believe you've rescued councillor Traun?" asked Marc.

"Yes! Would you come this way?" he replied turning to head away.

Tom looked about interested, as they followed Adam on up the corridor, leaving the Docking Bay doors of Amalthea to close behind them, until their returning arrival. They soon surfaced onto the main concord, crossing the Micacer Complex, passing through bustling crowds, some carrying out small experiments, holding note takers on the way to some class, or other destined point of duty. Marc glanced away at an experiment as they passed, then looked back to where they were heading. They eventually came to white winding stonex set of steps. Tom wondered where they were being taken. Wherever it was, it sure had taken a long time to get there, still the scenery wasn't bad on the way, he thought. Lots to look at over the sprawling picturesque complex.

General Dayarn was a man in overall charge of the Micacer Colony. A man of medium stout build, in his mid forties early fifties. He was with Lydia, who had taken a small rest in her quarters. General Dayarn looked the true authoritative man that he was and showed this by the way he stood, he was truly a man who looked like he knew his job and the responsibilities that came with it. He had been explaining to Lydia that he had contacted General Largon at Questa and informed him of her possible whereabouts and that General Largon had sent two men, from a new team, called the 'Amalthean Quests Team' to find her. Suddenly behind them the quarters doors drew apart. Lydia looked over the Generals shoulder in anticipation to see who it could be. To her utter stunned amazement, Marc was the first through the open doorway. An overwhelming feeling of pure ecstatic joy filled her very existence, she was stuck for a few minons, as to what to say, she was so overwhelmed. Both forgot the past ranking they held on Traun. Marc walked forth with a warm smile and almost tears of joy to see it was the true Lydia Traun after all. Both hugged in a true feeling of escalation to know that each other was alive and well. They stayed together for a few minons savouring the fact that they had found each other. Marc had always seemed like the son she could never have.

Lydia drew slightly away, taking note that he looked slightly more older than she last remembered him. She expressed how good it was to know, he was safe and that now she was not the only Traunian alive. She looked at Tom in a questioning manner, without prejudice. Who was this handsome man standing looking somewhat awkward in her presence.

"No sign of Tayce, I was hoping she would have found you and be here, please don't tell me she's dead," said Lydia hoping that above all else he wouldn't.

"No she's not, allow me to introduce you to the second member of our new crime fighting team, Tom Stavard," said Marc stepping back allowing Tom to walk forth.

"Councillor Traun, it's an honour to meet you, Tayce talks about you quite a lot," expressed Tom taking hold of Lydia's outstretched hand gently.

46

"Tom!... You both talk of Tayce as if she's with you, but where is she?" asked Lydia wanting to know just where her daughter was, looking extremely concerned.

"We'll take you to her, if your well enough to leave?" said Marc looking to the General for approval.

"You are free to go whenever you wish, it's been a pleasure to be able to help you back to health and rescue you from the perilous planet you were on," said the General in a forthright friendly way.

"Thank you General, thank you Adam for looking after me, you are a credit to Micacer and a good host, in fact would you thank all the people of this colony for their help in making me feel welcome and treating me, I really do appreciate what they and you have done to get me back to normal health," said Lydia.

"We've enjoyed having you here Councillor, good luck with your future endeavours, may that army get what's coming to them," expressed Adam sincerely.

With this Tom asked Adam to lead them back to Amalthea. Both walked ahead of Lydia and Marc who followed on behind. Marc began they would be going to pick Tayce up, and he knew she was going to be overjoyed to know she was alive. Lydia couldn't wait and as she walked, she realised that, that mornet when she had woken, she had no idea at the mid part of the dayon she would be meeting Marc and getting to know Tayce was alive after all. Marc on route explained that they would be boarding Amalthea One soon. Lydia gave a look of surprise to know that Tayce still had the same cruiser, with all the crime in the Universe that was going on. She couldn't wait.

*****

09:00 next mornet aboard the Intergalactic Medical Colony. Tayce had had a good nights sleep something she hadn't been able to get for a long time, though she had a feeling it was something they had slipped into her drink. She in the last houron, had been up and walking in the company of a young Medic in the Parkland Area. He'd been assigned to guide her back to normal health. Dressed in a beige leisure suit, she was now taking her daily exercise, that had been prescribed to tone up her muscles. Donaldo Tysonne was the young Medics name. He was of athletic build, as if he'd spent most of his off duty hourons in the nearest Gym. He was lightly putting her through some supple exercises that would get her toned up back to normal mobility. Tayce didn't see the point in this, she used these muscles every dayon, why should she want to exercise them just because Dr Sellecson said it had to be done. Okay, she'd do it under protest, just until Tom and Marc got back. This she hoped was soon, as she didn't know how much more of this treatment she could take. Donaldo studied her, he could see she was finding this whole thing annoying, he could understand her frustration, she was use to life in space and a hectic lifestyle, he'd read her background and admired her for what she'd gone through. He wondered what it would be like travelling the stars aboard a space cruiser, as all he'd known was the Intergalactic Medical Colony. Tayce looked up studying his jet black hair, that was neatly styled in a short off the face layered look, that swept to the nape of the neck. His eyes were Italian dark brown, but showed alertness and kindness. He had a sort of educated look about him, someone that wanted to go further in life, than what he currently was doing. Donaldo was twenty-nine yearons old. He wanted to ask her what it was like travelling the stars, it was kind of boring being just another physio medic for Dr Sellecson undertaking physio with people such as Tayce, but he figured she might think he was being nosey. He wasn't what you called tall in statue, he was around 1.75 metres in height. Tayce sighed she could take no more and stopped.

"I know that Dr Sellecson said you had to try these new exercises todayon, but are you sure your well enough to try them, there's no use running before you can walk, as they say," he put to her concerned she was pushing herself more than she needed to.

Tayce was under the assumption that the more she got better, the quicker, she would get out off her surroundings.

"Let's just get on with this, I'm not enjoying this no more than your enjoying making me suffer," she said looking at him with a look conveying she'd rather be some place else as he probably would.

"Shall I tell you the truth, I understand you don't like being in this position, well your not the only one, I don't much like being here on this colony any more, it's the same tedious duty every dayon, but I have to do it and I'm suggesting you do the same, until your team come back and collect you, sorry if that sounds spiteful but I'm trying to make you see, that your not the only one fed up here," pointed out Donaldo much to Tayces surprise.

"What do you mean you don't like being here any more, why don't you change your job, surely there must be other colonies crying out for someone like you?" said Tayce climbing to her feet, from the last exercise move.

"I've been here a lot of yearons under Dr Sellecson and I've just finished training in the medical field, there is nowhere else to go I've tried, believe me, if there was somewhere else to go, I would go," he replied calmly and in thought.

Tayce on this began thinking. Her cruiser could do with a proper medical man to take care of the sudden on board medical emergencies. Could Donaldo be suited for the position? She thought about it in silence for a moment. Donaldo looked at her realising maybe she needed a break.

"Donaldo what are your real qualifications besides doing this?" she asked in the true tone of Colonel.

"I've just passed my final medical exams to become a Medical Officer in space medicine, but doing this is all I could get at the end of my training, why?" he asked looking at her curious.

"What if I could change this situation for you, and I ask you to join me on Amalthea, you'd have your own medical facility known as the Life Ability Centre and that you would also be part of a crime fighting team known as the Amalthean Quests Team, you would be serving under the Questa Emblem, your job would be to take care of all the medical matters during voyage?" put Tayce.

"Are you serious about this, why I would jump at the chance, it's actually what I've been looking for, my own medical facility travelling the Universe as part of some kind of team, yes I would," he replied eagerly not worrying about what he'd be giving up.

"Then it's settled, I offer you the position of Medical Officer in the Life Ability Centre aboard Amalthea, welcome to the Amalthean Quests Team, you'll be my third new member, you'll meet the others later, Tom and Marc," said Tayce glad she had found another member of her new team.

"You won't be disappointed," assured Donaldo, ecstatic that at last he'd found what he was searching for.

He didn't know what to say. He instead suggested they call the exercise regime finished for the dayon they had been exercising long enough. Tayce agreed, feeling somewhat relieved, she couldn't see the benefit of this exercise lark. They both left the Parkland exercise area and headed back into the main stay complex.

Later that same dayon Marc Dayatso entered the Intergalactic Medical Colony reception area. Dr Sellecson was summoned and soon appeared. Marc crossed to meet with him, he knew it was a lot sooner than he had anticipated in returning for Tayce. Dr Sellecson listened to Marc's explanation for returning early. He was a bit apprehensive to let Tayce go. Marc could see there was a problem, he wondered if Tayces condition had become a lot worse, than first thought.

"What's the problem here doctor, Tayce is going to be all right isn't she?" asked Marc apprehensively.

"Yes, there's no problem, but for the time being I'm releasing one of my team to be on your cruiser, just to keep an eye on Tayce, she's a lot better, but it may happen again if she doesn't take care, so when Tayce asked for me to release one of my team to become your new Medical Officer, I figured this would be a good idea to let him join your team and at the same time keep an eye on her," explained Paclan.

"Why do I feel that your not particularly pleased to release her?" said Marc standing at ease.

"I feel she should be here another weekon, but now that Donaldo Tysonne is part of your team, I'm hoping it will suffice," he said not happy to be letting his patient leave without completing the treatment

"Don't worry we'll take care of her and we've someone on board Amalthea who will make sure she takes breaks, when she should, her Mother!" said Marc knowing that Lydia would do just that.

They both walked to the room where Tayce was staying. Paclan entered first and Marc walked on in to see Tayce sitting in a chair by the sight pane. She turned glad to see him, glad also that he'd returned early, now Dr Sellecson wouldn't be able to keep her where she was any longer, she could go back to Amalthea.

"Does this mean that I can go now?" asked Tayce standing up.

"Yes young woman your free to go," said Paclan he could see where she was coming from in that she couldn't wait to leave.

"I've a surprise for you on Amalthea, something you thought you'd lost forever," said Marc keeping her in suspense.

"Oh what?" asked Tayce intrigued to know.

"You'll have to wait," said Marc with a teasing smirk.

Paclan handed Tayce a small container of small pink capsules, that she had to take for the next two weekons until they were all gone. Donaldo walked into the room carrying his holdall and garment bag.

"Marc this is Donaldo Tysonne, he's going to be our new Medical Officer on the team," introduced Tayce.

"Welcome to the team," said Marc in a true friendly easy going manner

Tayce began towards the entrance. Paclan suggested she take it easy. Was he kidding thought Tayce with all the criminals there were out in the Universe! Everyone walked out into the corridor. Paclan shook hands with Marc, then all three walked down the corridor, back to Amalthea. Donaldo looked back at the place that had been his life since he was sixteen. Even though he had learnt everything he needed to learn, he was glad to be walking away and into what promised to be an exciting life.

Finally they arrived back at the Docking Bay doors. Not a moment to soon thought Tayce as she stepped aboard. Marc announced that her surprise was waiting in Organisation. No more needed to be said Tayce left him and ran at full pelt to find out what it was. Her mind was in total overwhelmed excited anticipation, as to what it might be. As she ran so her blonde hair blew out in the corridor warm air. Who was it? What was it that was waiting she thought? Upon approach to Organisation, she slowed. Cautiously walking along trying to get some indication of what was waiting for her. Pausing at the Organisation doorway, she looked about. Nothing out of the ordinary, was this some kind of joke Marc had played on her. Then she stood up. Tayce couldn't believe who she was seeing. Tears of utmost overwhelming joy filled her eyes. Her heart skipped a beat. Lydia held open her arms to her daughter.

"Don't I get a hug after all these yearons?" she asked in a true motherly loving tone.

"Sure you do," replied Tayce running into her Mother's open arms

Lydia closed her arms around her daughter and held her tightly and lovingly overwhelmed with emotion to know and see that Tayce was very much alive. Tears of joy were running down Tayces and her Mother's cheeks. Both Mother and daughter held each other in a loving affectionate way. After a few minons Lydia held Tayce a little way away from her, taking a good look at her. It had been yearons since she had last seen this young impressionable face of beauty and she had grown like a younger version of herself. She wished Darius could see what a grown up independent young woman Tayce had become.

"Oh Mother it's good to see you and know that your here back where you belong?" said Tayce hugging her Mother yet again.

"I'm not going anywhere from now on, now tell me more about this Amalthean Quests Team," said Lydia.

As they talked Lydia could see that it hadn't been easy for Tayce alone in the stars for the past yearons but she knew that it wouldn't be, this is why they had Midge designed to keep her company. But now she was back and things were going to look upwards and onwards for the both of them a new future would be made.

Tom Under Trial

Everyone on board Amalthea was engrossed in some kind of on board activity. Marc was in command of the cruiser with Midge, checking through the new update programming changes that had been made to his software. They were working as a mini team in taking the cruiser on to a new sector, heading across the Universe. It had been almost two weekons since leaving the Intergalactic Medical Colony and life on board was becoming more like a team environment. Lydia was settling in, not only in being Tayces Mother once more, but being an active member of the team, Mother and daughter were growing close again.

Tom Stavard was pacing up and down the floor of his living area, in his quarters in agitated fury because of a communicative print out he'd received. The more he paced, the more he became agitated at the contents. Who had done this sick thing to him and why? He was vastly progressing beyond the realms of trying to keep his cool about the communication in his hands. Midge who monitored everyone's vital signs on board was getting readings from Tom that were far from perfect. He informed Tayce immediately, something was badly wrong with Tom in his quarters. He was reading very unrealistic high adrenaline levels and it was a great cause for concern. Tayce felt something was wrong as well, she didn't know how, or why, but she did. It was unlike Tom to be showing this kind of strange behaviour, he was generally a calm person at the best of times. Lydia suggested she go, they could work together later. Tayce on this, left her Mother and walked along to Tom's quarters. The doors opened upon her approach under orders to Midge to open them in case anything was happening inside. Tom turned to face her. His eyes were like wildfire with anger. Tayce looked at him wondering how he was going to be towards her, she glanced to the computerized printout he had in his hands, she could see whatever the contents were, it had something to do with his extreme anger.

"You want to talk about it, it obviously seems to be connected with what your holding?" asked Tayce cautiously and calmly.

Tom sighed an exasperating sigh. He was trying to find the words to describe the false accusation that was stated before him. He couldn't, instead he thrust the printout at Tayce, almost making her flinch in the way in it came at her. Tayce grabbed it before it fell to the floor. The information had come from Tom's home planet. It summoned him to a trial at the Intergalactic Criminal Court Colony over the mysterious death of his wife Alenea Stavard. Tayce looked to Tom, she had to admit, that she'd assumed that Alenea had died of her injuries. But had she? It had also been Midges diagnosis, that Alenea had in fact died of her massive internal wounds was there something he wasn't telling her? She looked at Tom, not knowing quite what to say. He suggested she read further down. Tayce continued reading, the next paragraph stated that he was requested to appear, as he was the only suspect in the case.

"Believe me, I didn't kill Alenea, you know what my craft was like when you found me," he turned on her almost shouting at her.

"I know your sore over this and I would be too, you must keep your calm, you go to that trial and be like you are now and they'll think the worst, that you did kill Alenea," said Tayce forthrightly.

"What am I going to do, as far as they are concerned I'm sent to the Prison Colony before I have a chance to state my case at trial," he replied.

"Tom calm down, I know that you'll probably take this the wrong way, but I've got to tell you, when Midge and I found you Alenea was dead from serious injuries, anyone who didn't know you would assume that you did kill your wife, although Midge knows otherwise and we'll help clear your name," assured Tayce waiting for Tom to lose it with her again she felt awkward and was not sure of what to say for fear of him lashing out verbally again.

"Thanks! I know you probably have your doubts deep down, but I loved her, we were childhood sweethearts the last thing I would have done is kill her, I would have done anything to protect her from those barbarians that were attacking us," replied Tom calming down.

"You need to attend this trial as I see it and tell it like it was, exactly word for word, what happened, Midge and I will put together a report of his findings, when we rescued you and put this up as your evidence to sustain that you did not kill Alenea," said Tayce.

Tayce walked over to him. He reached out pulling her in close in a thankful gentle way. Looking down at her, now with calm warm gentle eyes again. He informed her he was no murderer, proof of the first night aboard Amalthea when they were on duty, officially, should prove this to her, also when she fell down the steps, how he came to her aide. A murderer would have taken his opportunity to take the chance to bump her off and steal her present surroundings. Tayce knew this was true, he had been really concerned and like he had said, a murderer would have finished her off at the bottom of the Level Steps and probably jettisoned her body into space without so much as a thought. She drew away from him and walked to the nearest mouldable chair and sat down. She began by suggesting he explain to her fully what occurred before she and Midge rescued him and Alenea, so that she could compile her report, how Alenea was killed. Midge would record it on Disc Chip. Tom agreed. She ordered Midge via Wristlink to record Tom's words of how Alenea died, ready for the report for trial. Midge agreed. Tom began explaining how the Universe they were travelling through had suddenly changed, one moment it was all calm, then the next they were hit by a meteorite, or what they thought was a meteorite. Then they appeared out of nowhere a bunch of fighters, coming fast. Alenea had been running tests on some samples they'd picked up on the last planet of call, that was her job, she took samples for analysis. Then they were hit by some real powerful weapon fire, that threw her across the deck hard against the front control panel. She'd fallen to the floor, blood oozing from her face and forehead and she was out cold. He'd tried to reach her, but one, his safety harness had jammed, and secondly he was fighting off the onslaught of the criminal band that were after their surroundings.

"Didn't you call for help, send out a distress call of some sort?" asked Tayce.

He continued that he had, but no one came. When he did finally win the dayon against the attackers the craft was in the condition she found it in, and he hadn't realised, he too, had been injured, how he never quite knew. But despite his injuries when all was calm and the criminal race had left, he managed to lift Alenea blood stained back into her seat. She was breathing very shallow. 'Cargo' was like Midge was to her and he had ordered a scan of Aleneas injuries. Cargo did it, confirming her injuries were life threatening. He'd ordered him as he lost his fight to stay conscious, to find a non hostile vessel to hopefully try and help out. Hence he found Amalthea, or she and Midge found him and what remained of the craft. To top it all life support was damaged and failing by the minon. Tom as he sat opposite Tayce was doing his utmost to hold back the tears recalling the past with pain. The whole incident was like it had been yesteron, it still hurt like hell he thought inside. Tayce could believe Tom's side of what had happened, she'd come up against some real lawbreakers in her travels, over the yearons until now.

"I hope that helps, because it's the truth Tayce," said Tom breaking down.

She stood to her feet and crossed to sit down beside him, ordering him to let the hurt go. Midge overhead confirmed that he had recorded the whole testament. Tayce, when Tom had gained his composure, stood to her feet and understandingly informed him.

"Don't worry what you've told me, Midge and I will have this report of evidence compiled, plus any medical records of that dayon what condition I found Alenea in, ready when we need it," she assured.

"Your one hell of a good friend Tayce Traun, thanks for believing in me," said Tom managing a small smile of thanks.

54

"I'm just doing my duty, you told the truth and I would do the same for any of this team, If I have to, I'll also give the evidence that I found verbally, if it should be called for," she replied.

She glanced at the date on the computerized document. The trial was tomorron. It didn't give them much time to play with. As she began towards the doors of the living area, so she suggested he take the rest of the time off duty until they reached the Intergalactic Criminal Court Colony where the trial would take place. Marc and herself would take care of getting him to the trial on time and when her Mother had heard what had happened, she too would want to help. With this she slipped out of the opening doors as they parted leaving Tom to sit in silence.

Marc was returning from a duty break and was half way up the Level Steps, when he heard Tayce running up behind him. He paused, turning. Tayce caught him up. Marc could see she had something on her mind by the look of preoccupied thought. Upon them both reaching the top of the steps Tayce guided him to the side of the corridor wall. She began by explaining what was on her mind. Then handed him the document that Tom had thrust at her earlier. Upon studying it, Marc found it hard to take in and gave her a look to match.

"This is absurd, he's no killer, okay so he's a little rough around the edges at times, but he's no murderer, he was even scared of how he was going to meet your Mother," expressed Marc.

"Really, so your on my side when I say I feel the same?" put Tayce.

"Sure he's a decent bloke, unless he's been fooling all of us into thinking as much," said Marc seriously.

"I definitely don't think so, you weren't there a minon ago, when he told me of what had happened, when Alenea died he was between you and me, fighting back the sheer emotional hurt of the situation that had unfolded aboard his craft."

"Then you get my help on this, where do we start?" replied Marc eagerly.

"The course to the Intergalactic Criminal Court Colony, we have to get there, the quickest route in time to be there for the trial tomorrow," replied Tayce turning and beginning off in the direction of Organisation.

Both stepped into Organisation and made their way to their seats. As soon as Tayce sat down Midge began informing Marc next time he went for a break, he'd like a little more warning, as he had wondered where he'd gone, he thought he was still on duty. Tayce sat in the pilot seat, ordering Midge to lock in a course to the Intergalactic Criminal Court Colony, the quickest available route to be there for a trial tomorrow. He agreed eagerly. Marc sat back relaxingly and exclaimed he'd been to the colony once for her Father and he wouldn't care to mix with them again. The personnel there, were not the easiest to get on with. Tayce recalled herself that she remembered going once at around the age of fifteen and one officer was giving her the evil eye, he felt that minors such as herself were considered not appropriate to be allowed on the colony that catered for criminals. She thought to herself, she hoped that same officer was not still present, when she went back with Amalthea now.

"Believe me Tom is going to go through a hard time, on that colony," said Marc warning her to expect the worse ahead.

"It does make me wonder what they'll do to him, in their eyes he's just like any other criminal that attended trial at the colony, but with our evidence and even if I have to take the stand, we should be able to convince them, Tom is no murderer," exclaimed Tayce.

Marc nodded in an understanding way, they both sat looking ahead, as Amalthea went into Hyper Thrust Turbo mode and headed on it's swift journey to the Intergalactic Criminal Court Colony to clear Tom's name.

The Intergalactic Criminal Court Colony sat in the dark depths of the known Universe, looking every inch what it stood for. Gun metal grey in colour, it covered five milons in diameter. It was the only Earthon 2 law colony of it's kind in the current space and time. It was known for it's tight rules and laws, anyone going there felt the wrath of sheer fear. Decent or otherwise. It upheld the most tight laws on murder and for any other crime committed in the known or unknown Universe. If you were found guilty of murder or had taken another persons life without good reason even accidentally, then you were taken to the termination point and put to death by electrical slow increasing current. Tom Stavard was not going to have an easy time of it. There was nothing attractive about the colony. It was hexagonal in shape, with a lot of smaller hexagonal shapes encircling one large central one. It had been constructed by human effort and of stealex and glassene construction. Withholding four small courts for small cases, and two large ones for cases to be heard like Tom's. Anyone who was found to be guilty, suffered either the electrical slow increasing current induced death, or were sent to the Prison Colony. Fines were steep, to say the least 20,000 for a light crime 40,000 for a serious crime. Some accused beings had been known to lose their vessels, in having them repossessed to pay for what crime they had committed. The courts were ultra modern inside. The witness would stand on a one step platform, which lit up on impact, then he or she would place their right or left hand on a small octagonal hand sized pad, set on a white tube shaped podium that lit on touch when the answer was given. In the centre of the frontal wall of the large courts, was a large Sight Screen, enabling playback of evidence that had been filmed for the trial. The Judge would sit up high, above the lawbreaker, looking down on him, or her, or alien for that matter. The Jury sat in a circle, around the court. There was a spot light fixed, where the lawbreaker would stand. This is the Intergalactic Criminal Court Colony.

Back across the Universe on board Amalthea Tayce took the computerized printout evidence from Midges main printer and studied what he and she had put together. She smiled and nodded her head, this was enough good evidence to confirm that Tom did not murder Alenea, the trial would no doubt go in their favour, as she saw it. He had nothing to be concerned about. Marc stood to his feet after putting the cruiser back under Midges guidance walking round to take a look.

"Good is it?" said Marc looking over her shoulder.

"Let's see their faces when they get this," said Tayce pleased.

"Quite convincing, I'd buy it," he replied agreeably.

Tayce handed him the printout. He took it studying it in more detail with interest, raising his eyes at what he was reading. He congratulated her on it being truly impressive to say the least. She exclaimed it wasn't down to just her, Midge helped too. Lydia walked into Organisation, wondering what all the excitement was. Marc turned giving her the printout and let Tayce explain. Tayce began that she had to share something important with her, that involved a member of the team. Lydia gave her a look of questioning interest.

"Tom is been accused of murdering his wife Alenea, but Midge and I found his craft badly damaged and his wife was dead from her injuries, which would confirm otherwise, he confided in me a while ago and told me the whole story what had happened in the fact they were ambushed by a criminal race who opened fire on them," explained Tayce.

"So what's this here?" said Lydia quite calmly

"It's the evidence compiled on what happened by myself and Midge, I believe it's sound enough to clear Tom's name, at the trial that's going to be tomorron at the Intergalactic Criminal Court Colony," said Tayce as Lydia studied what was before her.

"Marc a word alone with my daughter here a moment, please," said Lydia waiting until Marc had left the deck so that Mother and daughter could talk.

"I'll see you later, I want to check on some modifications I've done," he said walking from Organisation.

Lydia waited until Marc was out of earshot and she'd finished reading the report. Tayce had a feeling despite telling her Mother the whole story, she was going to come in for one of her famous lectures and it no doubt had something to do with trusting Tom. She stood ready, thinking her Mother had only been on board a couple of weekons and she was already trying to take command. How long did she think she'd been travelling the stars since leaving Traun and being in command of their present surroundings. She knew who to trust and not to trust.

"Are you sure that this Tom is as innocent as he claims to be?" asked Lydia quite sternly.

"Yes! I've been in charge of this cruiser for three yearons, I know when someone is telling the truth, I'm a woman now Mother and not the naïve little Traunian daughter of a Commodore that you knew I'm leader of this team and I know Tom well enough to know when he's telling the truth," retorted Tayce.

"Spy's and Pirates come in all kinds of guises Tayce," replied Lydia ignoring Tayces tone of voice.

"What are you getting at?" replied Tayce sharply, she resented the path that her Mother was going down over Tom.

"You don't know Tom didn't kill Alenea, you've only his word he didn't," replied Lydia trying to make Tayce look at it from another angle, that even the most convincing killers sounded truthful.

"Well my judgement tells me otherwise, I'm not prepared to discuss this any further Mother I've made up my mind over the truth and that's final," retorted Tayce turning away she didn't want to hear any more.

Midge had witnessed the whole thing, he considered Tayces side of the story the right side, he'd monitored Tom's vital signs all the time he'd told Tayce, what had happened on board his craft with Alenea and the levels he read stayed normal, if not a little stressed. Tayce walked from Organisation, she was not going to stand and argue any more with her Mother she didn't see the point. Lydia sighed thinking that sometimes Tayce was a bit too headstrong for her own good. She was just like her Father, Darius her husband. Still she'd learn. Lydia figured that fair enough if she was wrong about Tom, she would apologise, but only if she was wrong. She stood in thought looking out of the sight port. Midge remained silent, guiding Amalthea on to the destined port of the call, he was not going to get involved.

Marc walked up the Level Steps towards Tayce, he could see she'd had an argument with her Mother. He couldn't understand it, considering both had been apart for so long. He noticed Tayce looked like thunder about to erupt. He reached out and grabbed her by the arm, bringing her back to him. She came back to face him giving a look that said don't patronise me, I'm not interested. He had always been able to put her right when things became heated between her Mother and herself in the past, this appeared to be like one of those times.

"Take it easy, you look like your about to explode, this isn't good for you right now with your health in it's current state," said Marc softly.

"Why can't she realise that I'm not that naïve little girl from Traun any more and I know what is right aboard my own cruiser and especially when it comes to a member of this team, she doesn't know Tom like I do and you would think that for once she would believe in what I believe?" protested Tayce.

"This is hard for her, she has your best interests at heart, she probably wants to believe you, but your right she doesn't know Tom like you do, give her some time to get to know him, she probably feels also out of things she's hasn't been here when you've faced things, she doesn't realise the Universe has moved on from our dayons on Traun, it's going to take time for her to adjust to this new way of life, come on Tayce, she is trying," pointed out Marc.

"So you think it's okay for her to call Tom a liar, do you, you heard his story?" continued Tayce sharply.

"I'm not saying that, I believe Tom didn't kill Alenea, but you both need to realise that things have changed since you last saw each other three yearons ago, you've grown independent and she's trying to come to terms with that, there are two factors here, one that you've grown up and secondly you have someone, namely Tom, that you believe in, she knows the Universe and how convincing bad guys can be, until she finds that Tom's not guilty she is going to see the bad in him, later on your both going to regret the spat you've no doubt just had, patience is the key here Tayce try exercising it," said Marc quietly but firmly.

"Okay point taken," said Tayce with a sigh.

"You'll look back on this somewhere down the line, she only has your best interests at heart, come here," he said pulling Tayce into a comforting hug.

He smiled to himself things hadn't changed much between Mother and daughter, he could remember dayons on Traun when they had these argumentative moments of debate. It hadn't changed a bit. He released her seeing that she was a lot more at ease. They stood talking about the forth coming trial. Marc informed her everything was working as it should be aboard. Midge via Wristlink informed Marc that Lydia seemed upset and it would be a good idea to go and find her on board. Upon Tayce hearing this, she realised what Marc had just said was true she had to be patient with her Mother. She felt guilty in a way. Marc could see this and suggested in a joking tone whilst she return to Organisation, he went and found her Mother before she jumped cruiser. Tayce turned and walked back to Organisation Deck, she realised now she was acting no better than that spoilt Traunian child. Marc turned and went back down the Levels Steps asking Midge via Wristlink where Lydia was on board, so he could find her.

* * *

The Intergalactic Criminal Court Colony was now moving into orbital view of Amalthea One. Midge began going through the tough clearance to dock at the colony. The treatment he was receiving, as he went through the tight security procedures wasn't far short of being the equivalent of a strip search! Beams of sensory light ran over the cruisers hull probing every nook and cranny for something that wasn't there. He found the whole thing very undignified and near damn right draining on his circuits. Once through, he was informed by the operator at the colony, that an escort would meet the criminal for criminal transfer in a very abrupt tone, upon arrival, Midge explained what was happening as far as Tom's transfer was concerned and that there would be people travelling to the hearing with him. The operator paused and the air was filled with deadly silence. Then after a few minons the request was granted with an abrupt reply. Midge was glad he wasn't Tom. This was going to be tough, it was good that Tayce had managed to get Tom's sound evidence, he was going to need it, judging by the treatment he'd received just being the cruisers high IQ Computer. Docking procedures commenced. Midge found the attitude of the Control Centre for docking just as up tight as the scan search and in his estimation. It was about

59

time someone informed them, that there was an old Earth One saying where a trial was concerned. "Innocent until proven guilty" and they needed to take a crash course in customer care. Not everyone was coated with the same criminal coating. Tayce returned to Organisation. Upon entering she briskly crossed the deck, and slid into the pilot seat.

"Are you okay Midge, your silent?" asked Tayce noticing so.

"I have just endured the most undignified search, this side of the Universe, just to be cleared for docking, not a pleasant situation I want to be in again," he expressed in a disgusted tone.

"You won't have to endure it again, I promise," said Tayce feeling sorry he had to in the first place.

"I have requested your presence, they say they are sending an escort to meet Tom, though not quite in those words, they stated that they were sending an escort for criminal transfer of the criminal," said Midge.

"Tayce can we talk a minon?" asked Lydia softly walking back into Organisation.

"Mother can it wait, I'm trying to watch the final moments of docking," replied Tayce watching as the cruiser went into the final moments before docking at the Intergalactic Criminal Court Colony.

"No it can't," said Marc leaning round the chair at her.

"Fine, you take over then, right Mother let's talk," said Tayce leaving her seat letting Marc take over.

Both Mother and daughter walked to one side of Organisation. Both stood talking, then both hugged after a brief silence. Midge informed Marc quietly that his discussions with both Tayce and Lydia earlier might have worked. Marc explained that he had informed Lydia of how a good colonel Tayce had become in the yearons since leaving Traun. He had suggested she let Tayce handle things in general, she was a grown up girl now. He smiled at the fact that both of them had sorted the situation out and it looked like things were going to be on an even footing from that moment on. Tom appeared in the doorway, looking somewhat ashen faced and trying to hide his apprehension of the forthcoming trial. Tayce turned seeing his uneasiness feeling, sorry for what he was about to endure. All she could do was hand the evidence over to the officer in charge of handling Tom's case. She crossed and in full view of her Mother gave Tom a reassuring hug. He slowly hugged her back. He felt bad having to put her through this unnecessary mess.

"How long till we're there?" he asked nervously looking out the sight port at the approaching sight of the Intergalactic Criminal Court Colony.

"We're nearly there, they have announced an escort will meet you, to take you in to trial, but don't worry Tom we will be watching and as I said earlier, I will stand up and speak on your behalf, tell them like it was," insisted Tayce looking up at him.

"Thank you my love, he said calling her it for the first time.

"We'll all be there for you mate," spoke up Marc from the pilot seat.

Final docking concluded. Midge took control whilst they were in Docking Port. He wished Tom luck before he began out of the Organisation Deck. Tom acknowledged then walked on behind Tayce. Lydia and Marc followed with Donaldo at the rear, taking his Medic Emergency Kit, in case he needed it. They all began on the walk down to the Docking Bay doors.

On the Intergalactic Criminal Court Colony two strong looking sturdy officers in guard uniforms stood waiting the arrival of Tom. They had weapons in their holsters, ready to use if need be, to act at a moments notice if Tom proved awkward in any way. Their current stance until Tom arrived was at ease, one, watching for the first signs of the emerging team that would soon be coming down the walkway. Upon hearing the sound of footsteps, they moved to the foot of the walkway and began up placing their right hands to the powerful looking handguns, ready to withdraw should any trouble arise. The senior looking of the two officers with ginger hair upon seeing Tayce, stepped forward.

"Which one of you is in charge of the Amalthean prisoner?" he requested to the point.

"I'm Colonel Traun and the man you seek is Mr Stavard here," replied Tayce introducing Tom in a tone that matched the officers.

Without warning and in quick movement, the two officers roughly reached out and grabbed Tom on both sides. They dragged him away from the team. Tayce gave a look of shear alarm at the sudden behaviour she couldn't believe the way in which everything had happened so fast. Marc could, he'd seen it too many times before on previous visits for Darius Traun. Tom was out of sight within minons. Tayce turned to Marc. He slipped his arm around her shoulders, quietly informing her he had told her what the personnel were like. A young uniformed dark haired officer stepped into view and began towards them. Marc tried to calm Tayce down, she was fuming inside at the way in which one of her team had just been treated and it showed on her beautiful features.

"I apologise for that action Colonel, it must have come as quite a shock, but I'm afraid that is how everyone who goes for trial is treated here, until they are proven innocent," he explained, in a regretful tone seeing the look of utter displeasure cross her face

"My team member is no criminal, as you will find out soon enough," replied Tayce displeased at the way in which Tom had been treated.

The young officer would say no more, for fear of further anger from Tayce. He suggested they follow him and he would take them where they had to go and wait. The remaining Amalthean team members followed on. They walked through a large reception, then on across the courtyard. On the way, the young slim officer explained they would have to wait in the waiting area, until called for. Tayce was finding it tough to keep her cool as she walked along in silence. She wondered how Tom was bearing up, hating the thought they had been separated until the trial. As they walked down a walkway Tom could be seen being lead away in the distance roughly Tayce looked with alarm, helpless to do anything in the careless handling of one of her team that she was witnessing. Marc discretely informed her, she might as well take it easy, there was nothing she could do. She listened, but hated the fact it was out of her hands. They soon walked into a room that withheld three bench type seats. Lydia sat down on one whilst Tayce and Marc on the other. Donaldo looked concerned for Tayce. He sat beside, her, asking her if she was all right? She nodded in thought, even though she was Colonel and leader of the team, she hated situations such as this.

"This is disgusting keeping us in here like this, I shall be reporting this to General Largon when I get to Questa Tayce, don't worry," pointed out Lydia understanding her daughters anger.

"I wonder how long they'll keep us here?" asked Marc wonderingly.

"Until they send for us I should imagine it's a bit bare of comforts, if this is the waiting room," commented Donaldo looking about.

"If I knew we would have to wait, we would have done it on Amalthea," replied Tayce, she was growing fed up in which they had been treated.

"I know how you feel, but unfortunately Tayce they make the rules, and we have to abide by them or end up where Tom is, it's out of our hands," said Marc positively, but he also couldn't understand the long wait.

All four sat and waited in the barest of waiting rooms reserved for waiting members for watching the trial. Each Amalthean members thoughts were on something. Noise could be heard outside, people shouting, going by, some arguing. Tayce decided to stretch herself out on the long bench and lean against the wall, there was no telling how long they would have to be there. She decided to Wristlink Midge aboard the cruiser to see if he could find out just what was going on outside their current surroundings, they called a waiting room. He soon informed her that he would come back to her.

Tom was seated further down the corridor looking somewhat lost. The area he sat in looked just as sparse as the waiting area and furnished just as much. He was so bored, he was trying to make out the many amusing words of inscribe on the walls. Obviously put there by the past inhabitants waiting for the same thing he was. Some were very interesting to say the least and amusing. His thoughts kept drifting in and out of what he was going to say, when called. Also his thoughts were wondering what Tayce thought of all this and how she was bearing up. He glanced at his Wristlink, wondering if the trial was going to happen on this dayon at all, it was growing late and in a couple of hourons it would be the end of court session for the current dayon. It was fast becoming obvious, he was going to be present for the duration of night hourons. He turned pounding the hard square material block, that was supposed to be a pillet trying to mould it into a shape he could rest against and drop off in to some kind of sleep, not that he was going to do much of that, with the prospect of being grilled the next mornet for a murder, he did not commit. He found himself staring at the uninteresting ceiling the moment he lay down and put his head on the hard equivalent of a pillet. Sounds from other criminals rang through the echoing corridors outside, complaining about their accommodation. Tom drifted into an uneasy sleep. Lights dimmed to go out, the room soon filled with total darkness and the noise from other prisoners that had been loud to say the least, faded into the distance ending another dayon.

Mornet came round soon enough on the Intergalactic Criminal Court Colony. The two guards that had dragged Tom away to his current surroundings the dayon before, walked along to Tom's room. Where he'd had the most uneasy of nights. The doors opened and they marched in. Tom sat up wondering what they were going to do to him, this time. He managed to gather his thoughts and himself together, when they once more hauled him onto his feet and marched him out of his present surroundings. As he went he wondered where they were taking him. People in the area looked him up and down in a summoning cold way. This he couldn't understand. He was totally innocent, but he guessed in their eyes, he was guilty as charged. The two guards took him along a narrow corridor which was once again dimly lit. They turned the corner at the far end going on through double automatic opening doors. Once inside, they ordered him to freshen up, then left him. Without further delay. Tom began to do just as they had ordered and he soon found himself feeling better for it, ready to face whatever was thrown at him in the dayon ahead.

Marc slowly shook Tayce from her crooked neck sleep, resting on his shoulder. She slowly sat up coming awake, at first feeling refreshed, but that she soon changed to disgust, that they had spent the entire night hourons in their uncomfortable surroundings, namely the 'Waiting Room'. She stretched.

"What time is it?" asked Tayce to Marc.

"Hold on I'll check," he said checking the Wristlink time display on his wrist.

It read 08:37 and he turned to inform her as much. He began thinking how hungry he was. They all had to get something to eat before the trial, he thought, this was disgusting. They had been treated no better than if they were criminals themselves. Suddenly the doors opened to the waiting room in walked the young officer from yesteron. To everyone's surprise Tayce jumped to her feet.

"I demand to know why you have kept us locked in here all night, I could have returned to my cruiser until we were needed todayon?" asked Tayce angry.

"My apologies Colonel, you should have been allowed to return to your cruiser, I'm here to suggest you go for some refreshment and a freshen up and to report to the hearing at 09:15 at the main entrance, to Court Centre 2," announced the young officer feeling somewhat sorry for the way everyone present had been treated.

63

"I'm Lydia Traun young man and the way we have been treated here, this will not be the last you've heard over your conduct towards us," said Lydia as she walked passed him.

Marc knew what Lydia said, went. She was the kind of woman to carry out her words in a situation that displeased her greatly. He threw an unamused look also at the young officer that said it all, as he walked passed following the others out.

09:15 hourons the Court Centre where Tom's case was to be held. Inside there could be heard the noise of spectators noisily taking up their seats, to get a good look at the criminal, namely Tom, jury members and law enforcing officers were all preparing for the trial of murder, the first case that mornet. A case that was totally untrue in the Amalthean teams eyes. The doors opened and the Amalthean team entered the Court Centre, immediately finding themselves under the interested eye of the spectators. Tayce felt she was a germ under a microscope. The young officer that earlier had suggested they should go and have something to eat and freshen up returned, crossing over to them briskly. He soon paused, then turned beckoning for them to follow him. Which the team did, walking across to some white spiral steps. As Tayce began up the steps, so she looked over to the Viewing Area and thought to herself, considering Tom was innocent there certainly were a lot of people present, especially legal people, this did not look good for him. Her sight came round to the lonesome figure of Tom, now standing staring straight ahead to the Court Centre wall. She could see he was very uneasy, in the way he stood, he had every right to be. She certainly wouldn't want to stand where he was. He eventually glanced about at the many people and law enforcing personnel. Tayce hoped he would look her way. As if he read her thoughts, he looked up to her in the now Viewing Area. She smiled a small reassuring smile. He didn't change his solemn expression of nervous anticipation, he looked back in front of him, thinking back to the moment in hand. The Judge entered the Court Centre in all his regalia. He was a plump pompous looking man who looked like he had seen his fair share of cases over the yearons pass before him. He was dressed in white long robe with an orange and yellow stripe running down the right hand side. He walked along up three steps and came to his seat, up in front of Tom. Sitting down he summoned Tom up and down for a moment in thought of whether he could be considered a guilty man or not. Tayce thought to herself that his hair colouring was somewhat strange, a yellowish blonde, with a streak of grey running from back to front, on his right hand side. She guessed it must be something that was in his ancestral blood line. Suddenly from below the trial started.

"Stand in appreciation for our Judge Marchoyns, who is in residence, to hear the murder trial of Tom Barry Stavard," announced a law officer in a loud voice, that silenced the Court.

Everyone present stood to their feet in respect of the said named Judge, to mark his grand presence. Tayce watched an officer hand over what would be her sound evidence to Tom's Lawyer. The Judge looked at what was happening, then nodded to Tom's Lawyer. He then began the trial which would take an estimated time of roughly an houron and a half and take into consideration both lots of evidence, from Tom's home planet, and Tayce and Midge.

"You are Tom Barry Stavard, is this correct?" demanded the Judge looking down on Tom coldly.

"Yes sir, that's correct," replied Tom nervously his hand rested on the lit palm sized pad before him.

From somewhere in the Court of spectators someone yelled out "Murderer". The Judge looked up and quite firmly announced the next outcry from any spectator, would be pin pointed and be severely dealt with. He continued on, when silence had been restored.

"You are here todayon Mr Stavard, under trial for the murder of Alenea Stavard, on 24th Januan (January) 2417, how do you plead?" asked the Judge sternly.

"Not guilty sir, it was an accident," replied Tom seriously and sincerely.

The Judge allowed his staff, to continue. Tom's Lawyer stood to his feet, looking down at the evidence, and his questions on the Porto Compute putting together the first questions he was going to put to Tom. Then he began.

"Place your hand permanently on the panel before you Mr Stavard during this session, do not move your hand at any time during the following questions, I am about to put to you," he ordered.

Tom did as requested he didn't want to put a foot wrong in case it incriminated him further. His Lawyer began walking about the small area, before him holding the Porto Compute. He was an average looking man. A smartly dressed official, in all he stood for, in Law and rules in his position. There was no friendliness about him and it didn't look like he was the kind of man to crack a joke to often.

"Mr Stavard your Colonel of the cruiser you serve on has given me evidence here to substantiate the fact your wife's injuries were somewhat horrific, but I want you to tell me in your own words how it happened," he prompted paying full attention to what Tom was about to say.

Tom began explaining to the Lawyer before him, exactly what he'd told Tayce, back aboard Amalthea which he knew to be the utter truth. From the Viewing Area Tayce was hearing everything once more via a loud speaker from the Court Centre below. She sat feeling sorry for Tom, having to relieve the moments of his wife's death once more. Marc watched and figured he was glad he wasn't in Tom's shoes, being questioned on something that was so close to the bone and painful. Back down in the Court Centre the Lawyer asked Tom had his wife been strapped into her seat during the supposed onslaught of unsuspecting attack? Tom explained Alenea had been on her feet studying the meteorite samples collected earlier running constant checks via the computer scanner. As the questioning went on, so Tom found himself fighting back the tears of strong emotion, when he thought of his pretty wife and her horrific injuries of blood stained and gashed delicate skin. He wished he was somewhere else. The lawyer could see that Tom wanted a few minons to compose himself so looked down at his Porto Compute Screen, looking for the next point he wanted to question him on.

"Did you personally carry out the medical diagnostic on Alenea that made you come to the conclusion she had died immediately from her injuries?" put the lawyer.

Tom looked about the Court Centre at the spectators, the jury and their computer placed slim screens in front of them and flat keypads. He could see they were giving him scrutinizing attention. He could also see as he continued giving his account that what had seemed like a straight forward case in their eyes, was turning into something more sincere and truthful. They were beginning to see him in a whole different light. Once through Tom's lawyer turned.

"Call Colonel Traun of Amalthea One to the stand," he announced loudly.

Tayce was somewhat surprised, she had no idea she would be called this early, even though she said she would give evidence of her findings if she had to. She thought her sound evidence would have been sufficient just handing it over they were certainly giving Tom a hard time in her estimation. She stood to her feet quite prepared to speak. She was escorted by the young Court Officer that had shown her and the others of her team up to the seating area earlier down. He walked ahead going to the area where she would have to stand and speak on Tom's behalf. She felt she was under scrutiny rather like a microbe under a microscope, as she walked from the spectators. She stepped up onto the platform that was identical to Tom's.

"Colonel Traun, you say in your report that Alenea Stavard was dead when you found Mr Stavards craft, can you elaborate on this?" began the same lawyer that had questioned Tom.

"I was about to start my daily duty, my cruisers computer and myself always checked the Universe before we continued travelling on, hence when we looked, on the horizon there was Mr Stavards craft we went about undertaking a rescue, pirates were pretty much rampant in the current sector that we were passing through, so we had to proceed with caution, once decontamination was done and I could board the craft, I ventured in and found Mrs Stavard bloodstained and in the most horrific condition, I have ever seen, no one could have inflicted the injuries she sustained, I would say it was from impact, her face was badly disfigured and there was a blood stain to her uniform in the chest region," said Tayce in the true tone of Colonel.

"What did you do then?" prompted the lawyer as the Judge gave his full attention.

"I took a Counter Medical Disc, it's a device that gives a clear reading of patients condition, I placed it on Mrs Stavards wrist and waited, the reading soon came back as 'Deceased,'" said Tayce seriously.

"Your report states she died from her injuries of impact from the way in which she'd impounded with the control panel At force?" he prompted studying Tayce in a summoning way.

"Yes definitely, when I glanced towards the control panel, there was blood on the silver leaver and controls," replied Tayce.

"Tell me Colonel how long would you say Alenea was dead for, before you rescued Mr Stavard here?" he continued.

"On a true guess, roughly two hourons, her injuries would state as much, I would have been surprised if she had survived," expressed Tayce.

"That will be all thank you Colonel you may step down, thank you for your informative time," he announced with a slight thankful smile.

Tayce on the way back to the seating area asked the young Court Officer to be excused, she did not want to be present during the cross examination and she needed some air, even if it was recycled. The young officer nodded in agreement. Tayce slipped out the opening doors to the side of the Court glancing back at Tom hoping all would go well. Once outside she felt the rush of refreshing air, even if it wasn't truly fresh it felt good on her delicate skin, she crossed to the silver and glassene balcony and leaned on it relaxingly taking in view over the whole of the Intergalactic Criminal Court Colony. She stood trying to shake the thought of the way in which the lawyer had made her feel no better than Tom, from her mind. A young sandy blonde haired girl approached Tayce cautiously.

"Um excuse me, are you Colonel Traun, Colonel Tayce Traun of the Amalthea One?" she asked politely but nervously.

"Yes I'm Tayce Traun, Colonel of Amalthea One, you are?" asked Tayce plainly turning to face the young student in her late teens, leisurely dressed.

"Treketa Stavard… I'm Tom's sister, hello!" replied Treketa introducing herself full of gush like any young female student of her age.

"Hello, it's good to meet you, Tom talks about you with pride, but what are you doing here, are you here to give evidence for Tom in some way?" asked Tayce awkwardly, she found this young woman a little to full on for her.

Tayce had always been brought up for a life of command, and she found Treketa in a class that she hadn't encountered before, she was different to her friends on Traun and felt uncomfortable to say the least, sure enough she probably was a really nice girl, but just a bit extrovert and she took a bit of understanding, as she was so light and airy with her approach to everything.

"No not really and he won't be happy to know that I've been kicked out of College Colony, oh don't get me wrong Colonel, I didn't do anything wrong, it was Tom that I got kicked out over," explained Treketa she suddenly saw the prejudge mental way in which Tayce was looking at her, spelling trouble with a capital 'T' in that she was the kind of girl to just flit from post to post without a thought. Treketa was the typical leggy sandy blonde, with blue innocent eyes and gentle clear, model like features that conveyed her student like prowess. She wore leisure type trousers, a top that showed her midriff and her blonde hair was scraped up in a side ponytail. Her make-up was colourful to say the least. Both she and Tayce slowly began talking about the reason Treketa had been at College Colony. She was stopped by the appearance of the young Court Officer at the Court Centre entrance, beckoning Tayce to return. She suggested to Treketa that she go with her. Treketa agreed in a whole hearted way. Both women walked on across back to the trial. Tayce in the moments that she had been talking with Treketa had summoned her up and came to the conclusion that she was not a bad girl she just needed to get a little serious. She was in fact thinking of asking her to join the Amalthean Team as the next new member it may calm her down a little. It turned out what age Tayce thought Treketa was seventeen, was wrong. Treketa laughed upon Tayce saying how old she was and explained she was in fact twenty-four yearons old. Inside the Court the trial was coming to a conclusive end. The Judge was about to give his verdict. Tayce and Treketa stood just inside the entrance. Tayce put her hands behind her back and crossed her fingers in hope that what had been proven, would make Tom the innocent victim and he would be able to walk free and back to the team and Amalthea. The Judge began.

"Tom Barry Stavard, we have gathered all the evidence and heard your account of the untimely death of Alenea Stavard to support that you were not responsible, that it was purely an unfortunate accident as serious as her injuries were, I have come to the conclusion that you are an innocent man, I have decided that no more action needs be taken into account, it is my estimation, that whoever brought this charge against you, made you an unfortunate victim, it is quite clear you have had to endure unfairly this court time unnecessarily I therefore have no sentence to pass and declare you a free man," he announced.

During the final words of the Judge, the whole of the Court Centre had fallen into a gripped anticipated silence. Nothing could be heard, it was what old Earth One people would say "You could here a Pin drop" The Judge stood, turned and began down towards Tom. A smile of great relief crossed both Tayce and Treketas faces knowing that Tom had been proven innocent. Tayce ran across to him and he opened his arms to her. The spectators walked from the court, all avoiding eye contact with Tom, knowing they had been proven wrong, whatever they first thought. The Amalthean members came down from the view area and all met in the middle of the now near empty court. Judge Marchoyn made his way towards Tom. He came to a pause.

"Hello, so your the new crime fighting team that I'm hearing good rumours about?" he said in casual tone.

"Yes your honour, this is Marc Dayatso, Councillor Lydia Traun my Medical Officer Donaldo Tysonne and Tom Stavard you already know and our latest hoped recruit, Treketa Stavard," introduced Tayce seeing the surprised and excited look on Treketas face.

"It's good to meet such a team, I wish you luck with your endeavours Colonel, this Universe could do with a team such as yours, it's a pity there can't be more," he replied seriously in thought.

"Thank you for seeing that Tom was innocent," said Tayce sincerely.

"Not at all, well better go I've another case in another of our courts here, good bye all of you," he said heading off.

Tayce watched the Judge go, he was an impressive man she thought. Treketa hugged Tom like a sister would hug her brother, in not seeing him for a long time. She told him that she was back for good. Tom looked at her and discretely informed her she could explain later what she meant. With that he suggested they get off their present surroundings before they were arrested for loitering in a criminal court! Everyone turned and began walking on out of the Court Centre. Upon reaching the doorway Tom turned taking one last look back to where he had stood earlier to prove his innocence, realising things could have been a lot more different if Tayce hadn't been there to support him. He hoped he would never have to set foot in somewhere like it again! He slipped an arm around Treketa and they headed on back to the Amalthea One. Lydia walked with Tayce discretely informing her, that it looked like she had been proven wrong over her thoughts on Tom's innocence and she was really sorry for doubting her.

***

A while later as the team were about to walk up the walkway and head aboard the cruiser there came a male call for Tayce to wait up. She stopped. A good looking young man with dark brown short layered hair and resembling a younger version of Jonathan Largon came to a pause, out of breath. Treketa looked at him in impressed admiration. The most startling thing about this young man, was his dark brown Spanish eyes, they sparkled. He was around 1.75 metres in height and of trim build, but strong in physique.

"Lance Largon what are you doing here, your not in trouble are you?" asked Tayce surprised and delighted to see him.

"No Father sent me, for a minon I thought you were going to leave me stranded here," he said warmly glad to see her just as much.

"Mother you remember Lance, Jonathan's son when we were children we use to cause havoc with the security procedures on Questa," said Tayce recalling the past with a smile.

"You remember those dayons," said Lance amused, as he recalled the many things they got up to.

"Oh yes Lance of course, you've grown!" said Lydia in surprise.

"Let me say it's good to see after all you've gone through, your here and just as lovely as ever," said Lance impressively.

"Thank you Lance, nice of you to say that," replied Lydia kindly seeing he was still as cheeky as she remembered him.

"Father found out where you were via Midge, he sent me over because he wants me to be part of your new crime fighting team, that's if it's okay?" he put to Tayce carefully.

"Sure it is, welcome to the team, shall we proceed?" said Tayce light heartedly.

Lance slung his garment carrier over his shoulder and fell in with the others heading on the walk back aboard the cruiser. It had been a good dayon, Tom was cleared of the unlawful accusation of killing Alenea and now he could go on without the fear of being suspected of such a thing ever again. There was now five members plus Tayce and Lydia on the team. They all walked onto the cruiser as the Docking Bay doors opened. Tom stopped to take one last look at the colony for the last time, glad to be free. He continued on aboard allowing the doors to close. Soon Amalthea One was leaving the docking port, heading on out into the Universe to continue on to whatever lay ahead or in the next sector.

Arrival of the Countess

The Amalthean Quests Team was growing, there were now five members. Tayce wondered how many would be in her team eventually, as she stood looking around the Organisation Deck, at some of them working.

Amalthea was travelling on no fixed course across the Universe, but on alert just the same, considering there was the constant threat of Countess Vargon and her Warrior Army still at large, who wouldn't hesitate to find the cruiser and finish off their so called business and get rid of Tayce at a cencrons notice. The two team members that had just joined the team, Lance Largon and Treketa Stavard, were settling in well. Treketa surprising as it was to see, had calmed down a bit from when Tayce first met her. They were making their quarters their own personal domain. Lance was fixing up his, the way he personally wanted them to be, considering they were going to be his base for the foreseeable future. Both himself and Treketa had been given their new team titles Lance was Quest's Research and Information Officer, his duty would entail him to take care of research into the Quest and search for information that was requested to prepare for a visit to different ports of call. Treketa was to work with Donaldo, as his new trainee Nurse and assistant to assist him in the Life Ability Centre and on emergencies or Quest's, when needed. She was getting to know where everything was in the Life Ability Centre, ready for her new duty. Tayce entered Lance's quarters to find him standing on a stool, hanging his favourite images on the quarters wall, that he'd downloaded from his Porto Compute. Tayce stood for a moment, looking up at him, until he saw her and jumped down. He began explaining what the images were, in that they were taken on past missions for his Father. Tayce gave an impressive look she found them somewhat appealing, some were space scenes, some were planets from different angles and even one of himself and his Father Jonathan proudly stood together on a vacation.

"That's a nice one of you and your Father, I wish mine was still alive, there would be so much I'd love to talk to him about over what's been happening," confided Tayce.

"Thanks, it was taken last monthon when I was on a break after graduation from training at the Astrono Training Centre, you know they may find your Father one day, whose to say someone didn't rescue him like they did your Mother," replied Lance understanding how she felt, and trying to cheer her up.

"I came to ask you a personal question?" asked Tayce.

"This sounds ominous," replied Lance, light heartedly, he had always been able to kid Tayce.

"I need you to say your age so Midge can put it into your personal record in his memory system," she replied relaxing in his company.

"Thirty, and not a yearon older he replied cheekily.

"That's all I need for now officially, when you've finished making this place home, I want you up on duty in Organisation understood?" she replied heading back to the entrance.

"Absolutely! I'll be there in twenty minons," he said after her.

Tayce walked from the quarters as the doors opened leaving Lance to finish what he was doing. The doors closed after her. She began up the corridor in thought, that things were certainly coming together in her grand plan of a crime fighting team. The cruiser had seemed empty for far to long and a team was just what was needed to make it a first class exploration cruiser that it had been built for. Without warning which made her topple and almost gasp in sheer shock, an image flashed into her mind of the woman that had started it all Countess Vargon, looking at her in all her cold evilness. Tayce found her breathing quicken at the sudden onslaught of the evil bitch. She tried to calm herself, but wondered what it all meant. Had it something to do with the mysterious Wristlink call she'd had just before entering Lance's quarters, from Tom? He had informed her that a message was coming in from General Largon at Questa. Was this the first criminal orientated assignment they were going to undertake, she wondered. Treketa exited her quarters at Tayces sudden surprise, as she thought she was working with Donaldo.

"Hi, I spilt something on my uniform, and it had to be discarded, so I came back to change and sent the other one to the incinerating system, are you all right, you seem preoccupied by something, if you don't mind me asking?" asked Treketa in a caring tone.

"You know that feeling when you see something flash in your mind and it makes you wonder if something is about to happen because of it, well I just had an image flash of Countess Vargon do just that," explained Tayce as she walked beside Treketa.

"God, what an image, Tom told me about her, she sounds like a real Witch," replied Treketa feeling sorry for Tayce and what she'd gone through.

Both woman were abruptly halted in walking and talking, as Amalthea seemed to rock and shake for no apparent reason. Both reached for the wall chrome rail, that ran the length of the corridor and held on fast. Treketa looked at Tayce, in questioning alarm.

"What's happening?" she asked loudly, as things seem to fall from the corridor walls, smashing onto the floor.

"I think it must be some kind of spacial turbulence in this particular sector," replied Tayce unaware of what was really unfolding.

"When is it going to stop, we'll come apart at this rate," replied Treketa beginning to get scared.

Tayce raised her Wristlink and contacted Midge demanding to know what the hell was happening, what was causing their present situation. Midge explained he couldn't find any anything out of the ordinary to cause their sudden motion state but he was currently working on it and would let her know what it was the moment he discovered it, but he had defence safeguards in place in case they had an unscheduled visit from the Countess. Tayce broke communications, not liking the situation at all. She suggested to Treketa they both try and make their way to where they were heading, gripping the rail to get there. Treketa did as ordered and headed on back to the Life Ability Centre whilst Tayce made her way up to Organisation. Tayce soon passed Treketa, going on in urgency, grabbing the rail, heading on up the steps. Half way up Tayce called to Treketa and ordered her to forget heading to the Life Ability Centre, she may be needed in Organisation Treketa agreed and followed on. Both women continued up the Level Steps with determination and difficulty, all the way to Level 1. Once at the top of the Level Steps, they staggered like a pair of out of control drunks towards the Organisation Deck entrance. Once inside the entrance, Treketa crossed to the nearest seat and sat down and held on. Tayce staggered across to the pilot seat. Tom reached out and grabbed her in safely to the seat adjacent to his.

"What's causing this, the Universe looks clear?" said Tayce looking out the sight port.

"We had a message from Jonathan Largon about an houron ago and it was urgent, he was warning us that the Countess is at large again, he wants us to try and apprehend her, I think this is one of her little tricks to provoke you," he informed her above the intermittent engines and shaking surroundings.

Without warning Midge went into shut down mode. Everything on board crashed offline. Emergency power activated, this was getting out of hand thought Tayce, they were being tossed about like an air filled spheroid. Suddenly there was a blinding flash that filled Organisation and blinded the team on duty. Tom, Treketa and Tayce had vanished in the flash. Midge came back to emergency power and was immediately alerted to the fact that all three were missing, as he did a scan of the whole cruiser he was quickly aware that not only were Tayce Tom and Treketa missing, so were Marc, Lydia, Lance and Donaldo. The cruiser was crew less and he was in total charge. He was unsure as to what to do. Where had his mistress and the others disappeared to? What was he to do? Stay put until further notice, or contact General Largon and ask his advice? He decided to remain in a stationary orbit until orders came from Tayce on what to do next. It was the best thing to do, considering the unusual circumstances he was now in. Silent and on emergency power Midge waited

It was Some kind of chamber, cold and bare. Nothing but walls of solid beige marblex was where the whole team had materialized to. But where were they thought Tom, as he woke from the involuntary sleep they'd all been placed in? He moved slightly falling from the beige stonex slab type seat, that he'd been placed on, hitting the black shiny marblex floor, that was cold to the touch. He quickly staggered to his feet, looking around. He quickly found Tayce waking from her induced unexpected state. He stepped over Lance and went to her side, to check she was all right. Marc woke and quickly went about checking Lydia was also all right. Lance woke up and quickly checked on Treketa.

"Where are we, how did we get here?" asked Marc glancing around at the barren type chamber.

"Oh no not here, anywhere but here, please," said Lydia realising where they were.

"Where Lydia?" asked Marc, not liking the way in which she said, what she had.

"Yes Mother where?" asked Tayce becoming alarmed at her Mother's tone.

Out of nowhere came a voice to familiar to Tayce and Lydia. Marc cursed under his breath and lowered his head, thinking to himself, they had just landed via being abducted, in the biggest bitches patch in the whole of the known Universe, this was not going to be easy getting out of this one.

"I'm glad you know where you are Lydia, it saves introductions, welcome to my Lair, for those of you who don't know me, allow me to introduce myself," began Countess Vargon in a soft evil feminine tone.

"Please don't," cut in Marc under his breath in anger.

"I am Countess Vargon, leader of the Vargon Warrior Army, destroyer of the world of Traun," she announced sounding boastful, that she had done what she had, in taking Tayces home world as a kind of trophy.

"Why don't you show yourself Vargon, our meeting is long overdue, over what you did to my people and planet, I'm not afraid of you, make no mistake," said Tayce in outright hatefulness, to everyone's surprise even her Mother's.

The wall drew apart if by magic before them and she walked forth into the chamber. A witch of no mistake. Long black hair, thick, down to her shoulders. Slim in physique, but her curvy figure was not matched by her looks, that were cold with evil darker than dark eyes, that conveyed her true powerfulness. To most she was the most dreaded woman in all the known Universe and hated by people who sort justice. She undermined them left right and centre, they made a move, she would make one better to get what she wanted. Tayce looked at her coldly conveying her cold feelings of all the pent up hurt of what had happened to her friends and people of Traun, still fresh in her mind, like it was yesteron, she wanted to march on her, get the confrontation over with. Marc acted quickly, he could see she was seething ready to attack. He grabbed her back. Tayce struggled protestingly and threw him a displeased look, because of his actions. The Countess ignored Tayces childish looks and anger, as she considered them just that, and walked across to Lydia. She paused looking down her slender nose at her in a cold and uninterested way.

"So you survived, how long for?" she simply asked in a soft spiteful tone.

Lydia looked away, she refused to be intimidated by this evil woman and just pretended that she wasn't there. The Countess walked over to Tayce, still being held in Marc's strong hold. She studied Tayce coldly, not moving an inch, trying to make this mere child out as she considered her, make her cave in to her powerfulness but Vargon realised suddenly that there was more to this Tayce Traun than met the eye. She pretended not to see what she was seeing in her eyes. It was a sudden force that made her feel slightly unnerved which was something that she generally didn't feel.

"You have spirit child, but that is no match for me, you can never defeat me, there have been those who have tried just like you," she said motionless, looking right into Tayce's sapphire blue eyes, trying to sear right into her soul with powerful intent looking, past what she could see that was a possible threat to her.

"Easy Tayce, don't!" said Marc holding his tight restraining grip, he did not want her to be another victim of Vargon.

"I'm not scared by your prowess Countess like the others, because I, know you have a weakness, people like you normally do and it will be just a matter of time to find that weakness and bring you down, for what you did to my people," retorted Tayce just as emotionless.

Vargon laughed out loud, she found the whole thing funny, the daughter of Darius Traun, threatening her, it was too amusing to contemplate, she turned back to face Tayce.

"Be careful Tayce, your spirited nature will be your downfall," she warned, in a slow dragging tone.

She turned and walked away with a smug evil look on her face, she glanced in amusement over her shoulder suddenly at Tayce, thinking at last she held her and her Mother captive. When she was safely out of sight Marc released Tayce, who was furious to say the least. She had no intention of letting the likes of Vargon keep her in her current surroundings, and so began looking for a way to escape. Donaldo couldn't believe what had just happened, the whole occurrence was just bizarre. What a bitch, he thought and said as much under his breath. Treketa glanced at him nodding her head in agreement, at his look of total disbelief.

"Mother are you all right?" asked Tayce crossing over to her, whilst looking for some kind of escape route.

"I'll say one thing for her, she hasn't changed, it will take more than her to scare me now though, I've been through to much to be intimidated any more," said Lydia certain of it.

Marc suddenly had an idea, but then squashed it in thought, as they all thought of ways in which to escape out of their present unwanted surroundings. Time was moving on. Suddenly in marched six lime green platex clad guards. Marc wondered if he'd get the chance after all to try out his idea and overpower one of them, but figured there was too many of them, and not enough of Amalthean Quests team.

"You, female Traun, you are to come with us, now!" said the leader of the clad guards pointing to Tayce.

"No chance pal, your not taking her anywhere," said Marc springing to his feet to protect Tayce.

He nodded to commence attack to Tom, Lance and Donaldo. The lead guard as Tom came forth, struck him with his platex covered fist. Tom sailed off his feet through the air and came into contact with the far wall with a thud, where he dropped like a stone to the floor and stayed there out cold. Marc had no choice but to let Tayce handle the situation. She was grabbed by two guards and pushed forward in a careless action. She glanced back over her shoulder at her Mother, mouthing she would be fine. The wall that had drawn apart closed behind them, as they passed through. Treketa rushed to her brothers side, there was nothing she or Donaldo could do, they didn't have their Medic Emergency Kits to check what kind of injuries Tom had sustained, or to treat him. Coming back to consciousness, Donaldo in a caring tone asked if he could sit up? Tom nodded. Both Donaldo and Treketa carefully helped him up into a more comfortable sitting position. When Tom was fully aware of where he was, he looked around for Tayce. He sighed in anger, realising he hadn't been able to achieve the stopping of her leaving, in the unwanted care of the plaxtex clad creeps. He forgot his pain and was on his feet. He tore across the chamber and grabbed Marc, he turned him round and sternly informed him, that next time he had a brainwave, to think about Tayce and the repercussions it would cause. With that he angrily pushed him away and walked to the other side of the chamber in anger. Lydia tried to calm them both explaining that the Countess would like nothing more than to see they were turning on each other, she would have something else she could use against Tayce by informing her that her team were beginning to turn against her.

"I would suggest the both of you calm down, this is not helping the situation," pointed out Lydia sternly.

Both looked at each other trying to do what Lydia had suggested. She was right, they would be playing right into Vargons hands if she knew it would be easy to turn them against each other, she would feel she could use it to her advantage and turn them against Tayce.

Elsewhere in the vicinity they were all in. In a large almost empty Grand Chamber with Lime Green neon lighting and shiny black floor, was what could only be described a throne of sorts also in shiny black marblex with four steps in the same material leading up to it. On the throne sat the Countess, looking like a regal Queen, in all her evil glory, waiting for her confrontation with Tayce. She was soon forced into the room and brought before the Countess at the bottom of the steps. The Countess looked down her nose at Tayce plainly and uninterested with dark malicious eyes.

"You have your confrontation young woman, we are alone, what do you think of my Lair?" she asked in jubilant tone, gesturing with her right hand around the chamber.

"Quite convincing for a witch like you," replied Tayce to the point, with a touch of hatefulness in her words.

"You intrigue me Traun, you show no emotion being before me, your Father obviously taught you well when dealing with people of greatness such as me," she said standing up.

"My Father taught me well enough but when it came to treating people like you with respect, he taught me never to respect you at all, he felt you didn't deserve it and I know why," retorted Tayce unaffected by Vargons attitude towards her.

The Countess slowly began down the steps, one at a time, letting her long black satinex gown trail behind her as she came all the way to the bottom. Upon reaching Tayce, she nodded to her two present guards that had brought Tayce in. They each took hold of her on either side in a restraining hold. Tayce struggled in their tight grip.

"Getting someone else to do your dirty work Vargon, can't you handle me alone?" asked Tayce continuing to try and break free of the guards uncouth grip on her.

The guards made her stop struggling and the Countess put her slim cold slender fingers under Tayces delicate chin and studied her closely, the courageousness, and beauty, that Tayce conveyed.

"Looking at you Tayce, is like looking at your Father, you have his eyes, I can see a lot of him in you," said Vargon close to Tayces face, in front of her.

"That must bother you, considering what you did to my world, you forget I was there the night you destroyed Traun, leave my Father out of this, he's gone where you can do him no more harm, but let me inform you what my Father told me, never to let you get away with what you did," said Tayce calmly and unemotionally.

"You might think of where you are girl, I call the shots here, you will abide by what I wish of you otherwise you'll see your Father a lot quicker than you thought," said Vargon becoming agitated by Tayces unemotional attitude and words of threat.

"Get to the point, why have you brought me and my team here, if you want me, let's get this over and done with, just the two of us without your dogs here to protect you, but first let my team return to Amalthea along with my Mother," said Tayce suddenly and strangely feeling powerful within herself, though why she couldn't explain it, it had never happened before.

"In good time, as for your Mother I will decide when she returns to your cruiser, not you," said Vargon in her true tone of command and not liking being told what to do by a mere Traun.

"What have you done with Amalthea, Midge my guidance computer has orders to stop you taking it he'll destroy it before you get your hands on it?" informed Tayce.

The Countess let go of Tayces chin and turned, walking away, she still found Tayces behaviour no better than a child, not getting its own way and protesting about it, it was amusing to her, which she was enjoying every cencron, Tayce was before her.

"Amalthea is perfectly safe and in the orbit where you were taken from for the present time," replied Vargon

Tayce stood feeling really infuriated at Vargon. Why couldn't she just get to the point? After a few minons, the Countess turned ordering two of her other present guards to fetch the Amalthea Team, immediately!

Now what! thought Tayce? What game was Vargon planing or trying to achieve next. She over heard her orders to the leaving guards of her Mother to be left behind, this told Tayce she had something darn right vicious planned in store for her. But what was she planning? What was going on in that evil mind of hers, thought Tayce. The next orders from the Countess to her men were for the preparation of the Image Visualler. Tayce continued to watch wondering. Behind her, the rest of the team were soon lead in minus her Mother. They all came to a stop just inside the chambers.

"Are you all right Tayce?" asked Marc unafraid of Vargon, looking over to Tayce in the hold of the two guards.

"Oh how touching," said Vargon coming back towards Tayce, with a sarcastic look on her face.

Without warning Vargon turned towards Marc, raising her right hand palm facing him, a ball of red light emitted from the centre, heading straight at him. Marc was suddenly bathed in a red aura, which made him become under some strange trance, created by Vargon. His features took on a fixed motionless appearance. The Countess laughed evilly amused, thinking she'd rendered the first of the Amalthea team helpless.

"This is so easy, your team are easy to possess Traun," she coyly announced giving Tayce a prompting look, waiting for a reaction.

"You release him at once, he's no good to you, it's me you have a problem with," ordered Tayce sharply.

"In good time, he amuses me, I might decide to keep him this way, he's very pleasing to the eye," she said studying Marc interested for all the wrong reasons.

"Time is something your running out of, because by now General Largon of Questa would have been notified by Midge upon pin pointing where we are and will have a team on their way here," warned Tayce but as she said this, she wasn't sure whether Midge would have been able to determine where they were, or not, but she knew that it would frighten the Countess knowing that a large army from Questa would be on their way out and would stop at nothing to destroy her, once and for all, for what she'd done.

"Idol threats are no threat to me, you should know that, considering what I did to your world, your Father made the same mistake," said Vargon, she'd seen through Tayces lie, regarding the Questa Security on their way out.

But Tayce wondered if she was covering up her own fear, that deep down she was worried that Tayces threat could be true. She turned and walked back up the black marblex steps to her throne, just as slowly as she had walked down earlier.

Midge on board Amalthea was having success in finding his mistress and missing team. He had found a weak signal that seemed to be emanating from what could only be a weak Wristlink signal. He made sure that it wasn't coming from on board, then scanned the near vicinity of the Universe, pin pointing it finally to a small grey ugly looking planet. He primed what he wanted to do, releasing a Heat Seeking Quick Reaction Digit Bomb, upon discovering who was occupying the planet, but just before he did, he sent a signal to what he pin pointed to be Tayces Wristlink, to the sound of her alarm call, then flashed the words on the Wristlinks display as "MIDGE BOMB COMING" He hoped the bomb would damage the Countesses precious Lair and help in the escape of the team. He hated Vargon just as much as Tayce did. All he hoped was that Tayce saw the message in time.

Back on Vargons Lair in the Grand Chambers, Tayces Wristlink suddenly sounded on her wrist behind her back. One guard let go of her wrist, she pulled it free. Vargon glared down at her, now seated on her throne.

"What was that?" demanded Vargon barking down at Tayce.

"What's it to you?" replied Tayce, she wasn't going to let Vargon know it was her Wristlink.

"Don't hide it from me girl, I want to know what that infernal musical sound is, well?" demanded Vargon.

"It's an alarm, I must have forgot to deactivate it this mornet, does it bother you, too bad," retorted Tayce in spiteful tone.

"You man, remove it from her wrist, destroy it at once," ordered Vargon to the guard on Tayces right.

"No don't, let me go, ouch! Stop it, let go," protested Tayce fighting off the guard from taking it.

Treketa glanced at her Wristlink, though why she had no idea, something prompted her to look down. As she did, so the words that Midge had sent to Tayce, were now being displayed on hers, but were flashing on and off "MIDGE BOMB COMING IN MINONS, PREPARE" she nudged Lance next to her, then Tom, glancing in gesture to their wrist's. They each saw the urgency in Midges message and took their chance, not only did Tom, who was wounded, but everyone began to fight for their survival before the bomb struck their very surroundings. Even Donaldo forgot his medical ethics of taking a life in the line of duty began tackling the on coming guards. Tayce broke her grip, by the guard who held her as he was pulling her Wristlink off her right wrist and turned kicking him right between the legs, in combat fashion, sending him sprawling to the floor of the chamber. This was full scale fight back, on the teams behalf, to gain their freedom before they were all blown to smithereens. Kicks and punches flew in all directions, on both sides. Vargons guards against the Amalthean team, only it was difficult to know where to hit them, because of the platex armour they wore. The Countess was coming down the steps to try and make an attempt of escape. Tayce turned just right to see her trying to make a break for it. Now was her chance for that real one on one confrontation. Marc slowly came back to his normal state and as Tayce went for Vargon, Marc went for the guard that was heading for Tayce. She rushed forth finding she was suddenly very powerful once more and again could not explain it, she reached out, grabbing Vargon by the back of her dress.

"Not so fast you bitch, your not going to escape from this so easily," said Tayce yanking Vargon back sharply making her almost lose her balance.

"Let go of me you pathetic girl, you're no match for me, don't think you are," shouted Vargon in sheer hatred and anger.

Vargon spun round and unleashed her true powers on Tayce. Without warning, Tayce found herself fighting back with an unexpected powerful force of her own, that had suddenly risen within her and one she hadn't experienced before only this time for some reason more powerful. As the Countess unleashed her pure energy strikes on Tayce, so she blocked them and knocked them aside with little effort, or loss of her own sudden powerfulness. The confrontation between the two women was quite spectacular and explosive to watch in the colourful exchange of pure energy strikes against the other. Marc couldn't believe what he was witnessing, he was speechless to say the least, at what he was seeing, as he returned to normal. He was surprised to see Tayce was suddenly able to fight back using powers of her own. Tayce finally caught Vargon off guard and delivered what was to be the final blow against her. She took direct hit and dropped to her knees out cold. Tayce calmed down and almost felt like she wanted to pass out, as the sudden and unexpected powerful onslaught that had occurred subsided once more. She stumbled trying to come to terms with what had just unfolded. Marc quickly hurried to her side.

"What happened, what did I just do, where did that energy come from?" asked Tayce in utter sheer disbelief.

"It's all right, take it easy," reassured Marc comforting her.

"She's out cold, unconscious!" said Donaldo checking to see if Tayce had killed Vargon once and for all.

"I would suggest we get her out of here, considering the General wants her apprehended," said Tom.

Without warning the rest of Vargons Army began converging on the chambers where they were, there could be heard the sound of heavy boots heading the teams way.

"Let's get Lydia and get the hell out of here," suggested Marc.

Upon him announcing his words, a Slazer shot rang passed his left ear and he narrowly avoided being shot by the army that was now in view. Tom and Lance hauled the Countess off the floor, still out cold and dragged her out of the chambers through another entrance. At the entrance, Lance glanced back to see the army enter the chambers. A smile crossed his handsome features, as their demise was very instant, in the fact that Midges bomb hit home, sending the roof crashing in on them, killing them instantly. He quickly joined the team and they quickly ran in search of Lydia, as the Lair was falling apart around them. Lydia was by the entrance where they had all once been brought to, at the beginning. She looked coldly at the unconscious Countess, almost wishing she'd remain that way. She was about to ask how had Vargon been halted. Marc quickly explained it was a spectacular showdown, to say the least, then glanced at Tayce who was looking away.

"Tayce contact Midge, tell him to get us out of here at once," ordered Lydia worried.

"Don't worry Mother, I'm now about to," replied Tayce taking stock of the situation.

All stood ready to get off their current surroundings. Tayce in urgency requested via Wristlink to Midge to immediately get them out. Within minons the orange energy glow of the swirling Travelsport surrounded the entire group, plus Vargon and they de-materialized from the falling apart Lair.

The moment the team arrived back on the cruiser, Tayce went with Lance and Marc to get the Countess put where she would remain for the journey to Questa under strong hold. Tayce wanted to make sure Vargon was securely locked up with a very high level of energy security barrier as she didn't trust the evil witch to find some way of escape when she came back to a conscious state. Meantime Donaldo guided Tom along to the Life Ability Centre to treat him for his cuts and bruises. Lydia went on up to Organisation, to order Midge to get under way. For the next so many hourons things were going to be full on in getting Vargon to Questa.

A while later the Countess came round in the Confinement Cell. She looked furious. Tayce had ordered Midge to watch her and make sure if she tried to escape to give an energy shock to the entrance force field. Vargon stared at Tayce coldly as she had gone to check on her and was now stood before the entrance to her holding cell.

"As you can see Countess, you have a lovely view of the Lair from here and it's just in the same condition as what you left Traun in, I hope you enjoy it, because in exactly twenty minons you'll see and feel the way I felt when you destroyed Traun, desolate," said Tayce, with spiteful meaning in her words, she meant every word of what she said.

"What are you proposing to do with me, I will rise again, Traun, of that you can be sure," promised Vargon.

"Your going back to Questa to face trial for the murder of my people and not before time, the verdict I should imagine will be instant death, the strongest they can find," replied Tayce uninterested.

"Your a very brave girl, but you'll see the error of your ways, make no mistake," warned Vargon.

"Enjoy the view Vargon, I shall when your world explodes into nothingness, it will be one moment I'll enjoy because it will be pay back for my people," replied Tayce spitefully.

Tayce left Vargon to look at what was once her home and walked away, glad she apprehended her at last, after three yearons. She was going to face trial for all the people of Traun, the innocent children who never got a chance to grow up. No sentence would be long enough, or strong enough, for the likes of the evil witch she thought, as she headed on up to Level 1.

An houron later Lydia was in Organisation. Marc walked in still puzzled by what he had witnessed on the Lair, when Tayce was unleashing the pure retaliating balls of energy at Vargon. He decided to talk it through with Lydia. He crossed and began cautiously, but Lydia could see that something was bothering him.

"Can I share something with you, it's about Tayce," he began.

"Maybe it's Tayce you ought to be asking, whatever this is, that's bothering you," replied Lydia not sure whether Tayce would want him talking about her behind her back, but she could see it was serious.

"I'd rather discuss it with you, honestly," he continued.

"All right what is it?" asked Lydia giving him her full attention.

"When we were on Vargons Lair something really extraordinary happened to Tayce, I have never witnessed anything like it before, when she and Vargon were in full fight, Tayce was emitting would you believe pure energy fireballs, throwing them directly at Vargon, I've never known Tayce to act so hostile, what do you think it was occurred and should we be worried?" said Marc concerned.

"It looks like it's skipped a generation, we did wonder if Tayce would be the one to inherit the powerful force, and it looks like she may have, it skipped me and comes from her Grandfather, he was a powerful man and nothing would stop him from righting wrongs, he was a member of what was termed the Empire of Honitonia. Tayce entered Organisation and both Lydia and Marc parted pretending to talk about something totally different. Tayce walked straight across to the Weapons keypad and typed in a sequence, then pressed the button to activate the Slazer Cannons. As she did she announced.

"Enjoy this view Vargon, it will be the last you see of your precious Lair."

The Slazer Cannons of Amalthea unleashed twenty rounds of firepower at the Lair that Vargon once called home. The firepower struck the Lair in different directions. Upon this, the small grey looking planet that withheld the Lair burst into a million trillion pieces, giving out a spectacular shower of sparks and debris that spread out for milons Tayce didn't like destroying planets in the Universe, but she made an exception when it came to Vargon and this target it had been a strike for her people and what Vargon had done to them.

"Target successfully destroyed Tayce," announced Midge confirming the task to destroy Vargons Lair once and for all was done.

"Are you all right, our people would have been proud of you Tayce and I know your Father would have been, he would have said, a job well done," said Lydia suddenly and softly beside her.

"You've a nasty burn on your arm, Vargons aim wasn't as good as she thought it was, come and sit down and I'll get Donaldo up here," said Marc carefully guiding Tayce over to the nearest seat.

"No Marc, I think she'd better go down to the Life Ability Centre with that burm," said Lydia taking a look at her daughters right arm.

Tayce stood to her feet walking on out of Organisation. She had felt no pain with her arm, but realised that it must have been during the confrontation with Vargon, like Marc had said, she hadn't been as good as she thought she was with her aim.

Later Tom was finishing his treatment with Donaldo down in the Life Ability Centre, when Tayce walked in with her arm burn. Tom turned concerned. Tayce crossed as Donaldo, let Treketa take over with the final stage of the healing treatment. He gestured to Tayce, to get up on the Exam Bunk so he could examine the burn properly. Tayce did so without further word, as it was beginning to sting. She laid down on his request, so that he could guide the examination device over the injured area, whilst she relaxed. Treketa soon finished Tom and moved to assist Donaldo watching what he was doing with interest, so that she could learn. Tom walked to Tayces side, coming to a pause beside the bunk. He took hold of her left hand and squeezed it lovingly

"That was some feat out there you did, so she's the evil woman who destroyed your home world?" asked Tom looking down at her in a warm and caring way.

"Yes, that's her, and I'm glad she is where she belongs, heading to what she deserves, how are you feeling, you know Marc didn't mean for you to get injured, he just thought he was trying to help," said Tayce she'd heard about their fracas, from Lydia upon return.

"Oh I'll heal, I'm more concerned for you though, you were extremely brave coming up against the Countess, even if you did have a bit of unexpected help," he said referring to her powers from nowhere.

"Hate makes strange things happen and has some strange outcomes, I can't explain what happened, but I did what I felt was right to honour my people and what she did," replied Tayce, she didn't want to think about the sudden powerfulness she'd found.

"I think you were really spectacular, I couldn't have taken her on like you did," said Treketa handing Donaldo a gadget to heal Tayces arm.

"When faced with the prospect of repaying her for what she did to my people deep inside me, I felt about nothing more than putting an end to her evil ways, my Father once told me, she was a woman no one crossed but if you did, then you had to have the courage and the guts to stop her," replied Tayce.

Treketa nodded in agreement. Donaldo took great care and showed extreme gentleness in healing the small flesh burn, caused by one of the Countesses power strikes. Tayce glanced away as Donaldo concentrated near to the area with the hand held gadget. There was slight pain, but Tayce fought if off. She looked back up into Donaldo's warm caring eyes. He smiled back, exclaiming when they were on the Intergalactic Medical Colony, he or she had no idea he'd be treating her injuries so soon after his arrival on board. Tayce agreed. She had to admit, that more than anyone she had no idea she was going to come up against the Countess and feel her wrath so soon. Everyone present nodded in total agreement. Donaldo soon finished allowing Tayce to sit up. Tom helped her up into the sitting position. Donaldo, as he began to put back the gadgets for treatment, ordered her to take it easy for a while, her arm would seem sore. Tom assured, he would make sure she did. Tayce gave him an "Oh yes! I don't think so, look." Treketa tried not to laugh, she could see that Tayce was somewhat like herself, no one was going to boss her around. Donaldo knew Tayce and he had summed her up as being somewhat stubborn, to say the least. He knew Tom was not going to have an easy time of it. Tayce slid to the floor and she and Tom began on out of the Life Ability Centre leaving Donaldo and Treketa to clear away the treatment equipment used. The doors drew apart before them on approach and they both passed through. Once outside and walking along the corridor, without warning Tom gently grabbed Tayce and guided her back against the corridor wall. She was taken totally by surprise of what followed, when Tom did what he had wanted to do for a long time, and that was to plant a long lingering kiss on her delicate lips. Tayce found herself responding to him and found a rush of pure ecstatic pleasure sear through her. This was different from the boys she'd kissed on Traun. But was this wrong, she'd considered Tom just a friend, but could tell by the way he was kissing her, he wanted more than friendship. Tayce found herself being drawn into the moment of pure wanting tenderness and draped her arms around his strong neck. Everything around them seemed to melt away. They were totally lost in each other. Tayce did think however at the back of her mind, whether this was all too soon, after the death of his wife Alenea. Was this just a rebound feeling.

Countess Vargon sat in the Confinement Cell doing what only could be considered the equivalent of the licking of her wounds. Lydia had sent Lance to check on the current status of their on board unwelcome guest, that she hadn't tried to use her powers to escape despite the intense energy field. He paused outside the force field entrance studying her. She looked up feeling someone was looking at her. Lance looked back.

"Lance Largon isn't it, Jonathan's son, you've grown to be a fine young man, I'm still here, your Colonel has seen to that," she announced plainly.

"Why, I remember when I was a child, you were on the good side of the law, what made you switch?" asked Lance curious, he couldn't understand why she'd done what she had, to the people of Traun.

"Times change Largon, it's more fun being on the bad side," she replied giving him a dark eyed look.

"Yeah but once you were a good Councillor, you and your husband, where's he in all this?" asked Lance unbelieving what she had become and the fact her husband had left her to face the heat in going to trial.

"It is of no interest to you, where he is," she replied to the point, like she was hiding something, and was not going to let on.

Tom walked towards Lance with fresh Coffeen, informing him that Lydia in Tayces absence had ordered him to watch Vargon until they reached Questa. Tayce was resting. Lance nodded in agreement, taking the fresh Coffeen starting to drink it. Tom threw a cold look at the Countess wondering why such an attractive looking woman, was such a venomous snake. Tom knew that he shouldn't, but in a way he felt sorry for the way she looked at life and her attitude to the Traunians, it was hard to understand. Lance nudged him telling him not to be taken in by the looks, treacherous is, as treacherous does. Both went on to discuss what Tayce had done back on the Lair in her confrontation with their present guest, both could only put it down to a momentous fluke, maybe conjured up from some unknown force. Neither could think of how it could have happened. Tom left Lance with the confined Countess, with words of warning, not to trust anything she asked. Lance agreed sipping his Coffeen. Tom headed off back to Organisation Deck

Quite suddenly a while later there came an agonising horrific male cry. That was pin pointed coming from below decks on Level 3, rear of the cruiser. Midge announced, Lance was in trouble. Tayce who had just returned to duty, left

Organisation with Marc in hot pursuit. They both ran at full pelt to get down to Level 3. Donaldo had been requested by Midge, declaring an emergency situation. Donaldo emerged from the Life Ability Centre, with Treketa carrying a Medic Emergency Kit. He was controlling the Hover Trolley with the hand held keypad and walked behind it as they sped along the corridor. Both switched equipment half way, Treketa took over the Hover Trolley, so he could run on ahead. Tayce wasn't taking any chances, where the Countess was. On Level 2 she paused at the Slazer Emergency Cabinet on the corridor wall and retrieved two Slazers. She checked they were fully charged, then handed one to Marc, suggesting he keep alert. They continued on down to the rear of Amalthea, on alert. On the 3rd Level Tayce was met by the awesome sight of Lance trapped in the force field entrance door, to the Confinement Cell which was still activated. She took aim at the operation panel and open fired, to deactivate it. It shut down Lance dropping to the floor like a lead weight in a scorched and bleeding near unconscious mess.

"My God Lance it's okay, take it easy, Donaldo's on his way," said Tayce crouching beside him.

"She's escaped Tayce, sorry," he mouthed in pain.

"You stay with him, I'll check around," suggested Marc clasping his Slazer in his hands setting off with it primed ready to fire at a cencrons notice, at the sight of the Countess.

"Marc be careful, she's already had Lance, you know what she's capable of," warned Tayce.

"It's all right I know how that woman thinks, I'll be fine," he assured her setting off in search of Vargon.

As if Countess Vargon being on the loose aboard wasn't enough to worry about, overhead Midge announced they were going into boarding with Questa Headquarters Base. Tayce cursed, she knew now Vargon would escape to Questa and get lost in the crowds of people and aliens arriving and departing the base, she had to do something and fast. Donaldo rounded the corner, setting down his Medic Emergency Kit. Tayce Left Lance in his capable care and set off up the corridor. She had to stop Vargon escaping to Questa. Treketa could see the look of urgency and panic as she passed Tayce with the Hover Trolley on the way to Donaldo, but she didn't say anything. Tayce raised her Wristlink, contacting Midge. She ordered him to slow down the docking procedure, and no account, open Docking Bay doors until Vargon was at least not discovered on the cruiser. Midge agreed. Tayce ran, checking every doorway she came to and on every corridor junction. She Wristlinked to her Mother advising her to warn Jonathan Largon, the Countess was on the lose, she had broken confinement and she may exit to Questa. Lydia agreed cutting communication, she quickly contacted Questa and informed Adam the Generals aide of what was unfolding on board.

Marc was in suspicion, he'd pinned the Countess down, he crept around the corner on Level 2. His hunch had been right, the Countess was on her way to the Docking Bay doors. He wanted to pick her off right where she was, but figured if he did, she would not stand trial. He stepped out onto the Level, fully aiming his hand held Slazer directly at her with it set to Stun.

"Hold it, you've got no where to run, it's all over, stop where you are, or nothing would give me the greatest pleasure to change the setting on this gun, take this as my first and only warning," he said looking furiously at her.

"Go ahead Commander Dayatso, nothing would give me also the greatest pleasure of adding you to my list of dead Traunians, you'll never stop me," she retorted coldly.

Tayce stepped cautiously round the same corridor corner Marc had just ventured from, she saw Vargon was about to unleash another of her powerful fire balls, of pure red energy. She dived literally towards Marc pushing him out of the way of the on coming missile. Both she and Marc hit the deck floor. Marc's Slazer flew from his grasp, and slid away against the corridor wall. The Countess went on laughing callously Marc was far from impressed so Tayce had saved his life, but now they probably had lost the last chance of stopping Vargon gaining access to Questa, or had they? Further Up, Tom stepped out of the Deck Travel and smoothly and silently aimed his Slazer at the Countesses head, daring her to make another move, because if she did, it would give him the greatest pleasure to carry out the necessary, to put a stop to her once and for all. Tayce was on her feet and walking to join Tom, who now had Vargon in tight restricting grip.

"You won't be able to hold me forever, no one can stop me," she protested to no avail.

"We'll see about that Countess, there's a team waiting to meet the likes of you on Questa and I wouldn't advise struggling, considering our last encounter," warned Tayce.

Marc placed the force field handcuffs on the Countesses wrists and did it in an uncaring manner. Tayce Wristlinked to Midge ordering him to go on with the docking procedures. Amalthea continued on with the completion for docking home with Questa. Tayce handed over the responsibility of holding Vargon to Tom she then headed away heading off to see how Lance was in the Life Ability Centre. As she went, so she thought how glad she would be when Vargon was safely in the hands of the Questa Security Team.

Down in the Life Ability Centre Lance was protesting that he was fine. Donaldo knew though it was down to his quick thinking and quick treatment he was. It was hard to imagine less than forty-six cencrons ago Lance was in a near death grip on the corridor floor, on Level 3. Lance winced a bit, realising all his pain was not entirely gone, as he placed his polo-neck top back on with help from Treketa. Donaldo smiled to himself, he knew that there was some discomfort still and that Lance was just being brave showing off to Treketa. But if Lance assured him he was fine, then he was not going to argue with him. It was on his head be it if something happened later during duty, like he collapsed. The doors to the Life Ability Centre opened Tayce walked in, her face suddenly took on an angered look at the sight of Lance being brash and pretending he was fine, when he looked clearly like death warmed up. She crossed to him in a no nonsense way.

"Lance, where do you think your going?" she asked coming to a halt putting her hands on her hips in a true manner of command.

"I want to collect my things from home, when we dock," he began as he slid to the floor.

"Donaldo your the Medical Officer, do you think he's up to this?" confided Tayce questioningly.

"I've warned him and advised him, but he has insisted he's fine," replied Donaldo looking to Lance giving up any responsibility of what Lances actions were, in the fact he felt like Tayce, that Lance should be resting.

"Well all right if you insist that your fine, I'm not taking responsibility for you lets go," said Tayce plain and simple, heading towards the entrance doors.

Donaldo and Lance followed on behind, as did Treketa. Tayce didn't like the idea of Lance wanting to be on his feet so soon, after the serious injury he'd sustained, no more than Donaldo did. Fair enough, his wounds may have been healed on the surface, but they would still be sore underneath. After leaving the Life Ability Centre Lance was beginning to feel that maybe Tayce and Donaldo had been right, it was to soon to try anything strenuous, but he was not going to let on. He caught Tayce glancing back at him, truly displeased he was even attempting such a foolish act, he quickly smiled, brushing off the fact he was fine. As Treketa caught up with her, she ordered her to keep an eye on Lance on Questa the moment he showed strain he was to be escorted back to the cruiser in a no nonsense way, she gave her the authority to be tough with him. Treketa agreed wholeheartedly and confided that she too thought it would have been wise that Lance remain on board until he was strong enough, there would be other times to return home for his things.

Marc, Lydia and Tom stood at the Docking Bay doors with the Countess trying to break free of her force field restraints, but to no avail. She looked like thunder ready to erupt. As everyone grouped together Lance stayed at the back feeling both anger and pain towards the Countess, to think he had been taken in so foolishly by her treacherous ways, even though he had been warned by Tom. It was a good thing he still smarted and that he and she weren't in some lonely destination, he'd forget being a nice person and show her his dark side and how nasty he could get, if angered. It was nice to feel the rush of the Questa warm air meet them as the Docking Bay doors opened. On Questa Jonathan Largon awaited, with him was the promised amount of high level security guards ready and armed. There was also a strong presence of other armed guards spaced out around the immediate area, in case the Countess tried to escape. Jonathan Largon stood watching stern faced towards the entrance and walkway of Amalthea, he shared the hatred for the most devilish woman in all the galaxy, with Tayce, who was about to walk forth with the team. At the sight of the Countess in all her evil glory walking forth in front of Tom in force field restraints, Jonathan turned and nodded to his nearest officer. All the security guards present and around the immediate area immediately went to primed alert mode, with their weapons ready to shoot, if the Countess tried to escape. The spectators gathered had heard that she was arriving at Questa. They watched and ridiculed her cruelly as they saw her being lead off the Amalthea. The odd person catching who it was, as they were walking by paused and gave a plain look of surprise and disgust. Tayce paused in front of Jonathan.

"General I believe our first assignment is a success, here is the first of hoped many criminals being brought to justice from us," announced Tayce proudly.

"Good work Tayce, that goes for all off you, well done," praised Jonathan.

"I'm glad this criminal is one we've been able to apprehend first, she deserves everything that's coming to her don't you agree?" asked Tayce confidingly and loud enough to let the spectators gathered hear.

"Oh I totally agree, Countess Vargon your going where you deserve to be for the rest of your natural life and I will make sure that you remain there, you may have escaped from confinement on Amalthea One, but we've a strong well protected spot especially for you here, until you come to the trial you so rightfully deserve, men take her away," commanded Jonathan in a true tone of command.

Two guards stepped forth and one placed a high density force field belt around the Countess, then lead her away through the square under primed weapon sight and to the sound of boos and hisses and cold sharp spiteful innuendos. Jonathan Largon turned his attention back to welcoming the team, then his eyes caught sight of someone he thought he would never see again, in the group. He walked forth as the team parted to let Lydia walk forward

"Lydia, it's truly good to see you my God we thought we'd lost you, welcome to what I hope you will term as your new second home, Questa," said Jonathan in a warm loving way, then gave her a warm comforting hug.

"It's good to be here," replied Lydia hugging him back, as they had been friends for many yearons.

Upon releasing Lydia Jonathan invited everyone to his Officette. They began on their way leaving behind the cruiser with Midge in charge. All soon arrived at the Vacuum Lift to take them up to Jonathan's Officette. They boarded. Tayce stood next to Tom, noticing how quiet he was. She didn't say anything, she just stood feeling the welcome warmth of his alluring presence. Those of the team that hadn't been to Questa before stood watching as the Vacuum Lift rose above the city. Donaldo occasionally glanced at Lance checking he was holding up. The Vacuum Lift soon stopped. The doors parted and everyone walked out and along to Jonathan's Officette. Half way along the corridor, Lance paused, and called Tayce to one side.

"I'll see you later back on the cruiser," he announced.

"Fine, but take it easy, Treketa will go with you and if you start to feel unwell, she has my authority to take you back to Amalthea, is that understood?" pointed out Tayce in the tone of authority.

"Yes that's okay," agreed Lance.

Tayce before joining the others, watched both Treketa and Lance walk away, she was not pleased that Lance was hiding the fact he was in serious pain and would not give in. She continued on shaking her head at his stubbornness. Lance explained to Treketa, as they both walked along, about the many buildings at Questa and what they were used for. They both headed to the Vacuum Lift that would take them near to his and his Father's residence on the lower levels selected residential area. Treketa as well as keeping one eye on Lance, was admiring the many different spectacular sights around the base. In a way she felt proud to be with Lance, after all, he was the Generals son. Lance was spotted by old friends, especially girls, on the way to the Largon residence, they all gave Treketa the once over, something she found amusing, as she thought they must have thought, she was Lances latest flame. The girls tried to catch his eye and blew kisses telling him to look them up the next time he was home. Treketa just shook her head, thinking she thought Tom used to be bad enough for the fanciful eye of the ladies. Lance once the admiring glances etc. were over apologised to Treketa, she laughed and told him not to worry, she was use to Tom once being in his position. They soon arrived at a white modern architectural designed home of great splendour. Lance keyed in his command to enter the residence. The doors soon opened inward. He gestured for Treketa to go first. She was totally taken back by the lavish splendour within.

Up in Jonathan's Officette he enquired who would be remaining for the Countesses trial, to give evidence on what she had done to Traun, as it would carry great weight in her final sentence. Lydia stood suddenly to everyone's surprise and walked over to the sight pane. Donaldo looked at her, concerned she may be unwell. Lydia paused, looking out the sight pane, in thought. Tayce glanced to the General, then Tom in questioning manner. Lydia turned.

"I'll remain for the trial, nothing would give me the greatest pleasure of seeing that woman go where she belongs, you can pick me up in a monthon, I want to stay for this for your Father's sake Tayce."

"It's all right Mother I understand, really I do," replied Tayce in a true tone of understanding.

Even though Tayce could see where her Mother was coming from, she was concerned for the strain it would cause her when faced with bringing up that fateful night on Traun at trial, and the cruel treatment Vargons men put many of them through. She also realised leaving her Mother behind, when she had only just found her was not going to be easy, they had not had true time to get acquainted as Mother and daughter again. They were really close on Traun. Jonathan could see Tayces disappointment, that Lydia was not travelling on with them and she was genuinely concerned for her Mother's safety, should Vargon escape before trial. He assured her that Lydia would be a guest at the Largon Residence for no matter how long she decided to remain on Questa, and security would be of the most vital importance during her stay, she would be assigned someone to escort her everywhere for her own safety, whilst Vargon was awaiting trial. Tayce felt a lot more at ease knowing at least her Mother would have a good friend and the proper protection should she need it. She stood to her feet.

"If there's nothing else you want us for, we had better head back to the cruiser, criminals don't rest in the current times as you know and with us not out there to stop them, well who knows what will unfold," said Tayce.

"Quite!" replied Jonathan.

"Tayce I need some free time before we head off, I need to pick up some supplies," said Marc standing.

"Fine, but don't be late back," ordered Tayce.

Marc with this excused his presence, and headed off. Lydia and Tayce hugged in a goodbye way. She then ordered Tom to look after Tayce, she did not want to hear of any mishaps. Tom agreed wholeheartedly. They all headed over to the entrance of Jonathan's Officette. Just as the doors opened Treketa stood waiting. Without warning a Slazer shot went off. Treketa was shot in the upper arm and fell against the wall beside the entrance. Donaldo rushed forward, catching her before she crumpled to the floor. Lance quickly turned to try see who fired the shot, but they had vanished from sight. Jonathan ordered the two present security men who had arrived upon hearing Slazer fire, to search the base immediately, he wanted the culprit found.

"Treketa where are you hurt?" enquired Jonathan in true caring concern.

"It's my arm," she replied wincing every time she moved her right arm.

"Take her to our medical facility," ordered Jonathan.

"It's fine General, we'll take her back to Amalthea, thanks," replied Donaldo supporting Treketa taking her on out the entrance.

"Bye Mother, stay in touch and take care," said Tayce then walked on.

"General, until next time," said Tom following on behind Tayce.

"Look after yourselves, it's a treacherous Universe," replied Jonathan after the team, as they walked away.

Lydia watched Tayce proudly as she walked with the team on back to the cruiser, until she was out of sight hoping she was going to be all right, like any Mother would.

As Tayce went so she thought of how the last hourons had seemed. Countess Vargon was now rightfully where she belonged and was going to get what she deserved, coming to her for all the murderous actions she'd so freely enjoyed in her time of reign as leader of the Warrior Army. Marc soon rejoined the team at the Docking Bay doors. Midge made a crew check to make sure everyone, except Lydia had returned to the cruiser for departure then sealed the Docking Bay doors. Amalthea left Questa behind once more, heading off into the Universe.

Questa disappeared slowly, ebbing away behind them like a disappearing blot in the vast Universe.

Pilot From The Storm

In the dayons that followed Treketa returned to her healthy normal self, after the unfortunate incident of being shot outside the Generals Officette. It was night hourons to be exact, of the following weekon, Tayce's quarters, she was in deep sleep, but that deep sleep was tinged with the fact this night was an unusual one, because it was one of those nights where she was reliving the fateful night on Traun. A nightmare that made her relive the final moments before Trauns demise, from the moment she was ordered to be taken to her current surroundings by Marc. Her Father kissing her goodbye for what was thought to be the last time and her being thrust forward in the crowd, never to see her Father again. She tossed and turned in an agitated state, as she progressed through the dream sequence, which was heading to her looking back from Amalthea to see her home world explode in a million trillion pieces. Tears now ebbed down her delicate cheeks dropping onto the grey silkene pillet. Her body was perspiring from the agitated state, she'd slid into when going into the deep nightmare scenario. She tried to turn away from the same repeating scenes, of for some strange reason trying to find her Father against all odds. That he wasn't dead. She woke suddenly sitting up with a breathless start. Shaking like a leaf and looking around the dimly lit Repose Centre. Why had she had this recurring dream again she thought, there was no reason, it had been monthons since she'd dreamt about the last moments of Traun? She took a deep breath to try and relax herself. Then laid back down the bunk, trying to think of something else. She soon drifted back into a peaceful calm sleep.

Outside in the distant Universe, developing as it ebbed towards Amalthea and into the current spacial sector, was the most spectacular Intergalactic storm that ever was, which was being monitored by Midge as it headed in their direction. Bright flashes of red, yellow, orange and greens, with a crimson edge emitted from the storm in dagger shaped lightening, off into the Universe in no particular direction simultaneously. The more the storm developed, the stronger and more powerful it's energy strikes became.

On board Amalthea Midge was taking no chances for what might be and was putting preparations for Storm Attack in place. He being guidance and main operations computer never went to standby, he was on watch of the Universe the whole time to protect his mistress and crew at a moments notice. To his surprise Midge was picking up what he found to be a vessel of sorts, trapped in the heart of the moving storm. He wondered whether he should assist in a rescue, but he would have to do a scan first and identify the vessel in case it was a trap to gain his trust. He took no chances preparing to open fire the moment he did the scan if it proved hostile. The Universe was a treacherous and hostile place, at the best of times and it was growing harder to establish the friendly vessels from enemy type. He realised whoever, it was after the scan came back safe, this was an innocent victim of the storm being tossed around. He began trying to make contact. But because of the extreme powerful energy of the mass, it was increasingly hard to establish a solid contact. He was receiving what he was sending. The call was literally bouncing off the storms energy barrier. He continued to try undeterred increasing the signal strength each time he sent a call, that he was there to assist in anyway he could. He would continue to try and rescue the vessel, until Tayce came on duty, first light.

Tayce walked into Organisation next mornet feeling somewhat still agitated by the fact she'd had her recurring nightmare again and couldn't understand why, she wondered whether it had something to do with the trial and Vargon, as this was on her mind greatly, she wanted the witch out of circulation for good she thought. But did it mean that the evil witch would escape and return to get her again? She crossed to the sight port that was showing the immediate Universe. In the centre of the storm, that suddenly caught her immediate attention, was the vessel that Midge had been trying hard to communicate with. She crossed to her seat and sat down looking at the vessel caught in the colourful tempestuous sight.

"Midge report please, what have we got?" demanded Tayce not taking her sight from the small vessel.

"It materialised in the early hourons, while you were in sleep, I have been following it's progress and trying unsuccessfully to make contact with it, so far we have nothing coming back in returned communications and it continues to drift, I have also put into operation precautions for our protection from the oncoming storm I don't fancy their chances Tayce, whoever is inside that storm and vessel," said Midge.

"What is that?" said Marc in amazement, at the sight of the storm, as he entered Organisation.

"That Marc, is a storm to end all storms and what's more there's a small vessel caught right in the heart of it," explained Tayce glancing over her shoulder at him.

"Have we tried to contact it?" asked Marc looking out to the spectacular sight.

94

"I have tried many times without any success," replied Midge.

"What if we try extreme tractor mode AX-1," asked Marc.

Tayce watched, as did Marc, as to what would happen, when the tractor mode was applied. From the front of Amalthea, the familiar green intense energy force, that was the AX-1, shot from the cruiser across the sector they were currently occupying, straight into the heart of the storm. It locked on to the unidentified craft dragging it with unsteady awkwardness slowly out of the storms interior into clear space. Then slowly as the tractor beam withdrew back into Amalthea, it brought the vessel with it. Midge ran a scan over the vessel once within boarding distance. It was somewhat scorched, owing to the energy lightening strikes that had bombarded it, but it was sleek by design and considered to be a first class fighter type vessel. Tayce waited watching with great interest, as to what would unfold.

"One life sign on board, currently using standby Life Support," announced Midge informatively.

"Marc have Donaldo meet us down at Docking Bay doors on Level 2, in twenty minons, I'm heading down there," said Tayce leaving her seat, heading across the Organisation to the entrance.

"Be right with you, just as soon as I've done this," replied Marc continuing on with the orders for Donaldo to meet Tayce at the Docking Bay doors.

Tayce hurried on out and along Level 1 to the Level Steps towards Level 2. As she went, it had her thinking the nightmare she'd had last night hourons, may have been something to do with the strange vibes that were coming from the storm in their path and not Vargons trial after all. Some people in the past had reported experiencing strange phenomenal forces and experiences in the event of these strange type storms. The more Tayce thought about, it as she went, the more it seemed feasible. Tom soon joined her on the steps coming up from Level 2.

"What's happening, Midge said it was urgent, is something wrong?" asked Tom studying her concerned.

"No I'm fine it's just we have a vessel well a fighter to be exact, that we've hauled from the approaching storm, Midge is bringing it in to dock on Level 2, care to join me?" asked Tayce casually.

"Sure, of course," replied Tom.

Both continued on down the steps, stepping onto Level 2 on walking along they wondered what was awaiting them.

In time Donaldo came running briskly up the corridor to the Docking Bay doors, with a Hover Trolley and Medic Emergency Kit on top. Treketa was laughing and talking with Donaldo as they came. Tayce noticed that she and he were growing together, not just as working buddies, but close in friendship of the intimate kind. This she was glad to see. It was something that she had noticed a lot, ever since the team had come together, everyone seemed to work in unison.

It was understandable, that there were the odd dayons, they each had their problems and moments of agitation, but they soon got over it, if it couldn't be resolved then she wanted to hear about it, so it could be sorted. She appreciated the people that had come together to be considered for her team, they had all given up their spacial lives to try something new and that meant a lot in itself. Tayce Wristlinked Midge as she walked.

"Midge hows it coming?" she asked.

"Final docking in progress Tayce," replied Midge informatively.

Marc hurried down to join them at the Docking Bay doors. He soon stood waiting until decontamination was completed. It seemed to take ages. Midge ordered whoever was volunteering to go aboard the vessel, to get into special protection suits, the air according to his scan readings, was not breathable, very virulent. Tom and Marc agreed to go on board, so went off to get suited up in the nearby suiting up room. Tayce didn't like the sound of Midges findings and wondered whether she was putting both Tom and Marc in danger by letting them do, what they had volunteered to do, by going into the poisonous atmosphere, but they had no choice. Donaldo looked at Tayce and could see her uneasiness, he assured her that whatever happened he would more than be able to put it right. Tayce nodded, then began pacing impatiently. She wanted to get started, to see what, or who, was on board. Treketa could see Tayce was apprehensive at the thought of Tom going into the unsteady atmosphere and she understood that, she felt uneasy too. Tom and Marc soon returned. Tayce, discretely advised Tom the moment he felt they'd been in the bad atmosphere long enough, she wanted him out, she did not want to lose him. Tom pulled her to him and assured her he would. Both himself and Marc once Midge gave the all clear for them to step into the airlock proceeded with caution. Donaldo meantime prepared the Hover Trolley, ready to rush the pilot or being off to the Life Ability Centre, when he was brought from the fighter type vessel. Everyone stood waiting patiently.

Inside the fighter type vessel, it was cramped and the atmosphere was filled with a hazy and poisonous gas. Marc considered it impossible to almost see in front of his face, the air was so thick. But they had come aboard to do a rescue and that was just what they intended to do, they wouldn't give up until they found the pilot they had come to rescue. Upon finally discovering him, they quickly grabbed him from the seat on either side hauling him back to the entrance, watching their footing as they went.

"We don't want to be here to long, there's something leaking, this thing is going to go up, we need to jettison it before it takes Amalthea and us with it," said Marc as they returned to the entrance of the fighter.

Tom nodded. Once back at the entrance, they both dragged the pilot out into the airlock, letting the entrance hatch to the fighter close behind them. Tom ordered Midge via his suit comceive, to jettison the fighter before it blew and took them with it. The airlock soon returned to normal level and the Docking

Bay doors to Amalthea opened. Tom and Marc struggled out back aboard the cruiser, with the humanoid looking pilot. He was not a big built person. Tom and Marc helped lift him onto the Hover Trolley. He was unconscious. Donaldo quickly operated the hand held panel and took the pilot to the Life Ability Centre. Marc removed his protective head shield with much relief, after being in the hazardous atmosphere. Tom did the same. Just as Marc and Tom removed their head shields out in space the fighter that had been jettisoned and had drifted away to a safe distance, exploded from all the dangerous gases that had built up aboard. There came a wave of aftershock that rocked Amalthea. Tom slightly toppled as did Tayce.

"That is what you call a near miss, any longer aboard that thing and we would have gone with it," said Tom with relief he and Marc hadn't stayed aboard the dangerous fighter any longer.

"Have to agree with you there buddy," agreed Marc in utter relief of the fact.

"Besides the gaseous interior, did you find anything in the fighter that would help us identify who our on board guests might be?" enquired Tayce.

"Nope! Nothing except the pilot and the gaseous atmosphere," replied Marc pausing before beginning to walk off to get out of his suit.

"All right while you two go and get changed, I'll go and see what Midge has managed to turn up on this storm, Marc I want you to go to the Life Ability Centre, find out if the pilot has some ID on him," ordered Tayce.

"Yeah sure, if I find anything I let you know later in Organisation," replied Marc walking away.

Tayce began on the walk back to Organisation, wondering just who their on board guest might be. Tom followed Marc to go get cleansed and changed back into his uniform.

Outside the spectacular storm raged on, now much closer than before and right in front of Amalthea. The immense power strikes bounced off the outer hull and the high energy shields around the cruiser. Lightening shone through the cruisers sight ports like someone shining a flash torch of extreme magnitude and of many colours in intermittent succession of brilliance. Amalthea was now gripped by the force of the immense storm in it's path. The cruiser travelled through with great difficulty, jolting this way and that, especially as lightening bounced off the shields.

Lance was in Organisation running information research into the storms interior. He was working in unison with Midge in comparing readings, working as a small team. Tayce soon arrived, walking in, she walked to Lances position preparing to hear what research he had so far.

In the Life Ability Centre on the Exam Bunk lay the pilot from the fighter. He had been changed into medical overstay attire. He was young, no more than twenty-eight yearons old in appearance. But was this his real age? He was of slim athletic build and around 1.54 metres tall and of pleasant good looks.

A monitor above his head was giving Donaldo the readings, as the portable connected machine rid his lungs of the contaminated air he had breathed in after being caught in the storms interior. The air filtration system aboard his fighter had failed, hence he was rendered unconscious. Treketa noticed as she looked down at the young looking pilot, his mousy coloured short spiky hair. As her hand brushed pass it, so it felt rough to the touch. The doors to the Life Ability Centre opened. Marc entered walking briskly over looking at their on board guest curiously. He paused. He couldn't believe who he was seeing. He glanced at Donaldo in wide eyed amazement.

"Do you know who your treating here?" asked Marc in surprise at who they had before them.

"According to his ID in his suit, his name is Dean Addams and from somewhere known as Deltaline 4," replied Donaldo not quite sure of why Marc was near totally shocked, at who this young man was.

"Can I have his ID, Tayce is never going to believe this," said Marc not letting on who the patient was.

"Hold on Marc, is there something I should know about this Dean Addams?" asked Donaldo directly.

"He shouldn't even be in this sector, of space, his home is in the 4th sector on from this one, we're currently in he's also the son of Commodore Addams of Deltaline 4 a very elite bunch, so treat him with extra special care," replied Marc taking the ID from Treketa.

Donaldo raised his eyes, this kind of life for him was beginning to look ten times better than where he use to work on the Intergalactic Medical Colony, so far he'd met General Largons son and now he was treating the Commodores son of Deltaline 4. What next he thought, in amazement.

"So what's his injuries, nothing serious I hope?" asked Marc.

"Tell Tayce I'll give her a report in an houron, but there's nothing serious, I've already run a scan," exclaimed Donaldo.

Marc nodded in total understanding. He turned without further word, and began heading on back to the entrance to head back to Organisation, smiling to himself, amused of who they had just rescued. Treketa looked back down at Dean, as the final diagnosis came through. She continued to check and key in the instructions Donaldo gave her, as he read the young pilots injuries. Together they continued on to treat him to restore him to normal health.

Midge as the lightening was so brilliant, put into operation anti glare mode, tinting the sight ports around the whole cruiser, making the glassene slowly change to a darkened shade, like looking through polarised lens which would shield the teams eyes from the constant glare.

Marc returned to Organisation to find Tayce watching the information Lance was getting on the present storm situation. He crossed exclaiming he had what she requested earlier. Tayce not taking her sight from the Visual Slim Display

Screen, took it reading the final piece of storm information. Marc waited. Tayce stood up from bending down and crossed to the control seat, opening the beige wallet, as she went. Inside she found the Disc Chip that contained the young pilots personal information. She took it out. Placing it in the Disc Chip Reader, activating it. After a few bypass codes to gain access to the information stored. The screen came to life. But instead of an image of the young pilot, there was a cautionary message that flashed across the centre of the screen which read.

ANY FURTHER ACCESS ATTEMPTED BEYOND THIS POINT WILL BE A GROSS VIALATION OF THE DELTALINE 4 RULES OF PRIVACY, WITHOUT THE AUTHORISED CODES FOR ACCESS.

Tayce figured she had been warned, but this was not going to stop her. She ignored the warning and continued, there was no one to tell her otherwise, other than some printed warning notice especially someone from Deltaline 4. Marc glanced at her as he sat down beside her in the seat adjoining the control seat. Together they found a way to break into what they required from the Disc Chip. Up came all the personnel information with a flash.

"Name Dean Paul Addams, Pilot Elite Fleet, Son of Commodore Addams Deltaline 4," read Tayce casually it didn't bother her that this young man was almost royalty.

"You mean to tell me he doesn't impress you Tayce?".asked Marc looking at her surprised that she wasn't.

Marc was going to say more, but was cut short by Midge announcing that Donaldo wanted Tayce down in the Life Ability Centre. Tayce agreed. She stood to her feet, having a feeling it had something to do with their on board guest, maybe he had woken and didn't feel Amalthea was good enough for him to be on. She headed on out of Organisation knowing if this was so, he was going to be sharply informed that if they hadn't of rescued him, he would be dead. Marc shook his head, at her lack of interest not realising just who Dean Addams was and in space terms the Addams of Deltaline 4 were considered royalty of the first kind. But maybe Tayce was somewhat similar, considering Traun was the only planet known to have a paradise atmosphere and withheld a very high esteem with it's people.

Down in the Life Ability Centre Dean Addams was beginning to regain consciousness. He'd been out for more than two hourons. Treketa alerted Donaldo to the fact. He put down the progress report and crossed. Dean was looking far from amused, as his vision cleared. He focussed on his sterile surroundings of the Life Ability Centre. He glanced up at Treketa in an ordinary way. She gave him a reassuring smile. He returned it with a cold unimpressed look, where the hell was he, he thought? But it, didn't stop him also thinking that she was stunningly attractive for a medical woman. Donaldo checked Deans vital readings on the Counter Medical Disc. He then took his Medical Torch and shone it in Deans eyes, one at a time, checking for reaction in case there was more damage than he, or the diagnostic computer via Midge, had not detected. Dean didn't care for this bright light being shone in his eyes, who did this man think he was.

"What are you doing, stop that, do you know who I am?" protested Dean annoyed.

"Yes I do Captain Addams, I am Dr Tysonne, I have to check that your eyes are clear," insisted Donaldo persisting with a calm tone.

"I demand you stop this act at once, it's a violation of my personal being," persisted Dean in a royal upper class tone.

"Captain Addams I am aware that you are probably use to different treatment where you come from, but you are a patient on this cruiser and I am trying to treat you to the best of my ability, to get you well, to return you to your people in good health," said Donaldo becoming firm in his tone.

On this Dean said no more, he realised he had met his match, in this medical man. The doors to the Life Ability Centre opened, Tayce entered crossing in a true commanding way. She came to a pause at the foot of the Exam Bunk, she sensed an awkward atmosphere. She looked plainly at Dean. She considered herself to be on level footing with this Commodores son, as she was the only daughter of Commodore Traun.

"Captain Addams, I'm Colonel Traun, your on board Amalthea One, you've met my medical staff, I'd like an explanation as to what you thought you were doing putting your fighter in the heart of the storm we are currently experiencing, if it wasn't for my guidance and operations computer, you would not be here to tell the tale," said Tayce without any nonsense in her tone.

"I was on a routine flight and then out of nowhere this storm as you say your experiencing, materialised before me, before I knew it and could react and pull out, it was too late, my Father doesn't know I'm here though, does he?" asked Dean hoping not.

"Why would it bother you if he did?" asked Tayce plainly.

"No, it's fine," replied Dean, he figured this Colonel Traun was not going to let him treat her like he treated other people, he came across that were beneath him.

"I would take this time to rest and get well, we will talk again when your up on your feet," suggested Tayce leaving him to do just this.

Treketa made sure Dean was comfortable, then followed Donaldo into the Officette to talk with him and Tayce on Dean's injuries and what treatment he would receive, also his duration of stay in the Life Ability Centre.

Lance meantime in Organisation was constantly checking the readings on the progress of the storm in their path. Tom and Marc were working on getting the Amalthea safely through the storm, with Midges help in main guidance operational mode. Midge suddenly announced he was receiving a somewhat distorted call that was coming through from Questa, from Lydia Traun. Between himself and Midge, Marc worked to clean it up so that it could be seen and heard.

Finally after a lot of adjusting and blocking of the harmful forces of enduring storm, that was estimated to rage on for hourons. Success was achieved.

"We've got you Lydia, go ahead, what's the problem?"asked Marc ready to listen.

"Vargons trial is having some surprising results, so far some 250 people who have suffered at the evil hands of Carra Vargon, have given evidence against her, to convict her," explained Lydia informatively.

"You sound half optimistic, but why do I feel you wonder if she will still get away with what's she done to date?" asked Tom giving her his full listening attention.

"Your right, the trouble is the 250 people who have all given their evidence, it's not sound enough or serious enough to be classed in the same category as the attack on Traun, so far Traun is the only serious attack, she could still walk free after all she has done," replied Lydia.

"She'd better not do," said Tayce hearing the last words of her Mother, as she entered the Organisation Deck.

"Tayce are you all right?" asked Lydia seeing her daughter preoccupied by something important.

"Yes, you'll never believe who we've rescued in the heart of the storm, that we're currently encountering at the present time, Commodore Addams son. Dean, from Deltaline 4?"

Lydia gave a wide eyed surprise look and was about to say something, but was summoned back to the trial. She quickly ceased communication promising to contact them again when the trial was over. Tayce replied she looked forward to that moment with hoped anticipation, that Vargon was going to get what was coming. She thought to herself, she would have loved to have been present at the trial, to see Vargon receiving the most gruelling and probing questions, she could not escape from. Tom studied her, he knew what it would mean for her if Vargon got her just deserts, but he wondered if she had the feeling that somehow Vargon would evade being sent where she deserved to go.

"I've an uneasy feeling about this trial, I feel there isn't going to be enough people with serious cases to be taken into consideration, some may fear there could be retribution if they testified against her," said Tayce in thought.

"You can't worry Tayce, whatever will, be will be," replied Tom.

"Hows our on board guest doing?" asked Lance looking up from his research position.

"For some strange reason I get the feeling he's escaped something on Deltaline 4, by the way in which he asked, did his Father know where he was," said Tayce recalling the fact with suspicion.

Lance raised his eyes in surprise at the fact. The more she thought about it, the more Tayce realised she had to get to the bottom of the reason why Dean was wanting to know if his Father knew where he was. Her next move would surprise even herself. She walked into part of the Organisation Deck, that she never used much, the Meeting Centre, where there was a table large enough to seat about nine members of team around if called for. Tayce crossed to the Telelinkphone. She sat at the far end of the meeting table. Picking up the handset, she ordered Midge to push through the storm and get her connected to Deltaline 4. Midge agreed. After a lot more static that was interference from the storms energy, an official abrupt male voice of extreme authority came online.

"Deltaline 4, this is Commodore Addams, to whom am I addressing?" the voice demanded straight to the point.

"Commodore Addams this is Colonel Traun of the space cruiser Amalthea One, I'm calling you to inform you we have your son here on board, Dean, we rescued him from an energy storm we are currently travelling through, his fighter craft is something that could not be saved, due to being filled with toxic gasses I must point out it was not destroyed by ourselves, I ask you not to be concerned, he is under the expert care of my on board medical man and he is perfectly safe with us," explained Tayce politely.

"Colonel I do not have a son, you must have the wrong planet, or you have an imposter on your cruiser who claims he is," he replied coldly uncaring even.

"But Commodore the ID we retrieved states he is Dean Addams and if you'll pardon me for saying this as you state you do not have a son I have to argue that it clearly states that he, is, your son from your planet so someone here is not getting their facts right and I can assure you sir, it is not us," insisted Tayce not understanding why the Commodore should want to disown his own son, what was he hiding and what had this Dean done, that his Father did not want to take responsibility for him thought Tayce?

"No need for apologies Colonel, he maybe stating he's my son... Dean has decided to chose another way of life outside our world, therefore he is no longer classed as my son, I have nothing more to say on the matter, I ask you not to call Deltaline 4 again Colonel," he replied then abruptly cut communication.

Tayce was literally left speechless, the audacity of the man she thought, first lying then telling her he no longer wanted him. No wonder Dean didn't want his Father to know where he was. She wondered if the Commodore would have felt the same way if she had contacted him to inform him, that his son was dead. She placed the handset back in thought of wondering what had gone on between Father and son. She stood and walked back out into Organisation. Lance looked up seeing her somewhat shocked and in thought.

"Bad news, you look shocked, what's the problem?" he asked concerned and ready to listen.

"I just had a conversation with Commodore Addams, he denies all responsibility for being Dean Addams Father and in no certain terms, asked me not to contact Deltaline 4 again," said Tayce not believing what she had heard and the attitude of the Commodore she was glad her Father wasn't like it when he was alive.

"Denying it or not it's definitely him, Midge ran a check and it definitely states royal son and heir of Commodore Addams Deltaline 4, but Dean has a right to not want to know his Father any more, apparently I was once told his Father was a real royal pain the neck Dean wanted different to what his Father wanted for Deltaline 4 and they kind of fell out," expressed Lance.

"One minon he denied having a son and then said Dean had chosen his life and that was that and now what you've just told me about their relationship seems to match what he is saying, he did have a son but didn't want to know him any more judging by the attitude I just received, Deans got my sympathy, not wanting him to know where he was, I guess that's what I got for sticking my nose in, I think if Father had been like that, I would have escaped when I could too, I don't blame Dean, but to throw yourself into a raging storm, that's another thing," replied Tayce.

"Who's going to tell him his Father doesn't want him back?" asked Lance curious.

"I will, not that he probably doesn't already know, but there's no time like the present," expressed Tayce in true command.

Tayce walked from Organisation leaving Tom and Lance to look on in raised eyed gesture, in the way in which she had made her decision. But Tom had a feeling that the reason Tayce wanted to be the one to tell Dean is she wanted to know exactly just what it was that had made his Father disown him, there was no point in keeping him on board herself, if he was going to cause trouble, she'd have transport sent out from Questa and have him taken back there, she was not prepared to let trouble start on this new team.

Tayce as she went decided that if there was a genuine reason for Dean leaving his home world and he had not caused trouble, she would ask him to become a temporary guest member on the team, until such time he could leave of his own free will. Being a royal member of the Addams family, it would not be permissible for him to become a fully fledged member of her team, because of the crime fighting they had to do at times. He may have fallen out with his Father, but she did not want to get into trouble with his world for getting him killed. There was a lot to be taken into consideration, so he would remain as a guest member.

Dean was talking with Treketa about his home world and how it had become unbearable to stay under his Father's rule. Treketa listened with summoning interest about Deltaline 4 and the relationship between Dean and his Father, what she could concur, was a serious conflict of interest, between Father and son. Dean was very much for joining the other colonies in the Universe in some kind of shared contract, to enable the people of his world to travel to distant colonies, but his Father wanted to remain a single planet, with single policies and values, which was chocking the young people and people like himself to advance with the universal living. Donaldo found himself listening, also with interest and could understand why Dean had left this home world.

"If you don't mind me asking why did you leave it so long before leaving your home world?" asked Donaldo giving Dean his full attention, crossing to his bunk side.

"My Father is someone you don't escape from so easily especially as you are considered a royal elite member of the highest order of my people, it's frowned upon for being, dare I say this, difficult!" replied Dean a lot more calmly and politely.

"So you took your chance and ran for it, so to speak?" said Treketa.

"Yes I crept out one night, grabbed my fighter and took off, I just couldn't go on with Father's narrow minded singleness approach to the way he wanted to live," replied Dean thinking about it.

The doors to the Life Ability Centre behind them opened. Tayce walked in, in thought about how she was going to break the news to Dean, what his Father had just told her. Dean studied her on approach, thinking to himself for the leader of a team and Colonel, she was exceptionally beautiful. Too beautiful to be in charge of a crime fighting team. He still couldn't believe what Treketa had told him how Tayce had come to be where she was. In a way they were a little alike, she'd lost her home world through a war that was not her planets fault, where's he had lost his home because his Father no longer wanted to know him.

"Captain Addams!" Tayce began.

"Colonel Traun, I know what your going to say, it's my Father isn't it, believe me I know he has disowned me and doesn't want me back on Deltaline 4 I expected nothing else," began Dean.

"I'll leave you two to talk," said Donaldo walking away.

"Your correct, I spoke with your Father and he informed me that he did not have a son, and he did say he disowns you, his exact words were, that he did not have a son and that you had made your choice, care to explain?" said Tayce giving him her full attention.

She listened as Dean explained what he had told Treketa and Donaldo, about his Father wanting to stick to old structure instead of changing to a new way of life, that would benefit every young person on the planet his Father didn't see the need for change he was sticking to the old structure to do things and it didn't do him any harm growing up was the words he'd used when he questioned it. He further stated, that it had come to a head that he and his Father no longer agreed on anything. He was for the young people and hearing what they wanted and that was change for the better, but they could no longer agree on anything any more. So he up and left, but had unfortunately fallen into the hands of a raging storm, he wanted to apologise for causing any inconvenience, or rudeness all round, that may have been caused by himself and his Father.

"Believe me, I have experienced people like your Father in my past and what your telling me, in time he will have to change, or the people of your world will change it for him," replied Tayce.

"Oh I agree Colonel, but I for one will not return to help him, he has made his feelings quite clear to me and therefore he will have to deal with the consequences himself," replied Dean casually.

Both carried on talking about both his world and Traun. Tayce was trying to make sure she could trust this Captain Dean Addams.

Outside Amalthea was still enduring the wrath of the alarming influences of the interior of the storm. The effects were somewhat violent at times. The lightening strikes becoming more frequent, as they struck home. Suddenly without so much as any kind of warning, the protection shields failed around the cruiser. Amalthea was vulnerable to all the violent influences of the storm, that were being thrown at her, tossing the cruiser about in the force of energy, that seemed to hold the cruiser like a small ball in an air powered tornado like sphere.

On board in Organisation, Tom and Marc were getting explosions all over the deck, as circuits blew under the continued strain. Amalthea was failing by the cencron, they had to think and do something fast, otherwise the cruiser would become a destroyed victim of the storms interior. Tom and Marc both tried to find the break in the circuits, to try and bypass the break long enough to get the protection shields back online, so they could at least make it to the end of the storm, in one piece. Midge cut in announcing that if they could fix the break long enough, then they could hit the Hyper Thrust Turbo control and head off to clear Universe. Amaltheas interior equipment and loose belongings around the cruiser fell off places all over the place, some smashing on impact with the deck floor. In the Life Ability Centre, Treketa and Donaldo were trying to salvage any equipment they could get a hold of before it broke. Dean became anxious, beginning to think that maybe he should have remained in his fighter, as it looked like he was going to die anyway. Tayce helped in trying to hold Dean in his bunk, with one hand on the wall rail and gripping Deans arm with the other one. Amalthea was now spiralling out of control in a storm that was determined to claim the first class cruiser for it's next victim.

In Organisation Marc was on his back down under the main operations console. He was trying with great determination to get the protection shields back online, but every time he gained a connection sparks and shocks came back at him. Determined he continued, until the connection was achieved and it looked like it would hold until they would be clear of the storms interior. Marc soon sprang to his feet, giving the all clear to hit Hyper Thrust Turbo. Tom did as they proposed and sat back in the seat praying to the Gods of the Universe, that the connection that Marc had achieved, would hold in the next houron of the journey to freedom. Just as Tom had hit the button for Hyper Thrust Turbo the Protection Shields kicked in and climbed to full protection, degree by degree. The first class exploration cruiser shot off like a shot from a Slazer Cannon, heading through the ferocious lightening strikes, which occasionally shook the vast sized cruiser. Tom and Marc were now holding their breath, almost praying with every once of what faith they'd got, that calmness would not be far off ahead.

Calm space. The cruiser had made it through. On board it looked like, from Organisation to the Flight Hanger Bay it had been through a tornado. Broken equipment and personal belongings lay littered around the decks, sections and rooms. Tom and Marc in Organisation sighed a thankful sigh of relief that they had managed to pull off a somewhat tricky and miraculous manoeuvre. Lance put his hand out for Tom and Marc to shake in congratulations, on a near impossible task, well achieved.

"I think that's what Earth One people use to term, flying by the seat of the pants, right Marc?" said Tom in jovial tone.

"Oh to right, but it's something I don't recommend every dayon," replied Marc shaking Lances hand.

All three men surveyed the strewn mess, that was around the Organisation Deck. Midge announced that Amalthea had gone through the head of the storm, which had been the biggest source of power to strike at the cruiser. The storm was now behind them, heading on to some other unsuspecting victim, that crossed it's path. Tom stood to his feet and began to tidy up, with Lance, what they could salvage. Marc suggested he head down to the Life Ability Centre to see if the others were okay. Tom agreed leaving Marc to go on ahead. Marc exited the Organisation Deck, running at full pelt on the way down to Level 2, to the Life Ability Centre wondering what he was going to find. Mess that littered the corridor floor from broken circuit panels, felt like rubble under foot, as he went. The Level Steps were the only clear area not littered. Light Panels to show the way down had cracked but not smashed on to the steps, which he was glad of, otherwise it could have proven treacherous, the speed in which he was running down.

In the Life Ability Centre Tayce was rubbing her right arm bringing it back to circulation from aching in hanging on during the storms turbulence. Donaldo fetched the muscle repair treatment called Healentex. A small round unit, hand held and used for treatment of torn or pulled muscles in strain. He was treating Tayce while Treketa was sorting Dean out making him more comfortable in his bunk and that all monitoring discs were back where they should be. The doors opened and Marc entered expecting to find total pandemonium, but was somewhat surprised to see everything was well in hand. Both Tayce and Treketa laughed, upon seeing Marc's shocked and somewhat amazed expression.

"Looks like you did better down here, than we did up on Level 1," said Marc glancing around.

"We just held on, right Tayce?" said Treketa glancing to Tayce.

"Yes, I hope this cruiser is in one piece, did I detect that Hyper Trust Turbo was used?" said Tayce looking at Marc in a somewhat questioning manner.

"You did, the cruiser is in one piece yes, we've just got more mess than you upstairs right now," replied Marc, he had no idea Tayce was being somewhat teasing.

"Really! What have you been doing with my Organisation Deck Marc Dayatso?" said Tayce continuing to tease.

"Would you believe guiding this cruiser with Tom out of the last milons of the storm," he said catching on what she was up to.

Dean watched the easy happy atmosphere of the relationship between these members of the so called crime fighting Amalthean Quests team and he liked what he saw. Tayce introduced Marc to Dean. Marc crossed. Both men shook hands in greeting. Tayce explained that Dean would be remaining with the cruiser, as a temporary guest. Marc nodded in total understanding. But he wondered whether like Tayce, if Dean could be trusted, he would be keeping an eye on the Commodores son of Deltaline 4. If he stepped out of line in any way whatsoever, he would be feeling the wrath of himself or Tom of that he could count on.

"Thanks Donaldo let's hope I don't have to do that again too soon and we encounter any more of those kinds of storms for a while," said Tayce pulling her sleeve down.

"Your welcome, it was quite an experience, I don't think any of us want to encounter to soon again," replied Donaldo returning the Healentex to the stand, from where he'd picked it up from.

"I'll leave Captain Addams in your care, you can decide when to send him to Guest Quarters," ordered Tayce beginning back to the entrance with Marc.

The entrance doors opened on approach revealing a corridor of debris. Both Tayce and Marc walked out and immediately began picking up some of the large fragments, that were to big and dangerous to be left lying around. They began to talk in more detail about Dean, as they went. Marc found that what Tayce was saying, quite plausible in the single mindedness of Dean's Father, he'd heard reports he was not a man to be easily swayed into new policies. Both discussed whether they could ever consider Dean team material or not.

Tom was busy trying to get the cruiser back to full operational power. He was working with Midge in putting new replacement circuits where the others had simply exploded, due to the storms powerful energy force. Lance was running checks when Tom had replaced the new ones, to make sure they were fully operational. Midge kept an eye on the Universe so to speak, he was constantly scanning the on board systems as the new circuits became operative, to make sure that it stayed at a constant operational level as each circuit was replaced, watching the pathway ahead in case there was any unsuspecting nasty surprises arising.

Three hourons later the Amalthean Cruiser looked more like the first class cruiser, it should be and not a reminiscent of tornado alley. Tayce was back in command and had requested everyone gather in the Organisation Deck, Meeting Centre, as her Mother had sent live coverage to them of the trial of Countess Vargon. Tayce had found something very strange about what her Mother had said, in the outcome in that it was quite, quite exceptional and least expected. Tayce because of this, couldn't wait to see it with the rest of the team. Lance could see she was somewhat enthusiastic to get started though, in a way he couldn't blame her, as he would feel the same if it had happened to him and he wanted to see Countess Carra Vargon was going to get her comeuppance, because of what she had done to the planet Traun and others. Tayce and her family were good people he thought. Marc entered the Meeting Centre exclaiming he'd spoken with Dean about having another word with his Father personally, he had agreed, but said that he hadn't much hope of a successful answer. Tom joined Marc and Tayce in deciding what they would do in giving Dean a job on board for the duration that he was with them. They all discussed the best position to place him in temporarily.

Donaldo gave Dean the all clear, as he completed his final check on the points that put him in the Life Ability Centre in the first place, the inhaling of the fumes from the gaseous atmosphere aboard his fighter were gone and his lungs were fine. He ordered Treketa to take him to on board Guest Quarters, then she could join him in the Meeting Centre as Tayce had requested they meet her there. Treketa agreed wholeheartedly then began towards the entrance with Dean in tow. Treketas uniform was very attractive on her. A white knee length skirt. Calf length white high heeled boots, beige tights and a matching white top with a thin navy stripe running down the sleeve from shoulder to cuff. As the doors to the Life Ability Centre opened, Treketa let Dean go first, then followed on explaining that he'd find in his quarters somewhere he could relax and make himself comfortable and make his own. As they went Dean thanked her for being so patient with him, he must have been a real pain in the neck with attitude when he came round and he wanted her to know he truly didn't mean it. Treketa laughed it off. He studied her wondering if all women outside Deltaline 4 were like Treketa and Tayce, beautiful he hoped so! They soon stepped into the Deck Travel as the doors opened. Treketa waited until the doors closed, then depressed Level 4. Both stood in silence as the Deck Travel took them to the desired level.

When almost everyone had arrived in the Meeting Centre later, Treketa came running in apologising for keeping everyone waiting. She soon found a seat and fitted in.

"Did Captain Addams get to his quarters all right?" asked Tayce curious.

"Yes he's fine, he said Amalthea was a lovely cruiser and if his Father wasn't so awkward he could have a fleet of cruisers like it too," said Treketa.

"Mother and Jonathan Largon have sent us part of the trial that shows the outcome for Vargon, Mother says that the outcome is somewhat unexpected, so I have been told, shall we begin?" said Tayce.

On Tayces command Midge activated the Sight Screen on the main wall of the Centre. Everyone turned their attention to the screen, as the recording began with a shot of none other than Countess Vargon dressed in a brilliant red gown looking more like a well made up Queen, than the evil witch that she had come to be known as. The trial went on asking her probing questions of her attack on various planets, colonies and vessels. Not to anyone's surprise she denied she had done anything wrong. Tayce shook her head and gave a totally disgusted look, that said it all. Jonathan Largon came on the Vid recording explaining that after the following, he would leave what happened next to the teams imagination. The trial continued and abruptly without warning, a brilliant red aura surrounded Vargon. She gave the following statement then vanished.

"Thought you could all hold me forever, wrong, no one can hold me, not even you," she retorted pointing her slim finger in the direction of Jonathan Largon.

Tayce now knew what her Mother had said was true, that the outcome was somewhat exceptional. Vargons brilliant red aura became powerful to the extent it was near impossible to look at on the screen, then she vanished into nothing. Gone from the trial leaving everyone in the Meeting Centre and at the trial speechless.

"That's just like her, she can't get way with this," said Tayce angrily jumping to her feet.

"Take it easy Tayce, there's nothing you can do," said Tom standing taking hold of her in a soothing way, trying to calm her down, as she was shaking with anger and shock, at what had happened.

Everyone present was just as shocked as Tayce. So Countess Carra Vargon had escaped against all odds of sending her to a sentence befitting for what she stood for, crime of the highest degree. But where had she vanished too and would she make another appearance. Tayce for one hoped she would, deep inside so that next time she could finish her once and for all or bring her to justice with much more tighter security.

Amalthea had gained an on board guest team member, it was uncertain whether he would become permanent or not. The team were left in what was somewhat of a stunned silence as to the outcome of the trial in Vargons spectacular disappearance. It was a shame that Vargon had not been stopped. But there was always another dayon to do just that.

Searching for the Greymaren Victims – Part 1

Much to everyone's surprise Lydia was returning to the cruiser, her Launch from Questa was in the final stages of docking alongside. Because of her sudden arrival, Marc had been the one to go and meet her. Tayce had a meeting with Dean to discuss his on board duties, considering he had tried to talk to his Father again without much luck of him returning home under the grounds, that he would stand with the people of Deltaline 4 and change against what his Father was adamant not to change, this could not be allowed. Marc stood waiting at the Docking Bay doors patiently to ask Lydia why she had returned so eagerly? He in his estimation, thought now that Vargon was on the loose she'd want to stay in the safety of Questa. But that was Lydia, she was going to do what she wanted to do. He recalled how sometimes Darius her husband use to despair at the way if she set her mind to do something no matter what he advised, she'd go right ahead and do it regardless. He guessed this was one of those times and she didn't have Darius to stop her.

Tom was inspecting a newly arrived container down in the Flight Hanger Bay that housed a new fighter (a self assembly Kit) he figured in his off duty times he could put it together, as a means of a way to relax and it was something he could do when he and Tayce couldn't share off duty time together. Now he'd heard about the sudden arrival of Lydia, he had a feeling that he would be spending a lot of off duty time alone in the bay. But in one way he was glad she was returning for Tayces sake, he wondered also if her early return had to do with the fact that Vargon was back in the Universe again and someone aboard had informed her Tayce didn't take the news to well. But who could blame her, considering what she went through at the hands of the evil woman the night Traun was destroyed. He for one loved Tayce and understood her hurt after losing Alenea he'd like to get his hands on the creeps who attacked their craft, made him lose her. He continued in thought on the matter. It seemed strange to think monthons had passed since he'd lost his wife.

Lance was in Organisation at the cruisers operational main controls, something he hadn't had the chance to do since joining the team, even though he was an expert pilot. Midge was scanning the immediate path they were currently travelling. Something ahead didn't seem right as right in the centre of his vision field was a space station drifting with no power. The on board emergency alarm sounded suddenly, this was an emergency. The alarm sounded throughout the whole cruiser, in every corridor, section and deck. Lance nearly fell off his seat, had he done something, he thought until he realised that the alarm was warning him of the unexpected sight ahead.

"Relax Lance! We have trouble ahead, I've picked up a space station that appears to be powerless, no lights, nothing".announced Midge informatively.

"Midge run magnification scan, make sure this is not Vargons first elaborate trap, we have to be on our guard, considering she's back out here," ordered Lance.

"Running magnification scan, now," replied Midge.

Lance watched as the magnification view showed the whole station, as it glided over the whole structure. It came to rest on the name and a name that Lance was not expecting to see, but knew well.

"Oh my God Greymaren Station, this can't be right, she shouldn't be here," said Lance almost speechless at the thought that a station such as Greymaren, was generally a living thriving community in it's self, should be drifting void of all life.

"According to my research this station has been in the missing files of your Father's Lance, for some time, it has been missing for almost two yearons, it appears to be a long way from it's original orbit, but how it got here is unexplainable," informed Midge.

"Midge get the others up here now, Tayce is never going to believe this," commanded Lance.

Whilst Midge summoned the rest of the team to Organisation Deck, Lance carried on studying the somewhat deserted Greymaren Station. The station was roughly two milons in diameter over all. It was still as good in appearance as the first dayon she'd been placed completed in the Universe, for the sole purpose of galactic exploration. It catered for several aspects of space exploration, some termed it as scaled down version of Questa Headquarters Base. Tayce soon arrived on deck, walking briskly in. Dean followed on behind. Tayce immediately looked through the main sight port at the sight of the Greymaren Station in a stationary orbit and walked to the control seat. Lance quickly got out, allowing her to take over. As she did, so be began explaining that the station had been missing for almost two yearons, lost from it's original stationary orbit. Lance continued, that his Father had been great friends with Commodore Martin Travern, the head of the station as she too herself was familiar with the Traverns and Greymaren. Lance headed away to the research console suggesting to Dean on route, he watch and learn. He sat down and began to key in the request for more information, on their current subject of attention. A few minons passed, then it began coming in thick and fast.

"All life void aboard, according to this, there's no further information about what might have happened, or where the people of the station went," said Lance informatively glancing back at the screen from time to time.

"How many people should be on the station, when it's fully operational, I can't remember?" asked Tayce listening.

"According to this, roughly 460, give or take a few," read Lance.

Without warning Dean suddenly spoke up recalling one fact about the Greymaren and the inhabitants, the Commodore had a daughter her name was 'Kelly'. Lance nodded, he too remembered Kelly Travern. If she had managed to escape the demise of the station, she would be around twenty-four yearons old. Dean for a moment went into deep thought over the last encounter he'd had with Kelly, it hadn't been a happy one.

"Lance you say no lifeforms, try scanning for even the most smallest of life signs, anything that signifies a remote chance someone might be on their own over there, living rough, it might give us something to go on, as a base for a Quest to go over and investigate, that includes you trying anything Midge."

"You've got it scanning now," replied Lance.

Lance could see Tayce was hoping for a small miracle, but would it happen? Tom entered Organisation and glanced at the station through the sight port. He crossed and paused asking was their present sight the reason for being summoned? Tayce nodded and began to explain their current situation. Tom wondered what force had attacked the Greymaren Station, to put it in it's current state, whoever they were, they had to be a real deadly group of beings judging by what had occurred. Suddenly Lydia arriving on board and getting a top priority welcome had been put at the back of everyone's minds. Greymaren Station had now become a top priority instead.

Lydia was unpacking her holdall in her quarters. Marc was with her, he figured that Tayce could more than take care of anything that was currently under way. Lydia and himself were discussing the unforeseen abrupt ending to Vargons trial. Marc explained how it had shocked Tayce to the core, knowing what had happened. Tom however had helped her realise, that she would not be alone should Vargon make another appearance. She had the whole team, that would be therefore her, should Vargon try anything untoward.

"I had a feeling she'd take it badly, thanks for telling me Marc, that's one of the reasons I returned early," said Lydia softly.

"We've a new recruit on board, temporary as he maybe, 'Dean Addams,'" said Marc bringing Lydia up to date with what had been happening whilst she had been on Questa.

"The Ambassadors son of Deltaline 4, yes I had heard," said Lydia plainly.

112

Marc was about to go into the reason for Deans arrival when he was cut short by Tayce announcing overhead that his presence was requested, right then in the Organisation Deck. Marc could tell by Tayces tone, she was not amused. He stood to his feet exclaiming he'd continue their conversation later. Lydia nodded. She smiled to herself right from the first dayon he'd arrived on Traun, Tayce had always managed to make him jump to her command and nothing had changed. Marc briskly walked from the living area out through the opening doors, heading up to Organisation in urgency.

In Organisation it had been decided to contact Jonathan Largon at Questa. Tayce ordered Midge to contact Jonathan, she wanted to speak to him urgently. In the moments that followed Tayce sat studying the station wondering just what had gone on aboard. Jonathan suddenly appeared on screen. He wondered what was so urgent and it showed in his facial expression, by his questioning look.

"Tayce what's wrong, your Mother made it back all right, I was concerned that she wanted to head back out to you, so soon after the trial, that's why I had security fly her back?" explained Jonathan hoping that nothing unforeseen had happened to Lydia on route.

"Yes, she's fine and safely with us, I contacted you General on a different urgent matter," began Tayce.

Jonathan gave her his full attention, with Adam listening in, in the background. Tayce didn't quite know what to tell him. Jonathan prompted her to start at the beginning, it was generally a good place to start!

"It would be better if I show you the outside view of Amalthea right now," suggested Tayce.

Midge sent Jonathan a sight that he had not expected to see ever again. He was speechless, to say the least at the sight of the deserted in darkness Greymaren Exploration Station. He didn't know what to say.

"How come she's in your current orbit, I'm aware that she went missing two yearons ago, we lost all trace of her it was simply assumed she had met an untimely end, that everyone on board had perished in some unforeseen accident, any sign of life?" he asked greatly interested.

"At the moment both Lance and Midge are trying everything to determine if there's a small chance that there might be some kind of life, but it's unsure whether there will be," replied Tayce.

"I want you to treat this as your next Quest, I want you to go and investigate, go aboard, find out what's happened to the 460 or so crew and the Travern family," ordered Jonathan seriously.

"Don't worry, leave it with us, I'll come back to you the moment we uncover anything that may help us track down the crew if we can," replied Tayce.

"Good luck and be careful over there," said Jonathan then ceased communication.

The screen went blank. Tayce ordered Midge immediately to compile a suitable Quest team for investigation. He agreed undertaking to find the right team members for the Quest ahead. Meantime Lance continued on trying to find some in depth information, to help on the Quest, but all he had been able to find out so far, there was an atmosphere, but very thin. It was due to the stations current orbital state. This would mean that suits would have to be warn on the Quest and portable air containers would have to be taken along. He informed everyone present as much. All listened, plus Marc who had just walked into Organisation.

Greymaren Station. In total darkness. All that seemed to be on board was the patrolling Securidroids in operational mode, patrolling the corridor's for the first sign of trouble not knowing that there wasn't anyone on board. They had been in operation since the crew had gone missing, it was not quite clear where they were getting their power charge source from to keep in operational mode. It was possible they were still in their self sufficient programme, which enabled them to take care of their charging without the need for human operation. They were around 1.47 metres in height. But these Securidroids were still patrolling as if the crew were in night sleep mode. Something the team from Amalthea would have to try and avoid, as these Securidroids were programmed to kill any intruders on sight. To them the Quest team were going to be just this, intruders. It was not going to be easy. They were silver metallic grey in colour and had a tough shell that was hard wearing. They would prove not the easiest to bring down if need be. Amongst their many duties they would pick up corridor rubbish and patrol for intruders. Any intruders would be shot on sight and disintegrated. There was an extreme feeling of eeriness aboard. A cold feeling was felt in the thin atmosphere chilling even. Equipment and work surfaces around the many deserted sections, rooms and centres, looked like the crew had gone off duty, to return later. Empty Coffeen beakers sat on the work surfaces where people had been working. In the quarters of the once crew, bunks looked like they hadn't been slept in. Uniforms for the next shift discarded by the various members, never to return to change into them again. The whole station looked like somewhat of a ghost port, in space. Whatever had happened, happened without warning and fast. To add to the eerie feeling of desertion the stations structure, creaked and groaned. Was the team entering a somewhat perilous situation, were they about to put their own lives in danger, just stepping on board?

On Amalthea the Quest team had now been picked by Midge. They were suiting up in their specially made close fitting atmospheric suits. No sooner they were ready, they were heading along to the on board Travelsport Centre. Tayce, Tom, Lance, Dean and Treketa in case she was needed, all were in thought of the uncertainty of what lie ahead and what they would find on Greymaren. They took their Slazers, fully charged in case they needed them for protection, though Midge hadn't detected anything other than a small sign of life. They soon entered into the Travelsport Centre, crossing they stood in the Travelsport square, marked on the floor. Tayce raised her Wristlink giving command to Marc up in Organisation to commence Travelsport. The de-materialisation oscillated around the Quest team, and they de-materialised off Amalthea.

On arrival on board the Greymaren Station, the team were met by the dark and cold eerie atmosphere. Each Quest member took a moment to take in their surroundings. They activated their pencil shaped light hand held torches known as 'Light Pencil Torches'. Treketa suddenly shuddered as if someone had walked right through her, like a ghost. In the light beams from the torches, the team began looking about. They guided the torches over signs on the walls. Tayce walked forward into what must have been the Main Operational Hall where personnel obviously were always kept busy. Now dark and eerily lifeless, like most of the station. The computers silent, screens blank. Several chrome and black Leatherex chairs were dotted here and there, either pushed out, as if someone had got up to leave, some had even been tipped on the side. Tayce broke the unnatural silence of the atmosphere.

"Let's see if we can get some light and life support up and running," she suggested.

"This is a far cry from what this place should look like, it's generally full of life, people working, living their every dayon lives, like they should be," said Lance recollecting what it had been like in the past.

"Your more familiar with this place Lance, as from now on, your in charge of finding and restoring light and life support," ordered Tayce.

"You've got it," replied Lance.

"And while your at it, keep an eye out for that small sign of life we detected," said Tayce.

"Sure!" replied Lance.

Tom turned to Tayce suggesting that as soon as life support was up and running, assuming they could get it up and running, they should find their way around the station, maybe split into small groups. Tayce quickly informed him that she was in charge of the Quest, any decisions that were made, would be made by herself. She would tell him what they were, when ready. She was not prepared to put anyone's life in danger by walking off on their current surroundings, in the state that it was. There was no telling what was lurking in the dark, around the corridors. Tom fell silent, he could see her point. Lance announced that he had found the stations main operational panel. Dean was with him, shining his light pencil shaped torch, high enough for Lance to look over it. He searched for the activation switch. Tom felt he'd rubbed Tayce up the wrong way, so decided to wander off to the far wall, where there seemed to be a directional map of the entire station. He stood following the various routes with his torch, where they lead to. Tayce walked over to see what he was making sense of.

"This place is giving me the creeps, I can see Treketa feels the same," said Tayce discretely by his side.

"Scared of ghosts are you!?" he teased giving her an amused look.

"After all I've gone through in the last yearons since leaving Traun, never!" replied Tayce shuddering.

Tom looked down at her, he had feeling she was just being brave at the fact that maybe the station was haunted. Lance found the activation sequence. He pushed it home and waited along with Dean for the worst to happen. Suddenly the wide computer keypad began coming to life, as did all the computer keypads in the Main Operational Hall. He found that the key symbols for each command, was the same as Questa's computer language. He remembered the language from when he grew up and went on duty with his Father, he had in fact seen this particular console when he visited Greymaren with his Father in the old dayons. Dean shone the torch so Lance could key in the sequence for hopefully activating the life support. As Lance worked so the station began coming back to life, bit by bit.

"At last! Now things don't look so bad in the light," said Treketa as lighting overhead came on showing the vast size of the Main Operational Hall.

"But where are the crew, that's the main factor here," said Tom discretely, deactivating his torch, slipping it back into his suit pocket.

"Life support now operable, keying in the command to bring it up to full operating power," announced Lance keying away.

Tayce wanting to see what the console was like, walked over to him, leaving Tom studying the map. She also wanted to make sure in him bringing the station back to life, that he didn't accidentally activate the control to set the station in motion and it started moving off into another orbit with Amalthea chasing after them across the Universe trying to catch up as they headed on to wherever. Just to make sure that the atmosphere was gaining full strength, Tayce contacted Midge on the cruiser. Ordering him via Wristlink to double check life support was running and increasing as Lance was getting the readings as such, before they removed their head shields. A few moments lapsed.

"Air breathable Tayce, at the required human level of normal operation," replied Midge, over her Wristlink.

"Thanks Midge, contact you later," said Tayce deactivating her Wristlink.

She removed her head shield and shook her blonde hair back into place about her shoulders. The rest of the team discarded their head shields and placed them down. Tayce clapped Lance in a congratulating way on the shoulder. She then ordered Tom to stay in the Main Operational Hall and see what he could find out on the missing crew, if anything from the stations on board computer banks. He nodded agreeably. Tayce then suggested that she and Lance go one way and look around for the faint sign of life, whilst Treketa and Dean head off in the other direction, anyone who found anything, were to report back, using

Wristlinks. Lance left the console in Tom's hands and followed Tayce, while Dean and Treketa began off. Tom set about keying in a request for the last log entry.

Soon Tayce walked into a medium sized room. A room that withheld more station operations. There was a sight pane that showed the Amalthea, in all her white gracefulness. Tayce unexpectedly felt like someone or something was watching her. She spun round to see one of the stations Securidroids hovering in the doorway, looking at her with its blue luminous eyes. She knew that if she moved suddenly, she'd be toast, so she had to think and think fast, to stay alive. There was no telling what it's memory systems saw her as and she bet it was in the category of disintegration as an intruder. Lance appeared in the doorway just behind it. He saw Tayce was in danger and had to also think fast, he remembered what these giant robots were capable of. He gave a hefty shove to the side of the Securidroid, which sent it to the other side of the doorway, then reached out his left hand and grabbed Tayces right.

"Come on Tayce, run for it," said Lance in urgent whisper.

She didn't need telling twice, she ran across the room, out into the corridor past the Securidroid that was about to see what had caused him to be shoved aside and was turning to face her, as she passed. Lance pulled her round the next available corner down low out of sight. Here they stayed silent in close to the wall, just slightly peering around the walls edge. Tayces heart pounded in her chest, as the Securidroid exited the room slowly. Lance put his finger to his lips to silence Tayce in case she wanted to say something. The slightest move, would have had the Securidroid heading in their direction.

"We've got to find weaponry stronger than our Slazers, to throw those things off guard," said Lance close to Tayces right ear in whisper keeping one eye out for the Securidroid.

Tayce nodded. Just as both had thought the Securidroid had chosen to head down the corridor and it was safe to move off around the corner, came yet another Securidroid. Tayce ducked as did Lance, both running full pelt in the other direction, they didn't have a clue where they were heading and there was no chance to stop and read the wall signs, it was just a means to get away from the advancing Securidroid. Lance spotted a Weaponry Store. He quickly crossed kicking in the door, with a defence kick, straight at the door. Amazingly it shot from it's hold.

He raced inside, Tayce followed in search of a weapon, that was better than her Slazer. It called for some heavy duty firepower against these silver metallic monsters she thought.

Elsewhere on the station, Treketa and Dean were walking into what had to be the Service Area for the Securidroids and mechanical equipment, that was used around the station. The room was rather like a large Hanger. Equipped with every repairing bench, gadget and electronic crane that was needed for repairs and service. On one bench lay a Securidroid half taken apart and the pieces and equipment left as if the person working on it, would return any minon. Suddenly behind them, as they neared the centre of the vast service area. A Slazer shot just missed Treketa. She screamed. Dean grabbed her and ran with her to nearby crates big enough and tall enough to hide behind, Slazer shots hailed above and passed them, in quick succession. Dean recalled as they thought of a way in which to handle this giant patrolling monster, of an earlier time, when he had visited Greymaren for his Father. He'd arrived in the dead of night hourons and one of these Securidroids had taken an offence to him. He pulled out his Slazer, set it to stun and ordered Treketa to stay put, much to her horror he was an on board guest, what was he hoping to do she thought.

"Dean what are you going to do, your crazy, your a guest on this team?" she reminded him, flinching every time a Securidroid Slazer shot whizzed past her.

"Maybe so, but I'd rather be a live guest, than a memory for my Father, God I hate these things," he replied taking a look over the crate before him.

"What's it doing?" asked Treketa in a whisper.

"It's no doubt summoning up the crate in a scan mode, trying to find a weak spot, believe me, it knows we're here somewhere, it's just a matter of time," replied Dean.

As soon as Dean got high enough to aim for a weak spot in the Securidroids outer casing, the Securidroid fired, as did Dean. He dropped down cursing, he'd missed the point where he wanted to aim. Treketa thought he'd been shot and immediately was concerned.

"It's all right I'm fine, I just missed where I wanted to aim," he assured her.

There was only one thing left to do as Dean saw it, shoot and run. He suggesting they do just this Treketa got behind him, when he gave the word to run into the next room, they'd run like there was no tomorron.

"Ready? Let's go, stick close behind me," he whisperingly told her.

Both emerged from behind the crate, open firing on the Securidroid as they raced for the entrance and on out into the next adjoining room. Once inside the doors closed and they collapsed against the wall out of breath. But very much relieved, that at least they were away from the advancing Securidroid with death on it's mind. After getting their breath back Dean suggested they carry on going, there maybe more of the Securidroids advancing on them once they found them on heat scanner. This he was not prepared to stick around and find out if there were. He headed away with Treketa in hot pursuit, on out of the other side of the room checking both ways as they went. Both ran until they felt it was safe to slow to a casual walk and headed back to the Main Operational Hall. He felt they'd had a narrow escape.

Lance and Tayce now equipped with a much more powerful Slazer weapon, quickly unburdened themselves of the persisting Securidroid. Lance didn't want to damage someone else's property, but to stop it, he had to put a Slazer shot right between it's sight frontal panel. It stalled it's advance on them, giving off a spectacular small electronic zigzag display from side to side of the corridor, when it didn't do anything, only stop in the middle, facing in their direction, Lance took aim and sent a further shot into the same position, in the sight region. This brought it to an abrupt stop and total shut down. Tayce walked on into the nearest centre that seemed to look like a resources information room. Books and notes lined the many shelves and some were in preserved clear glassene topped drawers, so that people could admire them. Lance upon entering the room walked to what he considered more up to date material. It was a box marked 'GREYMAREN CHRONICALS' Lance opened the box and withdrew a Disc Chip and placed it in the Disc Chip Reader. He and Tayce were about to start studying it to see if there was an up to date entry for the last dayon the Greymaren crew were aboard, when Tayces Wristlink started to play it's musical notes signifying someone wanted her to answer. Lance continued to transfer the Disc Chip information to the nearby slim screen for reading, while Tayce raised her Wristlink depressing the Commun Button.

"Tayce here go ahead," she said waiting to hear what was wrong.

"It's Tom, I have something here I think you should come and take a look at," he said in a tone of urgency.

"On my way," she said ceasing communication, and lowering the Wristlink.

"Don't tell me, he's found a Securidroid, what's new, the place seems to be crawling with them, don't forget your gun, you may need it," he suggested in a caring tone.

"I'll leave you to carry on studying that, beware of those tin cans they term security," joked Tayce heading back on out.

"You to, remember, aim for the sight panel, it brings them to a halt fast, especially after the second shot," he replied.

Tayce left Lance to it and stepped cautiously back out into the corridor, she checked both ways to make sure she was not about to be under threat from patrolling Securidroids, then began on the walk back to the Main Operations Hall.

Tom was on his own. He was lucky to not have been in an encounter with the Securidroids, considering they were patrolling nearly everywhere. A couple had passed the Hall doorway, but none had entered. It hadn't stopped him putting his Slazer within a minons grasp, if he was suddenly confronted by one. He was now in what was considered Commodore Martin Traverns Officette, come work station. He had found a layout of who was in charge of the station, then he'd found Martin Traverns Personal Journal. On Screen, he had found information on Martins daughter Kelly. But as he studied the information, to his sheer surprise there was the mention of none other than their latest on board guest 'Dean Addams'. At this, Tom frowned something didn't ring true, especially as Dean had told them he hadn't ventured off Deltaline 4 for sometime when it appeared Kelly had seen him less than four monthons ago. It stated, it was somewhat of a parting of the ways. Something made Tom stop reading though he wanted to read more. He could hear the sound of approaching footsteps but they didn't sound like Tayces commanding walk. He cautiously deactivated the desktop light and stood waiting in the shadows to see what or who was going to enter his surroundings, surely it wasn't Tayce so soon? He waited alertly. He set his Slazer to stun. Slowly he aimed it round the corner, as the footsteps drew nearer by the cencron. Whoever they were, they entered. Tom took the moment and reached out, grabbing whoever it was roughly pushing the person across the room and hard up against the far wall. They struggled in his strong grasp. Suddenly a female cry of mumbled protest rang out.

"Get off me you idiot, let me go," she protested.

"Not till you tell me who you are, and what your business is on this station," demanded Tom.

"Tom it's me, what the hell are you playing at, get off me," replied Tayce fighting to break free.

Tom upon hearing it was Tayce, was shocked to the core, he gently loosened his tight grip on her neck and dropped her gently back on her feet. He didn't know what to say. She looked up at him, angry and ready to lay into him, what the hell was his problem, she decided to let him have it.

"You jerk, who did you think it was, I told you I was on my way back," she angrily blurted at him.

Tom felt the full force of her anger at him what he'd just done was totally unforgivable. She was far from amused. He expected to be thrown in confinement when they returned. He activated the desk light once more trying not to look at her not quite knowing what to say. He eventually glanced at her and could see the cold hurt look, she suddenly looked up at him in. He felt awkward, but it was a pure accident, that anyone could have made. He walked across the room towards her. She backed away, thinking what was he doing, did he think that she was going to let him get away with what he'd done. She pushed him away, but to no avail, he grabbed her into his strong arms and apologised most sincerely. They stayed together for a few minons. Tayce caved to his persuasiveness and looked up at him. He looked down and silently mouthed, he was sorry, then they kissed in a strong sincere way. She calmed in the warmth of his kiss, figuring mistakes were mistakes. They broke away. Tom crossed back to the desk, Tayce followed interested to see what he had found.

"Our newest temporary recruit lied when he said he hadn't been to this station in a long time, he was here a couple of monthons ago, seeing the Commodores daughter, for the last time," explained Tom.

"What makes you come to this conclusion?" asked Tayce, wondering where he got the information from.

"According to Martin Traverns Personal Journal, Kelly was in love with Dean," explained Tom.

"Sorry Tom, what are you saying?" said Tayce unsure of what point, he was trying to make.

"There's more to this than meets the eye," said Tom.

"Not necessarily, maybe Dean and Kelly were forced apart by his Father, hence it ended badly, and he doesn't want to talk about it, would you if it ended badly," replied Tayce.

"Okay, ignore the entry in the chronicles, take a look at this," he said, crossing the room to a grey floor standing cabinet, that had weaponry burn marks in a patten that looked like it had been scorched.

Tom bent down and rubbed away with his right hand. He pointed out that the burns were recent, he'd asked Midge to run a scan from Amalthea, he confirmed the burns were about three monthons old. Tayce looked him in surprise, what was he trying uncover, that perhaps Kelly had been a remaining member on the station, when the crew mysteriously vanished and Dean had somehow returned in a fit of rejected anger to finished her off. The whole thing seemed stupid or was it? Tom was not going to stop, he continued to explain that the weapon marks were that of a Pirate weapon but Deans finger prints were also on the cabinet. Tayce gave him a look of, do you really expect me to believe what your making out here that Dean was working with Pirates, this was too crazy to be true. But she didn't dismiss the Pirate fact. Her Wristlink sounded again, she turned away answering it far from pleased at what she figured Tom was driving at. That Dean was somehow connected to Pirates. Lydia's voice came through, she informed her that there was an urgent call coming in from Jonathan Largon, she was going to patch it through. Tayce waited.

"General what's the matter?" asked Tayce giving him her full attention.

"Tayce I hate to do this, but I need to pull my son off your team for a while, I need him for an important assignment," stated Jonathan.

As if by coincidence Lance walked in. He paused upon hearing his Father's voice, over the Wristlink. Tayce agreed with the request, but insisted that he return when the assignment was through, after all he was a much valued member of the team. Jonathan wholeheartedly agreed.

"Lance your needed back on Questa that was your Father, he needs you for an important assignment, you have to leave right now," announced Tayce

"Sure of course," replied Lance nodding understandingly as he glanced from her to Dean, noticing she was summoning him up in a suspicious kind of way for some reason.

Tayce was wondering if what Tom had said earlier about Dean as he and Treketa returned, was true, but something was telling her that Dean didn't look the kind to be Pirate material, but was there more to this Dean Addams than met the eye, that she knew nothing about, that he was keeping from her. Lance could see that Tayce was in deep thought. Treketa broke the moment by hugging Lance, in a goodbye manner, telling him she'd see him soon. Tayce Wristlinked to Marc on board Amalthea, ordering immediate Travelsport of Lance. A few minons later Lance vanished from the Greymaren Station to return to Amalthea in the oscillating Transport aura. Donaldo appeared to take Lances place on the investigation team. He brought with him, some real substantial evidence that would prove useful. He crossed setting it down on the desk top.

"This has just come in from Micacer research section, your Mother contacted them and told them of what had happened, could they provide any further information, that would be helpful, it states here, that Kelly Travern is still here somewhere on this station, that numerous passing vessels and cruisers had seen what appeared to be an apparition of Kelly, or the real thing even, there had been numerous Galactic Vision News reports that every time someone came out here, because of it, there was nothing to investigate," said Donaldo reading the report aloud.

"Perhaps this place is haunted after all and she was killed when whoever raided this station," said Treketa.

"Maybe Treketas right Kelly is a ghost, like the rest of the team gone never to return," spoke up Dean.

"Why would you think that?" said Tayce demandingly throwing a suspicious look Dean's way once more.

"It's just an idea that's all, maybe she was killed by a passing Pirate or someone that boarded".he replied he had suddenly sounded like his royal self, who could not be questioned because of who he was.

Tom found his suspicions were now screaming at him, so much so he lost it, pushing past Tayce, he grabbed Dean by the front chest region of his uniform and pushed him up against the computer console behind him.

Tayce didn't have time to react to what was happening.

"I'm beginning to think you do know exactly where Kelly Travern is, considering you only saw her a couple of monthons ago, you see Tayce this proves he lied when he said he hadn't been to Greymaren in a long time, you were also in love with her weren't you," said Tom angrily, almost throttling the truth out of Dean.

"Tom that's enough, release Dean at once, that's an order," said Tayce sharply.

"At least have the decency to tell us what really happened here Dean," backed up Treketa.

"All right, I and Kelly, yes, we were in love, not that it's anyone's business, but it was a relationship her Father had forbidden from the start, he was so strict, we tried to work it out behind both our parents backs, but it got harder and harder, we just ended up getting into fights verbally finally it ended one night after a blazing argument we swore we never wanted to see each other again, I returned four monthons ago to see if she would change her mind and yes she was alive then, she wouldn't budge on her decision though so I left her to her own devices going back home," explained Dean.

122

"Was the crew here then?" asked Tayce curious.

"Hard to say, I came down in the dead of night and the strangest thing was, she wouldn't have me board the station, she came out to me on my then launch to see me, she told me she didn't want her Father to find out she was meeting me for the final time," replied Dean

Tom apologised to Dean, he could see he was telling the full truth, as what he said made sense, that if there hadn't been any team then and that Kelly was the only one on board, she was not about to tell Dean she needed help, especially if she was being threatened by the real threatening being that had frightened her into keeping her mouth shut. Suddenly there was the sound of approaching footsteps. Tayce ordered everyone to remain calm and standby. Silence fell in the Officette of Martin Travern. Tayce stood her ground her hand rested on her handgun, ready to open fire if need be. Tom stood just behind her, as back up. In through the entrance to everyone's utter amazement, walked a very tired and near to death looking Kelly Travern. She had taken enough of the torture and it showed in her pretty doll like features. She was a Petit slim girl with dark brown curly hair, that hadn't seen a wash for some time, it was dusty and out of style, hanging around her shoulders carelessly in dark oily strands. She looked totally exhausted. She looked around at everyone present, with her doll like brown eyes. Treketa could see what Dean saw in her, she was very attractive to any man even in her current state.

"Who are you people, what are you doing in my Father's Officette, you've no right to be here, I should call a Securidroid".began Kelly slightly wavering with tiredness.

"I'm Colonel Tayce Traun you remember me and this is my team, we've been sent here by General Largon to investigate where you and your people are, why your so far off your original course," explained Tayce softly taking off her jacket and crossing to the frail looking Kelly.

Tayce draped her jacket around Kelly's slim shoulders, guiding her carefully over to her Father's chair. Here she sat her down gently. Donaldo, with soft gentle approach, took his Medic Emergency Kit and crossed to attend to her. Immediately Kelly began to panic.

"No don't come near me… don't touch me," she protested, frightened of Donaldo.

"Take it easy Kelly, come on, trust me this man is my Medical Officer, he'll help you, I promise he won't hurt you," assured Tayce gently by Kelly's side.

Kelly studied Donaldo apprehensively, as he approached, she wanted to run, she hadn't seen a man since seeing the barbarian who had threatened her and stole away her people and parents two yearons ago, this was not easy for her and Tayce could fully understand that. Donaldo gently began to examine her, giving her a reassuring smile each step he went reassuring her she was going to be all right, she was safe. He couldn't believe the state she was in. Treketa came forward on Tayces nod to do so carefully.

"Kelly I'm Treketa I'm a nurse with the team, we're going to take care of you," said Treketa softly crouching down beside her.

"Kelly can you tell me anything about what happened here, I know it's probably difficult for you, where are your parents, your people?" asked Tayce carefully.

"Gone, they're all gone, I hid, like Father told me to do, so, they wouldn't find me, especially the leader, he was awful what he would do to a woman to make them be submissive to him," said Kelly sadly and near breaking point.

Tayce shook her head, she didn't ask Kelly who this leader and group were, for fear that she would crumble beyond retrieval. As it was, she could see that this young woman had been to the equivalent of hell and back. She realised that the whole occurrence had to be on the same level of herself, being cast out into space all those yearons ago. She discretely beckoned Tom and Dean outside, out of earshot of Kelly. Both followed leaving Donaldo and Treketa to start on treating Kelly. Kelly nervously looked at Donaldo through tired eyes. For a moment a past flashback came into her mind, of their stations doctor, who had been a good man. He had healed many of her scrapes when she had been a child. It hurt like no one could imagine, that she would not see her parents, or her friends again.

"We had a doctor, his name was Locanna, Bobby Locanna, he was a good man," Kelly announced slowly.

Donaldo smiled kindly, assuring her that from this moment in time onwards, they were going to help her and that she could look forward to a better future and possible new life.

Outside the Officette Tayce hit one of the Main Operational Hall desks in anger, that Kelly had been reduced to the condition they had found her in, the fact that nobody had bothered to really search for this young woman made her furious beyond belief. Tom reached out and put a calming hand on her left shoulder and squeezed it, but he too could understand the anger, he couldn't understand how anyone couldn't of made a deep scan of the station to find Kelly sooner.

"How could they have left her here, I can't believe it," said Tayce in angered frustration.

"Maybe she didn't want to be found, till now, after all her Father had told her to hide because of the leader of the group that attacked this place could return, maybe she was staying put thinking that either her Father would return or the leader would catch on that she was not with the others and come back for her, whoever he is," said Tom.

He had a point thought Tayce, if this leader was as bad as she said he was, there was no telling what he would have put her through to gain her submissiveness. Also she could see how easy on this station it would be for someone to hide and not be found. She would probably feel the same as Kelly, if she were in her shoes. But she would like to come face to face with this so called brute of a leader, she wouldn't be quite so submissive as what he considered she should be in his presence.

"What are we going to do with her, we can't leave her here," asked Tom curious.

"She'll have to return with us and go to our Life Ability Centre for further treatment, we'll have to contact Questa and have the station taken back to the headquarters base orbit," replied Tayce.

Donaldo came to the doorway. He beckoned to Tayce once he'd gotten her attention. She crossed leaving Tom and Dean. Donaldo entered the Hall and walked well out of earshot with Tayce. He began that Kelly was in a bad state, for a start she was going to need nutritional injections and lot's of rest and recuperation, this could start on Amalthea, when they returned. Tayce nodded, thinking the sooner they returned, the better it would be for Kelly so that they could commence her journey back to full health. Without further word She contacted Marc on the cruiser via her Wristlink. He soon answered asking how things were progressing over on the station?

"We've found Kelly, she's in a bad way, but alive we're bringing her back to the cruiser for treatment, get ready to Travelsport when I give the word," ordered Tayce.

"All right, Lance has been picked up by Questa Security," he informed.

"Good let's hope he's not away to long, see you soon," said Tayce signing off.

She decided to explain to Kelly what was what. Briskly she headed back across the Main Operational Hall and into Martin Traverns Officette. Kelly looked up at her, as she walked back in. Tayce walked round the desk and crouched down and gently announced what was going to happen. Taking the young woman's gentle slender hand she began.

"Kelly we are going to help you in two ways, firstly were going to take you back to Amalthea, for medical treatment, then were going to help in the search for the crew and your parents of this station, believe me if they are out here somewhere, we will find them, you can be sure of that, we are known as the Amalthean Quests team and our job is to fight crime and bring to justice on behalf of Questa, criminals like the one that abducted your parents and the crew, do you understand?" said Tayce softly.

"Yes Tayce and thank you, I trust you will do what you can," replied Kelly in clear eloquent English

"Treketa look after Kelly become her aide, I'm putting you Donaldo in charge in getting her back to good health," ordered Tayce standing to her feet.

"You've got it," assured Donaldo sincerely.

Tayce walked back out into the Main Operational Hall and requested everyone should regroup ready to get off Greymaren. Donaldo slipped a heat sealant blanket around Kelly's shoulders covering her dirty and torn uniform. Treketa guided her on out to join the others, whilst Donaldo shut up his Medic

Emergency Kit and followed on behind. As everyone stood ready to Travelsport over to Amalthea, Treketa assured Kelly that there was nothing to fear. Kelly hadn't noticed Dean up until then, she looked at him coldly, then away again she did not want to know him. Tayce caught the look, but said nothing, she raised her Wristlink and ordered Midge to commence immediate Travelsport. The whole team and Kelly de materialised just in time as one Securidroid that hadn't bothered to enter the Main Operational Hall had decided to. The sudden power source of the Travelsport had been detected on it's immediate scanner.

On board Amalthea, the Hover Trolley that Donaldo had left prepared for when he returned, awaited the arrival of Kelly Travern. Marc stood ready waiting to tell Tayce upon her arrival what he had done in contacting Questa. He was joined by Lydia, who explained that she knew Kelly and wanted to be there for the young woman. Marc stood in re-collective thought about the old dayons, there were three men on the good council back then they General Jonathan Largon, Commodore Darius Traun and Martin Travern, he remembered the three sealing a kind of joint venture and celebrating well into the early hourons. It made him smile, at the fact that Martin Travern had flown home worse for wear, after so much celebratory drink and swore he would never do it again. But the threesome were a good trio, when it came to spacial matters, this he could well remember. He hoped that Martin Travern could be found, he was a good man. The Quest team materialised back on board. Donaldo and Treketa immediately helped Kelly up onto the Hover Trolley. Lydia waited patiently, then walked over to the young Greymaren woman, putting a gentle motherly arm around her slim shoulders. She assured her that until she reached Questa, she would be there for her.

"Thank you Lydia, I really appreciate that," replied Kelly glad to see someone she knew well from the past.

Donaldo started up the Hover Trolley as Lydia stepped back and headed with Kelly down to the Life Ability Centre. Marc waited until Lydia had gone with them. Then walked with Tayce and Tom heading back up to Organisation beginning to explain to Tayce that Jonathan Largon was on his way out especially when he'd heard that Kelly had been found.

"He's up graded this assignment, he is treating it as a top priority," began Marc.

"Really! I'm not surprised it is turning into somewhat of a serious matter," said Tayce thinking that it was.

Both left the Travelsport Centre in discussion about what she had found over on Greymaren and her possible theories what might of materialised on the station regarding the crew. Kelly had explained that it seemed like a group headed by some barbarian who liked nothing more than to over power women for his own pleasure. Marc raised his eyes at the thought. But continued to listen, as she explained her thoughts on the whole mess in hand.

Outside in the Universe an houron later, a group of vessels arrived in orbit of Greymaren Station. They were a tow service fleet. Twenty in all. Roughly a milon across in diameter and had arrived, flown out from the Service Division that undertook the job of manoeuvring the station back to an orbit outside of Questa. They had flown in fast and expertly gone about their work, manoeuvring into position on the four corners of the station, locking on their immense and powerful tractor beams, ready to pull the station from it's current orbit. Together they all moved forward on the slow return journey, monitoring the station from the tow vessels, and a special team aboard the station, that had also been sent in to deactivate the Securidroids. The Greymaren Station in all her lit deserted state, slowly moved with the tow vessels, heading of to the headquarters base, that would put her back to operational mode with new modifications, as it had been a while since her systems were updated.

Tayce walked into Organisation Deck, to be welcomed back by Midge. He informed her that he had General Largon on Satlelink waiting, She quickly crossed to her pilot seat sitting down, ordering him to put the call through. Jonathan soon appeared on screen. Tom turned as did Marc, as they had been discussing the moving of Greymaren.

"Tayce I'll be with you in roughly forty-five minons, I want to brief the team, when I arrive, if that's all right with you?" he asked seriously.

"Of course, I'll get everyone together, see you on arrival," assured Tayce.

The Screen went blank. All three knew by the way in which Jonathan had asked what he had, this latest Quest had turned extremely serious. Tom found that he could hold on no more to a question that had been bothering him the moment Kelly Travern had surfaced and he decided to out with it.

"I've got a question, it's not about Jonathan's arrival, it's about Kelly and it's been bugging me from moment she appeared," began Tom in thought.

"Go on, what is it?" asked Tayce interested.

"How come if there was no life support on that station, she managed to survive for long?"

"He's got a point," said Marc.

"Maybe she had some kind of portable system, where she was in hiding, when she found that she wasn't alone she came out," replied Tayce thinking about it.

"Midge have everyone report for a meeting in the Meeting Centre please, tell them General Largon is coming aboard and I want everyone to attend," ordered Marc.

Upon Midge beginning the request the team report for a meeting, Tayce stood to her feet and walked into the Meeting Centre. Tom followed on taking with him the entries he'd retrieved from the 'Greymaren Chronicles' file. As Tayce sat down, so he explained that she may find them useful. She took them and began sifting through them. One caught her eye it was headed in bold 'FORMED LOST FRIENDSHIP WITH JONATHAN LARGON'. Something that puzzled her, she thought that Martin Travern and Jonathan Largon had always been friends. What could it mean, she thought. She looked up at Tom for his input on the matter. He cocked his head, as if to say "what?"

"What do you make of this, you printed it off?" asked Tayce showing the printout to him.

"Maybe they fell out over something, then Jonathan thought about it again and got back in contact with him again and the friendship was back on," replied Tom shrugging his shoulders.

Midge suddenly announced that the high ranked cruiser of General Jonathan Largon was approaching for docking. Tayce stood up straightening her uniform, then began on out leaving Tom at the meeting table. She ordered him to make sure everyone was present, when Jonathan arrived. He nodded. Tayce headed off out of Organisation heading on down to meet Jonathan. She, as she walked realised this was the first time he was coming aboard the cruiser.

General Largon appeared via Transpot in the Travelsport Centre. He was far from pleased, the controls to dock along side Amalthea on his cruiser had suddenly failed, so he had to board by what he called the in personal means, using a Transpot. He sighed he hated that new Transpot, it gave him of all things indigestion especially if he'd had a big lunch before leaving Questa. He walked out of the Centre into the corridor just as Tayce was walking to meet him, concerned that he should make it aboard all right. He was wearing his high rank usual navy suit.

"Are you all right General?" asked Tayce.

"If that doesn't tell me to get a new cruiser, nothing will, I've had it for the best part of fifteen yearons," he said light heartedly.

"Just as long as we were able to bring you aboard for the reason your here, that's what counts," replied Tayce.

"Shall we walk, I have to apologise for removing Lance so quickly from the assignment in hand, he will be back, this I assure you," he said casually as they walked along.

Both talked as they made their way up to the Meeting Centre about Greymaren. Jonathan explained he wanted to talk about their next step. What needed to be done in searching for the Greymaren crew, that had obviously become victims of whoever had done what they had done. Tayce explained that Kelly was at the present time in the capable medical hands of Treketa and Donaldo Tysonne, plus her Mother was with Kelly to help her back to normal health. This pleased Jonathan, he expressed she was in safe caring hands, it was good. They turned at the top of the Level Steps and headed on into the Organisation Deck to enter the Meeting Centre to brief the team, what was to be the next move.

Searching for the Greymaren Victims – Part 2

When Jonathan Largon walked in, all but Treketa was seated around the meeting table. Donaldo apologised for her absence, but stated that he did not want Kelly left alone in her delicate frightened state. Jonathan nodded understandably. Everyone present stopped discussing the strangest of disappearing acts by the Greymarians when Jonathan walked to the head of the table. They gave him their full attention. Tayce and Tom exchanged glances conveying everything was all right between them after the incident on Greymaren. Both Marc and himself had decided, that as neither had the right to be Tayces second in command without her say so, they would share the duty load nearest the top together. Tayce seated herself, gesturing for Jonathan to start. He began by requesting Midge to place on Sight Screen the first of the suspected group responsible for the abduction of the Greymarians, a suspected Pirate colony that according to flight records from Greymarian Martin Traverns Journal, had sent ships pass the station on many occasions. Within a few cencrons Midge did as requested, firstly dimming the lights, so that the team could see the wall Sight Screen clearly, then placing up the information Jonathan had asked for. He began the race that they could see on screen, a cold hearted rough looking bunch, were known as the Boglayons. They were the worst form of pirates that everyone hated in all the known galaxy, they hunted generally in fleets and their motto was 'Take no prisoners, only leave enough debris around to state they had visited'. They would steal what they could, that would make a pretty sum of currency on the under market, use any female for their pleasure, but leave victims for the broken hearted, on discovering they had visited. Usually in the dead of night hourons. Jonathan continued that this particular bunch were usually drunk from the profits of their spoils. They had been known to use what was known as, slavery tactics, of the worst kind to the most vulnerable of people, women, stood no chance in the leaders hands. It had been discovered on many occasion from criminal records, that they had left women of planets vessels etc., naked, tortured beyond belief. They were not fast in coming forward, however when it came to designing the latest technology, they had been the first to create what was known as the Time Jump Dimensional Suspension Device, this was where a whole crew like the Greymarians would disappear into a Universe of the leader of the Boglayons choice. Probably a deserted area of space and left to fend for themselves as captives of the Boglayon leader. If he so decided, he could make them live horrifying recurring unrealistic dream sequences until he needed them.

"So you think this so called leader, used this Time Jump Dimensional Suspension device to send Kelly's parents and the Greymaren crew to uncharted space?" asked Marc interested.

"Quite, Donaldo I know Kelly is vulnerable right now, but what we need to do is show her an image of this Pirate Boglayon Army and ask her if she's familiar with any of the faces, ask her if she remembers when they went aboard by force," asked Jonathan knowing that it was not going to be easy.

"It would be chancy, but I think it could be done, as long as we keep in mind, she is still very frightened at the fact the leader would come back for her, should she say anything, as this is what she told me and Treketa in the last houron," said Donaldo in thought.

"I appreciate this, but we have to know," replied Jonathan in earnest.

Donaldo was far from pleased at having to lay this on Kelly so soon, but if it meant finding the crew of Greymaren, then it had to be done with great gentleness. Jonathan as much as he did not want to push it, he put it to Tayce that this should be done sooner, rather than later, so that they were clear on what they were up against. Jonathan thanked everyone for attending the meeting and stated that everyone present would be involved in this rescue, once the identification had taken place. As the others headed back to duty, Jonathan waited for Tayce as Tom paused for a moment, assuring her he would take charge of Organisation along with Marc, whilst she sorted out what was needed in tracking down the Boglayon Pirates, that's if they were identified as who abducted the Greymaren crew and the Traverns. Tayce nodded in agreement. As Tom walked on out into Organisation, she and Jonathan followed on, to head on down to the Life Ability Centre. Donaldo had hurried on ahead to prepare Kelly for her probing questions from Jonathan, even though he didn't like putting her through it.

"General tell me about the leader of the Boglayon Pirates, I've heard he can torture a woman for his pure pleasure, is there anything I need to know about him, after all there is Treketa and I on this team and I want to know what we're up against?" asked Tayce as she and Jonathan walked along.

"Dion is a man not to be trusted, extremely powerful, he uses his mind to seduce women, so much so that they don't know what's happening until it's to late, he possess great powers of the mind, just by thought he can destroy or make happen what he wants to, with what he has in sight at that particular moment just by looking at it, be it vessel, base or being, be extremely careful, this man is no fool Tayce, if you end up in his presence remember he will do anything to possess you and use you at will, you'll end up destroyed like all the other females he's had as a pleasurable pause in his greedy lifestyle," replied Jonathan warningly.

"Don't worry General, this female is not for the possessing, not by the likes of him anyway," said Tayce she knew just how she was going to play this Dion.

As they walked the rest of the way they both talked. Jonathan again apologised for removing Lance from the team so soon after joining, as he understood that he was settling in very well, but he would be back just as this urgent assignment was taken care of and it had been a top secret one, that needed one of the Largon family to take care of, it had been in the pipeline so to speak, for some time and Lance had volunteered to take it on. Jonathan without warning stopped walking in the corridor of Level 2. He put his hand to his chest. Tayce paused, concerned something was wrong. He merely brushed it off and light heartedly assured her that it was purely indigestion, it served him right to have a good meal before flying out and using the Transpot. He hated the Transpot, but it was the best alternative to put oneself on a vessel just not recommended after a full lunch! Tayce didn't push the matter any further, she couldn't tell him that maybe he should get himself checked over by his doctor on Questa, after all he was the General of the said base, it was not her place. They continued on. But Tayce was still worried and if Lance had been on board, she would have confided in him as much.

Donaldo was stood by Kelly in her bunk explaining carefully that the General of Questa was on his way down to ask her some questions, regarding the group that had visited her home, it was vital in finding her parents and crew, but he did not want her to become concerned, she only had to answer the questions once and Tayce and himself would be present, plus councillor Traun, so she was in safe hands. Kelly looked at him with a look of apprehensive panic in her eyes. Lydia reached out and clasped her hand in a kind assuring way. The Life Ability Centre doors opened, Jonathan and Tayce walked in. Tayce let the General walk forth towards Kelly, she stood out of the way whilst Jonathan in a kind understanding tone expressed that he was sorry that he had to make her recall a somewhat horrific experience, but it was absolutely vital in order to get the crew and her parents of her home back. He began as gently as he could and produced images of the race that it was assumed did the dirty on Greymaren. Tayce listened with interest.

Outside in the Universe and heading off into the distant future, was the Greymaren Station, now all in total darkness, as the on board team had done their work and shut the station down. It was a spectacular scene to be seen, the tow vessels manoeuvring the station at a cruise speed, back to Questa, keeping the right amount of travelling manoeuvrability, making the station look like it was gliding along.

On board Amalthea Treketa, had been ordered by Donaldo to take her break, as it was a convenient time to do so, as the General would be a while with his questioning and he was present and could take care of anything that may arise. Treketa stood sipping the much needed Coffeen in thought, in the Leisure Centre. She heard footsteps behind her, ones she recognised as Deans, but somehow she wondered if she should bother talking to him, considering he had been trying to get to know her better, than just a member of the team and as Kelly had suddenly materialised she had been turned off as galactic flavour of the monthon. She didn't much care for being treated like yesterons news. He glanced at her, as he entered the Centre and headed towards the drinks dispenser. Upon retrieving the fresh cup of Coffeen he'd come to grab, he turned studying her questioningly, feeling a sense of hostility in the air from her.

"Taking a break then?" he said trying to break the icet.

"I thought you'd be visiting your Greymaren girlfriend, especially as she's back on the scene it would appear that I seem to be yesterons news I don't much like being treated like it," she replied not the least bit emotional towards him, quite cold in fact.

"For Gods sake Treketa she's just been to the equivalent of hell and back, we had this out last night, she and I are no longer an item, it's in the past, let's just leave it there, shall we," he retorted somewhat surprised that she was so insensitive as to what Kelly had gone through and the fact he wanted to make amends with her. Treketa was something that just had to be put aside for the moment and he had hoped she understood that there was a past that needed sorting before they went on.

"Let's just forget the whole thing, shall we Dean?" said Treketa discarding her cup in the nearest incinerator shoot and beginning to storm out the entrance without further word.

"No, let's not we'll discuss this off duty later in my quarters, all right?" he said grabbing her arm mid stride and restraining her before letting her go on.

"Maybe!" she replied continuing on out the Leisure Centre, to head back to duty. Dean sighed shaking his head. She had surprised him with her cold hearted attitude about Kelly and him being friends again. He couldn't understand it, he had never had this problem on his world. Women on Deltaline 4 were a whole lot different to what they were in this Universe, that's for sure. He turned to look out of the sight port and sipped his Coffeen in thought. He was caught in a difficult position, he did like Treketa a lot, but he felt sorry for Kelly and understood what she had gone through and right now he figured, he had to be there, in case she wanted to talk to him.

Kelly Travern had confirmed identity, that it was none other than Dion and his Boglayon Pirates that had boarded the Greymaren Station, abducted the crew and her parents. She further explained that he, the leader had used the 'Time Jump Dimensional Suspension' device she heard him. Tayce stood in thought somewhat surprised at the way in which Kelly had described, what had happened to her parents and the crew, how the Boglayon Pirates headed by their leader boarded in the hourons of duty unexpectedly rounded up the crew in different sections, then fired a kind of weapon at the teams in each of those sections and they vanished where they stood. Even security didn't have time to react. It was the most amazing sight to see the weapon giving off a brilliant beam, almost equivalent of lightening. Upon seeing the first group vanish, she ran into the deep depths of the station and stayed there. Tayce walked away with Donaldo out of earshot.

"What's going to be your next move, surely your not thinking of taking on this Dion and his army single handedly, hearing what he did to Kelly's people, I hate to think what they'll do to this cruiser and us?" put Donaldo discretely, one eye on Kelly.

"I don't know, first I have to get a Quest team together, but don't concern yourself I have no intention of putting any of us in danger like the Greymarians," replied Tayce.

"If you want me along, you only have to say, I could cover all the medical needs," he volunteered.

"Fine, I'll let you know, well it looks like the Generals finished, take good care of Kelly, she's done well recalling something I know I couldn't," ordered Tayce.

"Sure I will," he assured casually.

Jonathan left Kelly asking for a discrete word in the Officette. Donaldo agreed, turning and heading off towards the Medical Officette, wondering what it was about? Jonathan once inside explained, that he wanted Kelly ready to be transferred to the Counselling Complex on Questa. Donaldo gave Jonathan a questionable look, much to say, why? Did the the General think that he wasn't doing a good enough job. Jonathan seeing the look on Donaldo's face, quickly assured him he'd done an excellent job. But going to the Counselling Complex would help Kelly adjust to a new life should they not be successful in rescuing the Greymaren crew and especially the Traverns, Kelly's parents. Donaldo much relieved nodded in total agreement. Tayce could see that both Jonathan and Donaldo were in an awkward situation. Jonathan felt he had insulted Donaldo, but hadn't meant to and Donaldo was trying to calm himself internally at not being pleased, that he had jumped to the wrong conclusion of what the General had implied. She quickly suggested to him, he continue with the preparations to transfer Kelly. He nodded glad to be heading away. Both herself and Jonathan followed on out of the Officette and across to the entrance leaving Kelly once again in Donaldo's hands. Jonathan outside the Life Ability Centre discretely put to her, he felt he had insulted her medical man, but hadn't meant to. She quickly suggested, he think nothing of it Donaldo had felt as awkward as he'd done. Tayce realised that under that tough Generals exterior, Jonathan was a man of great sincerity and kindness. Lance had a lot of his Father's qualities, she thought, as they walked along.

Two hourons later the Medical Launch from Questa manoeuvred into position to dock with Amalthea. Preparations had been done to get Kelly ready for her transfer, she waited the final moments of docked completion with Donaldo at the Docking Bay doors. Jonathan Largon had asked to be flying back with her as he had, to send his cruiser back to base for repairs. Both he and Tayce walked to meet up with Donaldo.

"Take care Tayce and above all else be careful, don't trust Dion, under no circumstance, he and his army only have one thing in mind and have an ill approach to people like you and this team," warned Jonathan.

"Oh I'm quite sure we'll be ready to handle the likes of him, he may find that I have a few tricks of my own when it comes to coming face to face with him," assured Tayce, she was thinking about her own powers.

The Docking Bay doors drew apart when docking had gone through final completion. A female medical therapist walked forth, with a gentle polite smile, which conveyed her kindness and warmth. She was in her mid forties, slim with dark brown short hair and pretty features. She was dressed in an all in one medical white close fitting suit.

"Donaldo Tysonne, how do you do, this is Kelly Travern," he announced lightly ushering Kelly forward.

"Trudy Carns therapist you can call me Trudy, okay Kelly I will be looking after you from now on, your in safe hands," assured Trudy in a gentle caring way.

"Colonel before I go, I want to thank you for finding me on Greymaren, all I ask now, is you find my parents and people, if you can't, make that barbarian Dion pay for what he's done," said Kelly

"You found us, but you can count on us to find your parents and people, we'll take care of Dion, if we don't find your parents can take it from me, justice will be served," assured Tayce.

Tayce watched with Donaldo as Kelly, the medical therapist and Jonathan all boarded the Medical Launch and the Docking Bay doors closed. Once the Medical Launch was safely away, Tayce left Donaldo to return to his duty and headed on the walk up to Organisation to start sorting the best way to take on Dion and his army to rescue the Greymaren crew and the Traverns.

Marc in Organisation was studying with Tom the information on the Boglayon Hideout. It was not what was considered the most interesting of planets to look at. Tom had made Marc laugh, by saying it looked like a muddy misshaped ball, that someone had put dents in. As far as Pirate bases went, it was far from impressive and especially as Dion was discovered to be a 'Lord'. They could see that it would be near than impossible to land on. Not that anyone would want to, for fear of being shot or worse. Armed to the teeth with every means of weaponry to hold off intruders, or Nosey Parker's who dared to venture where they were not invited. Some had and had never been seen again, for obvious reasons. This army were more ruthless than Vargon and her army. Their motto was their rule. The whole planet covered a rough diameter of a milon across. This was not going to be an easy Quest.

"As pirates go, this Lord Dion doesn't believe in an elaborate dwelling does he?" said Marc

"Pirates are pirates, hostile to the end, they are what they stand for, end of story," replied Tom.

"Jonathan's team on Questa have sent the coordinates and Midge has logged them in," said Marc.

Tayce walked into Organisation Deck, Dean not far behind, coming back from his break. Tayce glanced at the Boglayon Hideout on screen and gave an unimpressive stare. Marc looked up at her smiling, amused by her expression.

"Don't tell me that's Lord Dions Boglayon Hideout, I thought he'd have something a lot more elaborate than a muddy looking ball," said Tayce unimpressed.

"Afraid so, but don't let the appearance fool you, it's armed with every available weapon to fight of any unwanted intruders, which I might add, will be us," said Tom.

"Whose on the Quest this time, you'll need the members of this team, that are capable in handling the likes of that barbarian?" asked Marc.

"We will all go, except for Mother, she can be in charge here with Midge, ready to pull us out and hopefully the Greymarians too, at a moments notice," replied Tayce much to Marc's surprise.

"Are you sure we should take Treketa, considering what Lord Dion is capable of," said Marc in concern.

"Treketa is as much a part of this team, as any of us, we will be in just as much danger as she will," replied Tayce.

"Oh don't let Treketas nice calm act make you think she's a pussy cat, she'll stand up for herself apparently she gave Countess Vargons daughter at the College colony a good hiding for telling her friends that her brother namely me, was a murderer over Alenea, she can hold her own," spoke up Tom like any brother would do that knew his sister well.

Midge announced suddenly that he would be standing by when she was ready to leave, to do what was asked of him, on this somewhat dangerous Quest. Tayce acknowledged, then ordered Tom, Marc and Dean to head down and get some Slazer practice in, on a Boglayon simulation Midge would programme the tactics that would be needed into the simulator and they were to make sure that they would be able to handle the members of the pirate race even if it was just in a combat practice centre. They all began on out, Tayce ordered Tom to take Treketa and show her how to do the same, she needed all the skill she could get. Tom nodded in total understanding, he could see where she was coming from in the more experience Treketa got, the more she would find it easy to take on the likes of advancing Boglayon pirates. After the others left, Lydia entered Organisation and crossed to join Tayce, now sitting in the control seat. She sat in the adjacent one as the Amalthea changed course, for the new direction of the Boglayon Hideout.

Outside in the Universe Amalthea turned like a graceful bird in flight, making a change in course. Once in the right position, the cruiser went to Hyper Thrust Turbo and headed off in the direction of the Boglayon Hideout. The journey would have them in orbit in twenty-five hourons.

Aboard the cruiser an houron into the journey, everything was calm and smooth running. Tom was teaching Treketa firstly how to handle a Slazer. He was discovering quite quickly how she was picking up the certain moves to avoid being shot so much so, that he took her onto the next level of the simulation of the advancing Boglayon pirates, in all their mean and beardedness.

"Your doing well sis, your a real natural at this, watch his move and time it to the next, stay ahead of him, he'll take you if you don't, you cannot take chances," warned Tom watching his sister carefully.

Marc had exited his practice booth next to Treketa practising. He stood and watched her, amazed. He nodded to Tom and mouthed that she was proving quite good. Marc was the one on Traun to teach Tayce to shoot and watching Tom and Treketa, it took him back to how Tayce was like Treketa, naïve, but willing to do what was set before her. As he recalled it Tayce had become top of her combat class. But then she had to be, she was the Commodores daughter.

Midge was watching the Universe as they went. He was sorting out what preparations were required in an emergency act, if the Boglayons sent out a welcome committee, which they no doubt would. He listened in to the conversation between Lydia and Tayce, he found himself being part of that conversation, as they were discussing Traun in general. He took over full control allowing his mistress full concentration and time to relax before what lay ahead. Tom a while later at the end of his session with Treketa and duty time, returned to Organisation. Lydia left Tayce and Tom to be alone together, she figured they needed to discuss the Quest tomorron. She simply headed for the entrance of Organisation, informing them both that she would see them first light. With this she walked from the deck. Tom waited until he figured they were not going to be disturbed, then reached out and pulled Tayce out off the chair, up into his strong arms gently.

"You certainly seem happy, something I should know about?" asked Tayce draping her arms around his neck.

"We certainly don't have anything to worry about over my sister tomorron, let me tell you Treketa is one hell of a good shot, she surprised me and Marc during training just now, Dean was somewhat speechless and I think he was quite impressed," said Tom softly down at her.

"Good! thanks for teaching her," replied Tayce glad he had.

He softly studied her and suggested she forget all about the Boglayon pirates and tomorron, what would happen would happen, they had done all necessary preparations.

"Your one special woman to me Tayce Traun," he said in a alluring soft whisper.

He lowered his head and drew her into a long wanting passionate kiss. Tayce relaxed against him. She gave in and responded with just as much feeling and wanting tenderness for him. All thoughts of the dayon drifted away as she became lost in the moment. Tom scooped her up into his warm strong arms and carried her from Organisation, kissing her every few moments, with tentative kisses as they went. Tonight hourons had been a long time coming, since they had first discovered each other and he had got over the death of Alenea. Midge knew that this night would be the sealing of their relationship, on a personal level, so he decided to take full night time control of the cruiser, contact Marc should any on board emergency occur, which until they reached the Boglayons Hideout, he figured wouldn't happen anyway.

Next mornet Marc was the first to arrive on duty, Midge released full operational control to him, coming out of night standby mode. Marc took up his seat feeling a lot more refreshed for his nights sleep. Midge opened the main sight port shutters. They drew back to reveal a clear calm spacial view. Marc was about to take the cruiser to warp 10, when he noticed on the scanner, they were being watched by what would be termed and what they had expected, the welcome committee in the form of fifteen enemy fighters, from the Boglayon Hideout. They all hovered, looking menacingly thunderous with weapons primed in unison, waiting for Amalthea to make the first move. The fighters were like elongated Skulls, in shape lying on there sides. Slazer Cannons were mounted at the front like eyes and the rear like short stubby points.

"Looks like that welcome committee we were expecting, just arrived, right Midge?" asked Marc.

"That's them all right, they wouldn't win any prizes for the best looking fighter would they?" replied Midge.

"It's time for the first of our precaution measures, that was worked out yesteron," ordered Marc casually.

"Activating first precaution now Marc," confirmed Midge.

Tayce walked on deck feeling happier than she had felt for a long time. Tom followed on. Tayces happy feeling quickly disappeared as her eyes caught sight of the welcome committee through the main sight port. Play time was over, firmly. The matter of rescuing the Greymarians and taking on Lord Dion and his army was very much at the forefront. She crossed to Marc, whilst Tom took up the nearest seat at a computer console, which happened to be Lances position. He began keying in the sequence to find out what was what on the enemy fighters, hovering in a stationary orbit. Tayce moved into her seat, as Marc let her take over. Midge announced that defence precautions were in place. Marc flicked a switch to show Tayce the whole outside of Amalthea. The whole cruiser was surrounded in a bright red energy aura of defence and protection against the Boglayons. She congratulated Midge and Marc for acting quickly, especially as the welcome committee looked so menacing. It was time to show this Lord Dion, that he was not the only one calling all the shots in this area of the Universe, even if his planet was the only one for milons. She informed Midge they were going to play Lord Dion at his own tactics. By this, Midge knew what Tayce was driving at, she was about to give this Pirate leader as good as he was going to try and dish out. He confirmed that he was more than ready. Everyone present around Tayce looked at her, wondering what she was going to attempt. Without warning first. As Tayce began to manoeuvre the cruiser, to play an almost cat and mouse game with the fighters, something their obvious leader became infuriated about. Over the Aircom of Amalthea came a demanding powerful deep callous male tone.

"I don't know who you are, but your playing with fire, state the nature of your business here, before I grow tired of this tactics that your attempting upon my men and destroy you," he said growing tired and becoming increasingly frustrated.

Midge suddenly placed a visual of the male matching the demand on the Sight Screen. His black leatherex clad muscular upper torso almost filled the width of the screen. He looked at Tayce, as if he was burning right into her very existence, with his powerful dark brown eyes. He was not what she had expected for a Pirate leader and could see why women so easily fell under his powerful influence. He had jet black collar length curly hair and smouldering bearded features that gave him the devil may care look but even though she knew that she shouldn't think it, he was rather sexy to say the least. But Tayce realised that those features so easily could turn cold, that would show you no mercy if he so wished to.

"Be careful Tayce," whispered Tom over her shoulder.

"Am I addressing Lord Dion, leader of the Boglayon Pirates?" asked Tayce showing that she was not the least bit intimidated by his powerful appearance on screen.

"You haven't answered my question woman, time is growing close for your demise," he retorted his brown eyes showing their true fire and anger.

"You haven't confirmed that your the leader of the Boglayon Pirates and until you do, I am not prepared to divulge the nature of my reason for being in your Universe, so the longer you keep me waiting, the longer you'll discover my reason for being here," said Tayce enjoying this match.

After a brief pause, came an exasperating sigh of frustration from the Pirate leader on screen, this woman intrigued him and infuriated him all at the same time he thought. She wasn't like all the other females he had encountered. This pleased Tayce, she could see that she was getting to this Pirate Lord, like no other female had dared to attempt.

"I am Dion, you are?" he quickly turned the tables on Tayce playing her as she was him.

"Colonel Traun of Amalthea One, you have something that belongs to Questa Headquarters Base, in the form of the Greymaren Crew, I'm here to take them back," replied Tayce simply to the point.

"Colonel I am unable to full fill your request, do not come any closer to Boglayia, my men are on standby and from this moment on you have now outstayed your welcome," he said cutting communication abruptly.

Tayce knew by this, that he had just given her all she wanted to know. Now it was a case of going in, to get what they wanted. She turned ordering Marc to be prepared to go and tell the others, it was time. He agreed leaving the seat and going on out to get everyone ready. Dean entered Organisation, Tom turned informing him of what was happening. Without warning, the Boglayans in the welcome committee opened fire on the cruiser. Much to Midges relief, he was glad the protection shield was operative. The impact had little effect. One missile bounced off the shield and blew up the enemy fighter, blowing it to smithereens. Midge took overall control, advising Tayce to go on with the Quest, he could handle this bunch of unlawful vagabonds. Tayce knew that he wouldn't let her down, they had been through worse than the likes of the Boglayan Army, when they used to be on their own. Tom and Dean briskly fell in behind her walking on out of Organisation.

Amalthea outside was firing back at the welcome committee and dodging their constant bombardment of weapon fire, as the cruiser ploughed through the line of fighters, on its determined set course for Boglayia to rescue the Greymarians. An exchange of Slazer Cannon and energy missiles, between the Amalthea One and on coming fighters to stop them reaching their destination Boglayia was exchanged. But the protection shield around Amalthea held fast, as she ripped her pathway through to the Quest ahead.

On board Tayce and the Quest team had soon changed into their Combat Quest suits. They were all making their way to the Travelsport Centre, checking their Slazer handguns as they went. They looked every inch the crime fighting team they were, heading into battle, in order to get the Greymarians back. They, if they had to would destroy the device that had taken the Greymarians where they were being held captive, once the rescue had been achieved and everyone was safely back where they belonged. Tom glanced at Tayce, he could see she was more than prepared to take on the likes of Lord Dion face to face if she had to. He recalled the fact that she had fought Vargon using some kind of inner force, would she use this on this Lord Dion? It concerned him also that he may try and turn her power against her, if she did. But nothing would stop her. They all soon stepped into the Travelsport marked area and waited their Slazers primed, ready to shoot the moment they arrived on Boglayia.

"Midge activate Travelsport, now!" ordered Tayce via her Wristlink.

"Activating now, good luck Tayce," replied Midge.

The Travelsport activated sending the whole of the Quest team off to what was to be the most dangerous and life threatening quest to date.

Boglayia was dark upon arrival and the strong smell of musty male body odour hung in the air, along with the smell of Vardox. Judging by it's potency, it hadn't been long after the last celebration of victory spoils. In the caverns ahead men ran back and forth busy carrying what could only be described as expensive looking equipment. Obviously stolen during that last raid. The Quest team watched from the shadows as they materialised in the unpleasant atmosphere. Much to Tayces surprise, she was joined by a fighting group from Questa Headquarters Base, headed by a man who introduced himself as Combat Chief Paul Penfron. Tayce listened as the chief announced that General Largon had sent him and his team of thirty men to assist her in the rescue of the Greymarians. Tayce felt that even though Jonathan was only trying to protect her, this chief and his team were just going to get in the way of a very finely tuned and dangerous operation. He quickly and politely assured her.

"Colonel if you feel that this rescue is too dangerous to you and your team, we would be quite happy to take it out of your hands," he offered.

"No, it's fine, we can handle the likes of this Lord Dion, your men are more than welcome though to assist my team, but as far as your team or yourself taking over this Quest, General Largon asked myself and my team to come here and take care of this rescue and that's what were going to do," said Tayce to the point.

Who did this chief think he was she thought, did he think that she was some helpless female that couldn't take on the likes of Lord Dion? Well he was very much mistaken. But the chief was surprised that she hadn't been fooled by his wanting to take over the rescue of the Greymarians, from her, he considered her one gutsy woman. Tayce suggested they get going. Slowly the Amalthean Quests team, with the combat team from Questa crept along the dimly lit cavernous corridor, heading to the centre point of Lord Dions domain without hopefully being detected. Dean shielded Treketa, watching for the first sign of trouble. Tayce noticed that whatever bad feeling there had been between them, had now been resolved and they seemed to be close once more. She rounded a corridor kind of cross section and was grabbed swiftly and from sight in a matter of cencrons from the team, in a muffled gasp. A strong black leatherex gloved hand went over her mouth, whilst another dragged her quickly with strong grip out of sight and presence of the others. She tried to struggle and fight back to break loose, against the strong muscular extreme strength. Whoever this was, they were not prepared to let her escape at any cost. Marc was alarmed to say the least, that his worst fear had been proven, Tayce had been grabbed to God knows where and had it been by Lord Dion himself no doubt.

"Tayce is missing," said Marc in alarm, all kinds of nasty scenario thoughts, were rushing through his mind as to what might happen to her. Without warning overhead came the words Marc and the others did not want to hear. They came from none other than the Boglayon leader himself.

"Teams of apprehension, if you wish to see your beautiful Colonel alive and as you remember her, you had better try and find me, though I might add, I am not going to make it easy for you," said Lord Dion in plain tone.

Marc now knew where Tayce was, in the hands of Lord Dion himself. He gave an enraged look. They had to find this main point and get Tayce back before it was too late and she ended up like other women that had befallen Lord Dions spell. Everyone was now more eager than ever to get this Quest started. They continued on in alert in search of where Tayce was being held captive, in the powerful hands of a man she did not want to be. Chief Penfron didn't want to appear interfering, but informed Marc that he was quite prepared to send his men in, or offer expert advice in this situation, they now faced. Marc gave him a look much to say, that he was listening.

"Commander Dayatso I know the Colonel is probably in danger to you, but she strikes me as the kind of woman who would do her damnedest to keep the likes of this Dion at bay, my advice is let the Colonel keep this leader busy and we head off and find the machine and rescue the Greymarians, that we were both sent on this Quest to do, then we can go after this Lord Dion all together, rescue your Colonel," suggested Paul.

"You go on and take the Quest members here Donaldo and Treketa are medically trained, you might need them, I'll go on, see if I can find where this barbarian has Tayce, I don't like the idea of her being in his presence any longer than she needs to, considering what he's done to countless women before," said Marc.

"Very well, just as long as you feel that you don't need one of my men to assist you, we'll join up with you just as soon as we can," replied Paul.

"Yes I'll be fine, good luck mate," said Marc sure of himself.

"Don't take any chances Marc, shoot him if you have to," said Tom.

"If I have to take drastic measures to save Tayce, I will," replied Marc in a loyal way.

Paul a blonde tall and broad military type of man, began away with the members of the Quest team, mixed in with his men in the direction to search the cavernous corridors for the Time Jump Dimensional Suspension Device. Which was no doubt hid well. Lord Dion was not the kind of being to leave something that gave him an advantage in the situation such as holding the Greymarians capture for the fun of it on show. But the combat team had their own equipment that would be an equal match for any tricks that Lord Dion wanted to pull to try and stop them. Marc went on trying to search for Tayce, he knew it wasn't going to be easy, but he'd been trained for dayons like this when he was back on Traun. He would try and gain the knowledge he needed, by listening in to the Pirates chatter amongst themselves, without being caught then head in.

Deep within the caverns of the Boglayon Hideout in the domain of Lord Dion, Tayce stood before the man himself. She was finding the fact, she hadn't bargained on this Lord Dion being the most amazing handsome man she'd ever seen. He was tall, muscular and broad. He had the kind of eyes that could seduce any female and he was doing a good job on her right now. But, she was fighting back, she realised that he could so easily possess her if she dropped her guard for a moment, if he so wished. Right now those dark brown eyes felt like they were staring right into the heart of her, as she stood before him. Was he reading her mind, searching her memories for some weakness to which he could act on, even though she tried to resist. She knew one thing, that he was beginning to make her feel so wrong, in the most alluring soft surrendering feelings of ecstasy that she could ever feel. Somehow she wished he was not her enemy. But he was, she had to keep this in mind. He stood on a one step platform and looked down at her in a commanding greatly interested way pleased at what he was doing to her enjoying every minon. He stepped of the platform and began walking forth.

"For a woman, your amazingly beautiful and easy to possess," he said softly in a seducing charming way, reaching out to grab her with his leather clad hands as he came to a pause before her

Tayce couldn't resist, as he brought her in towards him. He knew that he was winning in overpowering this beauty before him. It was as if she was being possessed by some unknown immense powerful force, she found herself compelled to look into his dark eyes and was feeling lost of why she had to resist. She began to lose what sanity she had, but strangely without warning she found the powerful strength to fight inside rising again, against him. But he was proving to strong for her to hold off. It was an emotional tug of war. He was liking the fact she was becoming helpless as she dropped her guard for a cencron, until she concentrated harder managing to brake his overpowering hold on her with little effort. She felt the strength rising again with more power to resist the second time around and step back away from him. But as soon as she dropped her guard away from him, he was ready and went back at her with more powerful determination than before.

"What did you do with the Greymarians," she simply demanded fighting off his powerful seductiveness.

"All in good time Fairness," he said dismissing her question, continuing on to get what he wanted.

He reached out stroking her left cheek, then leaned in and tried to kiss her fully on the mouth, thinking that she was completely under his sexual powerful influence. Wrong! Tayce lashed out and broke free finding the power she possessed, rise in her enough to do so taking him totally by surprise. This made him angry beyond words and he sighed in sheer angered frustration, that Tayce had not been so under his influence, as he had hoped. She went for her Slazer, she figured it was up to her to put an end to this Lord Dion, once for an all. She drew her gun and aimed it directly at him. He shook his head, what did this female think she was doing, she was no match for the likes of him, why couldn't she see it. He held out his right hand opening it wide. Then slowly closed it. Tayce suddenly felt a strange feeling around her hand, that was holding the gun. Lord Dion tightened his grip using very little effort of his powers to crush her hold, invisibly. He plainly watched her as she felt the increasing pressure and pain as her hand was squeezed tightly around the gun. No mercy showed in his dark bearded features, as she felt the searing pain of his invisible yet powerful grip.

"Drop it Fairness before I crush your fingers, you cannot win," he said commandingly.

"No chance," she protested, fighting back against the searing pain she was experiencing.

"Don't make me crush your hand to dust Fairness, I will," he said coming to stop in front of her.

Tayce looked up at him. Tears in her delicate sapphire eyes, fighting against him at the immense force he held around her hand. With his left hand he reached out and gently gripped her under the chin making her keep looking into his powerful dark eyes, he was almost making her plead for him to stop the pressure. As both Lord Dion and Tayce stood in a stance in the middle of his elaborate dark and maroon marblex chamber, Marc had found Tayce upon the word of Dions men, that he had a beauty in his presence, fitting the description of Tayce and rounded the corner beginning to open fire in warning shots passed Dion.

"Let her go, now, or the next shot that comes from this weapon, will be one, with your name on it," warned Marc slowing and walking to the centre of the chamber.

On this Lord Dion known as just 'Dion' by his men, loosened his grip on Tayces delicate hand and stood where he was, he was letting Marc think he'd won, but he was not the kind of being to be easily terrorised by a mere mortal such as Marc. Marc ebbed forward reaching out his hand for Tayce to grab. Which she did like a life line. Marc holding the gun aimed at Dion, retreated back to the entrance taking Tayce with him. Once clear of the room he fired a warning shot into the ceiling of the chamber over Dions head. The ceiling cascaded around him, where he stood before he had a chance to make a run for it.

Tom and the other members of the Quest team, with the Questa Combat Team found the closely guarded device known as the Time Jump Dimensional Suspension Device and discovered it had held the Greymarians in another dimension. The Device was fully operational. Chief Penfron and his men were now working in unison with the Amalthean Quest team. It was decided that as the device was currently being guarded by forty of Dions men, they had to work together to take them out, in order to rescue the Greymarians. Everyone quickly got into position ready to open fire on the Boglayons. An exchange of fierce weapon fire between the two sides, brought the pirates down. Dean was shot in the upper arm, he dropped back against the cavernous rough wall gathering the strength for a moment to go on, then carried on shooting through the immense pain he was feeling. Donaldo glanced at Dean concerned, as he too shot back at the Boglayons. He could see Dean needed medical treatment, but could not get to him, because of the fierce onslaught, that was taking place. Dead silence filled the immediate surroundings, suddenly. Every guard was gone. Disintegrated by weapon fire. Both the chief and Tom hit hands in mid air, at the triumph of their success. He looked at the square device that sat on a stonex pillar, namely the Time Jump Dimensional Suspension Device.

"It's all yours Mr Stavard," he gestured for Tom to go ahead.

"Thanks for the assistance," said Tom striding forward, to deactivate the device and bring the Greymarians back to the current time.

Both teams stood ready to assist the Greymarians, as they came back. Tayce and Marc entered the room and entered the red marblex chamber, where the device had been kept. Tayce was trying to shake the thoughts that Lord Dion had placed in her mind, of him and her being totally lost in each other and him taking her to the end of the Universe in the strong sensual stakes. She was also trying to keep her fingers moving, after what he had done to them. She studied the square medium sized box, known as the Time Jump Dimensional suspension Device, finding it quite interesting. It was full of blinking lights and silver buttons. It was like the whole of the Greymarians had been held in a prison, suspended in another time. She began thinking that if she keyed in the code on the command, that was printed on the top, would it return the crew? Tom nodded to her to continue. She began keying in the seven digit sequence, then stood back, when it was done. Preying inside that it had worked. After a few minons, there was a blinding flash, Just the way Kelly Travern had described earlier, when they found her. The whole of the Greymaren crew along with Martin Travern and his lovely wife materialised in the room. Martin immediately, once they had gathered where they were, walked forth with his hand outstretched, glad to be back. He was a tall well built man, with brown short curly hair, just the same shade as Kelly's. He was a handsome man, with a certain look of authority about him.

"Tayce Traun, what are you doing here and who is this group?" began Martin enthusiastically.

"We're here to rescue you, this is my Amalthean Quests team and a Combat team from Questa, headed by Combat Chief Paul Penfron, your all safe now," said Tayce in reassuring tone.

"My daughter Kelly, where is she?" asked a slim woman with straight brown hair, that cascaded down the middle of her back, walking to stand beside Martin.

"Kelly is safe, she's gone to Questa with General Largon to the Counselling Complex, the General thought it would help considering what she's endured from Lord Dion and his men, unfortunately Kelly was in a bad state when we found her, but she'll be fine," assured Tayce in a kind warm tone.

"Commodore sir, if you would agree my vessel from Questa can more than hold your crew, I would be honoured to take you all back to Questa, where you can all get back to normality," spoke up Paul.

"Yes, yes good idea, what of Greymaren, is it… ?" began Martin Travern, but was cut off by Tayce.

"Greymaren is safe, she is currently at Questa awaiting your arrival."

"Your Father would be proud of you young woman, thank you for helping us return," said Martin in a kind soft educated tone.

He gathered the whole of his crew together and began off in the company of Combat Chief Paul Penfron and his men, on the journey back to normality. Martin paused at the entrance, turning he informed Tayce that there would be merits added to her and her teams records for what they'd done. Tayce smiled and informed him it was all part of their new duty, there was no need. With this the Greymaren crew under the guide of Paul Penfron, headed to a safe position, to de-materialise off the Boglayon Hideout back to a vessel that would take them back to where they belonged Tom was about to pick up the Time Jump Dimensional Suspension Device and place it in a nearby box, ready to take back to the cruiser. Tayce put her hand up to stop him, asking him what did he think of the device, should it be recovered for future beneficial use, or destroyed there and then, as earlier Jonathan Largon had left the decision with herself when it was found. Tom thought about it. He shook his head, Tayce for the first time ever found herself reading his thoughts, that it may fall into the wrong hands and start causing trouble all over again if it was left. With this, she took aim with her weapon and fired. Everyone ran from the room, leaving the devise to blow into a display of sparks flames and smoke.

Lord Dion wasn't dead, his immediate guards had pulled him free, alive but dusty, from the rubble. He'd heard the exchange of weapon fire earlier and recognised it to be his men in combat, this meant only one thing. The Time Jump Dimensional Suspension device had been claimed by the beautiful female, who he had in his enticing captivity. He ordered the twenty or so men remaining to patrol and find the source, that had taken the device. They began forward and he briskly followed after them. Upon rounding a corner, as luck would have it, he could see the Amalthean Quests team ahead and the female he had so much enjoyed, if only for a while she had been different from most females he had the pleasure of in his clutches, there was something about her. A wicked amused smile crossed his villainous features, at the thought, that he had found this female different from others he wanted more of her and somehow some dayon he would. He had so much enjoyed her, she had spirit and something else, what he couldn't quite put his finger on. He waited in the shadow of the eves, he couldn't believe it, the team, as luck would have it was truly on his side, was heading in his direction, The fools he thought. Tayce was running ahead, hoping to get out of their surroundings. Midge could not get a reading clear enough to Travelsport them off Boglayia where they were. So they had to make it to a much easier position. He stayed where he was, knowing that Tayce had not seen him. As the team became suddenly embroiled in firepower from his men once more, Tayce was backing up towards him, which he was finding most pleasing to say the least. As she dodged one of his men, she came straight back against him. Hitting him in the solid midriff, she spun and was alarmed to find he was alive and right in her way looking down at her. She raised her gun and was about to shoot him for real this time. But she found she couldn't, something made her stop. Lord Dion looking down at her in silence, grabbed her once more having overpowered her and spun her round, holding her facing the team with his right arm restraining her around the upper half. His broad strong left hand around her delicate throat. Tayce tried to once more to break free. He spoke close to her left ear in his soft seductive tone, that almost made her melt.

"Stop struggling Fairness, it won't do you any good, your helpless against me, you know that," he whispered in such a way it made Tayce feel helpless.

Dion bellowed for his men to cease fire, but there were none left, he was alone. Tom looked at Lord Dion in alarm who had now stepped out of the shadows with a restrained Tayce in his hold. He raised his Slazer and ordered him to let Tayce go, otherwise he would take him out with the team, where he stood. Dion gave a look of impatient disgust to think a mere mortal such as Tom could shoot him.

"You go ahead and shoot, one squeeze of Fairness's neck and you might take me out, but you'll say goodbye to her too," he said in cold warning.

Tom under Tayces orders to drop his Slazer, did. She continued to struggle with all her strength and might she didn't like feeling the powerful warm presence of this Lord Dion so closely, he was truly making her feel uncomfortable in sensing his powerfulness. Suddenly her mind flashed back to the encounter she had had with the Countess, she began feeling that same strange force of power, rise within her, she found that it was growing more stronger than before in the encounter back in the chambers. She tugged at his strong muscular arm. He would not give an inch in releasing her. He just ordered her close to her ear to stop her stubbornness it was getting her no where, nor would the power that was rising inside her. He glanced around, as he was the only one left of his world, he had to plan the next move carefully. But he was also angry to discover that the last of his men had vanished in the vapours of the de-materialisation of weapon fire, he'd lost. Something he didn't like. It was time to take a swift exit, to survive and return for this beauty some other time. Treketa to his surprise was in the right position to take Dion out, but not harm Tayce. She took aim at him.

"Release the Colonel before I take you down, where you stand," she said warningly.

On this Dion pushed Tayce straight towards Tom running off down the corridor out of sight into the darkened shadows. Treketa lowered her weapon and Tayce sighed in the warmth of Tom's hold. Treketa looked for Dean, he was on the floor out cold, with his eyes closed not moving, she had recalled that he had been shot a while ago and had kept going as long as he could. She hadn't realised it had been so serious. Marc checked the Travelsport reading with Midge. Whilst both Donaldo and Treketa began attending to Dean as best they could until they got back to the cruiser. Upon Midge confirming they could Travelsport safely from their current position, Marc ordered immediate Travelsport. Tom pulled from his pocket a Digit Bomb, set it and threw it down the corridor in the direction of where Dion had ran.

"That ought to keep him busy for a while," said Tom under his breath.

Travelsport took on just in the nick of time and the team de-materialised off Boglayia back to Amalthea One. Leaving Dion alone, with nothing more than his powers. He was the last Boglayon with nothing more than crumbling surroundings that was once his world as the Bomb Tom had set and had thrown exploded, causing untold damage. But was Dion still on the hideout? Had his exit meant he'd left in some form of transport of escape, living for another dayon?

Once on Amalthea, the Boglayon Pirate Hideout blew apart in the most awesome explosive sight. Rocks and debris spread far and wide, way out into the far flung Universe. The Amalthea and the Questa Combat Vessel were caught in the after shock that came from Boglayias destruction, it washed over the both vessels bathing them in a powerful purple vapourish wash. Tom stood watching the sight from the Travelsport sight port, but what he hadn't notice was that something resembling a ship, had flown clear and had gone in the blink of an eye.

Treketa walked from the Life Ability Centre a while later tears were streaming down her face. Tom walked towards her seeing she was distraught with hurt, he asked what was wrong? Like any brother would do, he slipped his arm around her slim shoulders.

"It's Dean, the injury he sustained from being shot by one of Lord Dions men was a lot more serious than we first thought… he's dead Tom," she broke down.

Tom pulled her into a brotherly comforting hug and guided her away to her quarters, where he would stay with her for a while for support, as he had heard how close they had been. Donaldo had emerged from the Life Ability Centre in concern of what Treketa might do, she was so distraught. He was glad to see that Tom had the situation in hand. He turned and walked back into the Life Ability Centre.

Lord Dion or as he was known by his men 'Dion' had escaped, but to where? Dean Addams had been killed, only into his second monthon as part of the

Amalthean Quests team, as a temporary member. Tayce was hoping that she never had to meet the likes of Dion again, but there was a feeling deep down that she would do some time in her future. She exchanged farewells over the Aircom with Commodore Martin Travern and wished him well Both the Amalthean Cruiser and the vessel from Questa went their separate ways. For a Quest that was thought to have been dangerous, it had turned out well.

Strike of the Yarrick Raider

It was almost a monthon since the sudden loss of temporary team member Dean Addams. Tayce and the team had committed his body to the stars, with a simple but respectful ceremony. Lance Largon had finished the assignment that his Father had asked him to take care of and was on his way back to the team, to resume his duty as Quests Research and Information Officer. He was bringing with him a further new recruit to the team named Duncan Leyres. Lydia much to Tayces disappointment had, decided that space was not where she wanted to spend the rest of her life after all. Jonathan Largon had offered her a new position at Questa, so she had decided to return there for good. She had explained to Tayce she could see that she had grown up and didn't need her on board the cruiser any more. Her time now was with her team and Tom. Tayce could see where she was coming from, she had to admit she would feel a lot more happier if Lydia was safe on Questa, because of the Vargon threat. She wished her luck with the new position, which was related to helping with planetary council matters. When she thought about it, Tayce realised that she and Lydia were putting their lives back together. She was Colonel of a good team and now her Mother was about to work for Jonathan and the council, it was good. She knew also that if her Father was looking down on both of them, he would be proud to see they were moving on with their lives, since the demise of their home world.

Lance and new recruit Duncan Leyres walked aboard Amalthea. Lydia upon Lances introduction, had just enough time to shake hands with Duncan and inform him that he was on a good team, before the boarding courier announced that they were ready to take her back to Questa. She hugged Tayce then let the courier take her garment carrier and holdall, then followed on, walking on board the high ranked Launch to return to Jonathan Largon and the commencement of her new duty and life style. Duncan could see the fact his new chief and Colonel was going to miss her Mother. When the Docking Bay doors closed Lance introduced Duncan to Tayce, leaving him with her, heading off to get ready for duty in Organisation.

"Welcome to my team, I hope you enjoy the time your working with us," said Tayce casually.

"I never knew Amalthea was so impressive Colonel, it's an honour to serve on board," he replied.

Tayce could see that this dark haired young man, was the kind of friend Treketa could do with. He was similar to Donaldo in looks but there was a certain friendly kind charm about him, that conveyed nothing was to much bother to attempt if asked. He was around 1.83 metres tall, of reasonable good looks, But she could also see he hadn't long been out of training in his field by the way he behaved so nervously before her. He was no doubt top of his class she thought. His most striking features were his smouldering dark eyes, that probably had plenty of young females vying for his attention and Tayce wondered if this was the reason he had decided to leave Questa and further his career aboard her cruiser.

"Shall we walk, I'll explain things as we go," gestured Tayce.

"Of course! Colonel," replied Duncan pleasantly.

Tayce found Duncan's nervousness of her quite amusing. She guessed that it was because she was his chief. For the first time out of Questa. But in time he would fit in as part of the team, his nervousness would soon fade when he'd been on a few Quests. They walked together along Level 2 heading down to what would be Duncan's new quarters, they talked on the way, firstly Tayce explained the on board procedures. Then they talked a bit about things in general.

"I hear you just took on the Boglayon Pirates Colonel, nasty bunch from what I've heard?" he said casually.

"Yes, but they no longer exist and we achieved good success from the Quest, we were asked to take on, as for the leader of the Boglayon Pirates, we're not quite sure if he perished or not, Midge our guidance computer picked up something that left the planet after it's destruction, but it couldn't be determined whether it was an escape vessel or not, why the sudden interest?" asked Tayce curious.

"I was in the section that the Greymarians returned to, one of the Greymarians explained what had happened to them, excuse me for saying this but the leader sounds like a real bastard, considering what he did to Kelly Travern," replied Duncan.

"We each have our own opinion of Lord Dion, believe me, I don't think he's someone I care to meet again too soon," replied Tayce feeling the feelings she'd felt whilst in his company, like it was yesteron.

They walked down the Level Steps and met with Treketa coming up. Tayce introduced Duncan to her and watched silently as Duncan gently expressed how sorry he was to hear of the loss of her friend Dean. Treketa managed a small smile of thanks, then welcomed him to the team with a gentle handshake, before excusing her presence and hurrying on up the steps to duty. Duncan watched after her, as she headed on up the rest of the Level Steps to the next level Level

2, then quickly turned back to Tayce continuing on down in discussion about the last Quest. Tayce began thinking that Treketa was not going to be sad over Dean for long, where Duncan was concerned she could already see there was a connection between the two. On the Quarters Level Tom walked towards them. Upon seeing Tayce with their latest team arrival, he paused to welcome him to the team. He began he couldn't stop he was testing out the new Quest Mark 2. One of the new fighters, that had arrived.

"I've heard their quite something, capable of roughly 700 milons a minon, their the fastest in service so far, reports say that they are considered quick and nippy," said Duncan remembering.

"Really thanks for telling me," replied Tom, glad to hear what Duncan had just told him.

With this Tom silently announced he'd see her later and continued in the direction of the Flight Hanger Bay. Tayce continued on towards what was to be Duncan's quarters. She suggested that he make the place like home and join them later upon deck. She handed him his Wristlink, briefly explaining the various commands to push to activate what he wanted to do, then left him to settle in. Tayce raised her Wristlink as she headed away ordering Midge that when Duncan had settled in, his name was to be entered into the quarters memory. Midge could be heard agreeing. As Tayce walked on so she suggested he fill her in about their latest recruit by giving her some in depth background information. Midge began explaining about Duncan in what he had received from Questa Recruitment Agency. If the information was anything to go by, he was going to turn out to be a good asset to the already growing team. Midge continued on going into Duncan's personal details. He was twenty-nine yearons old and had originally come from a human colony called Antraglex. It was a colony that withheld a band of Earth settlers, whose forefathers took over many yearons ago, after the original Earth was made nothing more than a barren wasteland, through the massive war, with the continents. His Grandfather was the first to discover the Astro Planes of Cartegran on the same world, that had come to be known as something of a phenomenon, similar to the northern lights on original Earth. Tayce remembered the sight on Cartegran, it was truly breathtaking and that people travelled from all over the Universe to see it. She walked up the Level Steps, listening to Midge via her Wristlink, until he was through.

No sooner had Lance returned to duty for the first time in ages, when Marc turned telling him he had an urgent communication from the Chief of the Medical Health Complex at Questa. Lance frowned, what was wrong he thought? Marc suggested he take the call in the privacy of the Meeting Centre. With this Lance hurried on in as quickly as possible in concerned thought. Marc tried not to appear nosey, but was concerned, also, as the call was about Jonathan Largon. Tayce entered the Organisation and looked around for Lance, as she had heard Marc talking with him, coming up the corridor. She looked to Marc and somehow she picked up that something was wrong. He discretely pointed to the Meeting Centre.

"What's wrong, what is it, what's going on, why is he in there?" asked Tayce looking in the direction of the Meeting Centre curious seeing Lance in discussion.

"It's a call from the Medical Health Complex at Questa, they said they wanted to talk to Lance, it was extremely urgent," replied Marc in a whisper.

The Meeting Centre doors soon opened, Lance came out looking somewhat shocked, shaking his head in utter disbelief at what he had just heard.

"Lance are you okay, what is it what's happened?" asked Tayce in true friendly concern.

"It's Father, he's been taken to the Medical Health Complex Cardiac Section as an emergency patient," said Lance in sheer total disbelief.

"Look sit down, I'll get you a drink," said Marc not liking the fact, Lance looked like he was about to drop from the sudden shock.

He hurried out to the corridor Plicetar dispenser and retrieved a beaker of Plicetar. He quickly returned and went straight to Lances side, handing it to him. He suggested he sip it slowly. Tayce waited to hear what his plans were regarding his Father, she didn't mind if he had to return back to Questa, as this was somewhat of an emergency.

"I hate to ask you this, but could you accompany me back to Questa, I don't think I can face the worst, if it happens before I get there alone, they tell me it's bad this time Tayce," said Lance holding back the tears for his Father and the thought that he may lose him. She was torn, she had to think of the team and unsuspecting Quests that might lay ahead, that could materialise in her absence. Marc stepped in and offered Tom to take command of the cruiser and team in her absence, he could contact her if she needed to return. She knew that Tom was capable he had been good at taking charge at such short notice, he'd done so on many an occasion when it was just the two of them and she was doing something else on board that needed her immediate attention. She agreed. Marc suggested they get going, time was not for the wasting. He'd contact Tom tell him what had happened, so that he could return to the cruiser and meet them down in the Flight Hanger Bay, he'd join them just as soon as he'd called Tom. Tayce her mind on Jonathan, nodded, ushering Lance on out. Marc continued to contact Tom over the Aircom and informed him of what had happened. Tom could be heard telling him that he was heading in as he spoke and would be on board soon.

Tom a while later in the new fighter came into land on the Flight Hanger Bay, floor, gliding in and setting down gently. Upon ceasing the engines of the beetle shaped new Quest, with a protruding point, he jumped out and walked to meet both Lance and Tayce, entering the bay.

"Marc just told me what's unfolded Lance, I hope everything is all right when you get there, your Father is a good man," expressed Tom in great sympathy.

"Is the Quest all right to fly long distance, I want to take it to Questa?" asked Tayce studying the first craft of her fleet.

"Yes! Are you sure your going to be all right, flying all the way alone?" asked Tom a little concerned, as Vargon was at large and she'd be an easy target for the picking in a Quest Fighter.

"She's not going alone, I'm flying them," said Marc walking into the bay

"You could stay if you wanted to, believe me I can handle her, flying this cruiser is not all I can fly, you ask Mother, see you when I get back?" she replied finding it not fair that Marc, was going to fly the first of her new fleet.

"Not while we've got the threat of Vargon out there, your Mother would kill me if anything happened to you," said Marc heading towards the new Quest ignoring her protest.

Tayce gave a look that said, you think your flying to Questa don't you, not if I've got anything to do with it, then followed on. Tom stood and watched Tayce, Marc and Lance board. He smiled to himself, as he saw Tayce got her own way and had dropped into the pilot seat, before Marc had, had a chance. She could be seen going through the various checks and starting the quick reaction turbo nuclear engines, lifting up turning to head off out of the Hanger Bay doors, that were opening once again, before them. He stood watching as the fighter headed on out through the doors into space, off towards Questa at immense speed. Walking back to Organisation, he thought to himself that it was a good thing he had tested the first Quest Fighter of the fleet. The only members on board Amalthea, were himself, new recruit Duncan, Treketa and Donaldo it was going to be quiet unless something happened, which he hoped it wouldn't.

At Questa in the Medical Health Complex General Jonathan Largon lay in a medical bunk. He'd been present in the complex for the best part of two hourons. Optic thin wires and Discs were attached to him, sending the necessary readings to a nearby heart machine, giving the medical staff all they needed to know to keep an eye on his condition. He was in a near unconscious state and seemed to drift in and out of consciousness, as whatever had struck him down with such force, had been fast. He looked frail and very ill. His face was pale and not the normal warm slightly tanned complexion that it generally was. A nearby Medical Officer of the cardiac knowledge was busy studying Jonathan's continuous heart rhythm, he looked concerned to say the least. The officer shook his head not liking what was unfolding by the minon, but made a note on his hand held Porto Compute. It concerned the young brown haired officer, that so far things were not improving as they should have been considering his time with them. The young brunette cardiac care nurse could see he was concerned, she glanced to the fluctuating readings and had to agree that the injections they had given Jonathan so far, were not improving his condition, which they should have been. But the young officer knew that Jonathan had, had this materialising for a long time, he had warned him to slow down in his duties, but Jonathan had refused to acknowledge that there was anything wrong with him. If only he had listened he thought.

"Councillor Traun is outside and wondered if she could see the General," said the young nurse softly.

"Only for a few minons, he needs no strain at the present time with long visits, has his son been informed?" said the officer with Dr Neekum on his name badge.

"Yes sir, he's on his way Amalthea contacted us a while ago to let us know," replied the young nurse.

"Good, show Councillor Traun in," he replied in a kind but educated voice.

Dr Neekum keyed in the necessary information that he wanted to continue to try and save Jonathan at all odds. He turned studying Jonathan wondering if he could pull through, even at this late stage of treatment, or would it be a case of to much to late. Finishing the notes he walked on out leaving Jonathan with an alert disc attached to wrist to rest undisturbed, the door closing behind him. Before Councillor Traun saw Jonathan he wanted a word with her.

Back on Amalthea Tom ran up the last of the Level Steps to reach Level 1. He turned at the top, walking on along and into Organisation. He was met by Duncan, busy at the research position, taking over for Lance. Midge suggested he take up his position and take care of research until Lance returned. Tom greeted Duncan with a nod of acknowledgement upon entering, then crossed to the control seat, ordering Midge to release controls to him.

"Are you on command duty?" asked Midge.

"Until Tayce gets back," replied Tom sitting down.

"I can continue to be in charge if you have anything else you want to attend to, I can call you if I need you in an emergency," offered Midge.

Tom was about to agree to Midge taking full command, when without warning below Levels there suddenly came a piercing scream from Treketa that could be heard through the open entrance doors of Organisation Deck followed by the sound of a Slazer being fired. Duncan and Tom both gave each other alarmed looks, then urgently flew out of their seats, grabbed their Slazers from their holsters, and raced on out of the deck. Midge was announcing as they went, that there was an intruder aboard and that all necessary precautions had failed in stopping the intruder. At the top of the Level Steps both men paused, either side poised ready to open fire. Tom over his Wristlink ordered Midge to seal off Organisation, but stay in touch. Midge could be heard agreeing. Both men began on down cautiously. Waiting for whoever was on board to appear. Just as Tom stepped onto the third stair, up from the Second Level. A masked armed raider, dressed in black all in one suit, looking rather like an original Earth Ninja warrior, but built like a Mr Universe of the first order, appeared armed to the teeth swinging his weapon around, that every time it touched the corridor wall gave off sparks. He was so fast on Tom he did not get the chance to retaliate, the weapon swung and the raider open fired at Tom. Excruciating pain rained through his whole body, as the weapon hit home, sending him through the air and hard up against the wall. Where he remained out cold. The raider turned his attention quickly to Duncan, Duncan quickly back tracked, but found that his footing slipped as he tried to avoid being the next victim. The raider gained on Duncan, with amazing fastness and as he neared the last steps to the top the raider fired at him and he felt all life drain from his whole body, everything went dark. He dropped onto the steps and rolled all the way passed the raider, uncontrollably to the bottom on Level 2 where he remained out cold. Blood oozing from his wounds. The raider stood for a moment then stepped onto Level 1. Back on Level 2 further towards the Life Ability Centre Treketa was sprawled out cold. Blood seeping from a severe gash to the side of her head. She had been the raiders first victim, he had thrown her hard against the corridor wall as she had tried to fight him off, using her own armed combat skills, from the dayons on College Colony. It could be seen that the next unsuspecting victim was Donaldo, who was slumped over the Hover Trolley head on one side, through the open doors of the Life Ability Centre out cold beaten and shot. There was blood slowly dripping from his nose, he like Treketa tried to put a fight, even though he had been caught off guard.

Midge felt powerless, as he watched the whole horrific scenario unfold. He began running over in his memory what he could do to deter this unwanted raider, who he had searched the data files to find fitting the description of their present unwanted guest and had come up as.

'YARRICK' known burglar type intruder-steals anything for the fancy – uses very high energy power rod and weapon on anyone who tries to deter him in his quest to take what he wants has been known to kill to gain the spoils of his raid.

Midge knew he had just seen the power rod act, unfortunately on several of the team plus the weapon via the Intruder Cam. He recorded all he could, he was somewhat surprised to discover that this raider was no alien, his body shape was of a human. Under the black head covering mask, with only slits for his eyes to see, he spoke very clear, but rough English. There was something mysterious about this unwanted burglar and why he had picked Amalthea, but what?

On Level 1, the Yarrick was studying a device in his hand, that looked somewhat like a Porto Compute. He was checking where he wanted to head next and steal what he had come for. He was abruptly interrupted when he heard a noise that made him suspicious, perhaps there was someone else fancying his or her chances against him, he had over looked on board.

"Any more of you want to surprise little olé Yarrick, come on out and give it a go, what are you waiting for?" he announced in a tormenting tone, standing poised ready both weapons primed.

Midge wished he could and face this jerk, teach him a lesson he wouldn't forget. As the Yarrick looked up so he caught sight of the small corridor Vid Cam lens, in the Intruder Cam. Midge knew he was about to lose his only way of spying on this no good vagrant. The Yarrick raised his weapon in hand and shot the lens of the Intruder Cam. Sparks flew as Midge lost all chance to track him. But the bad thing was, the main feed had also been blown and it sent an electrical surge to the rest of the Intruder Cams, throughout the rest of the cruisers corridors blowing each Intruder Cam it reached in succession. Now Midge had no way of tracking him, what was he to do?

On Questa Lydia was sitting by Jonathan Largons bunk side. He was now awake, but still very weak, talking with the greatest of strain. Lydia didn't like seeing him this way, he was a long standing family friend and had been very reassuring that she would adapt to a new way of life, when she came to Questa for good. The door opened behind her and much to Jonathan's relief Lance casually slipped into the room concerned to see his Father in his current condition. He walked across to his Father, shocked to see him like he was, they had only cracked a joke before he'd left for Amalthea One a while ago. Jonathan could see the shocked look on Lances face and reached out his left hand to his son. Father and son had always had a good relationship, since Lances Mother had been tragically killed, when he was just five yearons old, Jonathan knew it was hard for him to see him in this condition. Lydia stood and upon passing Lance, discretely informed him that she was there for him should he need her. Lance nodded, with this, Lydia walked from the room allowing Father and son to have quality time together.

Out in the corridor Marc was leaning against the white corridor wall in thought. Nothing in particular, just passing time. Lydia slipped out of Jonathan's room and immediately met him, asking had he come alone?

"No Tayce and I flew Lance out here, he wanted Tayces support, I though I was going to pilot the new fighter but Tayce beat me to it and flew us here, she hasn't lost her touch, are you all right?" he asked gently he could see that she was troubled by what was happening with Jonathan.

"Yes fine, though what has happened with Jonathan has surprised me he collapsed this mornet whilst I was in his Officette, there he was one minon talking about plans for Questa, the next clutching his chest and down he went right before me," explained Lydia softly.

"What a shock," replied Marc looking at her softly.

Tayce walked back from the outside overview balcony she had a look of great concern on her normally beautiful features. Marc studied her and could see something wasn't right she was in concerned thought.

"What's up?" he asked as she came to a pause.

"I thought I would contact Tom on Amalthea and make sure that everything was fine, but for some strange reason I can't get anyone to answer not even Midge," said Tayce extremely concerned something wasn't right back at the cruiser. She felt very uneasy.

"Maybe there's a galactic storm again, or a technical glitch, why don't you try later," suggested Lydia trying to be helpful.

"Yes, maybe your right I'll try later," replied Tayce in thought of what might be happening back at Amalthea.

Tayce for some strange reason felt that something was dreadfully wrong, she was feeling a nagging feeling that she wanted to head back there and then, but she knew she couldn't, because she was there for Lance and her Mother over Jonathan. She tried to push the feeling to the back of her mind and do what her Mother had suggested, call the cruiser later, maybe it was what her Mother said just a glitch and she was worrying over nothing. Marc could see she was troubled by the fact she couldn't call the cruiser and slipped his arm around her slim shoulders in a reassuring way. He knew that she thought a lot of the team and he understood her uneasiness. Lydia suggested that some light refreshment was in hand, back at her new Apart-House. Tayce agreed, there was nothing she could do for a while. Marc suggested he catch up with them later, as there was something he wanted to do, he would inform Lance where to find them, when he'd finished visiting his Father. Tayce agreed walking away with her Mother in the direction of where the new Apart-House was. But the uneasy feeling not getting a communication through to Amalthea resurfaced and nagged at her conscience, that there was something more to the fact she could not get a call through to her cruiser. Marc watched both women walk away, then went to tell the nurse in charge of Jonathan, to tell Lance, where he could find Lydia or Tayce later.

Back on board Amalthea One across space. New recruit Duncan Leyres regained consciousness. He lifted his head feeling the most amazing groggy effect he'd ever felt to date, everything spun dizzily before him. What in Gods name had that weapon been that had rendered him unconscious, he thought. He concentrated hard trying to look down the corridor, remaining in a sprawled position, because his body felt numb. He listened for any unusual noises. When he found that there was nothing more than the sound of the cruisers quick reaction engines, humming away, he figured the raider had gone. He'd obviously found what he had come for and jumped cruiser. He slowly gathered himself together, pushing the immense pain that he was feeling to the back of his mind. He had to try and find this jerk, if he was still on board before he took over the cruiser and flew them off to Gods know where. He gradually made it onto his feet, with bouts of sudden dizziness hitting him. The corridor seemed to sway. He closed his eyes for few minons then opened them, hoping he'd see straight. Everything was as normal as it could be. He looked around for Tom's Slazer, that had landed on the current Level, he'd ended up on. Looking for Tom, he saw him still out cold up against the corridor wall. Crossing he felt for Tom's pulse and was glad to find that he wasn't dead, but as he was when first took down by the raider, in an unconscious state. It looked like it was up to him to save the cruiser, before it fell into the wrong hands. He picked up the Slazer and proceeded off in search of their unwanted guest.

"Okay, you creep, I'm coming, you better think twice about taking this cruiser anywhere, if your still on board, because as far as I'm concerned, your not going to get the chance," he said beginning off.

Going along Level 2 he soon caught sight of Treketa, down the corridor. Her body laying motionless and looking like a rag doll that had been discarded by an unwanted child. Her blonde hair swept across her pretty round face, in a dishevelled way. Again he upon pausing at her side, reached down and felt if she was still alive. He felt sorry for her first she'd lost Dean, now she'd taken a beating from this on board raider. Relieved she was alive, he raised his Wristlink hoping that Midge would still be able to communicate with him. Depressing the Commun button, Midge much to his relief answered. He was relieved that not all the team had been rendered unattainable by this unwanted fiend even if it was just the guidance computer.

"At last someone to talk to, are you able to communicate Duncan?" asked Midge quietly.

"It's good to hear your voice too, yes I can talk, is that jerk still on board, if so can you pin point him?" asked Duncan in near whisper.

"I'm glad to inform you that he's no longer aboard he's done a lot of damage however to my Aircom circuitry by stealing my Transceiver, if Tayce calls, she'll think the worst, however I am able to communicate with you, but I cannot see you, as the raider caused all on board Intruder Cams to blow," said Midge.

"What would you like me to take care of first?" asked Duncan trying to sound helpful, even though he was feeling like death warmed up. He began thinking what a way to start his new career.

"Duncan you are injured according to my scan of you, you should not even be standing up, but take care of the team first they're your first priority above anything else," said Midge surprised he was still standing by the reading he was getting.

"I'll survive, there are worse sights than me down here," replied Duncan trying to ignore the pain searing through his ribs region, every time he moved.

"Before you start, I think I can activate the Life Ability Centre and administer something for the pain, if it is too much to bear," replied Midge.

"Believe me if it gets too much to bear, I'll let you know, I'll take care of things down here," replied Duncan ceasing communication.

He crossed to a stores cupboard and retrieved a Heat Sealant Blanket. Crossing back he draped it over Treketa, then took off his jacket, folding it into a makeshift pillet, gently placing it under her head lowering it back down. Without warning, she began to come to, moaning about how her head hurt.

He spoke softly and gently down at her.

"Treketa it's Duncan, your safe now, your going to be fine stay where you are," he assured her.

Treketa drifted back into a deep state of unconsciousness. Duncan was not sure if it was sleep, or something a lot more serious. He went on into the Life Ability Centre to find Donaldo, hoping that he fared better than Treketa, but it was not meant to be. He raised his eyes how much worse could this get he thought.

Tayce on Questa couldn't stand the uneasy feeling any more, it had been a houron since she'd tried to make contact with Amalthea to no avail, she was going to try again. Upon doing so, all that could be heard was static and the Questa Operator informing her once more, that all Aircom Satlelink communication link up with Amalthea was not possible at the present time, to try again later. Tayce slammed the handset down. This was not helping she thought. She decided to try and use her Wristlink and try again. She waited and once again all she got was static across the air waves, she was unsuccessful. It was Like Amalthea had disappeared off the face of the Universe, there was nothing to make her feel any less uneasy. Lance entered the Apart-House. He looked shocked beyond belief and greatly strained. Lydia crossed with a fresh Coffeen, ordering him to drink it. He took it and sat down on the nearby soffette, gathering for a moment what had occurred in the last hourons since his arrival and it was near impossible to comprehend. Taking a sip of the refreshing Coffeen he looked over at Tayce, he could see she was uneasy about something, he recalled that he'd seen Marc and he'd told him that she had been unable to make contact with the cruiser.

"I heard from Marc, your not getting contact with Amalthea when you call?" he asked, his mind really on his Father and what could be happening.

"I tried just now, there's still nothing, I don't like it," replied Tayce thinking all the worst thoughts.

"Do you want to head back I won't mind, I wouldn't want us to get back and all is gone, because of me, honestly Tayce go back if you have to," replied Lance in an understanding way.

"Thanks, you know I would love to stay and be there for you, but I don't know what I'll find when I get back considering I can't make a communication link-up, Vargon may have struck already," replied Tayce worried.

"You go, I would rather you find out what you think is bad, is not and that everything is okay, after all Amalthea is my home too," replied Lance, giving her a reassuring smile, even though it was a tired one.

"I'll be here to assist Lance and when things start to improve, I'll have him flown back out to the cruiser via Launch," promised Lydia, putting her hands on Lances shoulders in a reassuring way

"All right, Lance I'll contact you the moment I get to the bottom of this and get communications back up on the cruiser, and find out what's happened," said

Tayce thankful that Lance saw her point in the reason she was walking away, leaving him in his time of need.

She began towards the entrance doors. Pausing and turning, she asked Lance to give his Father her regards and explain her sudden departure. He nodded and assured her that his Father would understand. He continued to down the Coffeen Lydia had given him earlier. Lydia watched as the doors drew apart and her daughter and Marc almost collide in meeting. She smiled, thinking that she was glad Tayce had found Marc. Everyone laughed at the almost collision. Tayce turned him around, before he had a chance to say anything, telling him there was no time to stop, they were heading back to Amalthea there was a problem on board and they were going back to find out what. Marc gave her a somewhat surprised questionable look at the idea, but fell in with what she wanted, it could be just a break down in communications he thought, but he also understood that she would not return to the cruiser without good reason that something wasn't right. They soon crossed Questa Square, heading towards the Arrival and Departure Area. As soon as they entered, they ran through the busy throng of people and aliens coming and going from Questa. On over to the Quest Fighter. Marc on the way took the de-locking device out of his pocket aiming it at the entrance doors so they would unseal ready for boarding. Marc was first on board, followed by an eager Tayce. Both were soon strapped into their harnesses ready for take off, as the entrance doors closed. Marc started the Quest engines, he decided he was flying back, as Tayce had flown to Questa and he could fly much more expertly than she, when there was an emergency ahead. Upon Marc gaining clearance for take off he manoeuvred the Quest up slowly off the bay floor and turned to head down the departure tunnel for departure into space. Within the blink of an eye the Quest shot down the tunnel, under the experienced guidance of Marc, back into clear dark space.

***

Two hourons later on board Amalthea, Midge was able to at least watch the sector they were in, he was finding that something with immense speed was heading in their direction. He kept the scanner pointed on the fast moving object and was ready to activate weaponry if it was the returning Yarrick Raider, back for more spoils. This was something he was not going to allow to happen again. It was bad enough the first time around and after a self assessment of his many operations, he had found not only had his Aircom transceiver been stolen, also his detection scanner had partly been picked to pieces, that scanned who was on board, like the crew, had been. Plus many of his main operations computer boards had been damaged in the careless way in which the transceiver and main scan pack had been partially removed, he had to use Wristlink link-up facility and hope it held, so he could talk to Duncan.

Tayces stomach was doing uneasy somersaults, at the fact of not knowing what she was going to find upon arriving back at the cruiser if there was a cruiser to find. Even though they had flown at Hyper Thrust Turbo speed across the Universe, to get back quicker. Marc didn't like dosing the new engines so soon after a test flight, but they had no choice. Tayce after catching sight of Amalthea and seeing that there was only dim lighting coming from within was glad in one way that at least she was still in one piece and in the Universe, though she wondered if the worse was about to face them in the fact the team were all dead on board. Marc glanced at her and saw her greatly concerned expression, but said nothing. He brought the Quest in towards the cruiser, now at a more cautious speed, ready to fly into the Flight Hanger Bay. As they were unable to make contact he hoped that Midge had detected that it was them and he had opened the Flight Hanger Bay doors otherwise they would have to try docking along side.

"Something doesn't seem right here, I think you had every right to be uneasy," said Marc feeling as uneasy as Tayce, as to what they were about to face.

They headed towards the Flight Hanger Bay and the slowly opening doors. Marc breathed a sigh of relief, that Midge had detected them somehow, but it didn't stop him from being ready to abort boarding, if he had to. Nothing but near darkness was waiting as they entered into the bay cautiously. Marc activated the Quest search lights, so that they could see the interior of their surroundings. Nothing seemed to be waiting inside so they could tell, much to their relief, all that could be seen was the stationary fleet of Quests.

"Nothing out of the ordinary, so what's gone on here?" asked Marc casually.

"Let's set down and find out, I still feel something has happened here," said Tayce in reply.

As Marc expertly brought the Quest down in it's designated space, Tayce unstrapped herself and went to the on board weaponry store. She retrieved two fully charged Slazers, setting them to disintegrated kill. Marc walked through giving her a questionable look, when he saw what she'd set the guns to.

"We don't know what's laying in wait and I don't intend to let anyone take this cruiser," she pointed out.

"I guess we'll need our Light Pencil Torches, main power aboard failed several hourons ago, according to readings I checked just now in scan, whatever or whoever hit this cruiser, took out whatever he could, to cause the most damage according the readings," said Marc recalling.

Both stood ready as the entrance doors opened, in case someone or something was waiting in the shadows for their arrival. Marc suggested he go first, jumping out onto the Hanger Bay floor cautiously. He shone his torch and aimed his gun in the in every direction, checking that there was nothing out of the ordinary His finger was rested on the activation button, ready to fire at the first sign of intruder weapon fire. Nothing but silence greeted him! He walked forth suggesting to

Tayce in a whisper to follow on. She did so cautiously, her gun poised ready to shoot.

"We need to check out and find why lights are on low setting, these torches won't last long," said Marc.

He headed over to the emergency power box for lighting. Tayce halted him, in his idea as it had suddenly struck her whoever had boarded, if they were suddenly put in daylight, they would know that there was someone back aboard, it would also enable them to get a good shot at the both of them. Marc saw her point.

"How about you stand at the entrance and get ready to shoot the moment I activate lighting, if they think they have us, we'll have an advantage on them," suggested Marc.

"All right, but if someone starts shooting, shut it down again quickly," said Tayce.

"Right!" replied Marc

Tayce didn't much like the idea, Marc was using her as bait. It should have been the other way around, after all she was Colonel, but then she didn't have a clue what he was going to do to enable the cruisers lights to come back to full operating power, he knew more about computer gadgetry than her. She watched him, as he eyed the override sequence, that he hoped would work in their favour.

"Get ready, activating now," announced Marc in whisper.

The lights activated turning the Flight Hanger Bay, back into full operational daylight mode. The far Hanger Bay doors closed. Tayce glanced to Marc, he raised his eyes in surprise. Tayce glanced around the entrance doorway. Nothing but silence was ahead. Marc began that one thing was for sure, whoever might be still on board if they were in hiding, they were now locked in with them. Once all clear had been surmised, they both cautiously proceeded out of the Flight Hanger Bay, on up the corridor. Out of nowhere Duncan sprang. He thought he had trapped the Yarrick Raider, instead he and Marc collided in the middle of corridor and Duncan brought him to his knees, preparing to take him out, once and for all. Tayce yelled for Duncan to stop. Marc pushed him off. It didn't take much effort considering his injuries.

"Get of me, it's Marc," he said in protest.

"What! God Marc I'm so sorry mate, I was hoping you were the creep that raided us," said Duncan climbing to his feet, breathing with great difficulty

"Your hurt, just what's been going on here?" demanded Tayce in concerned alarm.

"We've been…," began Duncan he'd just used up his last ounce of strength he'd had.

He dropped to the corridor floor, between Marc and Tayce. Tayce ordered Marc to fetch a Medic Emergency Kit and hurry. She crouched down by Duncan, thinking this was a great way to start his first duty aboard. She lifted his head and shoulders supporting him until Marc returned. He soon came running back with a fully equipped Medical Emergency Kit. Setting it down, he suggested as Duncan was injured, maybe, he should head off and see who else had fallen victim to the intruder whoever he'd been. Tayce nodded. He suggested she keep her gun ready, just in case and to stay alert.

"You too you can see what whoever it was that boarded has done to Duncan," replied Tayce beginning to treat him.

Marc headed away his gun primed ready to shoot at a moments notice. Tayce retrieved the Healentex healing device and began treating Duncan's wound, after using the exam scan to determine if the wound was deeper than it looked. As all clear had been given, in the reading, she figured she would suggest that Donaldo if he hadn't been killed by the on board raider, would take a look at him. She realised that Duncan must have tried to track down the intruder himself, because of what he had done and she was proud of him, even if he had nearly taken Marc out in the process a while ago. Once the Healentex had done it's work, Duncan began to come back to consciousness. Tayce administered a relaxant and suggested he head to his quarters and take it easy for a while. She helped him to his feet and along to his quarters.

Marc ventured onto the 2nd Level. He couldn't believe the sight that greeted him ahead. Treketa was laying in the corridor not moving, covered with a Heat Sealant Blanket. He ran along and knelt down, taking hold of her wrist he checked her pulse. As his hand took hers, she woke groggily, looking up into his familiar eyes glad to see him.

"Take it easy, your safe, we're back now," he reassured her softly.

He scooped her up in his strong arms and once on his feet, carried her into what was left of the Life Ability Centre. Inside the Yarrick Raider had wrecked almost everything, in sight and took what he wanted. Marc crossed to the Exam Bunk and gently placed Treketa down. He glanced around for Donaldo and shook his head upon seeing him slumped over the far Hover Trolley out cold. He knew that he would not be able to help. Marc figured it was time to find out if Midge would answer his Wristlink. Raising it, he pressed commun button.

"Midge do you hear me, it's Marc, can you communicate?" he asked hoping so.

"Yes Marc I can communicate, welcome back, sorry it's under current circumstances, we were raided by a Yarrick Raider, I'm only able to communicate via Wristlink at this present time, as the raider took some of my parts, I saw you and Tayce arrive in the Quest and was able to open the Flight Hanger Bay doors, what would you like me to do?" asked Midge trying to be helpful.

"Can you activate the medical equipment in the Life Ability Centre, what's left of it down here?" said Marc hoping he could.

"If I am able to do so, I can scan Treketa and find out her injuries, if it is any help?" suggested Midge.

"Good, go for it, she's all yours," replied Marc.

Marc waited and upon the Life Ability Centre scanner coming to life on low power which wasn't easy and begin its scan of Treketa. He turned his attentions to Donaldo. Just as he was about to head over to find out if he was alive Tayce entered the Life Ability Centre, bringing with her the Medical Emergency Kit.

"I'd like to know just what's been going on here, while I was at Questa, I left Tom in charge... oh my God where's Tom!" she said in panic and alarm.

"Take it easy, he's probably going to be fine, wherever he is, Midge is able to contact us using Wristlink only," said Marc, though his words fell on deaf ears, Tayce had raced off to find Tom.

She'd gone back out into the 2nd Level corridor, ordering Midge via her Wristlink, to tell her where Tom was at that moment, if he could. A few cencrons lapsed, Midge informed her that he was actually along by the steps on her current Level. No more needed to be said, she broke into a sprint, calling back to Marc via Wristlink, that she needed a Hover Trolley and fast. Tayce was not prepared for the sight that greeted her ahead, especially of the man she had come to fall deeply in love with. He was still in the position the Yarrick Raider had left him in.

"No please... Tom, not like this," she said having a sinking feeling, that he had been the unlucky victim of the team to die at the hands of the intruder.

Thoughts that she did not want to think went through her mind, was she about to be alone without him. Tears appeared in her eyes, as she knelt beside him and took his head and shoulders supportingly. Shaking off the feeling, the worst had happened. She refused to believe she'd lost him forever. If by some pure coincidence she felt that inner feeling of immense power once more mysteriously rising within her she wished she knew what it was and why it happened. The feeling was the same as it had been on the Lair and in the unwanted company of Lord Dion. She looked down at her hands. They were glowing, an orange aura surrounded them. What was this she thought? What was she to do with this aura? If by some guidance from somewhere beyond her very existence, she immediately found herself placing her glowing hands, palms flat, above Tom's heart. She closed her eyes to concentrate. The orange glow grew in size over Tom, pulsating and growing to a great intenseness, minon by minon. But it didn't seem to faze her. As Marc arrived, he looked on in great amazement, at what he was witnessing, he couldn't believe what he was seeing, it was truly beyond belief. What was causing Tayce to do this, he thought? Then he remembered what Lydia had told him, that her great Grandfather had been gifted. It now looked like Tayce was the one to inherit her Grandfathers gift. He watched on stunned almost beyond words, at what he was seeing unfold. The orange glow formed a pencil thin beam and entered into Tom's body, into his heart region. This could be seen glowing from outside his body. Tayce continued unaware that Marc was present, watching what she was doing. Right before Marc's eyes,

Tom's wound began to heal, like it had never been. He guessed that the power was doing the same for his injured organs. Once it was achieved Tayce's hands brought the orange glow up out of Tom and slowed it down, to where it had started, just above his body. Slowly Tayce felt the glow fade and the immense power that had mysteriously arisen in her, die once more. Slowly she opened her eyes. Marc looked concerned at her wondering if she was all right.

"What did I just do?" she asked shocked at what had just occurred.

"Save Tom's life, he's coming round," replied Marc softly to her.

"What happened, I thought I was dead... Tayce!" said Tom looking up at her.

"Your alive mate and this little lady here just saved you," said Marc.

"What, how?" asked Tom in sheer disbelief.

Tayce sat not quite knowing how to explain what had occurred before her. That one minon Tom was dead and now he was very much alive all thanks to this mysterious power. All she remembered once more was feeling the amazing powerful force grow within her, but a different kind this time around. Tom could see she was somewhat stunned, he turned hugging her in a warm reassuring loving way, telling her it was all right. He stood up pulling Tayce up with him. Marc couldn't believe the fact that now Tayce had done what she had, there wasn't a wound mark or any kind of bruise on Tom, it was as if the Yarrick Raider hadn't existed. All three began on the walk back up the corridor to the Life Ability Centre. On the way Tom began that the last thing he remembered, was being viciously attacked by a really big black clad resemblance to a Earth One Ninja.

Marc an houron later whilst Tayce was still busy patching up the team, was back in Organisation undertaking Midges repairs, replacing the various damaged and missing computer boards and circuitry that the Yarrick had ripped out. He had found that not only had half his electronic panels been damaged, when the raider stole his main Aircom transceiver and scanner device, to scan the team or intruder on board, but he'd also damaged the main Intruder Cam relay system, which was going to take a further houron to fix as good as new. He knew one thing, he'd like to have come face to face with this so called Yarrick Raider, he would have given him as good as he dished out for damaging Midge so severely. One thing, Marc realised as he repaired Midge that the items the Yarrick had taken had been ones, that had been taken to order, as some would be classed as somewhat expensive on the wrong market. Time passed and soon Midge under Marc's orders was able to operate and open the Satlelink Relay Link. Midge soon announced that there was a call waiting to come in from Questa. Marc upon this, shot out from under the console, banging his head as he did so, cursing and rubbing it. Getting to his feet he gave Midge his full attention. Tayce entered asking was he all right. Midge ignoring Marc's expletive, commenced the call.

"At last, I was beginning to think that you had fallen victim of what was breaking the communications link when you were here, is everything all right, what happened when you returned?" asked Lydia curious.

"My uneasy feeling was right, we arrived back to find the cruiser ransacked by what is termed as a Yarrick Raider, he left the whole remaining team with injuries also wiping out the Aircom on board scanner and Intruder Cams, plus the Satlelink Relay Link that's why Midge couldn't call for help, Marc's just completed the repairs, what's the reason for calling Mother, is Jonathan no better?" asked Tayce preparing to hear the worst.

"Yes! He's actually stable about an houron ago he began to respond and the Cardiac Officer said there is no reason why with the proper care and advice he shouldn't restore to normal health."

"That's great news," said Marc relieved at what he was hearing.

"I agree," said Tayce pleased, that Jonathan was on the mend.

"Unfortunately you won't be getting Lance back as early as you might have hoped, Jonathan has asked me would you believe, to run Questa in his absence, I know I use to help your Father, but this place is on a grand scale, anyway Lance has offered to assist until I get use to doing the routine Jonathan did with Adam, then I promise I will send Lance back," she said sounding convincing.

"It's okay. Mother, it's good to hear Jonathan is on the mend, we're glad he's going to be all right, speak to you again soon," said Tayce cutting communication.

Marc was somewhat miffed as communications ceased between Mother and daughter, that she had not shared with her Mother the fact what she had done to Tom earlier. But he said nothing, as he figured perhaps she preferred it that way. Tayce began to undertake the task of completing a report on the Yarrick Raider to be sent to Questa Security Division, on what had happened aboard in her absence, she had heard from the rest of the team the many stories, that had to be taken into consideration. She suggested that she and Midge work together he could take down the report and she would dictate it to him, then he could send it to Questa for further investigation. Later when Tayce had figured that the report had been filed with Questa Security Division, she was somewhat surprised to have a message come back, stating that a team was on it's way out to question various members over what had happened. Something Tayce didn't like the idea of but had no choice, if it caught the vicious creep. Just when everything was looking like returning to normality on board Amalthea, out in space, to Midges utter stunned amazement, the Yarrick Raider returned. His vessel that looked like it had seen better dayons, rusty and somewhat along the lines of an old freight barge, came into the cruisers vicinity. Midge warned Tayce immediately. She waited till the raider came into weaponry sights, then opened fired. A hit was scored, in a region that would take the no good for nothing weekons to fix, if not longer in some unlawful dry dock. Tayce knew that her hit would teach this Yarrick a lesson, he would never forget. That was to pick on her cruiser, any time soon. Both watched as the rusty looking vessel spun out of control off into the far flung deep depths of uncharted space on fire in the damaged region. Marc over Tayces shoulder whispered.

"You can get in trouble for that you know," he teased but found the whole thing deserving to the raider.

"Very funny, that will teach him to pick on my cruiser again," she replied.

He laughed shaking his head. Over all the yearons he'd known her, she hadn't changed a bit, when it came to dishing out what someone had done to her, or something close to her. She had always found a way to retaliate.

An houron later Tom sat in the on board Leisure Centre in thought, looking out at the passing stars. Donaldo and Duncan soon joined him for a meal, but Donaldo was finding eating anything at the present time owing to the beating he'd taken from the Yarrick near damned impossible, because he'd been smacked in the mouth. It had been almost seven hourons since they had all been unsuspecting victims of the so called Yarrick Raider it was a miracle to think that they had come through the whole ordeal with their lives intact. Marc wandered in, he was glad to see that Donaldo was back to near normal, apart from a bruised cheek. He sauntered over as he wanted to ask his opinion on what he thought about Tayces latest feat, in bringing Tom back to life. He sat down next to Duncan.

"I know your away from duty right now, but I want to run something by you, it's about Tayce," began Marc cautiously.

"Sure what is it?" asked Donaldo giving Marc his full attention.

"I was fortunate to witness another of her power forces earlier, in where she brought Tom here back to life, I don't know how it started, but by the time I got to Tom, she was in full swing, it concerns me whatever this is that she has inherited, apparently from her Grandfather, she is scared of what it can do, I think she needs to confide in someone about it and I don't mean me," expressed Marc.

"Okay. I'll look into it for you, I'll see what I can find out from Lydia and discretely talk with Tayce, I'll find some way of getting her down to me, for a one to one, when I have all the information," assured Donaldo.

"What concerns me is, she's going to hurt herself, if we can't help her in some way, adjust to what she now unexpectedly possesses," confided Marc, much to the amazement and understanding of Tom and Duncan.

Both Donaldo and Tom glanced suddenly out of the sight port, as their sight had caught the arrival of the Questa Security Division Launch coming along side, to investigate the Yarrick attack on the cruiser. Marc thought to himself that really their journey had been a waste of time as Tayce had sent the law breaker off into the deep depths of the Universe earlier, but he guessed it still had to be done, in case he found a way to return using another more powerful vessel. Tom suggested he go and meet them, he had finished his meal and was ready to face duty again. He slid out from the table and upon discarding his utensils for hygiene recycling, headed on out to go and meet Tayce. Marc continued on talking with Donaldo and Duncan about what he'd seen Tayce achieve earlier.

Donaldo could pick up on the way Marc was talking about it, it had effected him also.

Tayce and Tom met half way along Level 2. They walked to meet the team leader and his team from Questa. No sooner had they arrived at the Docking Bay doors, when the Patrol Officer stepped forth through the open doorway and outstretched his hand to shake Tayces, in friendly but authoritative manner. He studied Tayce for a few minons, almost making her feel unsure of herself. She slightly blushed thinking to herself that he was quite rugged looking in a rough kind of way. He was tall with close cut short hair, in a layered style. He had the kind of features conveyed that he was a go getting action man, that if something needed to be sorted, then so be it. His eyes were narrow and grey, they held a certain cold icy look about them. He spoke to her in a gruff no nonsense tone, but to the point.

"Colonel, the names Barnford, I'm security officer for Questa Security, I'm here to question your team on the unsuspecting attack of a Yarrick Raider," he announced seriously.

"Officer Barnford, welcome to the Amalthea," said Tayce politely.

"If your team can check their belongings to find out if there is anything missing and can compile a list, I'll take these back when we return to Questa, meantime I and my team want to talk to the victims of this Yarrick and take prints of were he's been, to take back," he said to the point and almost commandingly.

Tayce wondered if this Officer Barnford ever relaxed, as at this moment in time, she felt like she was under investigation, not this Yarrick Raider. But she knew that in order to trace him, she had to comply with what he wanted, she nodded for him to commence. He turned ordering his team of male and female officers to go about their duty. Twenty five members of Questa Security Investigation team all ran aboard Amalthea and under Tom's explaining of where the various team members were headed, off to get what they needed to investigate the crime that had been caused.

The Patrol men and women took prints for testing all about the cruiser and interviewed the team. They knew their place though, in respect that they were classed as on board guests and had to work around the team whilst investigating. They mingled in and around the team, as they began to get the cruiser back to the first class exploration cruiser it should be. The men and women when they entered a room or centre, worked around the personnel of the Amalthea team, gaining samples left by the Yarrick in his raid. Within two hourons the whole crime evidence against the Yarrick had been obtained by the Patrol Investigation team. Officer Barnford took the reports that had been taken and the lists of belongings that had been stolen, with him. He apologised for any inconvenience that had been caused and thanked Tayce politely, much to her surprise, for her total cooperation, explaining that the evidence would go back to Questa, then get sent to all patrols within the Universal sector for apprehension of the Yarrick

Raider. He further added that if she could think of anything further that could help in the capture of this said felon, then to contact him asking for Officer Jan Barnford. Tayce nodded in agreement, as they paused at the Docking Bay doors. He ordered for his team to return aboard. With that he nodded obligingly, then headed on aboard, behind his team and left for Questa. Just as soon as the Patrol Launch left Amalthea, so the cruiser headed on across the Universe onto the next waiting Quest.

Tayce later down in her quarters after duty hourons, was summoning up the last dayons events, she was glad things were returning to near normality, Jonathan Largon was going to be okay after all. The Yarrick Raider was under investigation. How easily things could have been so different if she hadn't of returned to Amalthea when she had the notion to. Next time she would take the cruiser to Questa.

The Arrival of Vargons Daughter

In the weekons that followed after the attack by the Yarrick Raider, Donaldo Tysonne contacted Lydia at Questa to find out more on the sudden power ability Tayce seemed to have gained. It transpired that the source Marc had informed him of in where the power ability had originated from was confirmed as that of her Grandfather and it was also confirmed, that it had skipped a generation. The reason for it triggering in Tayce so suddenly, was the fact that she had built up such hatred towards Countess Vargon, over what she had done to Traun. The more he thought about the first time Tayce had used her powers, it was in fact against the Countess. Lydia discussed with him, that she was a little concerned in the fact she knew that Tayce would not use the sudden gift to harm anyone, in an evil way. But it was unsure just exactly how powerful that gift would become, if her anger grew overwhelmingly in an a moment of confrontation. They had to monitor the situation very carefully. Donaldo agreed and after talking with Lydia, summoned both Marc and Tayce to the Life Ability Centre, to inform them of what he had found out. Tayce found it hard to take and believe, that she was gifted in such a powerful way, even though she was quite a gutsy person, it shook her a little to know the uncertainty of the new force she possessed. She had to agree with Donaldo that the power did appear in moments of emotional control. He assured her, that they would monitor the situation and he would find out more. In the meantime, she should let her body naturally adjust to the new found ability and not fight against it when it happened, as it could end up causing her serious damage internally. In time no doubt, she would adjust and cope, everything was strange when it was new and took a little getting use to. Whatever happened, the gift would never leave. It was now apart of her life and existence, she would probably be surprised just how good the effects became. He suggested to Marc discretely that he keep an eye on the situation, other than Tom, because he had known her growing up on Traun and knew her well, He agreed. They talked on about what Donaldo had discovered and what she might find happening to her in the moments when her powers struck, at length, for another houron.

***

15:09 hourons, under Tom's guidance, Amalthea was slowly cruising through the current territory of space heading towards an Annual Achievements Ceremony, on Questa. Every yearon certain aliens and people in space were awarded for an achievement of some sort for what they had done during the past yearon. The event was titled the Annual Space Achievement Awards Ceremony or for short the A.S.A.A.C award. It was a rare chance for the team to try out their ceremonial attire. Tayce was in her quarters, she was standing before the Reflection Imager, studying every angle of her elegant appearance in the white body hugging gown, that was edged in silver thin piping. It fitted her perfectly she thought. She couldn't remember when she had dressed up so glamorously, it had to be back on Traun. A party thrown for her Father in being another yearon in power, before the war of possession, by the Countess. Tom entered the quarters and stood admiring the way she looked, she was certainly appealing to the eye, he thought. He crossed dressed in his navy close fitting ceremonial uniform of trousers and jacket and came to a pause just behind her. He softly and seductively whispered close to her right ear, something very sexy, which made her smile and come back to the present.

"You sure you want to go to this awards ceremony looking the way you are, we could make our own entertainment, send the others in your absence?" he teased her softly.

"Afraid so, I think we better get going, we'll be late," she replied softly pulling away from him.

Tayce picked up the small clutch silver purse and headed for the quarters entrance doors, walking across the living area. Tom smiled and shook his head, how he loved to tease her. He followed her on out of the quarters, as the doors drew apart and closed again as they walked to Organisation to watch their arrival at the Ceremonial Venue. All duty had been suspended until after the awards event. Midge would be in overall control, until they returned.

Elsewhere aboard, the other team members were all getting changed into their ceremonial attire for what was suppose to be a spectacular annual event. Each team member was wondering who was going to be the unexpected guest of honour. Treketa walked from her quarters feeling back to her normal happy self after the nasty run in with the Yarrick. It was hard to imagine she thought, that it was almost two weekons since the attack. She guessed it would be on her mind for some time. Maybe this spectacular awards ceremony was what they all needed to unwind for a while, she thought, as she made sure the satinex pink trouser suit she was wearing, fitted just so, on heading up to meet up with the others at the top of the Level Steps. Upon passing a glassene fronted cabinet, she

171

paused to check her hair, that was clasped up in a gold clasp. In a ponytail style. Checking that it was as exquisite as she thought it looked. This night was going to be a good one to remember.

Tom and Tayce entered Organisation. Duncan stood concealing a surprise for Tayce. It was something that Tom had nearly given up hope on completing in the last monthons. It was his walking talking four foot high robot called 'Cargo' from his vessel, that had been part of the crew. Duncan stepped aside to reveal a new shiny version of the little robot. Tom explained that Marc had helped him with a few modifications, to bring him up to date. As from that moment on, he could communicate with Midge, if ever the team were ever in danger, via high frequency link-up. The little robot walked forth and lifted his arm opening his hand. Tayce glanced at Tom, wondering what she should do. Tom smiled and gestured for her to go ahead, shake Cargo's hand. Tayce held out her hand cautiously to him, wondering what he would do to her. He slowly applied just the right amount of pressure to grasp Tayces hand and gently shook it. He lifted his head up to look at her, with his small round blue lens eyes.

"Hello Colonel I'm Cargo... lady your beautiful," he said in cheeky child like speech.

"Thank you Cargo, he's great Tom!" said Tayce laughing softly.

"He's ours and he's coming to the event with us, if that's okay?" put Tom, hoping Tayce would agree.

"All right, but I don't want any trouble with him, understand?" agreed Tayce in a meaningful way.

"You've got it," assured Tom.

"Midge we'll be down waiting at the Docking Bay doors, let us know when Docking is complete with Questa," ordered Marc.

"Of course, I'll let you know on route if need be," he offered eagerly, he did not want Tayce thinking this Cargo would be as equally good as he'd been to her so far.

"Okay," replied Tayce, as they went on out the entrance.

Tayce, Tom, Marc and Duncan walked from the Organisation Deck, briskly heading on along to the steps. Cargo walked behind like an obedient servant. Tayce found that every step she took, the bottom half of her long gown flowed in the breeze of her movement. Tom took hold of her right hand, as they began to walk down the Level Steps. She had to lift her gown slightly to avoid tripping down the steps, as she walked. Marc and Duncan discussed the forthcoming awards, as they followed on behind. On Level 2 Treketa, Donaldo and Lance were all waiting, talking amongst themselves. Lance looked nearly to tired to attend the ceremony thought Tayce, as she came down towards them. He had only arrived back on the team just on an houron ago, she had suggested earlier, that he remain at Questa and meet them there, but he had declined, saying that his ceremonial attire was on the cruiser, he had to travel back and change, he hadn't even had time to take a break thought Tayce, she could see he looked all in, but was putting a brave face on.

"Are you sure your up to going to this ceremony, I would fully understand if you feel that you would rather rest," she gently put it to him.

"No I'm fine, honest!" he replied giving her a reassuring smile.

With this they all walked on towards the Docking Bay doors discussing who might be up for an award and joking who would definitely not be ideal for an achievement award!. Tayce wondered if she would get one for the team, owing to what Martin Travern had said in rescuing the Greymarians, he was going to make sure there was a good word put in for what they had done on Dion's Hideout. Tayces Wristlink sounded on her wrist. She activated it to hear Midge announce, that the last moments of docking were under way. Tayce acknowledged saying she'd see him later, then deactivated the Wristlink. As they reached the Docking Bay doors, so the final part of docking commenced. Tayce proudly glanced around her team in their ceremonial attire and then to the new addition to the team 'Cargo' who stood by the side of Tom in an obedient kind of way, this finished what was the ideal scene of her newly formed crime fighting Team. The men's suits were well designed in a navy colour, with high collars and white thin piping going from shoulder to wrist and from waist to ankle of the trousers. It was topped off by slip on grey shiny leatherex flat shoes. The team would be the best there was this night, thought Tayce, even if it was just for their ceremonial attire. Docking was soon completed it was time to go.

"Everyone ready for a night of a lifetime?" said Tayce light heartedly.

"We're all ready and right behind you," confirmed Marc.

Tayce glanced at him, he was looking really handsome and was about to break a few female hearts tonight dressed the way he was. Poor girls, she thought. Her attention was brought back to the opening Docking Bay doors before her and the sudden waft of warm air rushing in from Questa. It was followed by the sight of a joyous occasion, mixed with the sound of music and various crew personnel and high ranked dignitaries all topped off in their glamorous attire, heading to the ceremony. Tayce slipped her hand through Tom's arm, in a linking way and they all began off Amalthea down the walkway into the spectacular colourfully decorated scene, that was the Annual Space Achievement Awards Night on Questa.

Vessels came and went at the headquarters base, bringing people and aliens in for the celebratory night from all over the Universe, then departed to allow others to come in to dock at the Arrival and Departure Area. It was turning out to be a night that many would remember for a long time to come.

She was young tall and slender and arrived dressed in a black sparkling suit. She would blend in with the crowd on this night. She had long straight jet black hair and conveyed a certain evil edge about her. She glanced around with dark brown eyes, that conveyed treachery and deceit. Eyeing everyone in a scrutinizing

173

interest, as if she was searching for someone in particular, which made her somewhat suspicious, to say the least. She was sent to seek out one person in particular. That person was wanted dead by her evil guardian, she moved with a certain prowess almost cat like, as she sauntered her way through the crowd of merry makers. Then as she neared the 'Check in' desk her sight homed in on the vary person of the coming and going, crowd she wanted as, her intended victim, that person was Tayce Traun. Her guardian had been right who had sent her on this task ahead, this Tayce Traun was everything she said she would be. The desk clerk gained her attention away from Tayce in a sudden spoken request, in asking her to sign in, which she did to stop any unwanted trouble so early in her plan. She signed in under a false name. The name 'Sallen Corford'. As she looked around she could see Tayce laughing with the team. Tayce coincidentally looked her way, she quickly glanced away pretending to look at something else.

"Excuse me, that women, who is she?" asked Sallen in an innocent way glancing back towards Tayce again.

"That ma'am is Colonel Traun, one of our top dignitaries, she heads a team that fights crime, known as the Amalthean Quests team," explained the young smart looking desk clerk.

He handed her, her overstay Apart-House key innocently. She snatched it with her black silkene gloved hand, then picked up her holdall and briskly began away with the first part of her plan done, she'd identified Tayce. Now she thought, she had to sum up and plan the next part of what her female guardian had required of her. As she walked away the young male desk clerk found her presence somewhat disturbing and cold. He was quickly distracted by another person, who was signing in for overstay accommodation, but when he looked back in her direction, she was gone.

Lydia and Jonathan walked towards the Amalthean team. Lydia looked regal in her appearance, she was truly stunning. Her gown was a low cut body hugging sparkly cream design, that showed her every curve. It was topped off by gold coloured shoes, that could be seen under the full length gown. Her hair was designed in the usual blonde bob style, that rested on her shoulders like a shinning hood. Her make up was perfect to emphasize her beauty and show off her beautiful sapphire blue eyes. Jonathan had hold of her arm gently in an escorting kind of way. Even though he was present for this auspicious occasion, he still looked pale thought Tayce as she walked to meet him. But she could see he was being brave for her Mother's sake. As she greeted him with a gentle hug she noticed that he was not well yet, but didn't say anything.

"You made it then?" asked Jonathan in a delighted way.

"Yes and it looks like it's going to be a fantastic night, judging by what I've seen so far," replied Tayce glancing around at the celebratory surroundings and the mingling of smartly dressed people and aliens with different coloured hair and the strangest of strange appearances.

"Whose this little chap?" asked Jonathan seeing Cargo.

"This is Cargo, our new addition to the team, he'll be no trouble we promise," promised Tom.

"He's quite something," said Jonathan impressed.

"Your all looking lovely tonight, a team to be proud of even," said Lydia.

"Thank you Mother," replied Tayce kissing her Mother gently on the cheek in greeting.

"Shall we get this night to remember under way then?" suggested Jonathan happy to do so.

"Yes!" replied Tayce.

Little did Jonathan know that this night to remember, would be one that would not be forgotten for a while, at least by what unfolded in the next so many hourons. They walked on into the Celebrational Hall and to the available seating area, where the audience were taking their seats ready for the awards announcements to commence. The Celebrational Hall was the largest gathering complex on Questa, especially constructed for social functions, on a grand scale from music concerts to awards functions, such as the one that was currently being held this night. It could seat around 600 people in the seating area, with an isle down the middle. A 15ft ceiling gave the hall a large roomy feel. There were coloured lights of reds, yellows and blues, giving the occasion a soft relaxing atmosphere. Golden banners hung here and there, from the silver stealex rafters, with the words 'QUESTA ANNUAL SPACE ACHIEVEMENTS AWARDS' in gold on a white background. A soft music played in the background, to match the grand occasion.

"This place is already getting full, where do you want us to sit?" asked Marc glancing around.

"Over there, so you have easy access should you need to leave for an emergency," replied Jonathan gesturing to the far side of the hallway.

Tayce glanced around, then back at Marc, meeting his questioning look. He was somewhat puzzled as to why Jonathan should think that there should be an emergency, was there something he knew that they didn't and wasn't saying? Tayce discretely whispered as Jonathan began away, that she had an uneasy feeling about this night, but she couldn't put her finger on it just yet. She suggested they all stay on alert. Marc suggested he pass it on to the others to be on their guard. Tayce nodded. Lydia after talking to some other people, made her way up to the front to be with Jonathan Largon on the platform. Tayce watched her go hoping that whatever this uneasy feeling was, she hoped it didn't involve her Mother, or Jonathan. She recalled the young woman that she had found herself staring at quite suddenly earlier, out in the foyer, cross her mind, where had she gone? Was she to do with the uneasy feeling, she was feeling? She certainly wasn't present at the present time she thought as she glanced around.

"Is anything wrong, only you look like your searching for someone?" asked Tom seeing her look about with a scrutinising look.

"No, it's just someone I saw earlier, she looked a bit suspicious, I wondered if she was in here with us that's all," replied Tayce.

"Will you relax, your off duty Colonel, perhaps she was an artist, there are quite a few out there in the foyer making the evening more entertaining," replied Tom trying to get Tayce to relax.

Tom was right she thought, but it didn't stop her from wanting to keep an eye on everyone that entered the hall on this night. Eventually the seating area was full. All the people and aliens that were going to attend were there and seated. Some jabbering on in a language that was impossible to understand. Silence filled the hall as Jonathan Largon stood to his feet and walked forward to the stand where a tiny pick up microphone no bigger that a small button, was built into the podium. He stood for a moment welcoming the many guests that had come from all over the Universe, picking out certain ones as he glanced around the 500 or so seated. Then he began the awards ceremony.

"Ladies, Gentlemen and Honoured planetary guests, we are gathered here like any past yearons to pay tribute to the many humanoids or alien races, teams or individuals who has made a difference in what they have achieved in serving Questa Headquarters Base, this past yearon, I would like to bring to your attention, a young woman who came to this base with just one other member of her crew, she had lost her home world less than three yearons ago, to cut a long story short, this young woman had promise, she put to me a new concept in fighting crime, a Quest orientated crime fighting team and this yearon to date, she has achieved great success in bringing some of the most notorious leaders to justice, my son Lance is part of this new concept, Ladies, Gentlemen and honoured planetary guests, please show your appreciation for the Amalthean Quests team," said Jonathan proudly gesturing for the team to stand up.

Tom stood to his feet first, followed by Tayce and the rest of the Amalthean Quests team. They all walked out with 'Cargo' down the isle towards the platform. A loud thunderous applause sounded around them as they went. Tayce had no idea that they were so widely recognised by so many seated guests, as she received nods of thank you, as she passed, from people she didn't even know.

Outside unbeknown to Tayce and the inside gathered audience of the award ceremony, the young woman that had entered Questa earlier with long dark hair and wearing a sparkly black suit, signing in as Sallen Corford, had now donned a sparkly mask and was back in the crowd. The mask she had donned made her look like one of the many entertainers present on this celebrated night. But she concealed something more under her jacket, something that would aid her in her forthcoming act asked by her guardian to undertake at all costs, this was a Slazer weapon and she was making her way to her point of mission. Her aim was to terminate one person in particular inside the hall. She carefully made sure she was not being eyed suspiciously, as she sauntered towards the halls entrance. Waiting until silence was heard from within, she stepped onto the under foot sensory pad in front of the entrance doors, bracing herself for the duty she had to do ahead. The glassene and stealex doors drew apart before her. She stood staring at the platform ahead coldly and unemotionally, at none other than Tayce. Everyone present inside turned to look in her direction, to see who it was. Silence filled the air, so much so it could be cut with a Slazer knife. For this young female assailant was none other than the evil daughter of Countess Vargon, not as she had booked in as Sallen Corford. Sallen outstretched her black gloved hand and in it was the powerful looking Slazer weapon. Aiming it at none other than Tayce. She began to prance forward warning that if anyone moved, they would join the target in question. Adam Burnford who had come from Micacer was seated in the area nearest to this black clad beauty, as she made her way forward. He discretely opened his jacket and reached in for his small handgun. He slowly withdrew it thinking it was a good idea that he always carried his gun for protection in the Universe. He was also thinking that he may have to use it. He had hoped to have a night off duty and claim his reward without any trouble but he had a hunch it was not meant to be, somehow it was all about to change. Sallen took aim at Tayce in the sudden sounds of gasped surprise around her. She announced, "This is one award you won't live to receive Colonel Traun," spoke Sallen coldly.

"Get down everyone," shouted Adam, as he sprang into action and took aim at Sallen.

Everyone in the Celebrational Hall bent forward, lowering themselves to avoid being shot. Adam open fired on Sallen. The shot struck her in the upper shoulder and for a few minons she grimaced in pain, at the feel of impact. She looked daggers in Adams direction. Then dropped her Slazer and ran from the hall, holding her arm. Everyone slowly sat up and looked at Adam in surprise thanking him.

"Damn I missed," cursed Adam under his breath, as he lowered his weapon.

Tayce was quickly comforted by Tom, as she was shaking at the sudden thought she could have died right there on the platform. Lance saw how hurt she was and left the platform, running up the isle to join Adam to go after female assailant. Jonathan crossed to Tayce and Lydia. He was disgusted to think that this had happened when security had been extremely tight all evening. He left Lydia and the others to comfort Tayce and address the audience, apologising sincerely.

"Ladies, Gentlemen and honoured planetary guests, apologies for our somewhat untimely and unnecessary entertainment, but I assure you it's all in hand and I ask you not to let it spoil what is planned to be a lovely occasion," said Jonathan hoping that it wouldn't.

"Colonel Traun, are you all right?" asked a Questa guard discretely, as he had come to her side.

"Yes… I'm fine a little shaken, but I'm fine," replied Tayce.

She found her heartbeat slowly coming back to normal she hated feeling like she did, she'd been a vulnerable victim. The team that was except for Lance, who had left the hall with Adam, in search and pursuit of Sallen. Regrouped on the platform, putting the intrusion behind them. They were pleasantly surprised when they were awarded the trophy for new concept in Universal crime busting. There was a special appreciation award for Tayce, in what she had undertaken in rescuing the Greymarians. The rest of the team all won awards for various achievements. Duncan received an award for single handedly trying to stop the Yarrick Raider from taking a cruiser of the Questa Fleet. He was stunned and totally taken by surprise to receive such an award it was his first ever. He had claps on the back and shoulder by the team of congratulations. The ceremony went on for almost two hourons. Various people and beings received awards for their various achievements. At the end of the ceremony, Jonathan Largon announced that refreshments were being served in the next room. With this, the audience slowly stood to their feet and sauntered on out, discussing the somewhat spectacular intrusion. Guests that weren't staying, sauntered on back to their vessels but stopped to talk with Jonathan Largon for a few minons before walking on. Upon Lance entering the hall with Adam, Jonathan walked down from the platform and towards them. All came to a slow pause in the middle of the near empty hall.

"Somehow she's disappeared, it's like she just vanished," said Lance mystified at the fact.

"Lance and I caught sight of her for a moment, then she was gone, we did go in pursuit, but rounding the walkway she'd gone down, there was nothing, sorry sir," backed up Adam.

"Never mind, nice work you two, Councillor Traun has your awards, what we want to know is, who was she and why did she threaten Tayce in such a way," expressed Jonathan in thought.

"I guess we'll have to wait and find out, I know one thing, I won't be off guard next time," assured Tayce coming to a stop by them.

She was convinced that whoever this young woman was, she was not out for a simple act of vengeance, there had to be someone behind her pulling her strings so to speak. Tayce thought about it and she couldn't be sure, but the young woman, Sallen, had more than a striking resemblance to Countess Vargon, of all people. Tom saw her in thought, as he approached.

"You think there's more to this unsuspecting outburst then we witnessed first hand, don't you?" he asked.

"My intuition says there is and she resembled someone I'd rather forget," replied Tayce glancing towards the Celebrational Hall entrance in thought.

"Colonel Traun, we haven't met, I'm Adam Burnford the pilot that rescued your Mother and returned her to Micacer." Adam introduced himself politely.

"Hello, thank you for what you did, it's just a shame you didn't find my Father out there," said Tayce grateful for what he had done in rescuing her Mother.

"Don't give up hope Colonel, if he's out there, he'll be found one dayon," assured Adam kindly.

"Thank you that's reassuring," replied Tayce feeling hopeful on his kind words.

Tayce turned once again looking towards the Celebrational Hall entrance, she had a feeling that this was not over with this young woman assailant. Tom shook hands with Adam thanking him for going in hot pursuit of the uninvited intruder. Lydia could see Tayce was unnerved by what had just unfolded she fully understood it as it, had slightly unnerved her too. As she approached she put her arm around her and guided her to the side of the hall comforting her as she went. Mother and daughter stood talking, Tayce talked and Lydia listened in an understanding way. The rest of the Amalthean Quests team walked on into the next room. Tom stayed waiting patiently in the hall, waiting for Tayce to finish talking with Lydia.

Elsewhere on Questa unbeknown to Tayce and the team, was the assailant, whose, true name was Sallen Vargon. The daughter of the notorious Countess. She was fighting off the burning pain of her injury. She was finding that the side effects of being shot were making it hard to concentrate on what she had to do next. She was drifting in and out of drowsiness and everything kept going from blurred to clear vision in cencrons, she knew she had to find some kind of medical help soon, otherwise she would end up dead and not her intended victim Tayce Traun. Once she'd completed her packing, in between fighting to stay conscious, she pulled her jacket over her wound, hiding it from prying and concerned eyes. She slipped out of the overstay Apart-House entrance, cautiously, making her way back down the corridor back to the 'Check In' desk, where she had booked in earlier as Sallen Corford, waiting for someone to spot her, for what she had done earlier in the hall. She could feel the pain worsening and throbbing by the minon, as she fought to stay on her feet and not look suspicious. She could hear her Mother's words telling her, to get on with it stop being such a snivelling child in her head. Vargons never gave into pain, it was insignificant. Avoiding eye contact with anyone that walked into her path, she pulled the hood of her jacket over her long black hair. No one seemed bothered by her, as she had changed attire and she merely looked like just another traveller passing through. Suddenly Sallen heard a male voice shout out that seemed to be aimed in her direction. She looked to where it was originating from discretely. It was Lance, he'd passed luckily not noticing who she was, just another traveller and he'd seen some friends, lucky for her she thought. Quickly she crossed to the 'Check In' desk quickly presenting her de-locking key the moment she came before the young desk clerk.

"Excuse me madam, you have to declare who you are by signing the screen as acknowledgement of your payment for the duration of your stay," he said, handing Sallen a pen shaped instrument to mark the screen.

Sallen signed the same name she'd signed in with, when she had arrived. Then picked up her holdall turned and ran back to the awaiting shuttle, that was about to leave. As she fought against the immense pain as she went, she began thinking ahead avoiding the prying eyes of Questa Security. Watching and mingling with the crowds of departing passengers, sauntering along with them like any other boarding passenger. All she wanted to do was sit down and close her eyes, as she felt like death warmed up. Lance couldn't believe his luck, as he left his friends, he spotted her. Adam Burnford who was with him, nodded to the fact that it was her that they were seeing. Both once again sprang into action, but unfortunately for them, they were on the next level up from where Sallen was, moving forward in the queue. Both broke into a sprint, running along the glassene balcony walkway taking their Slazer handguns out of their side holsters as they tried to make their way as quickly as possible down to where Sallen was.

"Guards stop that woman boarding," shouted Lance down to the nearest guards in Sallen's vicinity.

"Don't let that shuttle leave," backed up Adam in urgency.

Screams of panic rang out as Lance and Adam moved through the crowd on the moving walkway, that would take them to the ground level. One group of ceremonial guests were right in their way at the bottom and it didn't matter how hard Adam and Lance tried to push their way through, the people ended up nearly in a push and shove tussle, finally Lance ordered them to move by order of General Largon, telling them that they were in pursuit of an assailant, they needed to stop them. The group, three men and two women gave an unimpressed look and moved aside. Lance ran towards the port, where the departing Shuttle had been. It was slowly under way, moving forward and off into the stars.

"Damn it we've lost her again," said Lance in angry frustration, hitting the nearest wall with his hand.

"Take it easy mate, she's gone, there's nothing we can do," said Adam smacking Lance on the back in a calm down gesture, he understood his frustration.

"Look she didn't board, come on lets get her," said Lance thinking he was seeing who they were after.

Security now had joined in the pursuit, having heard the real reason such a commotion was being caused in the Arrival and Departure Area. They fell in with Lance and ran with him to where they thought Sallen was heading. Upon reaching her, as Lance was thinking that he had done Tayce a favour, this female assailant was not going to strike again, he reached out and grabbed her round roughly to face him, with the look of shear anger in his brown eyes. He was immediately cut dead, as this young woman was not the person he thought she was, she glared back at him.

"What the hell do you think your doing, let go of me," she retorted angrily

"Sorry ma'am, I thought you were someone else, my sincere apologies," said Lance extremely apologetic.

"I should think so, General Largon will here of this, who are you?" demanded the posh princess like beauty.

"Lance Largon, I'm General Largons son," he replied casually.

"Oh… then I accept your apology," she replied feeling somewhat awkward.

The young woman continued on leaving Lance somewhat amused. The guards all glanced about hoping that they would find some trace of Sallen, but it was hard to make out anyone properly on such a night like it was. The night of the awards ceremony, was the busiest time of the yearon. Lance ordered them to stand down, but suggested they keep an eye out for a young woman dressed in black, that had threatened Colonel Traun earlier. They agreed and headed away. Lance decided to head back disappointed that the young woman had not been who he had hoped she'd been. He guessed it was a case of being in the wrong place at the wrong time. On the walk back, half way he was greeted by Jonathan and Tayce. She looked far from amused. She had heard that one of her team had been brandishing a Slazer weapon and causing hysteria in the passenger hall. Jonathan when he had found out it was Lance, was also far from pleased, as it was against the rules to brandish any kind of weapon unnecessarily on Questa, unless you were security. He had told him time and time again, that it was against the rules and he hoped for his sake, that he had an extremely good explanation.

"What the devil is going on Lance, I have told you time and again about the ban on brandishing weapons unnecessarily on this base?" began Jonathan, giving his son an angry look.

"This isn't a good example of one of my Amalthean Quests team to behave in this way with all these innocent people around," backed up Tayce.

"We found the young woman who tried to shoot you earlier, but we were up on the next level, we thought we had pinned her down, but it turned out to be someone else, I'm sorry," expressed Lance.

"You involved innocent bystanders, Lance really?" said Jonathan furious, at his sons actions.

"It's all right General, I can see that Lance and Adam here were merely trying to protect me, there's no harm done," assured Tayce trying to calm down from being angry.

Lance knew what his Father said was true, he had warned him about the unnecessary use of weapons on Questa. It was a peace rule and he had just broken it, he could understand that he had done wrong and didn't know what to say, to make it right he had apologised to Tayce. He glanced at Adam, expressing that Adam was merely assisting him and that he should not be blamed for breaking the rules. Jonathan still looking far from amused which wasn't good for him, nodded understandingly. Tom walked out to meet them, curious about what happened and why Tayce had left his side in such an urgent manner. He came to a stop, listening in on the fact that if Lance had managed to apprehend the young woman and found out who it really was that wanted Tayce dead, it would have avoided putting her in any more danger. Jonathan calmed down, as he could see his son's point in his actions he'd done to try and apprehend Sallen. He suggested they return to the rest of the celebrational evening. Tayce walked beside Lance and informed him, that even though he had tried to apprehend her assailant, he was not to try anything like it ever again, especially in brandishing a weapon on Questa, was that understood. Lance nodded.

***

Sallen Vargon had made her mark, but had escaped. But only for the moment. She would return again. Now Tayce had another of the Vargon family to face. The shuttle that she had escaped on, was lucky for her, a long haul flight, that had a medical facility on board, where she could get away with being treated without questions being asked. Whether they believed that she had been in a shooting practice accident and hadn't had time to stop off at the Questa Medical facility, she didn't care. All she knew was, that she was on the way home to her Mother and by the time questions were asked about her injury, she would have left the shuttle and been picked up the connecting shuttle home.

***

When the party after the awards ceremony was finished and the evening had wound down, the Amalthean Quests team and Cargo, who many of the guests had been impressed with, returned to the cruiser. The team had, had one terrific celebration and were pleased with the awards that they hadn't expected to be awarded, including the one that was awarded to the whole team, in the shape of a golden 'Q' on a gold stand. It had been a night to remember, even if it had been marred by the intrusion of Sallen Vargon. Tayce had a feeling there was more to come from the young woman, that nearly ruined her evening, she may have caught her off guard this time, but next time she would be prepared for her sudden appearance should it happen. Once they boarded, the Docking Bay doors closed and Amalthea departed from Questa, heading out into deep space. Midge had set the cruiser in a smooth running warp 5, until a new destination had been decided.

In the dead of night aboard Amalthea One when everyone was asleep in their Repose Centres it materialised from the deep darkness of space. It was a pointed sleek design, in silver grey, firing as it came. Midge luckily for the team, had already seen the vessel and put up protection shields. He returned fire, he knew it was down to him to take care of this unprovoked attack, as he was in night control. But he found it near impossible even for his capabilities to get rid of this vessel intent on destroying the cruiser. Amalthea took on many of the strikes, bouncing off it's defence shield. The vessel was seen armed to the teeth with what could only be described as every kind of weapon imaginable to start a war, or the means to destroy anything that got in it's way, which at the present time was Amalthea. A Digit Bomb that had unleashed on the cruiser bounced off the Protection Shield once more, but not before putting the whole cruiser into a violent shaking vibration and causing most of the on board electronic functions to temporarily go to standby in operation. Midge tried with the utmost skill to keep the cruiser stable during the constant bombardment, but failed and everyone on the Quarters Level fell out of their bunks, in some kind of fashion.

Tayce in her quarters Repose Centre rolled out of her bunk landing face down on the floor, with a thud. She yelled in surprise, as she had been in a deep sleep. The electronics and lighting in her Repose Centre crashed, then flashed up, then down again. With the violent rocking, she was brought sharply awake and very aware that something was very wrong. Far from amused she clambered to her feet, rubbing her shoulder, that she had knocked on the corner of the built in night stand as she'd fallen. She grabbed her 'D'Gown (dressing gown) and headed furiously towards the outer entrance doors, slipping it on doing up the tie belt as she went.

"Midge you better have a good explanation for this, this had better not be one of your simulation drills for an emergency, I'm tired," she said aloud to herself.

She exited the quarters, just as soon as the doors drew apart upon her approach. Tom was already out in the corridor about to press her announcement system, to get her up. He looked half asleep and fighting by the minon to become fully alert, to what was going on around them. Tayce dodged him, telling him to follow on in a tone that told him she was far from pleased at what was unfolding. He did as asked and was quickly joined by Marc, Duncan, Lance, Donaldo and Treketa, all equally looking like they were fighting to stay awake and confused as to what was happening, as the cruiser continued to take the bombardment of firepower.

"Why do I get the feeling, I know who's behind this, she's taken long enough to find me," retorted Tayce.

"Do you think that young woman we tried to stop earlier is somehow connected to her if it is her?" asked Lance.

"I was thinking of Vargon, but as you come to mention it, that young woman earlier who threatened me was specifically out to shoot me and no one else, maybe your right, the two are connected," said Tayce thinking about the fact the young woman had the same kind of grating voice as the Countess.

"Well I didn't want to say anything earlier, but I had a friend do a photo identification of her at Questa in security, he came up with a name for your female assailant, your not going to like this," replied Lance as he steadied Tayce up as another direct hit bounced off the protection shield

"Tell me I probably won't be surprised," demanded Tayce.

"Sallen Vargon, she's Vargons daughter," said Lance straight to the point.

Tayce looked at him taken back for a few minons at the name, she didn't know what to say, but it certainly explained the fact behind what had happened on Questa. Vargon had obviously sent Sallen to put an end to her, once and for all. She had now stooped to an all time low, using her daughter as a means to get rid of her. Well Sallen was certainly living up to the Vargon Warrior image, shoot first, answer for it later, if caught.

"How come your friend knew of her?" asked Tayce, as they walked up the steps.

"He informed me off record that spies tell him, that Sallen Vargon has been at College Colony, training in the highest form of combat and tracking skills, she disappeared shortly after leaving College Colony, sources say that she was seen in the company of your arch rival the Countess," expressed Lance.

"Bitch," said Treketa under her breath without thought, upon hearing the mention of Sallen's name and what she did to her at College Colony, in getting her kicked off her course.

"It seems to me, the Countess had her in training, to come after you," said Tom.

"Quite, well I'm not bothered, she can send who she likes, I'm waiting," said Tayce bravely.

"What are going to do if she turns out to be the one firing on us now?" asked Marc falling in behind unsure of just what she would do if Vargon was behind the unprovoked attacks, on their present surroundings.

"Handle it like the last time she faced me, right until we find out whose attacking us, sleep is hereby put on hold, until we get to the bottom of this, back to your quarters and get changed for duty, Marc and I will head on up to Organisation, until Lance, you can get there," said Tayce.

"Right, won't be long," said Lance turning and running off in the direction of his quarters.

Both Marc and Tayce ran on up the Level Steps, to Level 1, leaving the rest of the team to return to their quarters and get ready for the unexpected night duty ahead.

Tayce a while later in Organisation stood looking straight into the face on screen of the young woman who had tried to kill her earlier on Questa. Lances friend had been right, she thought, this was Vargons daughter and she had identified herself as such. Marc glanced from Tayce to Sallen on screen and he could tell from the look on Tayces face, that she was not going to tolerate the daughter of the woman, she despised the most in all the Universe, one bit. Sallen was looking back at Tayce in a cold spiteful way, and one that would freeze Plicetar.

"So your Sallen Vargon, does your Mother know your out here doing her dirty work, what do you want?" demanded Tayce coldly, to the point.

"I do my own dirty work, as you call it Colonel, no one tells me what to do, least of all, Mother," retorted Sallen just as cool in tone.

"She wouldn't like hearing you say that, so why are you attacking my cruiser?" asked Tayce again getting impatient.

Marc studied Sallen on screen, thinking the resemblance to her evil Mother, was quite startling, it was like looking at a younger version. Her eyes were just as dark and evilly treacherous, as her Mother's. Behind him the team ran into Organisation now dressed. Duncan paused so abruptly seeing Sallen on screen, that Lance nearly ran into the back of him.

"I want to finish what Mother started, your Vessel or mine, let's get this over and done with, I hate to leave things undone and as Mother has given me this task to take care of, I want to draw a concluding line to finish what she started, then it will be a matter of going after your Mother," said Sallen sounding like a boastful child.

"Fine! Like you said your vessel or mine," replied Tayce throwing the ball back into Sallen's court unmoved by Sallen's spitefulness.

"Are you crazy, you can't trust her, she nearly tried to kill you a couple of hourons ago remember," said Marc in a whisper of alarm, just behind her.

"Your call Traun," said Sallen, without feeling in her voice.

"Here on board this cruiser, the Armed Combat Practice Centre, twenty minons, I don't like to be kept waiting Sallen don't disappoint," retorted Tayce.

Marc as communication ceased, couldn't believe what she had just done, he couldn't believe also, that she was thinking of taking Sallen on alone, it could be a fight to the death, considering how much hatred there was between the two of them. What would that evil miss try, just to get rid of Tayce he thought. He didn't like the idea at all. But she was in overall charge, he could not tell her what to do. But he was not the only one greatly concerned by the idea that she was going to take on Sallen Vargon alone. As she turned, so Tom was giving her an extremely worried look. Tayce passed him without saying a word, this was something she needed to take care of herself and she didn't feel that she wanted to involve the team, she had her own way of teaching this Countesses daughter a lesson she'd never forget and it began in the Armed Combat Practice Centre. She ran down the corridor and as she went, she found her whole form changing attire with help from her amazing powers, going, from her night attire into her uniform and realised that what she had done was for the first time by mere thought, that she needed to change attire. Was her thinking what she wanted to do the trigger to use this force she experienced in times of urgent need, she thought. Marc after Tayce had gone, ordered Lance and Duncan to follow on discretely with their Slazers, but to stay out of sight, just in case Tayce could feel they were present. They were to do nothing unless Tayce was put at a disadvantage. They agreed heading on out checking their Slazers as they went. Midge had been told to keep in contact with both Lance and Duncan on route and activate the Intruder Cam, so they could see what was unfolding as Sallen arrived.

Twenty minons later as stated by Tayce, Sallen materialised in the middle of the Armed Combat Practice Centre looking every inch the true evil Countesses daughter in her all in one black jumpsuit and matching black shiny high heeled boots. Her long jet black hair cascading about her shoulders once more. She held in her hands a weapon that looked like a gun, but was it something more sinister, to take Tayce down with. The wound she'd suffered earlier from Lances gun narrowly killing her, was gone. She meant business and could hardly contain her eagerness to take Tayce on. In through the opening doors of the Armed Combat Practice Centre walked Tayce dressed equally ready to finish this business of the Vargon family trying to wipe her off the face of the Universe, for good. She showed that she was the more least intimidated of the two of them. Gone was the naïve little girl on Traun. Tayce was an independent woman and after three yearons on her own in the perilous Universe, before the team, she was more than ready to handle this miss. As she walked forth and came to a pause in the middle of the Centre. Out of sight both Lance and Duncan watched from the small equipment stores, as a fight for good against evil, was about to erupt right before their vary eyes.

"We finally meet Traun, but it's a meeting that will seal the end to the Traun dynasty, soon the Vargons will have done what they had nearly achieved in destroying your world yearons ago, that's riding this Universe of you and your family," said Sallen spitefully.

"I thought you said you didn't do what your Mother told you Sallen, it seems that you do, or hasn't your Mother enough power for another confrontation like the last one with me, fancy sending you out to die for something she doesn't have enough guts to finish, what did I expect," replied Tayce sarcastically.

"Your no match for me Traun," retorted Sallen sounding brave.

"Let me show you what I did to your Mother, after all your here representing her, so I'm figuring your here to take her place and die in her place," said Tayce no mercy in her voice.

Duncan and Lance were willing Tayce on silently from the equipment stores. They looked out so they could get a better view and were amazed when Tayce unleashed a pure energy fire ball of her power ability straight at Sallen. The size of a small throw ball hurtled at Sallen, who dodged it, ending up on the floor on her side with a thud. She glared at Tayce in anger to think she'd struck the first blow. She activated the weapon in her grasp to strike the next one. Unbeknown to her, Treketa had entered the equipment stores from the corridor carrying a loaded gun. Lance upon seeing her, grabbed her down beside him. Sallen looked in the direction of where a muffled gasp had admitted from wondering what it was. But couldn't see anything. Lance discretely warned Treketa that if she went out and fired on Sallen, then Sallen, just may open fire on her or Tayce and Tayce could die just because she had a score to settle.

"I've waited for this moment since they kicked me out of College Colony, to take her on because of her bullying me over Tom," she replied angrily in a discrete whisper.

Treketa managed to get in to the right position to view clearly Sallen and to carry out what she'd come to do. Lance flipped the setting to stun. She looked at him surprised. He simply informed her, that she did not want to end up no better than Sallen. Treketa open fired ignoring Lance just as Sallen was going to fly at Tayce with a glowing weapon in her hand. Sallen dropped to her knees, looking up at Tayce, for a minon Tayce saw the innocence in her rival, that had been trained to hate her so much, then fade as she passed out onto the floor. She shook her head. Treketa walked out fully into view.

"What did you do that for, I didn't give you the order to back me up?" demanded Tayce displeased at Treketas actions, but glad she'd done it anyway.

"You weren't the only one with a score to settle with that family, remember I got kicked out of College Colony, when she called Tom a murderer over Alenea," explained Treketa, looking down at a silent and out cold Sallen, she was a threat no more or at least for the present time.

"Are you coming with me, I'm putting the second phase into operation to teach this miss a lesson she won't forget for a long time to come, I'm taking her back to her vessel and making sure she takes a one way trip home to the Countess with a reminder never to stray this way again?" asked Tayce to Treketas surprise.

"You bet, I'll never get this once in a lifetime chance again," replied Treketa eagerly.

Both women crossed and hauled an unconscious Sallen up onto her feet. While Treketa supported Sallen, Tayce raised her Wristlink contacting Midge.

"Midge put me, Sallen and Treketa over on Sallen's vessel, now, before she comes too do it from here if you're able to," ordered Tayce.

In no time at all, as both Tayce and Treketa placed their hands on their guns, ready in case there was other members on Sallen's vessel. Travelsport took on around the threesome and de materialised them from the Combat Practice Centre. Lance and Duncan, once both Treketa and Tayce had gone, turned and headed back to duty, wondering what would lie in wait for the two on Sallen's vessel.

It was near darkness on board Sallen's vessel and not the roomiest in size, there was only two control seats and wall to wall operational panels. Flashing lights greeted the two Amalthean Quest members upon arrival. They both dragged Sallen over to her pilot seat and strapped her in. Tayce stepped back and took aim with her Slazer, setting it to the first setting that was below stun, it was just enough firepower for what she wanted to achieve, she fired on the clasp that was securing Sallen into her seat, which would make it impossible to get out off, any time soon. Then to Treketas surprise, she turned the weapon on the main control panel, but not before keying in the return journey to her Mother, the Countess.

"Tayce are you sure that's wise, surely we'll all get blown to smithereens, you fire on that panel," said Treketa having a feeling that Tayces revenge had overcome her and she wasn't thinking straight, in what she was doing in firing on the operational panel and locking in the journey home.

"It's fine, I know just where to hit this panel, so that it locks her on a return journey back to where the vessel came from, every vessel of sorts, has a logged in position of origin, where it comes from when leaving a Mother ship or base, that's what I've done, sent Sallen home with a reminder to the Countess that she'll face me herself next time, instead of sending Sallen here," explained Tayce.

"Is there anything I can do?" said Treketa at a loss

"It's covered, just call Midge and tell him to stand by, to Travelsport us back, on my word," suggested Tayce.

Treketa did as asked and in no time at all, Tayce had fired on the Navigations and Operational panel and they were Travelsported off Sallen's Vessel in a split cencron, before the Vessel turned away from Amalthea and headed back across the Universe, where it had come from.

Once back on board Amalthea, both women ran to the nearest sight port, to watch the vessel head back into the deeps dark depths of space. A smile crossed Tayces face, as she thought of how the Countess would react to see what she had done to her daughter. It would take Sallen quite a while to return home, because Tayce had set her vessel on the longest route through pirate and dangerous space, sealed in her control seat, she would have to plead for her freedom in meeting any one that came across her, if she wanted to survive.

"What did you do?" asked Treketa seeing the amused look on Tayces face.

"Only sent her on a journey home she won't forget, that's if she survives," replied Tayce.

Marc came down the corridor as they exited the Travelsport Centre. He had the look of great concern on his handsome features, in that he thought they had gone with Sallen. Tom came behind, he had visions of not only losing the woman he loved, but his little sister too. Tom immediately crossed and pulled Tayce into a thank God your safe hug.

"Don't ever do that again, we thought you'd gone with our unwanted guest, what did you do?" asked Marc greatly interested.

"Let's just say, she's in for a long and life threatening journey home, with unavoidable encounters of the worse kind," replied Tayce finding what she'd done gratifying.

Marc couldn't believe it, but he didn't blame her, because of what Sallen had tried to do on Questa and the fact that Countess Vargon had been behind it. It seemed that Tayce was beginning to feel like it was pay back time in retaliation for what Vargon and her army had done to Traun, whether it was Mother or daughter she was not going to let Vargon carry on striking at her in the hope of getting rid of her, without some kind of retaliation. It never ceased to amaze him, what she got up to in her actions lately. Treketa before heading back to Donaldo, informed Tayce that next time she felt like having fun with Sallen, count her in. Tayce nodded then headed on up the corridor going back to duty, much to the surprise look of Tom as he thought they could go and catch up on their sleep. He realised that Tayce and Treketa were joining forces where the Vargons were concerned and knowing his sister, she would be taking the lead in the next escapade towards Sallen, he warned Marc as they followed Tayce back to Organisation, that they better keep an eye on them in case one got the other one killed for their daring actions! Marc nodded in total agreement.

When Tayce had returned to Organisation a while later Midge said nothing, when she told him what she had done. But he didn't blame her. He had known her to do worse, when they were travelling alone for the three yearons together and he knew how she felt about the Vargons in general, he didn't blame her. He could see that she felt a lot more at ease knowing that she had handled the arrival of Sallen Vargon. But he wondered what the Countess would have up her sleeve for revenge in the near future.

Crash Landing on Maldigri

Weekons passed and Amalthea was in a new sector of the Universe. Lance was busy analysing information on their orbital current surroundings, in Organisation. Duncan was now in his official position of Amaltheas Navigationalist and was watching the horizon for any unforeseen hostile arrivals. Everything was calm at present. As it always seemed to be when they entered a new sector of the Universe, they hadn't encountered before, but was it all that it appeared to be, he thought, as he sat studying the horizon.

Tayce was with Marc and Cargo, they were in the on board Lab Garden Dome. A place that Tayce hadn't had much time to spend in, since she'd first arrived on board three yearons ago. It had gone to ruin since she had last visited it some yearons previous, but Marc had suggested to take her mind off of the sudden arrival of Sallen in the Universe, they sort out the problems in the Dome and see about restoring it to it's former glory. Both had been trained in keeping a Garden Dome, which was like a large botanical greenhouse. The tending and care to make it a place to sit and contemplate in times of peaceful solace, would be worth it, he thought. Many of the plants and trees had come from Traun and had been specially grown to withstand a spacial atmosphere aboard Amalthea. Marc looked up at Tayce, as she trimmed the branches of a silvery leaf tree. He stood at the bottom of the small hover platform, to make sure she was not going to fall, as she had insisted she do the job. He looked out through the curved glassene domed roof into the dark blue yonder just beyond her wondering what this sector would hold.

"You better not be thinking mischievous thoughts while in on this platform Marc Dayatso, I don't want to fall from here," teased Tayce in light hearted tone, she knew what he was like for pranks.

"I'm not, I'm staring at that out there," he replied watching something strange looking that had suddenly appeared on the horizon, that hadn't been in his sight fifteen minons ago.

"What is it?" asked Tayce glancing to where he was staring, wondering what it could be.

Out through the domed roof and into the not to distant was a bright red funnel of burning fire. It swirled and seemed to spurt balls of pure white energy out in all directions. Tayce climbed down off the platform and came to a stop beside Marc, still looking at the strange phenomenon, wondering what on Earth it could be? Whatever it was, as she stood watching, so she could see that it was moving towards them at a steady speed. She raised her Wristlink and pressed the Commun button. Midge answered.

"Activate protection shields, we have an incoming phenomenon, which I would consider hostile," said Tayce in the true tone of command.

In the moments that followed, Marc grabbed Tayce as a ball of immense fire hurtled towards the Lab Garden Dome roof. He ordered her to run for it. They both dropped what they were doing and ran for the entrance to get back into the safety of the corridor. They had just made it out into the corridor, dragging Cargo on the way and the doors closing behind them, when the ball hit the outside Dome protection shield and dispersed itself travelling along Amaltheas outer hull, from bow to stern. Marc and Tayce fought to stay on their feet and keep Cargo on his, but the little robot toppled onto his side and rolled up against the far corridor wall and shut down. Tayce grabbed Marc's hand and they made their way under the strange immense force that was making it difficult to move, towards the little robot, helping him back onto his feet activating him.

Outside in the Universal sector the strange phenomenon that had unleashed it's fire balls was briskly gaining on Amalthea and as it came, was bombarding the cruiser protection shield with the pure white energy balls. On the near horizon a green and blue looking planet loomed large in front of Amalthea and it seemed that the cruiser was heading straight for it, as if under the influence of the strange phenomenon.

Tom was met by Treketa on the Level Steps coming up from the Quarters Level. She was trying to stay on her feet and hang on to the silver rail, that ran the length of the steps. Tom reached out and took her hand pulling her across into his steadying protection.

"What's happening, what's causing this?" asked Treketa reaching the safety of her brothers hold.

"I don't know, but have you seen Tayce on your way up, she was with Marc in the Lab Garden Dome?" asked Tom concerned that both Tayce and Marc were hurt in the Dome, as Midge had informed him he'd lost all communications shortly after and the Dome had taken full force from a strike.

"What shall we do?" asked Treketa holding Tom's arm to stop herself from falling down the steps.

"We better head up to Organisation wait there see if Midge can scan anything other than that phenomenon outside, we may need to rescue Marc and Tayce," he suggested above the din of strikes off the hull.

If by shear coincidence round the bottom of the Level Steps came Marc and Tayce with Cargo, much to Tom's relief. In between being jolted and shaken about every five minons, they all struggled up the steps with Cargo. Without warning a sudden increase in gravity began to make it impossible to fight against, for the foursome and Cargo making it on up the steps. The more they headed on up to Level 1, the harder it became. Tayce found her legs were quickly turning to lead, going numb with the immense strength of the force pushing against her. Marc held her hard, with his right hand. Cargo latched onto the rail in front of her and went up nearly blowing all his circuits, as he proceeded. All four were losing the battle to make it to Level 1 and Organisation.

Duncan and Lance were trying with the greatest of difficulty in Organisation to keep Amalthea under control. They had abandoned their normal duty positions and were now in the control seats. So far, they were failing as the white energy balls were now depleting the outside protection shield around the cruiser. Outside and looming even closer minon by minon was the blue and green planet that had materialised before Amalthea. Midge was standing by, to put emergency landing procedures into operation, to land on the planet where it looked like it was going to be their only hope for survival. Lance was an experienced pilot and was giving it all his might, but wasn't happy to the fact Midge had just informed him that at any moment the protection shield would fail and it was going to be a lot more tougher, he would have to give it everything he could, just to bring the cruiser into land safety. The gravitational force had now reached the Organisation. Both Lance and Duncan were pulled suddenly and sharply back in their seats, much to Lances fury that he couldn't save the cruiser. As if timing wasn't bad enough communications restored and a call was coming in from far off in the Universe. Lance tried with every ounce of muscular strength he could muster, to reach the activation button in front of him, but with no luck it was just out of reach. Duncan reached out with his right foot and luckily kicked the button home. Jonathan Largon's voice came through.

"Is anyone there, it's General Largon?" said Jonathan finding that he was not getting the usual sound of Tayces voice, or any of the team coming back to him asking how could they help.

"Father it's Lance, were going to crash..." said Lance as the planet that had been looming large before them was now looking like it was about to engulf them.

"Lance, did you say crash, what's going on out there?" demanded Jonathan to the sound of no reply.

Amalthea went into a crash nose dive towards the planet surface. Midge activated the landing gear hoping that they would land safely, little did he know, that it would prove hopeless because of the tremendous speed that they were travelling had frozen the landing hydraulics and the landing gear was half extended. The large cruiser dropped to the surface like a heavy object dropping from a great height, which it was.

Outside Amalthea, the cruiser impacted with the planet surface sliding out of control through tons of sand, dirt and rocks with the sound of scrapping as it slid past, denting the outside hull. It got caught up in the planetary vegetation and dragged it along sending blooms of all colours and sizes into the air and everywhere birds and animals hearing the onslaught of the vast cruiser heading their way, took to flight squawking as they went in shear fright. Smaller animals either shot down burrows or unfortunately were killed. It was an uncontrollable journey that seemed to go on and on, without anyway to stop. The Amalthea left a trail of devastation behind it. The landing gear that had half frozen had smashed back up into the cruiser, on hitting the surface, making the breaking system on board fail. Hence the uncontrollable slide to infinity, or when the cruiser ran out of force to keep going. All lights on board had failed, along with the on board power. Silence suddenly filled the air, Amalthea had stopped her journey, looking far from the once beautiful white graceful cruiser she was.

Silence and darkness filled the air on board with the sounds of creaking and moaning from impact. On the steps Tayce lifted her head slowly wondering if she was still alive, looking about cautiously, waiting for something further to occur. She couldn't understand why the Level Steps were where the ceiling should have been, did this signify that they had come to a stop upside down, she thought? She was careful how she sat up in case she fell somewhere. There was natural daylight filtering into the cruiser from somewhere. Had they landed on a daylight world she thought? Bits of the cruisers wall were covering her uniform, making it look dusty, but she didn't care, just as long as she was alive. Tom! She thought, as she glanced around where was he? Marc moaned beside her and made light of the moment.

"I'm going to have to give Lance some flying lessons, this landing qualifies as a definite fail!" said Marc.

"Are you okay?" asked Tayce.

"Yeah, but I think this Cruiser is a write-off," he replied looking about, sitting up carefully, wondering what would fall on him from above first if he moved to quickly, as there was hanging debris, that looked somewhat precarious. He kept one eye on it, as he began to move.

"Why us, that's what I'd like to know, why did that phenomenon target this cruiser?" asked Tayce unsure of why the phenomenon chose to make them target practice.

"Tom mate are you all right, we've landed," assured Marc.

Tom nodded and sat up surveying the immediate wrecked area. He found looking at Amalthea upside down gave it a whole new look, that was somewhat weird to say the least. Treketa slowly sat up brushing off the grit and dust from the broken debris, from the steps. Everyone slowly got back on to their feet. Cargo was smashed to smithereens much to Tom's disappointment. He guessed that the little robot was not meant to be. He turned his attention to Treketa and helped her back to her feet. But the moment she put weight on her right foot, pain shot straight up her leg and she immediately screamed. Tayce crossed and checked it out suggesting that she stay off it as much as possible, until they found a Medic Emergency kit, or Donaldo alive. Tom slipped his arm around Treketas waist supporting, her, helping her out of their current position. They all carefully began away from where they were. Suddenly it crossed Tayces mind, that Lance and Duncan were still up in Organisation. Were they still alive she thought, as he had called her earlier via Wristlink and told her that he was taking over control. Marc glanced across seeing her in deep alarmed thought.

"What's the matter, you look worried?" put Marc wondering what was on her mind.

"We have to go to Organisation, Lance and Duncan are still up there, Lance told me things were getting way out of Midges capable control, so he took over, we have to see if they are alive,"insisted Tayce in urgency.

"Okay, I'll help you, we'll make our way carefully on up together, but it's going to be tricky," said Marc glancing around realising it was not going to be an easy job considering the cruiser was up side down.

"We'll continue on, at least there's one thing the atmosphere must be breathable where we've landed, as we can still breath, we'll meet you outside when we've found Donaldo," suggested Tom.

"Check that the area is safe and take handguns, just in case, see you later?" said Tayce following Marc in the opposite direction.

They both split up, going their separate ways. Both pairs found it strange walking along on the ceiling of the deck, with the cruiser being upside down. Marc occasionally took hold of Tayces hand, helping her over debris to big to step over, as they climbed to Level 1 in hoped anticipation that Duncan and Lance would still be alive.

In Organisation Lance opened his eyes and found that he was upside down. It felt weird staring at the control panel from another angle. He glanced around for Duncan. He soon found him covered in broken sight port glassene and debris from the impact, they had sustained during landing. He had to find out if he was alive. He summed up his situation and figured if he was careful, he could get out of his safety harness. He began slowly removing the harness straps and carefully manoeuvring himself, so he didn't drop to the deck ceiling and knock himself out, he also didn't want to be left hanging by his fingers. In the midst of him trying to get out of the control seat, Duncan began to come too, pushing off the debris. He teased Lance.

"You want to learn to fly Largon, the Generals son and you land us like this, I wonder what your Father would say!" said Duncan winding Lance up.

"Didn't you know, this type of landing is classed as an emergency landing on the Questa text disc," replied Lance giving as good as he was getting.

"Give us a hand, I've got to get down from here, if I open this harness, I'll drop like a stone," said Lance.

"Right, can you slowly open the harness clasp, I've got hold of you?" assured Duncan, taking Lances arm.

Together they worked at getting Lance safely down. Slowly Lance dropped down onto his feet, on the deck ceiling into a standing position with help from Duncan. As Duncan had already been thrown out of his chair onto the ceiling, he was able to guide Lance down to standing. They both looked up at the daylight pouring through the smashed sight port and smelt the breathable air rushing in, at least they were alive, they thought. Out in the corridor they heard Tayce and Marc calling out to them. Lance lead the way and helped Duncan out over the top of the entrance doorway into the 1st Level corridor. Marc and Tayce quickly began moving the debris that blocked Duncan and Lance from getting to them.

"What caused us to crash?" asked Duncan.

"We were forced down by that strange phenomenon, we first saw it in the Lab Garden Dome, when it first started sending out white energy balls," said Tayce.

"We raised protection shields, when you told us, it became impossible for Midge to control the cruiser, as he was beginning to lose many of his functions so I took over for as long as I could, I tried against all odds to bring us in properly Tayce safe the cruiser, sorry," said Lance.

"Don't worry you did your best, whatever that thing was, it wanted us on this planet, dead or alive," said Tayce not blaming Lance for his landing, she knew he'd tried his best, it was far from perfect conditions to land in, they were forced down out of their control, at least they were alive.

"Are either one of you hurt?" asked Marc.

"I've just nicked myself, nothing serious though, I think it was the sight port glassene, or some object that hurtled past me during the rolling over process, all we could do was put our hands up to shield our faces," said Duncan.

"If we find Donaldo and he's fine, I'll have him take a look at you, come on we're all meeting outside, do you have Slazers, we may need them, just in case this is not a friendly environment," said Tayce.

Both Lance and Duncan upon finding a Weaponry store, paused and retrieved two Slazers. Everyone walked on along the ceiling of the 1st Level corridor climbing over stuff and dodging cables that were swinging. Upon reaching the steps Tayce let Marc go first, then sat down and slid down behind carefully. Lance coming down behind her, then Duncan, until they reached what was left of Level 2. Going through Level 2 was not easy, but they made it. As they went Tayce thought of Midge in the fact that if they couldn't salvage the cruiser, then she wanted Midge placed into the new one, should they get another vessel. She also felt saddened to think that their current surroundings was her first cruiser and the last vessel to be constructed on Traun, now it was gone and so was Midge unless he could be saved. She tried not to show her sadness in the fact she was holding back tears, as they progressed.

Tom and Treketa reached the Life Ability Centre, which they had found in a state of total wreckage. Donaldo could not be clearly found, there was debris everywhere. Tom pushed a Exam Bunk mattress away from the entrance, allowing him and Treketa access. After searching for what was the best part of twenty minons, Treketa spotted Donaldo. He was trapped under his desk, against the wall in his Officette. Tom quickly with what help Treketa could offer, pulled the desk away to get to him. He looked up and smiled glad to see them both. Figuring that he was probably the only one alive.

"You two are a sight for sore eyes," said Donaldo with relief.

"Just relax mate, we'll have you out of there in a minon," assured Tom moving further debris away.

Tom once the debris was cleared, bent down checking Donaldo could move and helped him up onto his feet. Treketa hobbling about quickly searched for a complete Medic Emergency Kit. She grabbed it from under a pile of debris still closed. Tom helped Donaldo on out of what was left of the Life Ability Centre, as Donaldo had said, that he felt he'd done something to his ribs. Treketa glanced back, as they all made their way out, wondering what would happen to the cruiser? Donaldo gripped Tom for support, as his side hurt from the injuries, that he had sustained from the force in which the desk had hit him, as it had sailed across towards him as the cruiser flipped over.

"How are we going to get off the cruiser?" asked Donaldo in between wincing, from the pain, as he walked along.

"The plan is that we head towards the Docking Bay doors, up ahead," said Tom, as he made sure they both made it safely over corridor debris.

Marc came into view and walked towards them seeing Tom struggling, he immediately went into action helping Treketa first, in taking the Medic Emergency Kit, then supporting her on the way out. Once everyone met at the Docking Bay doors, both Tom and Marc quickly set about getting them released and open. Marc moved one side and Tom the other. When Marc had managed to manually operate the doors getting them to move to a gap large enough to get in between, they pushed the rest of the way together until the doors opened fully. Warm air rushed in from the outside. Tom aimed his Slazer ready in case there was anyone unfriendly waiting the other side. But nothing, except the sound of bird song and animals greeted them. This Tayce was glad of. Lance took out his hand held scanner that was luckily still working and checking the outside readings. Everything came back with the reading of 'CLEAR-NORMAL' on the LCD screen. Tayce walked forward and soon found that the planet they had landed on, was along the lines of a paradise world. The rest of the team left what was left of the cruiser and followed Tayce. Tom and Marc kept their Slazers primed in case someone or something appeared without warning in a hostile way. Again nothing dangerous materialised. They placed their guns back in their holsters when they figured all was safe but kept on alert as they glanced around at the views.

"At least we seem to be safe, did you get to find out where we were, before we crashed Lance?" asked Tom interested.

"It's classed as the paradise world of 'Maldigri'. I managed to get enough information before things got to bad, it's uninhabited," replied Lance in an explanatory manner.

Tayce leaned on a large rock and looked back sorrowfully at what was left of her cruiser, as they had walked to a clearing. It was hard to imagine in it's current state, that she had been considered the first exploration cruiser of it's time on Traun. It had been built to last by the best team of Traunian designers and constructed by the most experienced construction workers, in their field now they were gone and so was Amalthea One, forced to land on this paradise world by a phenomenon looking a far cry from the graceful sleek design, she had been known by. Smashed, dented, scorched and looking no better than if she'd been ambushed by space vagabonds, what a way to end it's life she thought. Marc caught her looking on in thought at the cruiser and he shared her feelings he had watched it being built on Traun, now it was a wreck. He walked over to her and upon reaching her, he placed his right arm around her shoulders, hugging her to him, like a big brother.

"You know they can always build another one," he assured her trying to cheer her up.

"She won't be the same, there will always be only one Amalthea One, the first of her kind, but Midge I want them to salvage him if it's possible, he's always been there for me, right from the start," said Tayce, holding back the tears. Amalthea One had been her salvation, her home on that fatal night, until their present time.

"Come on, your team need you," he said softly trying to make her feel better.

"Your right, I shouldn't feel like this, there are injuries to take care of," replied Tayce standing and walking towards the others.

Tayce and Marc soon joined the others, but it didn't stop the thought crossing her mind whether Vargon was somehow connected with what had happened to them it would be her kind of powerful treachery for what she'd done to Sallen in sending her on the long journey home. Lance looked up as she approached.

"If it's any consolation, Father was in contact with us in the final stages, before we crashed, I also released a crash seeking beacon, so if it successfully launched Questa Patrol should be picking up a signal soon," said Lance trying to make her feel better.

197

"Thank you," replied Tayce giving him an appreciative smile.

Tom as Tayce picked up the Medic Emergency Kit and began treating the team, walked to see the sorry sight of Amalthea. He stood wondering what would become of it? Would it be salvageable, or would she become another large piece of spacial junk left on the surface? Would Jonathan Largon pick up the distress crash signal, or would they all be marooned on this planet Maldigri forever? Only time would tell.

Treketa was sitting on the ground when she felt something swipe her arm lightly. She shot around to see the most adorable bundle of brown fur, with big black eyes, no bigger than an Earth 1 kitten/cat looking at her waiting for her to do something. Treketa panicked and shot away. So did the small creature, then it carefully peered over the grassy type vegetation at her and when it discovered she was not going to hurt it, it slowly came back to her, on all fours. Pausing, it studied her, blinking it's big brown eyes, waiting to see what she would do? Treketa wondered if it was dangerous. Both she and the creature were stalemate both looking at each other. Tayce looked, as did Lance who immediately ran a scan of the creature, on the hand held scanner.

"What do I do, he's just looking at me?" asked Treketa apprehensively.

"Nothing, until I can identify it," said Lance.

"If it had wanted to attack her, I think it would have done it sooner Lance," said Tayce.

"Here goes, don't you attack me," said Treketa slowly putting her hand out towards the little creature.

She was quite prepared to spring back, on her now supportive encased ankle, if she had to, at a minons notice. The little creature remained calm sticking out it's small brown snout to sniff at her, then slowly came towards her hand and began to lick it, as if he or she was washing it in an affectionate way.

"I think he or she likes me," said Treketa softly amused.

"It's known as a Fetig and only known as one sex, Male apparently they are animals that could be trained to be the equivalent of a domesticated cat would you believe?" said Lance reading from his scanner.

"Looks like you've got yourself a pet sis," said Tom laughing, along with the others, as the creature playfully swiped at Treketa again.

"If we get rescued, can I take him with me?" asked Treketa to Tayce hoping so.

"I don't know, you know the Generals rules, no pets on board vessels during transit, as there are too many buttons and things, it could cause havoc, if it landed on anything vital in operation," said Tayce.

"I'll talk to Father, see if we can arrange something to safely transport him, leave it with me," said Lance seeing how happy Treketa was for the first time.

Marc remembered he had put his Porto Compute in his jacket pocket and checked to see if it was still there. He upon finding it was relieved and retrieved it, hoping that it still worked. Activating it, surprisingly it came to life, asking for his enquiry on the screen. He keyed in Treketas pet name and description and the answer came back as the same as Lances. He was glad at least the Porto Compute was working, he continued to key in other information, silently studying it, as there was nothing else to do at the present time. Tayce when she had finished treating Donaldo, closed the Medic Emergency Kit, as everyone was okay for the time being. Marc glanced at her, he could see that she had used some of her power ability to heal Donaldo, so that he could return to being well enough to help further with the others, by the look on her face, she looked drained. He was going to watch her, make sure she didn't get to exhausted, or they would have a repeat of the Astral Exhaustion. Something that he did not want to see. Nightfall on the planet came soon enough. Dusk fell over the landscape. Tayce walked over to Marc, concerned as she did not know what a night on Maldigri would entail.

"I don't know about you, but, I know that Amalthea is a write-off, I think we should set up some kind of on board shelter for the night, there's no telling what comes out here after dark," confided Tayce.

"Oh I agree, this place may seem like paradise by dayon, but as you say, there's no telling what goes on the night-time prowl," he replied glancing around at the exotic plants and blooms.

Upon this, Tayce ordered everyone to gather around. Slowly they all came around her. She began that there present surroundings may seem like paradise by dayon, but nightfall was approaching and as they knew paradise could so easily turn bad and there was no telling what could happen so for their safety they were going back aboard the cruiser, to set up sleeping arrangements of sorts. The team agreed wholeheartedly and understandingly. With this, they started back aboard Amalthea and began trying to find some sort of way to set up sleeping arrangements, for the approaching night ahead.

***

Out in the deep depths of the Universe and growing nearer to Maldigri was a fleet of Rescue Vessels from Questa Headquarters Base. The search rescue beacon Lance had, had the foresight to sent out from Amalthea was picked up by a Universal Patrol Team and relayed to Questa. The fleet flew in unison, ten tow service vessels and a Medical Cruiser, equipped for every known emergency and the Generals personal new High Ranked Cruiser. On board the Generals new cruiser, he was personally briefing his different heads of section. They all sat around the oval shaped meeting table, all had come from the various vessels, that were currently flying with him, to rescue the Amaltheans and tow the Amalthea back to Questa. Each looked experienced in his or her field and dressed for the job they were about to face. Jonathan explained that he wanted a swift and quick rescue in six hourons time.

"Maldigri gentlemen, has a night and dayon rotation sequence, we need to be in position to rescue the Amalthean Quests team first light tomorron, you each know what you have to do to make this a smooth rescue and I want to hear of such at the end of this, I leave you to go to work and do your final preparations that's all gentlemen," said Jonathan standing to his feet and walking from the room.

The heads of sections and vessels for rescuing the Amaltheans stood and ferried on out back to their duty. Adam Carford was present to answer any questions, until everyone was happy and had ferried from the Meeting Chamber. Jonathan once everyone had gone, requested an update on the situation on the surface of Maldigri. Adam went in search of what Jonathan wanted and soon returned, entering the Private Chambers living area. Coming to a pause at the side of the chair Jonathan was sitting in.

"General, latest update from Maldigri, you requested, it would appear that the Amalthean Quests team are preparing to bed down for the night hourons, on what is left of the Amalthea," informed Adam reading the research message.

"All right Adam, keep me informed, you know where I am," said Jonathan standing before the vessel wide sight pane, watching the Universe in thought.

Adam turned and began away back to his desk to, await further updates, so that they could be passed on to the General. He wondered how Tayce and the others were coping on Maldigri. He also knew that she loved Amalthea. It was going to be hard for her to adjust to, the fact that if the cruiser was not salvageable, then it would be the last link with Traun. He turned his thoughts to the rescue in hand and watched his screen for any further updates, from the scanning beacon, they had sent ahead to the planet, to relay back weather patterns as well as the update on what was happening with the team. It was going to be a long night he thought.

Tayce on Maldigri, entered the cruiser just as the last moments of dusk turned to full darkened night. Her thoughts were on Midge of all things, she had made up her mind, she was determined that he should be salvaged, even if the present surroundings were not. She was glad to see that the team had made make shift sleeping arrangements, in the corridor to try and get a good nights sleep. She wondered what Midge would say, seeing her and the team like this and sleeping up side down for the night? Poor Midge, the last thing he recorded was the crashing of the cruiser. She walked to the area where Tom had set up a makeshift mattress for her and him, to bed down on. She sat down on what appeared to be a comfy makeshift bunk. Tom put his arm around her shoulders and drew her to him against the corridor wall. It had been a hard seventeen hourons for all of them, thought Tom, as Tayce rested her head on his warm shoulder. Marc looked across to them especially Tayce, she looked tired he thought, any other woman would have given up, the moment they crashed, but not her she had drawn on the training she went through on Traun for situations like this and she had done well in his estimation. Tayce caught him looking in her direction and smiled a

200

soft tired smile, she was glad she had found him on Questa at the beginning of the team, she thought. Everyone soon settled down for an unexpected nights sleep on the corridor ceiling on what was left of the cruiser, on Maldigri.

Outside what was left of Amalthea, the Maldigrian night was quiet, nothing stirred. But the temperature suddenly plummeted to almost below zero. In the distance the sound of an animal, broke the silence of the air by obviously calling to the mate, in his or her species. It was a creepy far reaching howling hi pitched cry.

Tayce on board the cruiser, was woke by it. She lay half awake and half asleep, ready for anything. Marc was doing the same. Tayce pulled the heat sealant blanket around hers and Tom's shoulders, she felt safe in his strong arms, upon hearing the sudden cry of the animal. Suddenly a noise started and it didn't come from outside. Tayce looked about for Treketas adopted Fetig, it wasn't the creature. It was curled up in the fold of Treketas arm, with it's eyes closed, it's long ears not moving, it hadn't obviously heard the sudden sound, that sounded like a high pitched pip pip. It seemed to be coming from somewhere above them, like Level 1. But how thought Tayce? She looked up at Tom, who was sound asleep, then across to Marc, who was awake. She nudged him with her booted foot. He looked at her questioningly.

"Can you hear that sound from somewhere above us?" she whispered to him.

"Yeah where's it coming from?" he asked listening again.

"I reckon it's Level 1, do you think something is on board, or that Midge is somehow still working?"

"Want to take a look?" suggested Marc having a feeling she did.

"Yes I'd feel a lot more easier knowing what it could be," replied Tayce, sliding out from the protection of Tom's draped arm.

She and Marc soon stood and began stepping around the others, silently until clear, then walked off along the ceiling towards the Level Steps. Marc activated his hand held torch, when they had neared the ceiling up. They began on the walk up to the next level, which at times proved difficult and treacherous. He helped her where necessary taking her hand

In the darkness of Organisation, on the navigational panel, a small red light flashed on and off accompanied by an electronic sound that was playing in continuous succession. It was Lances beacon, signalling their whereabouts. Marc and Tayce stepped over the top of the doorway, on to the deck ceiling, looking about. Marc spotted the small flashing light and drew Tayces attention to it. It looked like someone somewhere was picking up their signal and help was on it's way he thought.

"Looks like our signal is being picked up, nice work Lance," said Marc, hoping it was being picked up by the right kind of help.

"I've a feeling Jonathan is on his way, I don't know how, but I can somehow see his face in my mind," replied Tayce suddenly looking dazed.

"That ability of yours seems to be getting better all the time, at least we've found the source of that sound now I suggest we head back and grab what hourons of sleep there is left," suggested Marc in reply.

"Want to know something else according to what I'm feeling right now, he'll be here first light tomorrow, or thereabouts," said Tayce sounding optimistic, as if for some strange reason she knew.

"Okay, I believe you, now can we go?" he said heading back to the upside down entrance.

"Sure!" replied Tayce heading back to join him.

Marc shook his head, he was wondering just what else she would develop from the strange ability she had inherited. They both left Organisation and slowly made their way back down the corridor towards the Level Steps ceiling, to the lower levels, to rejoin the others, for the rest of the nights sleep. Tayce as they went felt a lot more at ease to know they were going to be rescued, she did not want to stay another dayon on Maldigri, even though it was a paradise type world. Their job was back in the Universe and after a while they would probably go stark raving crazy just doing nothing, except surviving!

First light. The Amalthean Quests team woke to the sound of another dayon in paradise. Tayce walked out of Amalthea into the early mornet sun. She looked skyward for any sign of their rescuers. Nothing but clear hazy sky. After a few minons, she called for the team to gather round, explaining what she and Marc had found out during the night hourons in Organisation. The Team were as glad as Tayce to know that they would be rescued soon. Tayce suggested that until that rescue took place, they all took time to do what they wished.

"Donaldo how are you this mornet, any easier?" asked Tayce in a caring tone.

"After you used your gift on me yesteron, I feel a little easier so I'm ready to take a look at Treketas ankle and the others, see how their doing," he replied in a manner that showed he was pleased she done what she'd did.

Donaldo picked up the Medic Emergency Kit and headed off leaving Tayce to talk with Lance, on his genius idea of releasing a beacon before they were about to crash land on their present surroundings. Tom wondered off also. He decided to do some exploring of the surrounding area. As he passed Duncan, he informed him that he was off for a walk and to let Tayce know, should she wonder where he'd gone. Duncan nodded, then turned back to discussing a plant with Marc that was in full bloom. Tom headed off into a group of trees. It was some time before Tayce realised he disappeared. She glanced all about, then over to Duncan, who caught sight of what she was doing informing her of what Tom had done. She was far from pleased, that he had just taken it into his head to just wonder off and turned on Duncan.

"Why didn't you stop him, I specifically told everyone here when we crashed landed, to try and stay within the area," retorted Tayce with a hint of commanding anger in her voice.

She took out her hand held Slazer and walked off in the direction Duncan had told her Tom had headed off in and went in search of him. She was displeased to say the least, she carried the gun ready to open fire at a moments notice, just in case the planet was hiding any nasty surprises, that were away from where they had crash landed. Marc made a note of her leaving them, he was concerned for her safety and wondered when Tom was going to stop acting like a total idiot, just disappearing. It was totally out of the blue what occurred in the next few cencrons, but it happened fast without warning. The sky over Maldigri rapidly filled with thunderous dark clouds. In minons the normally clear sky was blocked out by clouds and rumbles of thunder like nothing the team had never heard before erupted across the sky, accompanied with spectacular green coloured lightening. They all looked skyward, wondering what was going to happen next. As the clouds drew nearer the thunder shook the ground under their feet. Treketa screamed and grabbed her new furry friend and ran with the others into the shell of Amalthea. Within minons the team minus Tayce and Tom, were back aboard what was left of the cruiser, with the ground shaking beneath them, with the rumbles of thunder and a wind building up outside. Rain hit the outside hull and sounded like they were being pelted by rocks. It was discovered it was hailstones the size of a small hand ball.

Tom out in amongst the sudden change in weather conditions grabbed Tayce, upon finding her and they ran on to what was a derelict stonex grey building, that looked like it once had been used for space colonization. All that remained of the building was the empty shell, though it looked like it was once an elaborate base, along the lines of Questa. Once inside Tayce shook her wet hair, that had been soaked and was resting on her uniform shoulders. Tom studied her, thinking how sexy she looked. But the way he was thinking about her, soon changed, as she through him a look that said she was far from pleased at the way he'd made a sudden departure from the group and wandered off. He looked away and walked away, to look around what was the wide expanse of what was probably the main square of the base. Tayce walked after him, to reprimand him and upon reaching him she reached out and grabbed him roughly by the sleeve of his jacket.

"What the hell did you think you were doing, you could have been killed by one of those lightening strikes out there, just wondering off and got me killed in the bargain coming after you?" she stated angrily.

"Well I didn't and I'm here," he retorted defensively giving her an unemotional look.

"Your lucky then," she said, not letting him off the hook, that she was furious, he had disobeyed orders to remain with the group earlier.

Tom could see she was panicking in the thought of losing him, he quickly reached out grabbing her, bringing her hard up against him with sudden force. Tayce did not want to get romantic, this was not the time, nor the place. She struggled against his restraining hold on her.

"No Tom stop it, it's not the time nor place," she angrily pushed against him looking up at him.

"Why? We're not going anywhere in this storm, I can't think of a better place to get cosy, just the two of us," he said looking down at her, with soft sexual intent on his mind.

"As I said this is not the time, now let go of me," said Tayce pushing hard against him.

This time without realising it she used her powers and he let go of her in a hurry, stepping a couple of spaces back with force. Tayce turned away from him and walked to what would have been a sight pane, that was now a gaping hole. She stood watching the spectacular storm erupting all around their present surroundings. She did not want to look at Tom, he'd made her use her powers on him, something she didn't want to do, but maybe it made him realise, that he had pushed her too far. After a few minons he walked to join her.

"I'm sorry, I had no idea that I had disobeyed your orders, I thought you meant the others considering I'm a senior member of the team, it's just this building caught my eye and I wanted to take a closer look I guess my interest got the better of me".he said coming to a pause behind her.

"What for?" she asked looking up at him.

"In case Amalthea didn't hold together and we'd needed somewhere solid, like this to shelter until help got here," he said calmly studying her.

"Good idea, but you could have told me or Marc, before wondering off, telling Duncan wasn't good enough he's a junior member of the team, but I accept your apology," she said calming down.

They both stood watching the storm reverberating all around them. Tayce realised that Tom had made a good point about finding somewhere else to shelter if Amalthea became unsafe to remain in, until help arrived. Tom didn't give up the notion that he was finding her present appearance somewhat strongly sexy. He slowly slipped his arms around her waist and pulled her back against him enjoying her warmth and softness. This time Tayce gave in to him wanting her and relaxed back against his warm body. As he held her, kissing her neck, so the rain gave way to the sound of approaching vessels, that broke their sudden interest in each other. Tom abruptly stopped making Tayce feel softly relaxed in his arms and looked skyward. She came back to the present as the rain stopped. They both broke apart crossing to the hole in the wall, where they had entered their surroundings. Both stepped out to confirm that they had heard right, that vessels were arriving. Both stood waiting for the first glimpse. To their delight Jonathan Largon's fleet came into full view. In one way Tayce was glad, she wondered if it was a band of freebooters who had found Amalthea on their scanner and had come to salvage her. The storm clouds that had gathered so frighteningly fast, were now ebbing away back to what the paradise weather conditions had been before. A Quest 2 came out of the storm clouds, it flew overhead, turning to come into land in a suitable clearing. Setting down on the sandy type soil about a milon from where they were, Tom grabbed Tayce and they ran to meet the rescue party.

"Not so fast Tom!" said Tayce as she slipped a couple of times.

They made it to the landing site, just as the Rescue Quest, Medical Cruiser and General Jonathan Largon's cruiser touched down. The Amalthean members, back at the clearing slowly began forth on their way to the arriving rescue fleet. The service tow vessels all hovered in the sky above, waiting until everyone was sorted on the surface and Jonathan Largon gave the word to commence their duty, to move in and take care of what was left of Amalthea One and place the tractor support beams around the cruiser, for departure.

On board the Generals cruiser Adam Carford entered the chambers with the much eagerly awaited news from the surface Quest, that the whole of the Amalthean Quests team were present, but some had sustained injuries. Upon this news Jonathan turned announcing it was time to go, he wanted to personally see that both Tayce and his son were all right. Adam nodded, stepping back allowing Jonathan to go first from the private chambers. Adam followed on behind. Jonathan immediately ordered Adam to fetch Lydia Traun as she would want to see her daughter. Adam nodded like an obedient servant and walked away to fetch Lydia from her on board chambers.

"General sir, there is another chance that another storm will be coming in, in the next houron according to weather reports, we have to work fast before that happens," informed Jonathan's chief of on board operations walking to meet him.

"Right then, inform everyone involved on the ground and in the air, that we have to move quickly," ordered Jonathan in his usual voice of command.

"Very well sir, I'll get on to it," said the chief heading away.

Outside in the presently calm sky, the tow Service Fleet soon swung into position, upon getting their orders from the operations chief. A group of men were placed on the outside hull of Amalthea, to properly prepare her for transportation back to Questa. They placed small round devices in various points on the cruiser enabling the support beams to pick up the Amalthea in a supporting almost cradle like way, of pure energy. Once the men had completed their task they were picked up ready to commence the final task of removing the cruiser from the planet surface. The high energy beams of the tow vessels soon locked on to the devices attached to Amalthea once activated. The damaged Amalthea soon began to rise slowly up off the planet surface. The tow vessels working in total unison with each other. Bits and pieces fell from the cruiser through the specially constructed cradle. Tayce stood and watched from afar, shaking her head, she and Amalthea had come through some real dicey action in the last yearons, it was hard to imagine that it had taken a phenomenon to knock her out of the Universe. Suddenly she recognised a voice behind her, it was her

Mother coming towards her. She turned to see her, dressed in a navy Questa Uniform and boots. She came to a pause with a gentle sigh.

"She was quite a cruiser and she will be again, I'm sure," said Lydia putting a motherly arm around Tayce.

"I want Midge saved, If there is to be another cruiser after this one, or this one can be repaired, but I still want him as Guidance and Operations Computer no matter what," said Tayce determined.

"If she can't be saved, I'm quite sure Jonathan will be in total agreement to place Midge aboard a new Amalthea, or restoring him on this one, he will do his utmost and he has a lot of clout as you know," replied Lydia assuringly.

"Tayce, she'll be as good as new, if not I will make sure you get another," said Jonathan coming up behind.

"Tayce was just saying that she wants Midge saved no matter what," said Lydia turning to Jonathan.

"Of course Amalthea would not be the cruiser she is without Midge," said Jonathan in a way trying to cheer Tayce up as she looked sad by what had happened to Amalthea One.

"Thank you Jonathan," replied Tayce continuing to watch Amalthea rise into the sky and beyond.

"From now on young woman, you leave everything to me," said Jonathan.

Amalthea as the three of them watched soon, made it into the sky over Maldigri. Tayce, Lydia and Jonathan stood as she was taken away into the sky and on into orbit, on the slow journey to Questa Construction Port. Jonathan explained that the rescue and the lifting of the cruiser had to be brought forward a lot more quicker than it would have been, because there was another storm front moving in. In the distance it confirmed his words, as the sound of thunder rumbled overhead and the ground slightly shook under foot. He continued that the cruiser would be taken back to the construction port at Questa. There it would be decided what could be done with her, either way, the Amalthean Quests would continue, of that she could be sure of. Tayce nodded in understanding feeling a lot more at ease knowing that she and the team would not be disbanded and it wouldn't be the end of the Amalthean Quest. As another more powerful rumble of thunder shook the ground under foot, Jonathan suggested they get out of their surroundings, time was something that they didn't have, considering the sound of the nearing storm. With this, both Lydia and Tayce followed Jonathan off back across to the clearing that was busy with preparations for the Amaltheans to be taken off the surface. Lydia walked with Jonathan towards the his cruiser and upon noticing Tayce was not with them paused and turned.

"I want to check on my team first, before we leave," she began determined.

"Very well, we'll see you later," said Jonathan continuing on.

"Either way, just get off this planet Tayce, before it's too late, we don't want to return for you again," said Lydia in stern concerned tone.

As Tayce approached the Medical Cruisers entrance, the doctor turned. He was a tall man, but it could be seen he was a man that knew his job well in his field. His features surprisingly enough were not what you would consider the look of a doctor, he was rugged, rough looking even. She could see that this was a man that didn't have a lot of patience. But she guessed he had to be like it, considering he probably was what they called a field doctor, any space emergency and he was there, she guessed, he had probably come up against quite a few gruesome scenes in his career to date. Tayce figured he was in his late 40's, as he looked at her. His brown eyes showed no warmth. As he spoke, he spoke directly to her, no nonsense.

"Colonel Traun your members of team that were injured, will be flown back to Questa Health Complex," he said to the point without even a slight smile.

Tayce nodded in acknowledgement, leaving him to continue on with his duty. Tayce before Jonathan entered the cruiser called out was she ready to go? He paused waiting for her. Then looked skyward as the clouds began to gather. Tayce ran across to him beginning to say what was on her mind as she neared.

"I would appreciate it if you let Marc be in charge of dismantling Midge and help rebuild him, should we need a new cruiser as he was head of the design on Traun, when Midge was designed and constructed," she said hoping that he would agree.

"I think that can be done, I'll talk to whoever will be in charge of the job, when it comes to it," he assured.

"Sir the storm is less than half an houron from here, we have to leave," said the young Questa Rescue Officer concerned coming up to Jonathan.

"Fine, lets leave, we don't want to be here when it arrives, otherwise someone will be rescuing us," said Jonathan ushering Tayce aboard his cruiser, letting the entrance close.

Tom was waiting inside as Tayce entered. He'd been talking with Marc. They had both decided that Tom should go with her, whilst Marc would accompany the injured team members to the Questa Health Complex. Tayce nodded totally in agreement. Marc quickly went about transferring to the other cruiser whilst the Generals cruiser took to the sky, under the expert guidance of his chief pilot.

Once out of Maldigrian Orbit, the Generals cruiser headed off across the Universe, behind the tow vessels and the badly damaged Amalthea One, looking a real sorry state, not the sight she normally looked, graceful. Behind the Generals cruiser travelled the Medical Cruiser, with most of the Amalthean Quests team and Treketas caged new friend, the Fetig, that was in quarantine until it had passed tests, to make sure that it didn't bring any deceases to Questa.

Tayce a while later sat down in the temporary quarters, she and Tom had been assigned. She looked out of the sight pane back at Maldigri in thought, whilst Tom cleansed and changed into a clean uniform. She could see the spectacular lightening effect going off on the surface and was glad that at least they were not back down where they where, having to go through the storm yet again. She thought about how Jonathan had explained that the ruins she and Tom had taken shelter in, were in fact Questaline 6 Headquarters Base. Where the storms had unleashed tremendous terror yearons ago, killing thousands of people and destroying everything in it's path, she and Tom had been lucky, considering the once inhabitants, had met a cruel ending in being burnt or buried alive. It reminded her again of her people, that the same fate of being burnt alive on that fateful night on Traun, but it hadn't been a freak of nature, it had been Vargon and she was still trying to destroy her and her Mother.

Three hourons lapsed. The Generals cruiser glided into the High Ranked Private Area and slowly descended down onto the bay floor. The docking entrance opened. Jonathan was first off, followed by Adam and Lydia. Tayce followed on with Tom. A pair of escorts took Tayce and Tom away to be checked by the Planetary Health Check Team, just as a precaution, in case they had picked up anything off the Maldigrian surface, that couldn't be detected by the Med staff on the cruiser. It was just a formality.

Outside in the Universe and being manoeuvred into position by the tow vessels, was the sorry state of what was left of Amalthea One. Other suited individuals of the construction workforce, soon manoeuvred into position using special power manoeuvring packs, to secure the once graceful cruiser into locked position until it could be decided what was to become of her. Many of the Questa personnel watched from the base. Shaking their heads and talking amongst themselves, wondering what had happened to bring the cruiser home in it's current state. The Amalthean members that had been injured, docked aboard the Medical Cruiser and were immediately transferred to the medical team awaiting on Questa. Marc caught sight of the cruiser in her dusty and dented state, from the Medical Cruisers sight port, he didn't hold out much hope of getting the same cruiser back any time soon, it would take a miracle to restore her to her former glory he thought.

***

Roughly an houron later on Questa the doors to the Medical Health Check Examinations Centre opened and Tayce emerged with a total look of utter disgust on her normally beautiful face, she felt as if she'd been totally purged as there hadn't been a part of her, that hadn't been probed, scanned and miroscanned for any spacial and planetary viruses. She had found the whole experience, one she wouldn't care to endure again at any cost. Tom had been through the same and as he stood up at the outside seating area, he could see that she hadn't bargained for feeling quite so undignified. He'd been through the process before and he had to admit, the first time was always the most intimidating, where they shoved the probes and scanning equipment. He gave her a reassuring smile much to say, it's all over. Duncan walked to join them, he explained that Donaldo would

208

have to remain in the overstay wing for a couple of dayons at least owing to the severity of his internal injuries despite Tayce helping to heal him. On this, Tayce knew what Duncan had meant, but she had only healed him enough to survive, until help arrived. It would have been to draining for her to completely heal him. Treketa and Lance soon came forth meeting with Tayce and the others in the Q'City. Everyone sat around discussing what had happened on Maldigri and what a narrow escape they had all had, considering the shape of Amalthea. After a while, all five of them walked to the chambers to meet up with Jonathan Largon, to find out what was going to happen with the Amalthean Quests future.

The Tristarcan Power Crystal

The decision was made unanimously by the Intergalactic planetary council for Intergalactic matters. The Amalthean Quests should continue. So for the next three monthons Jonathan Largon assigned every available man in the design, construction and electronics field to strip Amalthea One down and rebuild her. The men worked around the clock every dayon and sometimes in shifts, with the promise of a bonus in salary, to get the cruiser ready for the three monthons deadline. Three monthons passed and Amalthea now finished was in stationary position in the construction port, ready to be space bound again in all her white gracefulness.

08:00 flashed up on the 'Q'City large central clock. The dayon had arrived for returning to Amalthea. First to head for Amalthea, was Tayce, accompanied by Tom and Donaldo, who was back to his normal healthy self after breaking four ribs in the crash landing on Maldigri. Donaldo headed straight to the Life Ability Centre the moment he stepped aboard. He wanted to see and make sure that everything was as it should be before they departed. There had been a few changes to team and cruiser. One was Donaldo. Jonathan Largon had upgraded him in rank, he was now known by the official title of Medic Doctor/surgeon, this he felt proud of, it had been a long time coming. He felt that he had now reached the rank he had been trained in at long last and it felt good, he thought, as he walked down the new corridor towards the new Life Ability Centre. Tayce walked on board, still at the rank of Colonel and leader of the team. She was glad also to be back on what she considered, home. Both she and Tom headed straight on up to Organisation Deck. Tom was going to do a final systems check with the Computer Techs from the Reconstruction Electronics Team. Upon arrival Tayce found Marc under Midges new console, checking over the last of the new operations circuitry. Marc was another member of the team to receive a new rank, this was Computer Analysing Technical Officer. This meant that all on board computer functions, were his total responsibility. He had worked closely with the men installing and programming the whole of Amaltheas new

210

computer systems, during the last monthons to familiarise himself with the way they functioned. One new change, that had occurred had been between Tom and Tayce. They had both decided to be legally joined in a coupling ceremony. Tayce was now Tom's wife and her new title was now Colonel Stavard Traun, Jonathan Largon had officiated the Coupling Ceremony, which had been held just on two weekons previously, all the Amalthean Quests team had been present. All the team arrived on board, firstly heading to their new quarters to get unpacked with view to heading on back to duty once more.

***

Two hourons later the Amalthea was ready to depart Questa Construction Port. Midge was back to his full operational self. One casualty that had not made it through the Maldigri crash, was 'Cargo', Tom's robot his damage had been to far gone to retrieve, so Tom had decided to ditch any attempt to restore him because of the cost. Upon Midge scanning around the cruiser to make sure that everyone was present and finding that they were, operated the closing of the Docking Bay doors. Sealing off Questa, that had been home for the past three monthons. The on board Tech teams that had been present for final check, had left to return to their next job, or duty. Lance and Duncan returned to Organisation, heading to their new duty positions. Both were glad to be back on board, both were returning in their regular duty positions, Duncan, Navigationalist and Lance, Quests Research and Information Officer. He had informed his Father, that he was doing the same duty, so he would keep the same title. Tayce was sitting in the new Control seat and watching the many vessels arrive and depart at Questa of all shapes and sizes, waiting for her permission to pull out into the Universal pathway, off on the continuing voyage.

"Midge hows clearance going, while we're waiting, will you do a crew check, I don't want to leave anyone behind," requested Tayce.

"All ready done Tayce, everyone is present and accounted for, it's good to be back where I belong and it's good to know that you pulled through the crash landing too," said Midge.

"I'm glad we were able to save you, if anything happened to this team, I'd be lost without you," replied Tayce glad to have him working and hearing his voice once more.

"I believe congratulations are in order, Colonel Stavard!" said Midge sounding as if he was pleased for his mistress.

"Thank you Midge," replied Tayce thinking about her new status.

Tom next to her in the adjacent seat turned his head and as she glanced in his direction. He winked lovingly at her. Midge cut the air of the moment by announcing that clearance had been granted and it was time to depart. Tayce suggested that he take the cruiser out slowly to begin with. Midge obliged.

The new Amalthea One slowly began going through the disembarkation procedure to manoeuvre them out of the construction port, that she'd been in from the dayon she'd arrived from Maldigri. Questa Headquarters Base began to fall away behind them and the cruiser went into position, to head off out into the dark blue yonder. Everyone involved with the rebuilding of the cruiser, stood watching their work leave with pride. Even Jonathan Largon and Lydia watched proudly, as Amalthea got under way for the continuing of the Amalthean Quests.

No sooner had Amalthea left the headquarters base continuing on voyage when Jonathan Largon reached his desk and contacted Tayce and the team via Satlelink. Tayce had a strong feeling that they were about embark on their first Quest back in space. She gave him her full attention as he appeared on screen before her.

"Hows she handling Tayce?" asked Jonathan enquiringly.

"Better than she did before, a lot more smoother, how can we help?" replied Tayce calmly.

"Just checking in making sure everything is okay..." replied Jonathan.

"Actually sir she handles just like Tayce, smooth and easy to control!" said Tom playfully.

"Tom, sorry Jonathan Tom does get carried away sometimes," said Tayce hitting Tom playfully.

"It's all right you two, I was coupled once you know," replied Jonathan laughing.

"You know I always wondered how I came to be here," quipped Lance from behind, at his duty position.

"Enough you two, we're ready for our next Quest," said Tayce laughing about banter between Father and son.

"Your Mother wants a word, I'll leave you two to talk and will be in touch shortly.

Jonathan moved away from the screen to allow Lydia and Tayce to talk for a while for the time being. Lydia wished Tayce luck, suggesting that they stay in touch, when she had a moment. Tayce agreed, then signed off. Amalthea headed on into the Universe, waiting for the first signs of trouble, or a rescue to cross it's path.

For the next dayon or so, Amalthea just headed back into deep space and explored the new area of space they'd ventured into. After what happened the last time, when they ventured into a new space territory Midge kept a close scan, as they progressed on, any sign of what had happened before and this time around he had more than enough new weaponry to put the phenomenon into oblivion, where it would belong, if it was considered a threat with the new modifications done to the cruiser. The team on board were able to check out a lot of the new equipment that had been brought up to date. From the outside the cruiser looked graceful once more, as she travelled at a slow speed onwards, it was hard to imagine that three monthons ago Amalthea looked more like a crushed, dented and ambushed pile of scrap.

It was mornet of the third dayon. Marc was sipping his first cup of Coffeen of the dayon, on Organisation Deck, watching the unchanged area of space through the main sight port, as Tayce and the other members of the team present expressed their concerns and shared general discussion on different matters, past and present. Tayce had stipulated that as there was a Meeting Centre on board still then every dayon they would come together first thing in duty time, to air any problems or what was on everyone's mind. Without warning the on board alarm sounded, stopping the discussion abruptly. The alarm signified that there was a vessel in distress in the near vicinity. Tayce ran out of the Meeting Centre coming to a pause before her chair.

"Midge scan the vessel and give me what information you can please," she ordered.

"It would appear that the vessel has lost all engine and operational power," replied Midge informatively.

"Put up a scan view, let's have a look," suggested Tayce wanting to know more.

The main sight port soon revealed a sleek looking arrow shaped Space Launch, in sapphire blue. Big enough to withhold a small crew. By the appearance of the Launch, it could be seen, it was in no ordinary class, but one of extreme high ranking. Midge informed Tayce that it had originated from somewhere in the present sector and it hadn't been in space to long. Marc next to Tayce, studied the drifting sight on screen, in a scrutinising way and ordered Midge to do a further magnification. The view moved a step closer and froze. The Launch was from whom Marc had suspected.

"What's she doing out here, this is not right, it's from the twin world of Traun, Tristarcas, it's generally flown by the supreme chief of Tristarcas, Empress Tricara," informed Marc revealingly.

"Surely she should be flying with an escort," said Tom joining Marc in curiousness.

"Quite! Something is badly wrong she hardly ever leaves Tristarcas, unless it's an emergency," said Marc agreeing.

"She's escaped from a terrifying ordeal," replied Tayce suddenly, her eyes glazed as if someone or something had told her as much.

"Right!" said Marc glancing to her, seeing she was obviously under another of her powerful influences.

"Bring it in on extreme power tractor beam, Donaldo you and Treketa go and get ready for an emergency, I'll meet you down at the Hanger Bay," ordered Tayce seriously.

No more needed to be said, both Donaldo and Treketa walked briskly from the Organisation Deck heading on down to Level 2, to carry out Tayces orders. Lance began to key in various commands to find out just what the Empresses on board computer had on why she had left the Tristarcan world alone, something she rarely did without some kind of close escort. Tayce was about to order Tom and Marc to head off down to the Flight Hanger Bay, when she was cut off by Lance, suddenly announcing over her shoulder in utter alarm that the Tristarcan Launch was suddenly becoming vary unstable, in the grip of their tractor beam, they had to do something and fast or the craft would implode and Empress Tricara would go with it. Upon these words Tayce went into action.

"Get her out of there using the new Transpot, now Midge, hurry!" said Tayce in alarm.

"Come on Tayce, we'll head down to the Transpot Centre, tell Donaldo what's happened Tom," said Marc heading on out the entrance, Tayce following on in hot pursuit.

"Sure!" replied Tom.

Both Marc and Tayce ran as fast as their legs would take them, they knew the urgency of the moment there was no telling what condition the Empress would be in, considering her vessel had been found drifting. They soon stepped on to Level 4 and ran along to the Transpot Centre. Upon reaching the doorway, as soon as the red overhead sensor, picked up their presence the doors parted. Inside on the Transpot area was Empress Tricara in an unconscious state, laying on the floor dishevelled, scorched and bloodied. A far cry from what she generally looked like. Both Marc and Tayce glanced at each other, in questioning wonder of what had been going on, on Tristarcus, or who had attacked the Empress so viciously. Before Marc and Tayce had a chance to enter the Transpot Centre, Donaldo and Treketa came rushing in. Donaldo manoeuvred the Hover Trolley into position, whilst Treketa set down the Medic Emergency Kit, readying it for Donaldo.

"She's beautiful, but how come she looks like this, it looks like she's been in a fight or something?" asked Treketa to Tayce.

"I've no idea, but I think something has gone wrong on Tristarcus," said Tayce, studying her family friend.

Donaldo began to get the Empress ready for transferring back to the Life Ability Centre. She was a vary graceful and beautiful looking woman. She had long straight brown thick shiny hair, that cascaded down to her waist. Her features were as pure as snow and her make-up just rightly applied to make her true beauty shine through conveying who she was. She was of slender build, but not as to be classed as skinny, she was an Empress by breed and an Empress by rank and name. Tricara was thirty-eight yearons old in her appearance, but it was wondered whether this was her true age, no one ever knew otherwise and she never divulged. She had held head supremacy of her world for the past twenty or so yearons and there was always a certain mystery, which surrounded the true creation of the twin world of Traun and Tricara's true age. Tricara was a very powerful woman, other than just being the supreme person in charge of her planet, she withheld a very powerful blue coloured crystal, known as the Tristarcan Power Crystal, which withheld great immense energy, that if it fell into the wrong hands, would cause untold devastation, throughout the galaxy. Both Marc and Donaldo gently lifted the unconscious Empress in her white chiffonex lined gown, onto the Hover Trolley. Tayce looked on. She wanted answers. Donaldo quickly rushed Tricara off to the Life Ability Centre, with Treketa in tow, carrying the Medic Emergency kit.

"This is not right, I want some answers, she would not be out here in this part of the Universe and in this terrible state without some desperate reason, considering she had no royal escort, it's not like her to travel without one," pointed out Tayce knowing there had to be more to why the Empress was out where she was, alone and it didn't look good.

"So what are you thinking?" asked Marc wondering.

"I know what I'm thinking, our worlds were joined in many planetary matters…," began Tayce.

"Don't tell me you think that Countess Vargon is somehow connected to this, come on Tayce, she can't be everywhere," said Marc.

"Well the Empress did try and help stop her from taking Traun, by giving us her men and forces to halt the attack on our world, if you remember the Empress was threatened by Vargon, perhaps the Countess has gone back to finish what she started, casting Tricara out into the Universe, like she did me you know what Vargons like," said Tayce seriously.

"Yes but, she has magnificent powers and her men were a slight cut above ours, remember, if you ask me, I think she would have quite swiftly done away with the Countess if it was her, if it meant protecting her people," replied Marc thinking over what Tayce was thinking.

"I think we need to hear her side of the story, when she gains consciousness," said Tayce.

"I agree," replied Marc, as they both turned and walked from the Transpot Centre.

As Tayce and Marc began on the walk to the Life Ability Centre, so she began thinking back to past times and the fact that a lot happened back on the last dayons of Trauns existence, when both Tristarcas and Traun were in joint entente treaty with each other. It was a good joint union, as she recalled, they used to exchange materials with each other, they both worked together in lots of joint ventures. People and technologies were the main source. She remembered how the relationship between Empress Tricara and her parents was very strong, in fact her Mother had told her, that Tricara had been present when she was born and had declared that one dayon she would discover, if the generations were as they should be, she would be gifted. She had been right about that. Tayce suddenly recalled to mind how Empress Tricara had treated her like the daughter she could never have as through a freak accident when she was in her teens, she was not able to have children of her own. Marc noticed that she was quiet in thought and didn't say anything. He figured if she wanted to share her thoughts she would.

Up in Organisation Lance and Duncan were in deep discussion over the sudden and unexpected arrival of the Empress. Duncan was finding Lances explanation over the origin of Empress Tricara and Tristarcus quite extraordinary. Lance like Tayce had wondered if the Countess had anything to do with the sudden departure Tricara had made from the Tristarcan realm? He put it to Duncan.

"You've a good point, but the last report we looked into about the Countesses whereabouts, was, she was on Carafax 7, wherever that is," said Duncan.

"Okay, so if Tristarcus was under attack, and it's not who we suspect, it has to be someone who has a lot of clout to match Vargons capabilities and has it in for the Empress, don't you agree?" asked Lance.

"Oh I agree, but who, that's the big question?" replied Duncan.

"Yeah, your right," said Lance thinking on who it might be.

Both went back to their duty not bothering to think about the fact any longer, or at least Duncan didn't, Lance found that it was on his mind and decided to do a bit of off the cuff research into what was going on with Tristarcus, he knew Tayce would be glad he did, should it be needed and he could find anything out.

Marc and Tayce soon entered the Life Ability Centre to find Donaldo running checks with the assistance of Treketa. They stood out of the way, whilst Tricara was brought back to normal health and consciousness, under Donaldo's expert guidance. Marc studied Tricara. Secretly deep down, he had always liked Tricara, he had always felt a certain deep respect for her and wished somehow she would have seen him more than Just Darius Trauns aide. Tricara began to come round. Donaldo turned beckoning to Tayce and Marc. Tayce crossed with Marc not far behind. Upon Tricara looking at Tayce, she could immediately tell that she was gifted and her words had come true, what she had foretold all those yearons ago, when Tayce was born.

"Your gifted, my prophecy came true," announced Tricara softly before saying anything else.

"Yes!" replied Tayce somewhat stunned that Tricara should know and say as the first words to her.

"Marc, still as dashingly handsome as I last remember seeing you," said Tricara.

"Empress, it's good to see you again, after all these yearons," replied Marc in a somewhat reserved way.

"Tell me, is this Amalthea the same cruiser, you had when you left Traun?"

"By name, but this is a newer cruiser, she was rebuilt after a crash on a planet recently," replied Tayce.

"It's good to know that you were the one's to rescue me, my worst fear was to be picked up by corsairs if you know what I mean, thank you!" she said in a thankful tone sounding weak.

"Well your safe now, all you need to do for a while is rest," said Donaldo in his true doctors tone of authority.

"I have some questions, but they can wait till your rested," said Tayce.

Tayce walked away leaving Treketa to move in and make the Empress more comfortable. Treketa figured that she was going to treat the Empress like royalty, as in her books, that's just what she was the equivalent too. Donaldo crossed to Tayce discretely calling her to stop, just before she was about to leave. Discretely he began that the Empress would be fine in a couple of hourons. Tayce nodded understandingly. He further assured her that all the Empress needed was a little time to get over what had happened. The doors drew apart in front of Marc and herself and they left Donaldo to take care of the Empress, walking on out on up the corridor to Organisation. Marc like Tayce was thinking over the reasons of why the Empress was so far from home. On route to Organisation Tayce raised her Wristlink and pressed the Commun button. Midge answered, she requested Lance. He quickly transferred her to him.

Lance was in the new on board Computer Study Centre when Midge informed him that Tayce wanted a word. He left what he was studying and ran out of the Centre back into Organisation, to find out what she wanted. He took up his regular duty position and asked Tayce what was the request.

"Where were you?" asked Tayce curious over the commun channel.

"Computer Study Centre, doing some in depth research that I couldn't do at my position, what can I do for you?" he replied casually.

"I need you to find out more on what has made Empress Tricara leave her home world, only I feel she's not prepared to divulge the real reason why she was out here alone," said Tayce discretely.

"Actually that's just what I'm trying to do, I knew that you would want to know why, so I'll go back and continue to find out, I'll let you know when I come up with something, are you on the way back up here?" he asked curiously.

"Yes, I want to talk to your Father, inform him of what's materialised, see you soon?" said Tayce ceasing communications.

Lance left his duty position once more and briskly headed back into the Computer Study Centre to continue researching about Tristarcus and the present situation. He had a feeling that this research was going to be for the first Quest back in space, in their new surroundings.

Both Tayce and Marc ran up the last steps and walked along the corridor back into Organisation. The moment Tayce entered the deck she requested communication with Questa and Jonathan Largon, she wanted to inform him of what had unfolded with the Empress, to see if he knew what had been happening. Lance a while later came back into Organisation in a hurry and went straight to his console, keying the combination to transfer the information he had found, to his duty position. He waited for it to arrive. Upon Tayce finishing the call with his Father he called her over to his screen, beginning to explain he had managed to hack into Tristarcus computer systems and found the real reason for theEmpresses departure from her home world. Both Tayce and Marc came to a pause at Lances side waiting. He keyed in a sequence that after a few minons brought up the information after transfer. Tayce after reading the first frame of the displayed information couldn't believe the image that was staring her in the face. She ordered Lance to magnify it, put clarity on it. Slowly the image became clearer and more dominant, on screen, it made her angry.

"Deltaline fighters, what the hell are they doing near Tristarcus?" said Marc before Tayce could say a word.

"Looks like we've found a flaw in Commodore Addams after all, he had better have a good explanation behind this as I recall what they are doing, is termed invasion of a no fly zone around the home world, Midge get Deltaline 4 on satellink, I want to speak to that obnoxious Commodore, now!" requested Tayce angrily.

"Deans Father is somewhat of a dark horse, as they use to say in old Earth times," said Marc to Lance.

"Yeah, but what Tayce said is true, Tristarcus has a milon radius around the planet that is a no fly zone, unless permission is granted by high command, their fighters are either breaking the law, or up to something that could have caused the Empress to suddenly depart her home world," confided Lance.

Tayce had no sooner sat back in her seat, when Midge announced that the Commodore from Deltaline 4 was on Satlelink waiting to talk to her. Tayce sat ready to address him, giving a far from amused look. He was a man she didn't care for much, considering how he had treated Dean when he was alive and how rude he was to her the last time they had spoken over Dean.

"Colonel Traun I hope this communication with you is important, I have an emergency meeting to attend to and I do not want to be late, pleasantries are at this time unnecessary," he began in his usual obnoxious way.

"This won't take long Commodore, what were your fighters doing in what is classed as a restricted fly zone around Tristarcus?" asked Tayce, getting straight to the point, without any politeness in her tone.

"Oh dear, Colonel what can I say… It all happened about less than a monthon ago, fifteen of our newly delivered Deltonian Fighters were stolen in transit, we did all we could to trace them, but whoever stole them covered their tracks, we came to the conclusion that a band of freebooters had staged the whole thing, If something bad has happened I would like to offer my sincere apologies right here and now and you must let us know if there is anything that we can do to make amends to those effected by this incident," said the Commodore much to Tayce's surprise in a much more pleasant tone.

"That is not for me to decide, however, whoever has these fighters used them to attack the planet Tristarcus and cause Empress Tricara to flee without any warning and any escort, lucky for her, we picked up her space Launch otherwise she wouldn't be here to tell what happened," replied Tayce informatively.

The Commodores face gave a look of utter surprise and shock, at what Tayce had just told him. This Tayce considered had to be the first time ever. He was glad in one way that the fighters however were still in space even if they were in the wrong hands of another race. He expressed his apologies once more to the Empress and assured Tayce that the meeting that he had to leave for, was one where they could look at retrieving the fighters and now look at ways in which to help the Empress. A wrong had to be put right. He suggested that any further updates on the whereabouts of the fighters would be very welcome. Tayce agreed, that if the fighters were discovered again, she would inform him where they could be found and what race to go after. He nodded and for the first time ever managed a slight thankful smile. He informed further that the moment she discovered who had the fighters, then he would have a team standing by, to fly out and take them out of the lawbreakers hands. Communications ceased and the screen went blank.

"Midge where's Tom right now, he should be here on duty?" said Tayce.

"I let him go for his duty refreshment break," replied Midge informatively.

"Have him meet me down in the Life Ability Centre, it's time for questions, that need answering."

"Yes Tayce, requesting him now," replied Midge.

Tayce left the control seat and began across the deck heading on out, leaving Marc in charge. Things had taken a drastic turn, in finding why the Empress was in the state she was in, milons from her home world. Deltaline 4 had now become involved. Just what was going on thought Tayce as she headed on down to meet up with Tom.

***

Treketa Stavard in the Life Ability Centre (L.A.C.) was standing by Tricara's bunk, unaware that Tayce was on her way down. She was running constant health checks on the Empresses progress, back to normal. As requested by Donaldo. He took the information and keyed in the progress to the Porto Compute as Treketa relayed it to him. He was finding the rapid speed at which the Empress was healing somewhat amazing to say the least. He had a feeling that Tayce would evolve to be as great in powers as her one dayon. He crossed and explained about how Tayce had suddenly developed her ability and listened to what Tricara had to say. Both Treketa and himself found the whole explanation far fetching, but believable. Tricara explained that she herself was linked to the realm of great power and energy and served under a greater being, who resided in a place called Hyperspace on a Empire world that was greater than her home world, of Tristarcus. He ruled over Tristarcus from this place and once he learned of Tayce and her abilities, he would visit her in a time to come, or send one of his people to work with her, to train her in the use of her gift, to a greater good. She and Tayce shared some of the same powers, in the fact she could heal herself and others if need be, but above all else, there was no need to be afraid of the power that Tayce possessed. It would do her no harm or the team around her. This Donaldo was glad to hear. He thanked her for her understanding, exclaiming that at least he knew Tayce would be all right. She smiled gently. The doors to the L.A.C. opened. Tayce briskly walked in with Tom at her side, who had waited for her outside. They both crossed to Tricara.

"Tayce, Dr Tysonne has been sharing with me his concerns for your welfare over your newly gained powers and I have assured him, as I am about to you, there is no danger to yourself, in time you will get use to this new gift, it's strange I know at the moment to adjust, but in time you will use them like anything else in your normal life, you won't even notice that your different," began Tricara assuringly.

"Thank you for telling me, I've contacted General Largon at Questa, he informs me that we are to take on the reason behind your attack and sudden departure from Tristarcus and try and help, we're to treat it as our next Quest, he's also looking forward to seeing you when you reach Questa," replied Tayce seriously.

"I fear it may be to late for Tristarcus Tayce, but thank you all the same," said Tricara softly.

"Tom this is Empress Tricara, of our sister home world Traun, Tristarcus, Empress this my new husband Tom Stavard," said Tayce introducing Tom proudly.

"Your highness, it's an honour to meet you," said Tom politely, nervous of her.

"Relax Tom, I'm no different to anyone else, only my title, tell me what's your rank?" asked Tricara plainly and softly, she didn't like to think Tayce had legally joined beneath her standing.

"I've just become Lieutenant, your highness," replied Tom again politely, but a little more relaxed.

"If your up to it now, I have questions that need answers, we've discovered that Tristarcus was attacked by stolen fighters, that were the proposed property of Deltaline 4, they apparently were stolen whilst being delivered to Deltaline 4, Commodore Addams wants to help you in anyway he can, for what's happened, I need to know from you, if you have any idea who was firing on Tristarcus using those fighters to investigate this further," said Tayce calmly, but hoping that the Empress could answer the question.

Tricara could see that Tayce hadn't changed in her eagerness to take something on and sought it, so began by asking, did she remember the blue Power Crystal of Tristarcus, that was once in her chambers for all to see? Tayce nodded wholeheartedly, giving Tricara her full attention. She urged the Empress to continue, so she did by explaining that there was an evil being more ruthless than any known lawbreaker in the Universe. His name was Norgan. He was greedy beyond all recognition and if the crystal had fallen into his hands, there was no telling what use he would put it to. Tayce knew what the crystal meant to the people of Tristarcus. It was part of their every dayon existence, because of the properties it withheld in it's immense power. She also knew that if it had been stolen by this being Norgan, during the attack, he probably was going to use it for no good purposes and not for which it was suppose to be used for. To protect the people of Tristarcus. This Norgan seemed to be along the same lines of Lord Dion of the Boglayon Pirates thought Tayce. It was her estimation that Norgan had lead the attack on Tristarcus, using the Deltaline 4 Fighters as an elaborate cover and it had obviously worked, considering the fact the Empress was where she was. This didn't look good and it made her angry beyond words.

"What happened to your people?" asked Tom curious over Tayces shoulder.

"Norgan attacked in a minons notice, we had no time to save ourselves, my people were struck down in their every dayon activities, with no time to retaliate, we were caught totally unprepared," replied Tricara a tear forming in her eyes, as she thought of her people perishing.

"I'm sorry to put you threw this," said Tayce putting a friendly arm around her friend, who was finding it hard to fight back the tears.

"There's one thing you need to know now your gifted, in that one dayon you will inherit this blue Power Crystal, you must try and recover it at all odds, to regain it's power of good," said Tricara sincerely.

"Don't worry Norgan has just carried out his last unprovoked attack, we'll find him and get the Power Crystal back where it belongs, this I promise you," said Tayce in a determined way.

Tayce knew that now she was going to be handed down the blue Power Crystal, it was up to her to find this notorious criminal, Norgan, and get back what will rightfully belong to her one dayon. It was time to get the Quest under way, she softly advised Tricara to rest then ordered Tom to follow. Both headed back to the main entrance. Upon the doors opening before them, they continued on out into the corridor. Once outside Tom informed Tayce he could see the seriousness of the matter in hand, anything she decided to do, then he would willingly back her up. Together they briskly headed back to Organisation Deck, to put into place the journey to Tristarcus and the hoped recovery of the Power Crystal. Tayce was hoping to catch Norgan in the act, if he was still on the surface.

It was roughly an houron later Tayce was in Organisation at the main controls working with Lance in having constant updates on what was unfolding on Tristarcus, on the long range scanning device, that could scan into the next Universe and beyond. By keying in the planets, or destination of the desired scan. Tom was beside her, as updates were fed through from the research console. The cruiser picked up speed and headed at a much quicker rate across the milons to Tristarcus. Upon receiving the latest update. Tayce occasionally looked out the sight port, for the first sign of trouble, as Lance had said Norgan was still very much on the planet surface, much to their gladness.

"Arrival time to Tristarcus Midge?" demanded Tayce.

"Two hourons and fifty six cencrons, to be exact are we going in to land may I ask, or are we remaining in orbit?" asked Midge.

"We'll put up protection shields and go into a stationary orbit, I don't trust Norgan, if we land and he's in full swing of taking over Tristarcus, as well as the Crystal, we'd be setting down in a battle zone," replied Tayce.

"Did you just say Norgan?" said Lance suddenly from his console over Tayces shoulder.

"Yes why?" asked Tayce curious.

"You must remember him Tayce, he was around when you and I were teenage buddies, he must be really old I would have thought by now, he was in his middle age back then," said Lance recalling the fact and thinking about it shaking his head to know the notorious Norgan was still around.

"Well he's back, unless he has a son and he's carrying on the evil lawbreaking ways of his Father, apparently he's either stolen the blue Power Crystal by now, or is still searching for it," replied Tayce thinking about what Lance was driving at, in the fact of Norgan, if it was the original one he, would be very old, something didn't add up.

"If you remember, if it is the original Norgan and he's obviously found some way to preserve his yearons, he never was any good, I figured he'd pulled his last stint yearons ago and got his comeuppence, when he got involved with that deadly bunch back in 2411, as we never saw him again after that time, I for one had thought he was dead," said Lance thinking about the no good law piece of work.

"He sounds a bad lot from what your both saying," spoke up Duncan, interested.

"You bet he is or was, he's in the same class as Lord Dion and Vargon," said Lance disgusted.

Duncan raised his eyes in surprise. Marc walked on deck. He'd brought with him much to everyone's surprise Empress Tricara. Tayce decided to put him in charge of looking after her whilst she was on board. This he obligingly accepted. He guided her to a nearby seat, after she had acquainted herself with Duncan and Lance. She sat silently and poised as if she was sitting on the throne of Tristarcus, which she normally did, but she was an active Empress, not one that ruled from the throne all dayon she liked to meet her people and help in anyway she could, she wouldn't have it any other way. Midge announced that they would be arriving in orbit of Tristarcus in roughly over two hourons at their current Hyper Thrust Turbo speed. Suddenly the Empresses face took on a saddened expression, at the thought of seeing her home world. Tayce felt her sadness, she glanced over her shoulder and assured her, that everything would work out well, she'd see.

Tristarcus came into view just on the two hourons later. The view to everyone's surprise was one of almost total destruction, flames, smoke and scorched debris was all that could be seen from the cruiser. Flames were leaping high into the Tristarcan orange sky. The once beautiful buildings that were truly something in architectural splendour that had been admired for many yearons, were in total ruin. Tayce shook her head at the shocking sight, suddenly it sent her back to the night of Trauns destruction once more.

"My God!" said Lance, he was almost speechless, at the sight of devastation.

"My beautiful world, my people… all gone, no…," said Tricara devastated, so much so, she had to be comforted by Marc.

"Midge put us in a stationary orbit, there maybe some slim chance that Norgan will be on the surface and we can reclaim the Crystal, before he escapes with it," ordered Tayce in straightforward tone, as she watched the surface of total chaos below.

"Atmosphere on the planet surface would you believe, is still breathable, but it would be advisable to take portable breathing containers, because of the smoke and poisonous gasses that are now slowly releasing into the atmosphere," said Lance checking out their status to head down to the planet surface.

"Right! Tom, you and Marc come with me to the surface, Lance your in overall charge, whilst we're down on Tristarcus, if you find a vessel leaving the surface in the form of a Deltaline 4 Fighter, destroy it, let's just hope we're not to late to retrieve the Power Crystal, before Norgan escapes to cause untold turmoil with it," said Tayce leaving her seat, looking down at Tricara understanding her pain and sorrow.

"Don't worry anything with a Deltaline 4 label won't get far, if we pick it up," promised Lance.

"Let's go," said Tayce heading over to the entrance.

Marc and Tom followed on in urgency, leaving the Empress in the hands of Lance. He gave her a reassuring smile and informed her, that if anyone could put a stop to Norgan, it was Tayce. Duncan fetched her a drink of Plicetar, as she looked shocked at what she had just witnessed, upon seeing her home world in the throws of total annihilation. Both men were determined to look after Tricara, as she was one special on board guest.

"Stationary orbit has been obtained," declared Midge.

"Activate the protection shields Midge, maximum status and keep your scanner on alert for any signs of departing Deltaline Fighters," ordered Lance.

"Activating protection shields now," confirmed Midge.

Duncan soon returned with the Plicetar carefully handing it to Tricara. He then sat down back at navigations talking with her about Tristarcus, listening to the many things, that happened there, especially its once link to Traun and what

Traun was like. Tricara found that after a while, she was becoming much more relaxed. Duncan got the impression this Empress was a truly special person, easy to get along with and understand, not the usual stuck up kind of spacial royalty, that he had encountered in his past.

Down in the Hanger Bay Tayce, Marc and Tom walked briskly to the Quest, carrying the portable breathing containers for the surface and loaded handguns, ready to find Norgan. Marc boarded the Quest taking Tayces hand, he helped her up inside. Tom followed on and the entrance sealed behind him, once aboard. The hatch soon closed and the Quest began going into procedure to leave the Hanger Bay floor and head off in to orbit of Tristarcus. The engines started with a powerful sound, then climbed to a crescendo, which stated that they were at full power. The Hanger Bay doors drew apart before the Quest, revealing the darkness of space and the sight of a burning in battle Tristarcus. Over the Aircom, as Tom lifted the small new Quest Shuttle/fighter off the bay floor and headed out into space, Lance announced that in the last houron scan had returned that Norgan and his men were very much still causing utter chaos on the surface below them.

"I want to be on that planet now Tom, hurry! Before Norgan gets the chance to depart," ordered Tayce.

Once clear, the Quest under Tom's expert control headed for the Tristarcan surface, at incredible speed. The protection shield around Amalthea deactivated for the passing through of the Shuttle/fighter, then activated again at full power. As the Quest headed down so it's protective shield of blue aura, activated, protecting the team members on board.

***

Back on Amalthea the Empress in Organisation decided she wanted to speak with General Jonathan Largon so Lance set it up for her in the privacy of the Meeting Centre. She soon stood and sauntered on in to the Centre in an elegant regal way. No sooner had she sat on one of the chairs, Lance called out to her that his Father's Officette was waiting online. Without warning the wall sight screen activated at the same time the clear vision doors to the Meeting Centre closed and Lydia came on screen. Both women were surprised yet overjoyed to see the other, was alive. Lydia couldn't believe that she was seeing her long lost friend and confidante, it had been almost three yearons since they had spoken and not by choice. It had been a situation beyond their control. Tricara expressed that she was not being rude, but she wanted to talk to Jonathan. Lydia agreed leaving the screen area, letting Jonathan come into view, showing surprise and delight at seeing that she was at least safe, as he'd heard what had been unfolding on Tristarcus, in the last five hourons.

"Jonathan it's bad, it's as simple as that, apparently its a criminal by the name of Norgan he's trying to take control of the blue crystal, you know of him, of old,

Tayce Marc and Tom have gone to the planet surface to try and stop him, though I am concerned for their safety, I have to admit," expressed Tricara.

"Tayce is a good leader and she knows what she's doing and knows who to take on Quests, I believe for one minon that she'll recover the crystal, if she can," assured Jonathan in a reassuring way.

"As soon as Tayce and the others return to the cruiser and have managed to recover the Tristarcan Crystal I intend to be at Questa in a weekon," replied Tricara.

"I look forward to your arrival, I'll have a place prepared for you to reside," promised Jonathan sincerely.

"Thank you, Jonathan, there is just one thing before I go, Tayce should have a much higher rank than she currently holds of Colonel, as part of the Planetary Matters Council, I would like this put forth for discussion as soon as possible," said Tricara with the sound of powerful command in her voice.

"As you wish, as a member of the Planetary Matters Council you have a certain power of casting such a request, though I must admit, it's about time that young woman changed her rank, she's held it since leaving Traun and believes me, she deserves a change, better go, duty calls, see you soon," said Jonathan signing off.

The screen went blank and Tricara walked back out into Organisation Centre. Tricara felt stronger for talking to Jonathan. She didn't for some strange reason feel quite so isolated. Tayce and the team had made her feel welcome, they couldn't have done more since her rescue, but it was nice to talk to long lost friends such as Lydia and Jonathan that understood where she was coming from in her responsibility to her people. Lance smiled as she walked out through the opening doors of the Meeting Centre, he hadn't meant to eavesdrop, but he had heard via Midge about Tayces possible rank advancement. He told her that he would keep it quiet until it happened. Tricara smiled.

***

On the surface of Tristarcus Tom brought the Quest down in shaded area, away from the turmoil. All three climbed out with their guns poised ready to open fire on any of Norgans men, that had seen them come in to land. It was an horrific scene of rubble glassene and scorched dead bodies of men women and children. It was everywhere, so much so it almost made Tayce want to heave. She gasped as she came across a young woman dead, scorched with a burnt infant in her arms. There was a look of terror on her once beautiful face. Tayce had to look away but there was just no getting away from the fact the people of Tristarcus hadn't stood a chance. Tricara had been right thought Tayce, she had always been allowed to call her merely by her name instead of who she was in rank, because of the friendship with her parents. The Tristarcans were caught totally unaware of what was about to hit them. Bodies were strewn this way and that, some unrecognisable, guards even of the palatial palace, lay blood stained, limbs missing, in many places. The smell was becoming somewhat nauseating. They all had to swallow hard. Marc glanced around at the once classy buildings, that formed a clean modern world, to be proud of he shook his head as many of those buildings were smashed to smithereens beyond any recognition of what they once stood for. There was no saving this planet, he thought, it was a second Traun all over again. Tayce one hand on her gun, poised looked about through the chaos for some sight of somewhere they could get under cover, enough to judge for themselves where to go from in the search of Norgan.

"Can't see anything in this smoke, not even Norgan," said Marc taking in a breath of the air from the portable breathing container, rather like an aerosol can, with built in mask.

Luckily they made it to a sheltered area. It had been horrendous getting to their current destination, but they had made it. Tom looked at Tayce, as she changed the setting on her gun to disintegrate, somehow he had a feeling that what she had witnessed in the people laying around scorched and dead, had hit close to home and she was not prepared to show any mercy towards this Norgan character. Marc watching the area around them, suddenly caught sight of a darkly clad figure and opened fired. A long burst of Slazer fire flew from Marc's gun. But it was the wrong move on his part, as no sooner had the firing started, so all three of them were engrossed in a total onslaught of pinned down retaliating weapon fire. All three sheltered behind the various pillars, firing back. Norgans troupers were everywhere, it was like they were crawling out of the ruins and firing as they came, but there was no sign of the man himself.

"Well that shot certainly got their attention, well done Marc," said Tom firing back as weapon fire showered all around them.

"I thought he was one alone, sorry!" replied Marc, above the weapon fire.

"No sign of Norgan, where do you suppose the crystal is, do you think he's got it and gone?" asked Tayce.

"Well if he hasn't, it's generally kept in the Palace, Tricara's home," replied Marc.

Tayce had had enough, this was getting them nowhere, these men belonging to Norgan were just as good as herself, Tom and Marc. She raised her Wristlink and contacted Midge. She ordered him to pin point the Palace as all the buildings were partly destroyed and alike. Within a few cencrons Midge came back and explained that the building that was to the left of their current status, about two buildings forward, was what remained of the Palace. Tayce acknowledged signing off. All three of them proceeded cautiously keeping out of shot of Norgans advancing men, which wasn't easy. The ground was awkward under foot from all the broken rubble and various concretex type rocks, that had been smashed to the ground along with glassene and stealex. Upon reaching what was left of the Palace, they all lined up close to the wall and slowly manoeuvred round into the entrance, Slazers poised ready to shoot. Tayce soon entered what was left of the

Grand Hall. It had turned into a far cry from it's original splendour. Gone was the white gleaming pillars and gold drapes. It was a total sight of a half burnt out shell. Tayce shook her head. Rubble crunched under foot as they walked fully into the Hall.

"My God, he certainly didn't mess around, when it came to destroying this room," said Marc glancing around almost speechless at what he was seeing

"Where is the crystal generally kept?" asked Tom, lighting his hand held torch, as it was becoming difficult to see as the planetary twilight was setting in.

"It should be over there, through the archway, there's a small door," said Tayce pointing to an archway on the far side of the hall.

"Looking for this little lady by any chance?" said a voice, Tayce recognised behind her.

"Norgan!" said Tayce spinning round to face him disgusted at what he was holding.

He still had the same bearded unkempt appearance, she thought. He was in the company of two of his men that stood either side of him, looking just as vagrant as himself. They held their weapons ready to shoot on their masters words to do so, neither one interested who they were in the company of.

"Hand it over Norgan, it doesn't belong to you," said Tayce with total disgust in her voice.

"I don't believe who I'm seeing, Tayce Traun daughter of the once Commodore Traun, a man who stopped what I was trying to achieve on our old world, I figured you of all your people would be the last to make it off daddies domain, tell me what's your interest in this, It really doesn't have any true significance, though hold on, you know Empress Tricara, that's right, I give you this and you give it back to her, how stupid do you think I am Missy?" said Norgan finding the who thing evilly amusing, giving an amused smirk to match.

"If you think you are stupid, then you must be, do you know what happens to anyone unlawful who tries to possess the power of the blue Tristarcan Crystal, you imagine your worst nightmare Norgan and treble it ten times, that's what the power does to anyone who holds it for evil purposes," said Tayce plainly, she could see this was the original Norgan all right, but how had he preserved his age, this was another matter.

Norgans men dropped back they had already pictured their worst fears and nightmares coming true. They began to feel uneasy to say the least, at what Tayce had just said. They had both done things in their lives that they did not want to exaggerate, because of the power, from some crystal, just because their master wanted to possess it for his own gotten gains. Tayce could see the look in Norgans dark eyes, that he too had under estimated what the crystal was capable of in the wrong hands. He probably had figured he could just open its velveteen purple box, take it out and give it a command to do something bad and it would do it, but it had been in the Tristarcan Power Force for centuries and anyone who had dared to use it for bad purposes was rewarded for their evil greed, she certainly didn't want to be in his boots.

"All right, what would you be willing to sacrifice for this precious crystal?" asked Norgan holding the box in his right hand in mid air.

Tayce was not willing to sacrifice anything, as far as she was concerned it was Norgan who would become the sacrifice in the most horrific kind of way. Unbeknown to Norgan, she began to concentrate with her ability. Marc and Tom exchanged glances that said it all. They knew what she was up to. The velveteen lid of the box began to open and rise up fully exposing the powerful crystal within. It began to glow more powerful by the cencron and if by magic Tayce could feel it communicating with her, on a higher level. Norgan looked at Tayce trying to make out, what she was doing, he began to get nervous at first, then he caught on to what she was attempting, he was both furious and alarmed to think that she was somehow gifted herself. Before Tayce could use the Power Crystal for her own defence, he pulled it from the box holding it tightly in his right hand, giving her a look, much to say I don't think so.

"Your wasting your time, once in my grasp like this, it is under my request to do whatever I so choose to do with it," he retorted feeling the thrill of holding a powerful force, he could use to his advantage.

"You haven't been listening, your men seem to know what I meant when I said about your worst nightmares coming true, look their backing away," said Tayce standing her ground.

Norgan glanced to see his two men back up towards the entrance, then scarper. He gave a look of anger and impatience, in their direction, they would pay later for deserting him.

"Give it up Norgan before I demonstrate the true power of the blue Tristarcan Power Crystal," warned Tayce and it came as a final warning.

What happened next amazed both Tom and Marc. In the following moments as Norgan failed to give up what was rightfully property of the Tristarcan Power Force and the Empress, the crystal put forth a brilliant white aura that grew by the cencron. Tayce continued to concentrate and communicate with the crystal via her mind. For the first time she felt the power she possessed as part of her and found that she was bringing it forth like turning on a tap. The power of the crystal, with her power had formed as one, with her inner self and it felt like a soft sereneness, beyond all comprehension. A swirl of powerful light rose around Norgan and travelled up his body to his neck wrapping itself around, forming an noose of pure energy. Norgan found for probably the first time ever in his evil life, that he was vastly becoming scared out of his very existence, of what was going on and what might happen. Marc and Tom watched on in disbelief, as Norgan realised he had bitten off more than he could chew, as the saying went this time around.

"I'm giving you a chance to hand back what does not belong to you, before it's to late, not like you did to the people of that space cruiser, all those yearons ago that you let perish because of your greediness to possess, some of those people were my friends, you so mercifully let perish at your command and that goes for the people of this world, which is it to be, hand me the crystal, or suffer your own fate for trying to possess something that doesn't belong to you?" said Tayce for the first time her eyes took on an illuminated sapphire look.

"I refuse to be intimidated by a bitch like you Traun," he retorted, holding on to any bravery he had left.

"Then your last chance has gone, you leave me no choice, you hereby pay the price for trying to possess what is not yours," said Tayce continuing on, she was being guided by an inner force to do what she had to do to save the crystal and what it stood for.

The noose of pure energy tightened around Norgans chunky neck and entered into his mouth and up his nose his eyes bulged and his face turned red, as he gasped for air, as the full power of the crystal joined with Tayce and taught him a lesson he'd never recover from again. Tayce found she was one with the crystal signifying the end of Norgans vary existence, finally. Tom became alarmed and wanted to try and stop Tayce, but Marc grabbed him back, informing him that any sudden break in Tayce joining with the crystal could probably kill her. Norgan cried out in shear terror, as the power took hold of his brain and made him live his nightmares in the worse form he could ever imagine. Tom couldn't let Tayce feel awful when it was all over that she had killed Norgan what was he to do? It was the power force that was making her do what she was doing, he knew that she would never live with herself when she realised that she had killed a man in cold blood, using her powers. He raised his Slazer and set it to disintegrate taking aim, he open fired on Norgan. Norgan disintegrated in the blaze of power, crying out as he did. The Power Crystal dispersed it's power but not before magically travelling through the air and into Tayces held out hands. It rested and died to a sparkling blue calmness once more like any other crystal. Tayces eyes returned to their normal look and she almost fainted from the unexpected onslaught. Marc caught her steadying her. Dawn soon broke over the surface of the destroyed city of Tristarcus. The outline of the palace could be half seen. The orange sunrise began to light up the smoke filled sky.

"You okay Tayce?" asked Tom in a true caring tone.

"Now that I have what we came for, let's just get out of here," she replied plain and simple.

"What about Norgans men?" asked Marc noticing they'd gone from the surface.

Without warning explosions began going off around Tristarcus. The three Amaltheans realised that Norgan and his men must have set self timer bombs to go off to cover their tracks, to eventually destroy the planet. Tayce, Tom and

Marc quickly ran at full pelt, for their Quest Shuttle/fighter. Upon reaching it they quickly hurried aboard. Marc immediately took control and in the moments that followed, the Quest and themselves were airborne heading for the stars. Below them Tristarcus erupted in explosions going off in quick rapid succession, which shook the Quest several times in after shocks. Once back in the stars Tayce contacted Lance via Aircom. Lance upon hearing that they were safe informed her that Norgan's battle cruiser had left orbit at a hell of a speed and disappeared in a blink of an eye, to another sector. Tayce smiled to herself, she guessed that Norgans men had seen enough, but would they return with a new leader? Time would tell and if she knew, she'd be waiting for them.

"Lance tell Tricara we have what is rightfully hers," said Tayce over the Aircom, holding the crystal in her hand, now calm and softly glowing.

"Of course," replied Lance happy to pass on the good news.

Tayce ceased communications and looked at Tom. He winked at her affectionately. She sank back in the seat still feeling a little exhausted from the joining with Tristarcan Power Crystal. She glanced out the sight port as the Quest left behind what was left of Tristarcus, in it's final moments, before total oblivion occurred.

***

On approach to Amalthea the cruiser opened it's Hanger Bay doors ready for boarding. As the Quest came into land on the bay floor, Marc raised his Wristlink and ordered Midge to hit Hyper Thrust Turbo speed and get them away from the shock wave, that would happen in the matter of minons. Empress Tricara could be seen waiting. Tayce was the first one off the Quest, she walked over to Tricara holding the Power Crystal. Tricara could see as Tayce neared that she had witnessed the power force of the crystal. She didn't say anything but could see that she had handled it well.

"This is for you, back where it belongs," said Tayce handing it gently to the Empress.

"Thank you, what of Norgan?" asked Tricara softly.

"Let's just say, he's gone where he belongs and won't be coming back," replied Tayce.

Tricara slipped a friendly arm around Tayces shoulders, suggesting that it was time to tell her a bit about the crystal and what she would one dayon inherit, also find it a temporary safe place on board to store it. Tayce agreed. As they sauntered away Tom who had heard what Tricara had just said as he and Marc were securing the Quest, shook his head and laughed. After what he'd witnessed on Tristarcus, it would appear that Tayce had already felt it's immense force, what more was there to learn?

Forced Trip to Arkanoss

Empress Tricara was collected by Private Launch from Questa, she, had insisted she would rather return under security than hold Tayce up in her Quest filled voyage. Before leaving, she thanked everyone that had gathered for their kind hospitality and Tayce, Tom and Marc for recovering the blue crystal. Tayce in one way was sad to see her friend go, it had been too long time since they had got together and really talked. It had been good to know that her powers were going to serve her well, over the future yearons. Everyone returned to duty once the Empress had walked aboard the Private Launch and departed for Questa.

***

It was one weekon later and nothing out of the ordinary was happening, the cruiser was running smoothly as usual. Tayce received her new rank via Jonathan over the Satlelink and everyone raised a toast to the new rank she had been awarded of Lieutenant Commander. She felt proud in a way, she wished her Father could see that she had gained a new footing on the road of leader. She knew that she shouldn't, at the happy time that it was, but she wished she could tell him. After the celebration everyone returned to what they were doing around the cruiser, this left herself and Midge to be alone in Organisation for a change. Something that she didn't mind, it reminded her of the old dayons, when they use to cruise the Universe alone. But now that she had a good team, she wouldn't trade those past empty yearons, for anything, especially now, that she had Tom and a new life. Midge gave her a blow by blow account of what everyone was up to on board, for her interest. Tom and Marc were undertaking armed combat practice. Lance was along the corridor in the Computer Resources Centre studying. Duncan was also studying navigational sectors for future reference in the Centre. Donaldo and Treketa were down in the L.A.C. going through some new medical techniques. As Tayce listened she thought to herself, it was good to know that her team were busy in something that they enjoyed. She thanked Midge, then went back to watching the Universe, undertaking the first of the new duty rota stints. Each team member was going to eventually undertake time in charge so that if anything happened and they were the one left they could so easily take over the cruiser and head back to Questa. Tayce found her time in command was extremely calm, nothing out of the ordinary had surfaced and it seemed a little to unreal she thought, as she sat relaxed. Then just as she had thought how calm it was, something darted past the main sight port in a blink of an eye, so fast, it was almost to fast to pick up, but Midge did. Tayce gave a taken back look, wondering if she had seen what had happened in the first place. Midge informed her that on the not to far of distant horizon and closing was a silver metallic formation, of the same small object that had shot past the sight port.

"Activating protection shields as a precaution Tayce," said Midge.

"Well done, get Lance back in here, I want to know what we're up against!" ordered Tayce sitting up in her seat now paying attention to what was unfolding before her.

"Requesting him now, though I can tell you that the largest of the round objects, is in fact a vessel," informed Midge.

"Scan for any life forms, compare them with any species that might be in this sector," ordered Tayce.

"Scanning now," replied Midge, as Lance walked in and slid into his seat.

Duncan hurried in behind and went straight to navigations. Lance glanced out the main sight port and saw the sight of the small objects darting here and there, raising his eyes in wonder of what they might be, then began keying in the request sequence to try and identify their sudden guests.

"Main vessel is giving off too much energy and static, as if it's blocking me trying to obtain information," said Lance trying a number of sequences.

"Okay. Midge take control, Lance and I are going out in Quests to see if we can get a closer look at just who we're dealing with," said Tayce standing to her feet.

"I'm not opposed to this, but do you think it's wise going out there, there might be a reason they don't want us to find out who they are and are just studying us," replied Lance wondering if it was a good idea.

"It's a chance we're going to have to take and what better way for you to keep up to date on your research and informational knowledge, than close up, shall we go," ordered Tayce heading for the entrance without further word.

Lance said no more, after all, she was his superior, even though they had known each other for yearons, duty was duty. But over this latest mysterious occurrence, he was still having doubts about what they were attempting. For some strange reason he was having a feeling of uneasiness. He soon caught up with her as she headed on down the corridor to head down to the Flight Hanger Bay.

Roughly 45 minons later in the Flight Hanger Bay two Quest Shuttle/fighters flew from Amalthea out into the immediate Universe. Tayce soon came along side Lance. Once away from the cruiser flying towards the now clearly visible mysterious main vessel. Over the Aircom Tayce began communications.

"It looks like it's been the victim of an attack, judging by it's scorched appearance, but were they innocent or the instigator?" asked Tayce, studying the vessel and it's many attack points.

"I'll try and do another scan from here," replied Lance, wondering if it would work.

But Just as Lance reached out to key in the sequence on the panel in front of him, for another scan, the main Vessel of the group emitted a blinding multi coloured flash, that blinded the pair of them. Tayce found that she lost all focus for a matter of cencrons. When she did eventually regain full focus, she looked to Lances Quest, only to discover much to her horror, he was not in the pilot seat. He'd vanished.

"Oh my God..." said Tayce in shear speechless horror, whatever the flash, it had taken Lance in the process.

Lances Quest went into uncontrollable flight spin, not having Lance at the controls. Tayce knew that in order not to lose the Shuttle/fighter she had to act fast. She began to use her mind ability and try and put the Quest under auto computer pilot, keying in, that it should return to the cruiser. It was difficult at first, but she accomplished what she desired, the Quest soon regained flight control and headed back to the cruisers Flight Hanger Bay minus Lance. She followed back not far behind, thinking that in a way Lance had tried to warn her what they were attempting was not wise, she'd been a total idiot, maybe she should have listened she thought.

Tom upon hearing from Midge that one of the Quests was returning without it's pilot, dropped what he was doing and began running until he ran into the Flight Hanger Bay. He waited with extreme concern that it was Tayces Quest that was the one returning empty. Marc as he too had heard from Midge, walked into join Tom in a furious mood. He couldn't believe that Tayce had acted so irresponsible in taking matters that she was unsure about into her own hands to head out and investigate without consulting himself or Tom first. What the hell was she thinking, he thought. He found it near impossible to keep his temper in check, as he stood beside Tom. First Quest into the Flight Hanger Bay, was Lances, returning empty. Midge placed it down on the Flight Hanger Bay floor, from where it had lifted off earlier. Tayces Quest came in behind. It was flying erratically. Tom hurried to a safe area and ordered her to straighten up, or she wouldn't land properly. He briskly with Marc not far behind headed towards it, when it safely set down and all engines had ceased. The entrance opened. Tayce came out shaking with what had just happened out in the Universe.

"What the hell did you think you were doing going out there without finding out about that vessel first, have you taken leave of your senses Tayce?" demanded Marc angrily, she'd acted irresponsibly in his eyes.

"What happened out there?" asked Tom more calmly, throwing Marc an angry look.

"Firstly Marc, we tried to find out about our visitors and they wouldn't let us scan them, so I said to Lance that it might be better to head out and get a closer look, I couldn't foretell what was going to happen could I otherwise I wouldn't of gone," snapped Tayce back at Marc trying to stop shaking.

"Calm down the both of you, this is not going to help the fact whoever they are out there, have obviously snatched Lance, we've just got to play this along, maybe they don't want to harm him, maybe they just want to find out who we are, let's not look on the dark side here," said Tom trying to calm the anger in both Tayce and Marc, as both were now almost in a face off situation.

"That main vessel I want it stopped from leaving this sector at any cost," said Tayce with meaning in her voice.

Tom raised his Wristlink and ordered Midge to somehow find a way to knock out all the main power on the egg shaped main vessel. Midge could be heard suggesting he leave it with him he would see what he could do. Without warning a few cencrons later, a small vessel of egg shape and the same colour of the group of vessels out in the Universe materialised in the Flight Hanger Bay. Tayce drew out her Slazer, furious beyond words, firstly that whoever they were had kidnapped Lance, now they were on board. She wanted answers and as far as she was concerned there was no time like the present. Marc walked from the Hanger Bay to head on back to Organisation, leaving Tom to assist Tayce. The small egg shaped Vessel large enough to normally withhold six people, opened it's circular entrance hatch. There was a long pause, then much to Tayces gasped surprise, first to walk out was Lance. She was about to rush to him, thinking that he'd come back, then Tom saw it was not what it appeared and reached out grabbing Tayce back swiftly by the upper arm. Five bald headed beings of slim build all dressed in silvery and white robes followed Lance out. Their eyes were an illuminated shade of white, with pin sized pupils. They slowly came to a stop in a line just a way away from Tayce and Tom. Tayce looked to Lance and found that Tom had been right to pull her back, for he'd been taken over by this intruding group behind Lance. His eyes were illuminated like the beings that stood behind him and he looked unemotional. His eyes were fixed and empty looking, the same illuminated shade of white. Tayce fought back her feeling of irresponsible guilt, seeing Lance locked in this taken over state. Maybe Marc had been right, she had been a total idiot, but nobody could have foreseen what was going to happen.

"We are the Arkarans of Arkanoss we come in peace," they all said together.

"I am Lieutenant Commander Traun, your on the Amalthea One, what do you want from us and my officer what are your reasons for crossing our journey?" demanded Tayce playing it cool, she did not want them killing Lance, even though they had said they had come in peace, she'd had dealings with beings like this before where they said they came in peace.

Much to Tom and Tayces surprise they suddenly began speaking through Lance and announced they had taken over his form so that they could communicate openly. If she and her team cooperated and followed their requested orders then the form they the were communicating through would be returned unharmed. If however, she and the team did not comply with what they wished, then she would be minus one of her crew who would die in an agonizing death, through their force of power, which would be her fault.

"You may request what you wish, as long as it does not interfere with the operations of this cruiser, or harm my officer in any way, because as we've scanned your main vessel, it's you who are at the mercy of us and don't think for one minon, that your the only one who has powers to stop you, in your wrong doings, should you try," warned Tayce feeling the least bit scared at the Arkarans threat.

"You have our word that we will request your permission and make clear our intentions before attempting anything necessary to achieve, what we wish for our purpose," said the Arkaran leader through Lance in broken speech, the best way he could.

"What is your purpose?" asked Tom.

"Merely to gain means to get us home to our world of Arkanoss and study more about your race on the way," explained the head Arkaran through Lance.

Treketa ran into the Flight Hanger Bay to find out if anyone was hurt, carrying the Medic Emergency Kit. She abruptly stopped in her tracks seeing the strange beings in the bay and gave a wide eyed look at the sight before her and especially Lance having eyes like the strange looking beings, that stood behind him. She continued cautiously towards Tom and came to a pause.

"What's happening?" she asked him in near whisper.

"These are the Arkarans and they are taking over Amalthea, we have no choice, they say that if we don't do what they want, they'll kill Lance," he replied straight to the point.

The Arkarans walked away behind Lance, who was heading to where they wanted him to head off to first. Tayce inside felt helpless she hated this situation, Marc had been right she had been so irresponsible and now it had put Lance where he was. She wanted to stop what was happening, but she knew at the present time she had to play along with what the Arkarans wanted, until she could see a moment when she could turn it to her advantage, taking the matter into her hands, ridding Lance of the Arkarans hold on him and getting them off

Amalthea. At the moment she knew that she couldn't put Lances life at risk, if anything happened to him Jonathan would never forgive her and it would not look good on her personal record, that she let her judgement get the better of her and killed the General's son.

"I don't know about you, I never expected this to happen, are you all right, I wonder what they have in store for us all?" asked Tom waiting for her thoughts on the sudden unwanted situation

"I'm fine, I want to see how this plays out first and when they least expect it and I feel the moments right, I will take the situation in hand and believe me this Arkaran Leader and his accomplices will wish they hadn't strayed into this sector," said Tayce angrily.

"You know what your doing, only this time think it over before you do," suggested Tom gently.

"I second that, especially as they have Lance under their hold," backed up Treketa.

"I suggest that everyone except Lance, meet up in the Leisure Centre in twenty minons, out of earshot of those body snatchers," suggested Tayce.

Tom and Treketa agreed, Tom suggested they head on back to Organisation to get Duncan. Tayce shook her head halting him explaining that the Arkarans would suspect that something untoward was going on behind their backs this would cause trouble for Lance, something she did not want to do, at any cost. It would be better to summon the others, except Lance via Wristlink. Tom agreed, he immediately began contacting Marc first, then the others in turn. Marc informed him he would find a way to ask Duncan to help him with something on the lower levels, this would not raise suspicion. As Tom sorted the gathering together of the team Tayce thought about her next move. She figured that it would be a good idea to find out something on their unwanted guests, so at least she would have some idea of what and who they were handling and it would give her something to work on, when the time was right to take back her cruiser. Treketa called Donaldo telling him to meet her in the Leisure Centre, in twenty minons. Tayce wanted to gather everyone there. Donaldo could be heard agreeing.

The Leisure Centre Twenty Minons Later:

Marc, Tom, Tayce, Treketa and Duncan all stood around waiting for Donaldo, who rushed in apologizing for keeping everyone waiting. Tayce for a few minons, gathered her thoughts on what she was going to say.

"Right we're faced with a sudden and unexpected situation, which I am very much against, it involves Lance and our sudden on board guests, the situation as much as it goes against what I would normally put up with in time we have to find a way to oust these beings in to space, but at present its unavoidable to tamper with their plans, the Arkarans have taken over Lance in a means to make us do what they wish in order to secure passage home, if we don't cooperate with the Arkarans, as they have a hold over Lance, they will kill him, however if you are asked to cooperate, do it to a certain degree, but if they ask for anything that you feel would jeopardize yourself or any of us, or effect this cruiser in anyway, check with me first understand?" said Tayce in the true tone of team leader.

"What happens if they don't give us time to contact you and start to harm us?" asked Treketa.

"It's not going to be easy I know, I suggest that if you feel you have no choice, knowing that if you don't do what is asked, then you won't be the only one that suffers, it will be the end of Lance also, I do understand that you have to do what you feel is right at that particular moment, but remember you'll have to answer to Jonathan should the outcome be Lances death," said Tayce seriously.

"I'm worried about Lances well being over this," said Donaldo giving a thoughtful look.

"There's nothing we can do, but I suggest you stand by in case needed when they leave," replied Tayce.

"Let's hope they don't stay longer than they have to," said Duncan.

"I agree, let's get back to duty and hope this ends soon, or if I can find a quick solution I will contact you all," assured Tayce.

She noticed as the others went back to duty, how uneasy the air was and it was understandable. Marc advised Duncan to act normal when they entered Organisation Deck so as not to raise suspicion. Duncan nodded in total understanding and agreement. Tayce crossed to the nearest sight port in thought, it was at times like this she wished her Father was alive and she could confide in him, what to do she thought. Tom, who was still present could see she was finding it hard and understood that she was caught in a total dilemma she wanted to get rid of the Arkarans but she was tied by the fact that any sudden move to do so would put Lance in danger, it wasn't easy. He walked over to her. Upon coming to a pause, he reached out and pulled her into a reassuring hug.

"I wish there was something I could do, I could try using my own powers but upon thinking about it I realise I'm tied whatever I do against them, Lance would be history," she confided resting her head on his chest.

"It's a no win situation it could have happened to anyone, you can't feel bad about this, Marc was wrong earlier having a go at you for going out in the Universe to take a look you couldn't see they would abduct Lance and put all of us through this, you were just acting as you saw right to do without thought of the repercussions, we all do it now and then," he assured calmly.

"We're changing course," said Tayce becoming alarmed and alert.

"Looks like they're setting their course for home, let's hope it's a quick journey," said Tom letting her go.

"I want to be up in Organisation in case they try anything else, come on," said Tayce heading over to the entrance of the Leisure Centre.

Tom followed on, wondering what she was going to do. She walked from the Leisure Centre on up the corridor to Level 1. The Leisure Centre was a room with several tables and chairs, a large wall screen and meal and refreshments computers. It was also a place to relax out of the quarters and off duty.

Marc had gone to the Computer Study Centre, leaving Duncan feeling uneasy at his navigations position, as the Arkarans were almost breathing down his neck, stood in the middle of Organisation. Marc was keying in the information to report that the locked in course to Arkanoss was under way, and also to log a record on the cruisers computer Journal of the unexpected journey. He discretely locked out all knowledge of what was happening, so that the Arkarans wouldn't probe the computer systems and discover he was also trying to link with the Arkanoss Home world and find out more on their unwanted travelling companions.

"Midge secure a translink with the Arkanoss home world, I want to find out more on our travellers," ordered Marc discretely over his Wristlink to Midge.

Midge did what was required, on screen the word 'Arkanoss' flashed in bold lettering followed by the words underneath, which stated Marc was entering a restricted database, that would need a security clearance number, after any initial enquiry. Marc probed further, entering the universal code that would hopefully gain him access to where he wanted to go, then sat back. A few minons lapsed and the words 'PLANETARY INFORMATION' flashed up on screen before him. Marc hit the chair in silent cheer, as the screen began to scroll and all the information he wanted was scrolling down before him. The information stated how many beings were on the planet, 26000. Marc decided to enter into the category that in so many words explained what made an Arkaran tick. Just as he did so, the word WARNING flashed up in bright red letters and the following information was displayed that Arkarans had incredible powers and would stop at nothing to achieve what they so wished, at any cost of life. He stared at the information in an alarmed way. He had to warn Tayce, just in case she was thinking of using her powers against them. He quickly disengaged his link with the Arkanoss home world and ordered Midge to terminate link up. Midge did and the screen went blank. Marc stood to his feet in urgency and walked from the Computer Study Centre, the doors opening and closing behind him as he went.

Tayce glanced about as she entered Organisation Deck, she had the distinct impression she was the invading person on her own cruiser, not the Arkarans. One of the Arkarans glanced at her and studied her with a suspicious eye for a moment, as if she was under scrutiny. Sensing him looking at her, Tayce looked back, she refused to be intimidated on her own cruiser. Marc walked back into Organisation requesting a brief word with her. The scrutinizing Arkaran that had been watching Tayce, looked to Marc, upon his words. Tayce ignored him and followed Marc into the Meeting Centre. The doors closed and inside Tayce breathed a sigh of relief, then sat at the meeting table to hear what he had to say He began to explain what he'd found out about the Arkarans.

Tayce wasn't the only one under scrutiny, down in the L.A.C. Donaldo and Treketa were about to get an unexpected visitor and it was not one for medical treatment. Donaldo was busy reading up notes on the computer when one of the Arkarans walked in. Treketa looked up, wondering what he was going to do. It was the Arkaran Leader, that had taken over Lance. He stood motionless for a moment. Donaldo and Treketa exchanged uneasy questioning looks.

"Can I help you, this is a medical facility, your in the wrong place if your looking for the Organisation Deck, is there something your particularly looking for?" asked Donaldo seeing that the Arkaran/Lance was looking about, as if he was searching for something.

"There is nothing here that your humanoid techniques could enlighten us to, our medical procedures are yearons ahead of yours," replied the Arkaran through Lance.

Treketa like Tayce found the whole thing creepy, the Arkaran speaking through Lance. He turned as if he'd read what she was thinking, staring at her for a few minons in a creepy blank way, that sent a shiver through her, then walked back out the L.A.C. leaving Donaldo and Treketa looking on in stunned silence, at what had just taken place.

"That's one weird being," said Treketa almost shuddering at the way in which the Arkaran had made Lance look at her so motionless and cold.

"What's Lance going to be like when we get him back, it must be hell for him locked inside his own form unable to say anything against what is going on before him, that the Arkarans have in mind," said Donaldo.

"He's my friend, but it's just so weird".said Treketa feeling sorry for Lance.

"Take it easy, it will be all right, you'll see," assured Donaldo putting his arm around her slim shoulders and squeezing her to him reassuringly.

Somehow it was just what she needed right at that moment and she and Donaldo were becoming firm friends as well as duty colleagues. It was hard for her to see her close friend in this Arkaran guise, it hurt to think that she couldn't communicate with him like normal times. They had grown close friends since they had met, as they had both joined the team at the same time. They had the kind of relationship that each one was there for the other in times of trouble or needing someone to confide in. Right now, she'd love to make him understand that everyone was there for him when it was over, when he got free of the force he was under. She broke free of Donaldo's gentle hold and went back to work, trying to push to the back of her mind what had happened.

It was night hourons soon enough aboard Amalthea. Tayce lay in her quarters bunk, not really sleeping, she couldn't, knowing that these invading Arkarans were up above her in Organisation up to God knows what without her knowing. She had ordered Midge via Wristlink to keep an eye on them, which he willingly confirmed he would. She hadn't even changed for sleep, she wasn't going to, just in case she needed to act fast, should Midge alert her to something that would be classed as an emergency. She lay thinking about all the worse possible things that the Arkarans were doing up in Organisation, she also began to think about what they were hiding in that silver metallic vessel that was in the Flight Hanger Bay. Maybe she should take a look. She sat up and slid to the Repose Centre floor. Standing she quickly made her way out through the living area to the corridor. Upon approach the quarters entrance doors opened and she slipped out into the dimly lit corridor. She was surprised to find that Treketa was doing the same from her quarters also.

"Can't you sleep either?" asked Tayce almost in a whisper.

"No and for all the wrong reasons, for the past houron it's been bugging me just why they should use this cruiser, I'm off for a look inside their so called vessel, coming?" replied Treketa also in near whisper.

Tayce nodded in agreement. The two Amalthean women cautiously began along Level 4 heading towards the Hanger Bay. After a while Tayce got the feeling they were being followed. Arkarans she thought, she was fed up with this feeling, like she was an intruder on her own cruiser and Lances life under threat, if she did try to stop them from obtaining what they wanted, she spun with a split cencron motion and was about to lash out and knock the Arkaran from his feet, when Marc's hand came out and blocked her avoiding the kick she was about to land on him.

"Take it easy, it's me," he said in alarmed whisper, dodging her kick with quick reacting block with his hand.

"Your lucky I was in the mood to put an Arkaran out of his misery for good, what are you doing out here this houron of night?" retorted Tayce questioningly.

"I could ask you two the same thing, where are you two heading, it's 00.300 hourons?" he said glancing at his Wristlink time display.

"I want to know what's in that silver metallic vessel, in our Hanger Bay and why should they want to take over Lance and this cruiser to get home to Arkanoss?" he asked in a whisper.

All three continued along Level 4 cautiously stepping onto the Level Steps. They began cautiously close to the wall in case they were spotted and had to turn back in a hurry. All that could be heard from above and all around them was the sound of Amaltheas fission engines, humming away. They were still moving thought Tayce, as she followed Marc up to Level 3. They all listened. There was a chanting sound and it seemed to be coming from the Flight Hanger Bay. They, at the top of the Level Steps, ran discretely along towards the entrance, but staying alert in case they needed to turn tail and run at the moment they were discovered. They reached the entrance. Marc cautiously put his head round the open entrance, just so he could see what was going on. He couldn't believe what he was seeing. In the bay stood around a hexagonal shaped pillar which was three foot high, stood the Arkarans. What was going on here he thought? He discretely pulled Tayce round so that she could get a look at what he was seeing. She came in just below his head and couldn't believe what she was seeing either, she gave a look of disbelief. Now the Pillar was giving off some kind of multi coloured light display, as the Arkarans chanted around it. Treketa looked and was about to gasp in awe at what she was seeing, when Marc put his hand gently over her mouth and muffled it. The Arkarans stopped suddenly chanting. Had they heard Treketa thought Tayce? Marc quickly grabbed them both and in urgent whisper suggesting they make a run for it. All three ran back to the Level Steps, as fast as their feet would take them Marc nearing an alcove before the steps, grabbed them both back in out of sight. The Arkarans exited the Flight Hanger Bay walking towards the Amalthean hidden three and the Level Steps. Tayce, Marc and Treketa watched on in silence, in the darkness of the alcove, wondering where they were going back to. Once out of sight Tayce stepped out into the corridor, followed by Marc and Treketa.

"Let's take a look at what's going on in that Flight Hanger Bay, I know for one, I'm not going to sleep not knowing what they're up to," said Marc.

"Your right, let's go, this is my cruiser and I have a right to know what their up to," said Tayce following on in determination with Treketa.

They headed back to the Flight Hanger Bay. Entering in, they walked a short way from the pillar and paused studying the now grey silver metallic looking object, that was now in an inoperable mode. Tayce raised her Wristlink and ordered Midge to scan it. A few cencrons later Midge who was surprised to hear from his mistress in the middle of the night hourons returned informing her, he couldn't scan it.

"What do you think it is?" said Treketa, walking around it in a studying kind of way.

"Maybe it's some kind of communication device, with their planet," replied Marc.

"It might even be watching us right now," said Treketa thinking about it.

"What happens if it's a bomb of some sorts?" said Marc serious.

"Would you both stop it, your giving me the creeps, thinking that maybe it's watching us, but you do have a point Marc, maybe it is a bomb primed to go off, when we reach their home world, but if I find out that it is somehow, believe me they won't be going home," said Tayce damned if she was going to lose this cruiser to the likes of a bunch of bald headed aliens.

Treketa walked around the pillar, it didn't matter which angle you looked at it, the sight was still the same, silver metallic grey and uninteresting with a point to it's top. She stopped suddenly, she'd found a name, it was engraved finely and indented for some strange reason. She said it in a normal tone not whispering.

"Natican, What does it mean?" she asked, looking at both Marc and Tayce questioningly.

"Treketa what did you do, it's opening up, let's get behind those containers, run, come on!" suggested Marc in alarm grabbing her to do so.

They all sprinted over to the right side of the Hanger Bay and ran behind some storage containers. Staying low for a minon, they waited for the weaponry to start firing in their direction. Nothing. Silence was all that was heard. Cautiously all three stuck their heads round the corner of the containers to take a look. A multi coloured light display was operational, it illuminated the whole Hanger Bay. Tayce decided that whatever it did to her she could equally match in powers, even though Marc had told her earlier to tread careful the Arkarans were extremely powerful and didn't mess around when it came to taking out something or someone that messed around with their race, if they didn't want you prying. She walked out. Marc felt she was being irresponsible again, in her actions. But what was new, he followed on behind, then Treketa behind him. She looked at the device as they progressed to the area where the pillar sat. As they all stood wondering what the object was going to do next, the Arkarans took them by surprise, by entering the Hanger Bay. The Arkaran/Lance grabbed Treketa from behind, pulling her back in a restraining grip. She lashed out to no avail. Tayce and Marc turned.

"Let her go she can do you no harm," ordered Tayce commandingly.

"Prying into matters that don't concern you Lieutenant Commander is really not wise, it is an houron when you should be in what your race term as sleep, why are you here intruding in matters that do not belong to you?" said the Arkaran Leader holding Treketa.

"You let her go and I'll tell you, and as for intruding, it's you that came aboard my cruiser and laid down your request of what you wanted, I have a right to know what that thing is and if it puts my team in any more danger than your already doing," began Tayce but was cut off.

"I am unable to divulge the nature of this piece of technology of our existence, it is forbidden," replied the Arkaran Leader through Lance coldly.

"I'd like to point out to you, that you seem to think this cruiser is solely here for you and treat it as it's yours, but from this moment onwards, enough is enough, I'm in command and you are classed as intruders I would think seriously about any further decisions you make regarding my team and cruiser, if you refuse to cooperate with me you might try and take the life of Officer Largon, but in return, I will make things very difficult for you to return to Arkanoss." With this Tayce reached into her uniform holster and withdrew her gun, much to Marc and Treketas astonishment, aiming it at the silver tone pillar.

"Your threat will only cost you your life firing on our technology will not harm us, but it will harm you," said the Arkaran in reply.

"Then tell me what is the use of this thing, because you see Arkarans are not the only ones to have powers there's a person on this cruiser who would match you make no mistake and like your technology here I like you are not prepared to divulge who it is," retorted Tayce trying to keep her cool and playing the Arkarans at their own game.

Marc lowered his head thinking that the Arkaran Leader could consider he had had his last warning. He knew what Tayce said, she meant. It was something he would like to see. Tayce match them power for power in gaining the Amalthea and Lance back. After a few minons the Arkaran/Lance who had grabbed Treketa released her. She ran to the safety of Marc. He slipped his arm around her protectively.

"Lieutenant Commander I have no wish to harm you or your team, we merely need this passage of which we are nearly coming to an end now, all we ask of you, is to allow us to continue in peace, in control of your cruiser and your officer, who we have had to use as a means to communicate with you, you have my word all will come to an end soon and will end well, if you allow it to," began the Arkaran through Lance.

Marc could see that the Arkaran leader had just met his match in Tayce. She hated being vindictive to Lance it went against all they meant to each other, all she hoped was somewhere deep inside, he was urging her to continue on against these possessive beings.

"Let me tell you Arkaran, the way in which you've handled your gaining of forced passage, is not how we do things in our Universe, I and my team, if you had gone about gaining a passage to your home world the proper way, I would have cooperated with you to get you to Arkanoss, though the way you have done this act against the team is considered hostile," stated Tayce, as far as she was concerned, it was time to clear the air between them.

"Lieutenant Commander, these words that you speak make me realise, that we have acted with the wrong approach to this situation, I therefore apologise… a brief word with you if I may?" requested the leader.

"Of course," said Tayce with Marc giving a look much to say, what are you doing?

She lead the leader out of earshot and out of the Flight Hanger Bay. Marc suggested to Treketa to return to her quarters to get the rest of her sleep, he could handle anything from that moment on. He followed on at a discrete distance after Tayce. Treketa did as ordered and headed back to her quarters, thinking how well Tayce had handled the situation. The Arkarans followed behind Marc, leaving the grey silver metallic pillar to revert back to it's standby state. Tayce and the Arkaran Leader walked along with a slight distance between them, towards the Deck Travel. Soon they all boarded and the doors drew closed behind them. The Deck Travel ascended to Level 1. Marc had decided to take the Level Steps and on the way up he Wristlinked Midge informing him of what was happening, that he wanted the whole meeting with the Arkaran leader recorded just in case there was any nasty outcome, when they reached Arkanoss. Midge agreed wholeheartedly. The Meeting Centre roughly thirty minons later. She crossed to the meeting table with Marc and gestured for the Arkarans to sit on the opposite side. She and Marc sat in seats next to each other. She thought to herself it was a good job Jonathan didn't call and want to speak to Lance, at the present time, somehow he would never believe what was occurring on board and to his son. In fact he would probably have a crack security team heading straight for them on finding out, to tackle this uninvited race.

"Lieutenant Commander, I would like to explain something to you, if I may, on why we treat your race with the hostility, but first we have one last request…" began the Arkaran Leader then looked at Marc.

"If it means jeopardizing any more of this team, you know my answer to that question and if you don't know what that is it's a flat, no!" replied Tayce she could almost see what he was proposing.

"Your people many centuries ago came to our world and left it in a devastated state, it was classed as exploratory investigation, we called it destroying our evolution, thousands of our powerful kind perished in the many tests they carried out, using various poisonous gasses, many of our kind were in hibernated state and many died there, as a result, they used us and this is why we show no compassion when dealing with your kind to date, so as your Officer Largon is a low ranked officer, allow us to find out if your kind have changed, we need to gain the knowledge and understanding of Commander Dayatso, if you cannot agree I still have control of this Lance form and it would be a pity to end such a young life," explained the Arkaran Leader.

"No way Tayce," said Marc standing to his feet angry without thought.

She was caught in a no win situation, once more. This race were a treacherous unpredictable lot she thought and cunning with it. She didn't want to lose Lance and she didn't want any more of the team coming under the influence of the uninvited bunch of beings, she sat in thought for a moment, then began, even though it went very much against her authority to allow what they had proposed, to occur.

"I want you to take note of this, you harm Commander Dayatso in any way and I'll send an emergency report to my headquarters base, they in turn, will have a security team visit your world and arrest you upon your return home for trial of killing an General's son and a high ranked officer of the Questa fleet, is that understood?" pointed out Tayce, in a tone that showed no patience.

"You have my solemn promise, no harm will come to your Commander here and we thank you in advance," said the leader nodding obligingly, knowing that he had fooled Tayce once more into getting what he wanted.

All the Arkarans grabbed Marc under protest, with immense force, stronger than his own, as he fought back to stop them attempting the same thing on him, that they had done to Lance. Tayce felt her heart rip right out of her chest at what happened in the following cencrons. One Arkaran took hold of Marc on either side holding him against his will, the deputy being next to the leader walked straight into Marc's form. Marc cried out and Tayce had to look away. For a few minons, there was a white wavering glow, as the Arkaran adjusted to Marc's form. Tayce wanted to be physically sick. She swallowed hard to keep what she was feeling from surfacing. Marc looked at her, as she looked back, motionless and with the eyes of an Arkaran. illuminate white with the pin sized pupil. What had she done, she thought, Marc would surely leave the team when he came back to himself for this. She had let him down badly, but she had no choice, as the leader still had hold over Lance and she couldn't let him die at any cost. Marc was now much against her wishes in the hands of the Arkarans, she felt awful.

Mornet came round soon enough and as soon as she entered Organisation, she was quickly reminded of what had unfolded the night hourons before, in the Meeting Centre by seeing Marc under the influence of the second of the Arkaran race. She hadn't told Tom, what had happened when she had returned to their quarters after the incident, she felt too terrible and had lain awake torturing herself thoughtfully for the rest of the night as Tom slept unaware of what had unfolded beside her. Tom and Duncan walked into Organisation next mornet. Both could not believe what they were seeing in Marc's current condition. Duncan looked to Tayce questioningly, as did Tom. Tayce looked away. Duncan went to his duty position, Tom asked for a private word in the Meeting Centre. He discretely grabbed Tayce by the arm, and ushered her inside. The sound proof doors closed.

"When did this happen?" he demanded in a impatient way, glancing over her shoulder.

"Last night hourons Treketa, myself and Marc decided that we wanted to know what was going on in the Flight Hanger Bay, take a closer look at what the Arkarans were up to there," she began.

"How come Marc's now under the influence of these damn Arkarans explain Tayce?" he continued far from amused at what had greeted him on arrival on duty.

"It's only short term, they asked for Marc because he is a high ranked officer, they said they could gain a better knowledge from him about us, they have promised that no harm will come to him and he will return upon them arriving home," protested Tayce, she wished he would stop being so defensive she felt bad enough as it was having put Marc through what she had.

"How many more of this team are going to fall under their influence, to get home Tayce," he retorted in near whisper. He and Marc had become good buddies.

"I had to do it, they would have killed Lance, I couldn't take that chance, I tried to give them an ultimatum in aiming my Slazer at their pillar type object in the bay, but they renewed their threat on Lance, I'm caught between wanting to rid this cruiser of them forever and wanting to keep Lance and now Marc alive, how do you think I feel, think about it Tom, would you have done any different?"

replied Tayce angrily shouting at him, she'd taken enough and she didn't care who heard.

Tom sighed in exasperation, but knew she had a point, she was trapped, he had to admit it and even though she probably wanted to use her powers couldn't, at the present time for fear of reprise. He reached out and pulled her in towards him, apologising feeling angry at the unwanted guests.

"You should have told me last night," he said softly, holding her now close to his warm chest his breathing slowly calming they had just had their first disagreement as a legally joined couple.

"I couldn't, oh Tom, it was horrible what they did, I witnessed the whole takeover moment between the Arkaran and Marc," she said near to tears, on his uniformed warm chest.

Tom thought about why they had taken over Marc, there had to be a deeper reason, than just gaining a better understanding of the human race so many yearons later. Tayce began explaining, the human race had visited Arkanoss and did tests that wrecked their planet for centuries, this had made them mistrust humans, so when they were rescued by humans centuries on taking over Lance was their first human since the last encounter centuries ago and it meant a way to find out if humans had changed, for the better, but they could only learn a certain level of knowledge in Lances form, hence them asking to upgrade to Marc, to gain a much more higher understanding of Marc's thoughts and memories of the past, to get a better understanding of the human race in the present time. Tom fell silent, he understood, but didn't like it. Tayce went on to explain that the Lance/Arkaran Leader had explained after the takeover of Marc, they had lost twelve home worlds to humans during the tests performed on them. Tom raised his eyes in surprise at the fact, maybe he was misjudging this uninvited bunch. Twelve worlds was a large amount of people to lose in any race. He suggested after all that she'd been through during the night hourons, she go and take some time off duty, get some sleep that she'd missed all night, he would take charge until she returned. Tayce agreed heading on out, not looking at the Arkaran Deputy/Marc, as she walked from the Meeting Centre on out of Organisation. Tom shook his head, this whole situation was one sorry mess.

***

Two hourons had passed, the Arkaran Leader/Lance entered Organisation and headed towards the controls gesturing for a takeover to his fellow Arkarans. The Arkaran Deputy/Marc ushered Duncan carelessly off his seat. Duncan wanted to answer back, but Tom shook his head, seeing what was happening. Tayce entered back into Organisation, she felt rested. Midge had informed her, that he had heard an Arkaran saying that the final duty was about to commence and figured that she would want to be there for it. She cringed at the sight of Marc still linked with the second Arkaran. She for one, couldn't wait for this whole affair to cease and everything return to normal. She looked out the sight port at the immediate view, the sight was the obvious home world of the Arkarans. She listened to the conversation between the Arkaran Leader/Lance and the Planetary Control Complex, what was being discussed in a cold precise dull tone, in that they had taken over Amalthea to return home. The Arkaran Leader turned to face Tayce and began.

"Lieutenant Commander Traun, my people on Arkanoss need further knowledge from your Officer Largon and Commander Dayatso and have stated that they will not allow us entrance back to our home world, unless we take these two members of your team, with us," he said plainly.

"You can tell your people Arkaran, passage ends here, as you have asked for, you stated that you and your three Arkarans the moment you arrived back in orbit of your home world you would release my two officers, this is now, and not for further negotiation, at any cost," said Tayce without further word.

Upon these words the Arkaran Leader stood leaving the control seat in silence, he commanded his men to follow with one commanding nod. He could see that he had done enough with Tayce and the team. Tayce felt she had gone beyond the borderline of endurance to suffer their passage. He walked from the Organisation Deck. Duncan took back his seat and Tom gave a look of speechless surprise. Before Duncan's backside got a chance to hit the seat, Tayce called him and Tom, she ordered them to check their Slazers and follow on. Tom, as he did so wondered if Tayce would be using her powers, as she had said earlier, if the worst came to the worst to get the Arkarans off the cruiser, then so be it, he thought. All three headed down the corridor determined to do everything possible to stop the Arkarans leaving Amalthea with Lance and Marc's bodies. On the way down to the Flight Hanger Bay, Tayce Wristlinked Midge.

"When I give the order you pull this cruiser out of our current orbit away from the Arkaran world understand?" said Tayce in a tone that sounded like the true leader she was.

"I'm ready, you just give the word," replied Midge.

They headed down the Level Steps two at a time, but kept a discrete distance behind the Arkarans as not to raise suspicion, that they were being followed.

"What do you have in mind?" Tom asked Tayce.

"I've decided that the time has come, the Arkarans have outstayed their welcome and I intend to make sure that Lance and Marc are left behind, when they leave," replied Tayce determined.

"Isn't that going to be dangerous for you, Marc and Lance, after all, Marc did find out they stop at nothing with their amazing powers, you could be in for a tough time," said Tom concerned.

"I believe I'm more than a match for them and I'm willing to give it a try, if it means bringing this team back together and getting the Arkarans out of our lives forever," replied Tayce.

They all stepped onto Level 3 cautiously and discretely going on along to the entrance to the Flight Hanger Bay. Upon reaching the open doorway they put their heads slowly around the opening, looking inside to get some idea of what the Arkarans were up to, so that they would have some idea of what they were up against. Inside the Hanger Bay, the Arkarans were preparing to shut down the pillar and move it into it's storage container to move it back aboard the craft, they had materialised aboard in. Suddenly the Arkaran Leader could be seen communicating with the main vessel. Tayce heard him and whoever it was confirming that all power had been restored and the Amalthean crew had been fools to think they were dead in space. Tayce felt like she and the team had been used for nothing more than a hostile mind fix. She decided it was time to bring this mess to an end, they had just hit a sore spot in being used, as far as she was concerned, she stepped out and walked over to the middle of the bay. Tom and Duncan followed coming to stand either side of her as she paused. Tayce looked at the Arkaran Leader far from impressed. He left the others packing to leave and crossed.

"Lieutenant Commander your here, I presume to tell me that you have changed your mind, in allowing us to take your two members with us to Arkanoss?" he began

"No I have not Arkaran," retorted Tayce feeling hostile.

"You've noticed that we are packing our vessel to head back into space...," he began.

"Your wasting your time Arkaran I heard you communicating with your main vessel, it appears that you have restored your power supply, you have been using me and my team in a hostile situation that Questa Headquarters Base would very much like to hear about, I want you off this cruiser and I want my two team members released from your total control, this is not for negotiation," stated Tayce commandingly.

"As far as your team members are concerned, we have made a decision that we are not going to give them up from this moment forward, until we are on our world, we shall be using them as a guarantee to getting us home, without you or your guidance computer destroying our main vessel, they will gain us entry back on to our own world, without them, we will be terminated of life, for failing to gain your knowledge," he replied plainly.

"I'm not interested in what your intending to do, like I said, I want you off this cruiser, now, without my two men," said Tayce in just as much plain tone.

Tayce suddenly felt her power ability rising within her. Tom and Duncan stepped away a bit. A sudden white protection aura surrounded her whole body. She raised her hands ready to emit the pure energy of her gift and warned Arkaran that he had given her no choice, but to end this charade, there and then. As if by some unknown force of extreme magic, a wind suddenly began that blew the gowns of the Arkarans, Marc and Lances hair. The force of wind grew to such a super strength, it was tough to hold their footing.

"Arkaran leave while you still can and hand back my two members of team, free them now from your link otherwise I will show you just what I can to do regarding powers, to keep what is rightfully mine," said Tayce almost shouting through the wind.

"Since you insist Lieutenant Commander, you leave us no choice but to return power, to retain your team members forms, say goodbye to your men," retorted Arkaran his men falling in with him and beginning their own powers against Tayces.

Tayce unleashed a ball of pure white energy against the Arkaran Leader, she figured if she could take him down first, the others would follow. She then closed her eyes to concentrate on a much higher degree of power source within her, to withhold her own against the Arkarans. She concentrated on breaking the link between Lance and the Arkaran Leader and Marc and the Deputy Arkaran. Lance writhed in the torture as the Arkaran fought to hold onto his form, it was a full scale power struggle between Tayce, the Arkarans and separating the Amalthean members. Treketa and Donaldo walked into the bay, not believing what they were witnessing.

"Give it up now Arkaran, give my officers back to me, or you will suffer in your own power struggle to an ultimate death," warned Tayce in the commotion, her face taking on the look that conveyed she was using her highest degree of power.

He refused to be intimidated by Tayce and her threats. He looked upon them as childish wishes of a naive beginner in dealing in powers. An Orange glow appeared and travelled towards the Arkarans from Tayce, she had gained the higher degree, she wanted to obtain. It enlarged as it neared them, they tried to fight back but for probably the first time in their lives, they were losing big time. Tayce found herself using every once of her power strength, just to gain what she wanted, she was not prepared to lose Lance or Marc at any cost. The Arkarans were failing in their power struggle and it began to slowly decline. Treketa couldn't believe what she was seeing, Tayce use her powers so violently. The Orange immense power aura swallowed the Arkarans, bathing them in a brilliant almost blinding light. Suddenly, they and their ship vanished in that blinding light. Tayce dropped to the floor out cold, her power immediately diminished. Donaldo rushed forth with his Medic Emergency Kit, bending down next to Tayce. Marc was slowly trying to adjust to life back in his own body, once more. He couldn't understand what he was doing in the Flight Hanger Bay, as the last thing he recalled was being in a meeting with the Arkarans. Lance who had been under the influence of the Arkaran leader the longest, stumbled. Treketa hurried over to quickly steady him and assure him that he was safe, back where he belonged.

"Take it easy Tayce, that was some power feat you just pulled off," said Donaldo softly down at her, as he began to check her over upon her coming to.

"I'm fine, just give me a moment, see to the others," she ordered.

"You pulled off what you set out to accomplish, the Arkarans and their vessel are gone, both Marc and Lance are back," informed Tom softly proud of her.

Tom raised his Wristlink ordering Midge to get Amalthea out of orbit of Arkanoss, then go to Hyper Thrust Turbo. Midge could be heard agreeing.

"Despite you all probably wanting to return to duty, I want all three of you to rest in your quarters for a while, that's an order," said Donaldo addressing Tayce, Lance and Marc.

Marc crossed to Tayce, she wondered what he was going to say to her, considering she had volunteered his body to the Arkarans, much against his protest not to be part of them. She stood up. He paused before her for a moment giving her a plain look that was making her feel not quite sure of what he was going to say. Everyone fell silent around them, so much so that the atmosphere could have been cut with a Slazer knife wondering what was going to happen. He then reached out and pulled her into a warm hug and informed her jokingly if she ever did anything like that again, he'd throttle her. The experience was somewhat unnerving to say the least. He guided her on out of the Flight Hanger Bay, suggesting that he tell her, what life was like being part of an Arkaran. Tom followed on laughing to himself silently, Marc was going to teasingly make Tayce suffer. Lance and Treketa walked slowly on out behind to head off to his quarters, Donaldo had given him a Vit Boost to bring his system back to good normal strength and also a relaxant injection to aid him in his recovery. The bay was soon empty and silent once more, with just the Quests being the only vessels present. It was hard to imagine that the Arkarans had even been on board. But it was an experience that the Amalthean Team would not forget for a long time to come, Tayce especially had been taught a lesson she would not forget in a hurry, before going out on a whim to investigate, find out more first.

The Arkarans were now on their home world, whether they would be accepted back was another thing. As far as the Amalthean Quests team were concerned, they really didn't care but their encounter with the race would live on for some time to come in their memories.

Generals End and a Newly Elected Chief

The news had come as a total shock a weekon later for the Amalthean Quests Team, from Adam Carford at Questa via Satlelink. Jonathan Largon had been rushed as an emergency back into the Cardiac Complex with a severe heart attack again and was not expected not to survive. The team waited with uneasiness for the outcome. Lance found it hard to concentrate on his duty and it was understandable. Adam an houron later after the notification had been received over the Satlelink, came on screen. He looked like he was fighting back great sadness and looked ashen faced. He gathered himself together on what he was going to say to deliver the news he had to deliver. Tayce picked up on the way in which he was stuck for words, he felt totally awkward, she guessed it wasn't good news. He began trying not to sound shocked and shaken.

"It's not good I'm afraid, the Generals in a critical condition, it's serious this time, he's asking to see Lance, could you come to Questa as soon as possible?" said Adam in a solemn tone.

"Of course, we're on our way, we will be there as soon as we can," assured Tayce.

She didn't need to ask Midge to lay in the course to Questa, he was locking it in the moment Adam had requested if they could head to Questa. She turned to see that Lance had left his duty position and left Organisation, this meant one thing, he had taken the news badly, she figured he'd need her support. Leaving her seat she put Tom in command of getting them to Questa, explaining as she walked across Organisation that she was off to find and support Lance, she had a feeling he was taking the news badly. Tom nodded in total understanding and continued taking command in her absence. As he sat, strangely enough and quite out of the blue he, found the thoughts of the accident and death of Alenea his first wife, rushing into his mind how she had died so tragically. He quickly concentrated on the journey ahead, trying to forget what had just occurred. Telling himself he had a new life now with Tayce.

Tayce as she made her way down the Levels Steps to find Lance, knew if the outcome was the death of his Father, it was going to be a real tear in Lances life and one where he was going to need a lot of support to pull him through. All she could do was be there as a friend, she thought. She Wristlinked Midge trying to find exactly where Lance was at that precise moment on board. Midge soon came back after searching Lances whereabouts, announcing that Lance was in his quarters. She hurried on there.

Lance stood looking out of the sight port, in the living area of his quarters, in thought. His Father worked too hard and everyone that knew him, had said as much, urging him to take more breaks. He wished he could somehow magically Transpot straight to his Father's side, there and then. But it wasn't possible, he just had to wait. God it hurt to think of the inevitable, that this was it, the end of the last relative he had and the end of the best man in charge of Questa. Tears swelled in his dark brown eyes and began to ebb down his face. The emotion was getting to much for him, his head was filled with the sole thought of his Father no longer being there for him to talk to, to confide in and someone to look up to when undertaking something complex on Questa. He crossed to the soffette and sat down putting his head in his hands. Thoughts raced through his mind past and present, one above them all was the fact that he was going to be the last known Largon alive. The quarters doors opened. Tayce entered to find the quarters lighting on the twilight mode.

"Lance, it's Tayce, are you in here, Midge said you were here?" she said walking fully into the silent interior.

"I'm here, sorry for walking off duty, I just couldn't stay hearing Adam talk about Father in such a solemn way, it's bad isn't it, tell me Tayce?" began Lance looking to her with tear stained eyes, fighting back the onslaught of the hurt.

"We've no way of knowing yet, but I'll be honest, it doesn't look good this time," replied Tayce understanding Lances sadness.

"It feels so wrong, I feel so helpless, it's not fair Tayce, he's the last member of my family I've have," he said looking at her deeply in pain of the fact he could lose his Father.

"I'm here for you, you know that, come here," said Tayce crossing quickly, she softly pulled Lance into a friendly hug of understanding support, as he broke down.

"I'm sorry," he said crying on her shoulder.

"Don't be, Duncan will take over your duty, whilst this is happening and I'm here for as long as you need me Tom's in command and he understands where your coming from over this, he lost his wife at the beginning of this voyage he knows exactly what your suffering right now," she replied reassuringly.

"Tayce I feel so alone, the possible emptiness is unbelievable," he said pulling away from her gently looking at her.

"You'll never be alone, of that you can be sure, we Trauns have always considered you as a member of our family too, you also have this team and we will be there for you and you know this deep down," said Tayce in an soft assuring manner.

"Thanks, it means a lot," he replied managing a slight smile.

"You know your Father may still pull through, he did the last time remember?" said Tayce.

Tayce could see that he would not rest until his feet were on Questa and he was heading to be with Jonathan, maybe in the final hourons. She thought about if for a few cencrons and decided that even though they were travelling at Hyper Thrust Turbo speed, it would be a couple of hourons before they docked at Questa, so she decided to let him take her Quest Shuttle/fighter. Taking the de-locking key from her jacket pocket, she handed it to him.

"Here, take my Quest we'll join you just as soon as we can get there," she said planting the square slim key in his hand and closing it.

"Are you serious, I can't take your Quest, it's yours...?" he began surprised.

"This is classed as an emergency, go before I change my mind, I don't make a habit of lending it to anyone you know," she replied light heartedly.

"Your one in a million Tayce Traun, thanks!" he replied taking the de-locking key and reaching for his jacket he headed on out of the quarters.

He paused briefly in the doorway for a minon, to tell her he'd see her later, then hurried on out. Tayce walked from the quarters slowly in thought about Jonathan, hoping that for Lances sake, he would somehow recover again, but if it meant Jonathan spending the rest of his dayons in pain and unable to live his life to the fullest, then the outcome that was meant to be, would be the right one. Her Mother crossed her thoughts and she wondered how she was coping with what had happened to Jonathan, it couldn't be easy for her. After all it hadn't been proven whether her Father, her Mother's coupling partner had perished after the destruction of Traun and maybe he was still alive somehow, somewhere, in the Universe. Poor Mother thought Tayce, she and Jonathan were close friends and always had had a great relationship, it would be a wrench if anything happened to him for her. Once out of Lance's quarters. Tayce walked up the Level Steps in thought on the way back to Organisation.

Lance was soon manoeuvring the Quest up off the Hanger Bay floor. Once in position, he turned the Quest and shot off out the open Hanger Doors into deep space, using the highest degree of manoeuvring speed. Destination was Questa and the quicker he could get there, the better it was. Amalthea ebbed away behind him continuing on in the Hyper Thrust Turbo speed it was currently in. In a short period, Lance was gone off the scanner and out of orbital sight.

On Questa the atmosphere was very sombre, with the news of General Largons sudden decline in health once more. Personnel were talking about it amongst themselves. Lydia Traun dressed in her long close fitting council robes of navy blue, with decorative white trim and stand up collar, entered the room where Jonathan was connected to the breathing and monitoring equipment silent. She had been allowed to see him briefly. He opened his eyes slowly, looking up at Lydia's breathtaking beauty. She clasped his hand gently, hoping that he would hold out until Lance arrived.

"Your a sight for sore eyes Lydia Traun, but you always were, Darius beat me to it you know," he said with difficulty, teasing her.

"Lance is on his way, Tom just informed me, he's using Tayces new Quest Shuttle/fighter to get here ahead of everyone else, Tayce is following on behind," informed Lydia in soft caring tone.

"He's a son to be proud of Lydia, if anything happens to me, promise you'll be there for him," asked Jonathan in a sincere way.

"You have my word, I promise, I'll treat him like he was my own," replied Lydia feeling the hurt of seeing her friend in such a frail way.

She sat on the stool that a young female nurse had brought her. She would stay by Jonathan's side until Lance had arrived to be by his Father instead. The young nurse moved around checking Jonathan's equipment. The male Medical Officer in charge of Jonathan, who was an extremely experienced in cardiac knowledge and had been handed his case to take on, was present and he was far from impressed at Jonathan being back before his team in his cardiac section, through no fault of his own. Lydia glanced at him, understanding his displeasure. 'Morganforn' was his name on his uniform Lapel badge and underneath the words, CARDIAC CONSULTANT GRADE 1. This thought Lydia meant he was top of his field and it also meant one thing. This was serious this time around. He shook his head in an impatient way. Lydia stood, walking over to meet him on the far side of room, as he studied the latest computer notes, out of earshot of Jonathan.

"Mr Morganforn I'm Councillor Traun, how bad is he really?" she asked softly, giving the consultant her full attention.

"Councillor, I'm afraid it's not good news and it's all his own fault, he's not expected to make it through the night hourons I'm afraid," replied the Consultant softly and quietly to her.

"His son Lance will be here soon, he's coming all the way from Amalthea One," expressed Lydia hoping that at least Jonathan could hold out until then.

"We'll keep an eye out for his arrival, nurse make sure that when General Largons son arrives, he is to be shown in immediately," ordered the Consultant.

"Yes sir of course sir," replied the young female nurse, in an understanding tone.

She finished running her final checks and suggested that with Mr Morganforns approval, as Councillor Traun was known to both the General and his son, she remain present whilst she took a brief break until the Generals son arrived. Mr Morganforn thought about if for a moment, then looked to Lydia in a questioning way. Lydia nodded agreeably. It was settled. She crossed back to Jonathan's side, whilst the young nurse went for her break. As she walked from the room so she passed Adam Carford walking in. Mr Morganforn turned.

"Mr Carford, only one person at a time with the General please!" he began.

"I won't be long, I wanted a word with Councillor Traun here," said Adam discretely.

Mr Morganforn nodded in understanding. Adam calmly and discretely enquired how Jonathan was doing, to Lydia. He at this moment opened his eyes and looked up at his loyal assistant questioningly.

"I'm not gone yet Adam, is there a problem?" he asked, as if he was still on duty.

"General sir, I for one, am glad that you still are and I hope that your here for a long time to come yet Questa would be lost without you, you don't have to worry about problems, Questa is as usual running well and I have taken care of all the things that you asked me to take care of earlier," said Adam sounding like the real reliable aide that he was.

"Very well…" replied Jonathan drifting back into a sleeping state.

Both Lydia and Adam moved away from Jonathan to talk discretely on the far side of the vast room, fit for a General. But not to far away just in case Jonathan would pass away suddenly. Both looked back at him occasionally saddened at what was unfolding before them. It had appeared and was well known, that even though Jonathan was generally a strong man, deep down after the sudden horrific death of his late wife, it put a great strain on his heart from the effect of the shock of losing her so suddenly. As they had been together since childhood, back when the Universe was a lot more dangerous and crime was a way of life just to scrape by for some. But Jonathan had been brought up by decent parents and what he saw, had made him more determined, that his headquarters base would up hold the law and make it a pleasant place to stay, work and also travel through. Both Adam and Lydia knew that the loss of Jonathan Largon would signify a great change for the whole base and it's run of things. Lydia wondered if Lance, would turn out to be like Jonathan in leadership one dayon, she hoped so.

***

Down in the Questa Arrival and Departure Area, Lance climbed from Tayces Quest and glanced around as he locked it up. It was busy he thought, watching the many people and aliens passing through and heading aboard flights of various shapes and sizes. Once he'd locked the Quest he headed off. There was a certain eerie silence in the air. That he put down to his Father's possible demise, many people on Questa respected his Father and thought a lot of him, for the things he had done for them in making the base proud to work and live on. As he went people that knew him as Jonathan Largons son, expressed their sympathy and assured him they were around should he need a friend, someone to talk to.

Lance politely thanked them, as some were old friends of his Father, some were even his own friends, before he left Questa for Amalthea One. He crossed over to the moving stealex steps that would take him to the City Level and would take him the shortest walk to the Medical Health Complex. He glanced at his Wristlink time display as he headed up the moving steps that ascended to the next Level. He'd made good flying time. Something suddenly down deep in the heart of him egged him on quicker, as if he could sense his Father was calling out to him to hurry. He crossed to the Medical Health Complex in shear urgency, narrowly escaping collision with other people on route. Passing through the glassene and stealex doors, with the same urgency, he was pleased to see that Adam had received his message and was waiting for him.

"Where is he Adam?" began Lance as he walked towards him.

"Follow me, he's through here," said Adam beginning away towards the room where Jonathan was laying.

"How is he really Adam, the truth?" demanded Lance as he walked with him.

"Straight, it's not good," replied Adam, he knew that Lance hated a sugary version of telling things to soften the blow, if it was bad news, it was bad news and he wanted to hear it as it was.

Both men rounded the far end of the corridor corner and came to the double doors, that were the entrance to the room where his Father lay. Lance upon reaching the doors, drew a deep breath and tried to calm himself. He found that he was beginning to feel really strange, at the thought, his Father was near to death the other side of the entrance. He entered leaving Adam outside. Lydia inside stood giving him a reassuring and understanding smile, to try and make him see she knew what he was going through. They both hugged and Lydia then informed him, she'd be around if he should need her. Lance nodded, then walked on to his Father's frail side. Jonathan held out his hands to him, glad he had made it in time. Lance quickly took hold of Jonathan's hands and came to sit down on the stool by his bunk. He tried to hide the pain that he felt inside at seeing his Father the way he was, ashen and near to death. It hurt like nothing he could describe. He fought back the tears. He had decided to tell him of the last Quest the team had endured, he figured that even though his Father was near to death, he would enjoy hearing the latest great feat, the Amalthean Quests team had pulled off. He began and found his Father listening with fighting interest.

Outside Lydia turned to look at the doors to Jonathan's room. She could hear Lance explaining the last Quest. She thanked God he had made it, to be by his Father's side in the final moments that there were. Adam crossed suggesting that maybe she should have some refreshment, as she had had nothing since first light that mornet before the Council Meeting, when Jonathan's trouble had struck suddenly. Lydia knew that Adam was trying to look after her and agreed, she walked with him on to the Refreshments Hall, but whether she would be able to eat, was another thing, thinking about what the outcome would be for Jonathan.

Mr Morganforn entered back into the room, as the silent alarm had sounded no sooner had he left the room earlier. He asked Lance for a discrete word. Lance agreed standing to his feet, he crossed with the Consultant to the other side of the room, where Morganforn explained that his Father had not taken the advice in taking things easy, hence his current condition, but there was something that he figured Lance should know, that had come to light. His Father's latest heart trouble had been brought on by an extreme heated argument in the chambers earlier, but what over his Father wouldn't divulge. Lance listened with great interest as he knew his Father to be one that never lost his patience, he was an extremely placid man. Jonathan behind them began going into the final moments before death. He called Lance with great difficulty in his voice and began going into the wheezing difficult to breath stage. Lance hurried to take hold of his Father hand and sit by his side for one last time.

"I'm right here Father," said Lance fighting back the tears of shear uncontrollable emotion.

"Lance my son, your now the last known Largon, I'm proud of you, serve Tayce well, she and Lydia will be like a family to you now, be good^e," said Jonathan then he faded again for the last time.

"I'm sorry Lance, he's in the final decline, there's nothing more we can do," said Morganforn in an apologetic tone putting a comforting hand on Lances shoulder.

"I want to know one thing?" asked Lance resting his Father's hand back down on the bunk.

"Of course what is it?" asked Morganforn giving Lance his full attention.

"Why couldn't he have had a new heart?" asked Lance, he found it strange that his Father hadn't been offered one.

"Your Father's organs surrounding his heart were too badly damaged, believe me Lance when I say, we advised your Father on his health many times, but you know what he was like, more than anyone, he was too stubborn for his own good and neglected his health a lot, sorry to say this, but he was his own destructive force," said Morganforn calmly and as gently as he could, he did not want to offend Lance.

"Dad, why didn't you listen?" said Lance turning back to Jonathan now gone.

Lance broke down, just as the young nurse that had been helping in Jonathan's care, entered the room. She glanced to Lance and then the still lifeless form of Jonathan Largon and felt Lances sorrow. She felt a certain sinking feeling in her own heart, Jonathan Largon had always been a good kind and understanding man, he would be missed. Lance stood to his feet tears showing clearly on his face, the hurt beyond all reason in his brown eyes. He slowly subconsciously turned to his Father. Looking at him for one last time.

"Bye Father, say hello to Mother for me," said Lance fighting another onslaught of emotional tears.

He walked away under the caring eyes of Mr Morganforn and the young nurse out of the room into the corridor. The founder and first leader of the Questa Headquarters Base, was gone he thought and everything good had gone with his Father, as he walked towards the open area balcony and looked to the wide open area beneath on the next level. He fought hard not to let go of the emotions, that were tugging at his heart making him cave in to tears, clouding his vision. He shook his head to try and fight the strong emotional loss. He didn't care if someone saw him, it didn't matter, people that knew what had been unfolding in the last hourons, would put two and two together and understand.

"Lance!" said a familiar female voice coming up behind him.

He turned to see Tayce, looking at him in a questioning way. Then she read his face and could see all that she wanted to know. Jonathan was gone. She opened her arms in a true understanding way. Lance walked into them, glad she was there. She knew what it was like to be going through what he was suffering, at that moment and she knew also, he was hurting beyond control. She reassured him again, that she and the team were there for him. He suddenly let go off all the hurt inside, pouring his heart out on her shoulder once more. Tayce let him go ahead, she realised that no one more than Lance, loved his Father the way he did and that special bond was now broken of Father and son forever. After a few minons Tayce let him go.

"I felt that something was wrong when I arrived and ran on ahead of the others, leaving Tom and Marc to take care of final procedures, security gave me a bit of a funny look, running, but I didn't care, I had this burning feeling that all was not right," she explained.

"Thanks for the loan of your Quest Shuttle/fighter, it gave me time to get here and spend time with him, before he said went," said Lance upset, holding back the tears with difficulty.

"Your welcome, my Quest is faster than the others in the fleet, I specifically asked for a faster model, I'm glad you made it on time," said Tayce studying him.

"I can't believe this has happened," said Lance not believing, what had occurred in the last hourons.

The doors to Jonathan's room opened and the medical internment team began out with Jonathan's body. Without warning it seemed like everything had suddenly gone very silent in the section and throughout the base. All noise around the area became deathly quiet, as if the whole base seemed to know that Jonathan Largon had gone never to return. Lance watched his Father leave for the last time, feeling the sudden emptiness as he passed on the Hover Trans Bunk, off to be prepared for the final ceremony of his life. Adam Carford and Lydia walked into view, both looked shocked at what they were witnessing. Both shook their heads at the loss. Adam forgot protocol and put an understanding arm around Lydia's shoulders to comfort her, as she had tears forming in her eyes. Treketa also soon came into view, she was surprised to see what was happening, she immediately crossed to Lance with support in mind as a friend, which he was glad of. Tayce crossed to her Mother, she couldn't believe Jonathan had gone so quickly.

"I think we better head to what was Jonathan's Officette, have you told the others where to meet us?" asked Lydia quietly.

"No, I just left Tom and Marc when I felt that something was wrong and Lance needed me," replied Tayce.

"I'll arrange everything for the General with our new assistant Aidan at the Officette, Lance won't need to worry about a thing, please tell him all will be taken care of, as his Father asked me to do this on his behalf, recently, after his last belt of heart trouble," explained Adam lightly.

"I'll contact the others, just to tell them where we're heading on to," suggested Tayce turning away to Wristlink Tom, to tell him what had happened and where they would be.

Tayce discreetly raised her Wristlink calling Tom on route as they all began away from the Cardiac Area of the Medical Health Complex off to what would now be termed as the Generals once Officette, until a new replacement could be found, to run the whole of Questa. They passed people who quickly offered their sincere sympathy and condolences to Lance at his loss of such a wonderful man, his Father. Workers in all aspects of Questonian life who knew Jonathan and Lance and respected them, acknowledged Lance with a smile and a reassuring nod. Once out of the Medical Health Complex area, they headed on across the square, enduring more sympathetic sincerities along the way, until they could see a vacant Vacuum Lift much to Lances relief. Lydia, Treketa and Tayce watched Lance concerned under great strain. They soon boarded the lift and were ascending to the Level where Jonathan's Officette was situated. Tayce thought about the first time when she had arrived on Questa and how Jonathan had made her very welcome, it was a shame that he would no longer be around, she thought. As the lift stopped on the destined level, everyone walked out the opening doors. The others were waiting for them, from the cruiser. Adam lead the way on into the Officette. Tom glanced at Lance, not quite knowing what to say, he understood his loss and what he was going through at that moment though, as he himself had been through just as much pain when Alenea died. Tayce followed on upon meeting Tom, falling in behind with the team. They soon walked through the opening doors into what was Jonathan's Officette. It felt strange, there was a certain deathly stillness, that hung in the air. Aidan Lord, newly appointed Assistant to Jonathan and Adam, in the Business section, stepped forth offering his extreme condolences. Lance accepted his words with a sorrowful nod, walking to the nearest seat sitting down. Adam gestured for everyone else to be seated. Lydia having temporary authority now that Jonathan had gone. It had been something Jonathan had made a condition, in the event should anything happen to him that Lydia would have immediate authority to take care of matters until a new replacement for his position could be found and recruited. Began giving orders to Adam and Aidan.

"Aidan you will be requested to take any orders as necessary, regarding ceremonial internment preparations from Adam here, when all is taken care of report back to me, with the final time and place," ordered Lydia in a true soft spoken tone of command.

"Would you like me to assist Aidan?" asked Adam as he could see that Aidan was looking unsure of what he was requested to do, as he had informed Lydia earlier, that he would take care of everything, but she had decided otherwise.

"No, I want you here to help me, you know what Jonathan put in place, should this situation unfold, you are to become my right hand man, in this instance," said Lydia straight she felt it was time Aidan did things on his own.

Adam nodded. Tayce looked at her Mother and recalled something that her Father had once said, when she was in her teens, that her Mother could quite easily take command in any situation should the reason for it arise. Adam stood by patiently waiting for his first orders, he was quite happy to become assistant to Lydia, as Jonathan had told him, tread carefully and she would treat him fairly. Lydia soon after her orders of what she wanted him to undertake, left him to continue, while she talked with Tayce and the team. Tayce crossed over to her, she could see that this wasn't going to be easy for her Mother, to adjust to.

"Mother, are you going to be all right?" she asked concerned.

"Yes I'll be fine, as unexpected as this situation is, it's something Jonathan has been training me up for, so even though I know I'm going to find it difficult to start with, until a replacement can be found, it will be strange but rewarding," replied Lydia assuringly.

Treketa crossed and sat by a sorrowful looking Lance, putting a friendly arm around his shoulders. Marc grabbed a cup of Coffeen handing it to Lance, suggesting he drink something, he hadn't had anything earlier so he'd been told. Lance accepted it with a nod of thanks, then began to drink the refreshing beverage. Marc headed back to the refreshments tray, that had been brought in to get himself a cup of refreshing Coffeen, asking if anyone else wanted one at the same time.

"Listen up everyone, one thing Jonathan did put into place was the written promise that in the event of what has happened, the Amalthean Quests are perfectly safe, so there is no threat at present of them taking the success of crime fighting away from any of you," explained Lydia.

"That's great news Mother," said Tayce greatly relieved at the fact, she was not about to lose the Amalthean Quests voyage at the present time anyway.

Lydia suggested that as they were all required to remain on the base for the internment, then it would be wise to use this out of space time, as shore leave. Tayce didn't like the idea of her Mother telling her team what to do, but on this occasion she would allow it. She agreed and the team split up heading on out under the words from herself, to stay out of trouble. Lance remained behind with Tayce, Tom and Lydia, there was much to do.

***

Two dayons later Questa Headquarters Base continued on in morning over the unexpected death of Jonathan Largon. In 'Q' City Square, black flags hung that had replaced the Questa colourful ones, in honour of the occasion. Many personnel walked around with black or grey arm bands on, in respect of the dayon. It was the mornet of the internment, Questa was having what was classed as a 'Break Dayon', where only the few personnel worked. Enabling others to attend the ceremony of Jonathan and pay their respects. The Docking Bay doors on Amalthea opened. Tayce walked forth with Tom on her arm, dressed in a black close fitting suit. The whole team as they ferried out, were dressed in dark colours of some sort, as a mark of respect to the founder of Amalthean Quests and Questa. Lance walked with Donaldo and Treketa. Tayce had suggested to Donaldo that he should keep an eye on Lance, as there was no telling which way his shock was going to surface, considering it hadn't surfaced as yet and he was bottling it up. Everyone walked through the Arrival and Departure Area, to meet up with Lydia in the square, with Adam and Aidan. It could be seen that it was going to be an elaborate affair, even as sad as it was. Both male and female delegates that knew Jonathan on the planetary council were heading to the Ceremonial Hall. The team followed on behind the delegates to be greeted by the sight of Jonathan's silver lead casket, ahead of them down the isle to the front area of the Hall. Tayce glanced to Lance and then Donaldo, watching understandingly the way Lance was feeling. There was a seating area up both sides of the isle, with elaborate displays of flowers around here and there, in colours befitting for the occasion. Tayce suggested the team go and find seats. She paused to speak to Adam who was walking in.

"Is everything all right, no questions needing answers?" he asked discretely as he approached her.

"I'd like to say a few words about Jonathan, if I may, is that possible?" asked Tayce.

"Of course, I'll call you up when it's time," replied Adam agreeably.

Empress Tricara acknowledged the teams presence, as she gracefully entered the Hall. She like others who knew Jonathan on a personnel basis, offered her condolences to Lance, then headed on to the front to take up her seat. Time slipped by in waiting for all the mourners to arrive, that were going to arrive. Finally the almost floor to ceiling doors to the Hall closed. An uncanny Silence filled the air and after a few minons Adam walked down the centre isle to the front. He bowed in respect of Jonathan, before his Casket then moved to one side, to wait to go and pick Tayce out for her speech later

261

"Call Deputy Councillor Lydia Traun to make a speech," came a stern to the point, eloquent male voice.

Everyone in the Hall glanced around as Lydia stood to her feet feeling nervous and walked up the steps to the platform and the small podium where a small built in microphone would relay her speech to the mourners both inside the Hall and out in the square. She stood for a few minons, gathering what she wanted to say.

"I look at you all before me here todayon, on this sad occasion and see rightfully, the grief we all share over a great man such as Jonathan Largon, some more than others, Jonathan will be remembered for the good he has done for both the base and you all here present, he put Questa on the Intergalactic map would you believe, but most of all Jonathan was a man that gave us his patience and time, when we asked for it, he made a lot of peoples ideas and incentives a reality, one being we all know as the Amalthean Quests crime fighting team, headed by my daughter Tayce, yes Jonathan you are a man that will go down in history and we will all miss you," said Lydia turning to Jonathan's Casket.

Upon Lydia finishing Adam began on walk down the isle to inform Tayce it was time for her speech. Tayce unexpectedly turned to Lance, suggesting he join her up front for her speech. He agreed, as he didn't feel that he could stand up at the front alone and face all the people his Father knew. He followed Tayce out down the isle under the concerned watchful eye of the gathered congregation. Silence was still very much apart of the atmosphere around the great Hall, whilst Tayce and Lance walked up onto the platform. Tayce let her Mother step back then began.

"It's an honour to be here todayon, to show mine and the teams respects to Jonathan on this sad occasion, he was a good man and without him my idea of a crime fighting team to clean up this Universe, would not have taken flight, he was like a second Father to me, but then he knew my Father, they were the best of friends in dealing with the many troubles that came up in the every dayon life that we lived back then, before my world was destroyed, Lance Largon here is a fine example of his Father, in the way he handles situations with the same amount of confidence and ease, General Largon will be remembered for yearons to come and I feel sorry for the next person who gets his position, as he'll have a lot to look up to, Thank you General for giving us a bright future and your time, we will miss you," said Tayce turning to bow to Jonathan's Casket.

Lance discretely thanked her then bowed in respect too.

"I have but one thing to say, no one could have wanted for a better Father than mine, he gave me something to aim for in my life, Father if your listening up there, thanks for everything," said Lance fighting back the tears.

Tayce draped her arm around his shoulders reassuringly and suggested discretely they head back to their seats. They both walked off the platform and received praise from many of Lances Father's delegates, as he passed, on his words. Another councillor that knew Jonathan stood up and began on how good a son Lance had been and how Jonathan had talked about him with nothing but praise. He went on to talk about how Jonathan had made Questa what it was and that was a base to be proud of, to be part of, if something needed to be done, then it was taken care of, to put a building, complex, or Dome up whatever needed to be done to restore it's glory, Questa had become the best it could ever be, in it's rising thirty-eight yearon history, thanks to one man who had a lot of scope for the future. He went on to express that whoever filled Jonathan's boots, then he hoped that they had the same forward thinking approach and could continue with the foresight to see things in the same way the great man himself did. He finally told funny story's and happenings, that got many of the congregation laughing. Finally a councillor who was near retirement stood and walked to the microphone. He began speaking on planetary matters of past and present that had a good outcome, thanks to intervention by Jonathan. It had been a sad couple of yearons, where members of the council had left places never to return namely Darius Traun, as yet his whereabouts unknown, whether he was in fact dead, or alive and now Jonathan Largon that laid before them. At the end of the ceremony Adam walked back to Lance asking him to accompany him back to the front. Two smartly dressed guards folded the Largon crest designed flag from being draped over Jonathan's Casket, then they walked forth in precise movement, as Lance came to a stop just ahead of them, out in the front area before the congregation. They handed the flag to him, then saluted a Questa military salute, then stepped back. Lance walked on to the Casket placing the folded flag down on top, then stepped back and bowed to his Father for the last time. He was still fighting the strong emotion of great loss as it tore at his heart. The memories of good times and tough times flashed in his thoughts, the many laughs he'd shared with his Father, when growing up, until the present dayon. His Father personally teaching him to fly a fighter, helping him in his studies to reach an 'A' Grade in the Complex of Learning. Donaldo walked out of the seating area, he could see that Lance was straining and had informed Tayce that Lance in his current state was not going to take much more. He walked down to meet him and walked back with him concerned. Lydia from where she was, looked to Lance also concerned, she considered him like the son she could never have and she felt he was being extremely brave. She stood to her feet walking back to the Microphone.

"Let us pray for a peaceful eternity for Jonathan Largon, Father and General," said Lydia.

Everyone around the hall lowered their heads and closed their eyes to pray for the Journey of peace. Tayce before doing so glanced at Tom, he was looking back at her. He winked affectionately and reached out to clasp her hand. Once he had hold of her hand, he squeezed it reassuringly. Slowly up front Jonathan's Casket began to move on a suspended cushion cold energy beam towards the jettison hatch, then as it slowly opened, the Casket headed on through until out of sight and jettisoned into space. The jettison hatch closed and the founder of Questa Headquarters Base was no more. The various aliens and human people that had come to pay their final respects stood and began on the walk out of the Hall. Many shook hands with Lance on the way. Donaldo in the capacity of watchful cruisers medical man, stayed with him as did Treketa. Tayce stepped out of the seating area waiting for her Mother. Tom followed on. Aidan kindly stepped forward offering to take anyone who wanted to leave, up to the Celebration of Passing. The celebration of passing was very much like an old Earthon tradition called a 'Wake' but this century, it was a means to say that the person was on their way to an eternity of peace. It signified that the celebration of friends and family gave a guiding light, by which that person would be guided to the peace and tranquil existence, such as it was, in the other realm. Tayce turned to the team suggesting that they go on. Donaldo asked was she sure, they could wait? Tayce nodded. Tom stayed behind also, whilst Aidan lead the others away on out behind the many people leaving. Once the Hall was empty Tayce stood in thought for a while.

"You know the way your Mother conducted herself at this ceremony, she would make a good contender for Jonathan's position," said Tom suddenly.

"Tom for Gods sake, Jonathan's only passed to eternity two dayons ago," said Tayce in surprised reprimanding whisper.

"Sorry, I wasn't thinking!" he said, feeling somewhat awkward that he'd said what he had without thinking.

"No it's all right, it's just I was surprised the way you came out with it, but when you come down to it you do have a point, she apparently has that certain commanding knack for the position and I think she could settle in nicely," replied Tayce seeing his point.

Tom walked across the row of the seating area and gently turned Tayce around. He gently advised her that maybe they ought to catch her Mother later and join the others at the 'Celebration of Passing' Tayce nodded. Tom slipped his arm around her waist lovingly and guided her on out, leaving Adam talking with her Mother. Neither one noticing, that both he and Tayce had left.

People were mingling with drinks of various colours and in various designed shaped glassene's, a while later at the Celebration of Passing. Treketa sat watching the different ranked members of Questa personnel talk with Lance. She was quite surprised to find out that he knew so many influential men and women. Empress Tricara crossed and began talking with her, noticing that she looked lost and alone. Tayce and Tom walked in and were immediately offered drinks by a welcoming hostess, to toast a farewell toast to be announced soon. Tayce wasn't much for drinking, but on this occasion, she would make an exception. She accepted the tall stemmed glass with sparkling Stavern in, then crossed to talk with Tricara. Tom took his drink and did the same, only while Tayce was talking with Tricara he caught up with Marc and Lydia. The elderly councillor that had spoken earlier for Jonathan, soon crossed to join the discussion about Jonathan and what might happen with Questa in general.

"Tayce, I'd like you to meet someone your Father use to talk about when you were growing up, this is Councillor Waynard Bayden, do you remember my daughter Councillor, Tayce, well she's now Lieutenant Commander of the Amalthean Quests team?" introduced Lydia in friendly manner.

"Yes, I remember young Tayce, how are you, Jonathan told me about the good you and your team were doing, he was truly amazed at some of the things you've taken on, especially the one where you took on Countess Vargon, your a credit to your Father young woman, he would be very proud of you," said Waynard glad to see her.

"I'm fine Councillor, it's good to see you again, Countess Vargon as you know, is at large once more, she's a tricky person to trap, but should she appear, we'll be ready for her," assured Tayce.

"I have no doubt, you will, you're like your Father, he wouldn't stop when he had to tackle something important that had to be stopped, or brought to justice," said Waynard in polite tone.

"Marc Dayatso you managed to survive the onslaught attack on Traun then, it's good to see you again," said Waynard turning to Marc glad to know he had made it off Traun alive.

"Yes sir, I'm part of Tayces team now, as Commander and wouldn't trade it for anything," said Marc.

"Tell me Marc is Tayce here like her Father, keeps you on your toes," asked Waynard discretely with a grin.

"Yes sir, she certainly does," replied Marc light-heartedly.

"You must be Tom Stavard, Tayces Legal Intimate Joining partner?" asked Waynard turning to Tom.

"Yes sir that's correct and I wouldn't have it any other way, Tayce here is one special lady," said Tom drawing Tayce to him with a gentle squeeze.

Waynard smiled a gentle smile. He was a kind mellow looking man of round statue and average height, he had whitish blonde hair and a beard rather like an old professor. It was assumed that he was in his late 60s to mid 70s as he never let his age be known to anyone and no one had dared to ask him, but it was a known fact he had started at Questa roughly before Jonathan Largon took over, as General, he had taught Jonathan all he needed to know in running an Earthon 2 type base, such as Questa. Suddenly there came the sound of three single gong type sounds. This signified the farewell toast to Jonathan. Waynard took his glassene of Stavern and walked to the centre of the room, asking for everyone's immediate attention. When the room had fallen silent and everyone was looking at Waynard, he began in a well educated voice.

"I have known Jonathan for many yearons and it gives me great pleasure to do this farewell toast, so please each and everyone of you raise your glassenes… to Jonathan Largon, Father, General and good friend also founder of this base, may he find happiness in the realm of Eternity, to Jonathan!" said Waynard raising his glassene to a Image representation of Jonathan, high on the wall at the front of the room.

The guests gathered around him, also raised their glassenes in a final salute, to the great man, then drank down the final drink of the celebration. Tayce glanced around for Lance. She saw him alone, walking out of the open glassene doors and leaning over the chrome rail, of the outside balcony. She excused her presence and took her glassene walking on out through the gathered mingling guests, leaving the rest of the team to mingle. She walked on through the open doorway, out onto the balcony, coming to a pause beside Lance.

"You okay, do you want to talk, I'm proud of the way in which you've held it together todayon," said Tayce in an understanding and quiet tone beside him.

"Thanks, I can't believe Father knew so many influential people," he began, continuing to look down into the City Square below them.

"Your Father was a man of great importance and had a lot of influence, everyone that's back in there knows that, that's why they all came, he's helped them in so many ways and they appreciate that, I for one would not have the Amalthean Quests team if your Father hadn't seen the potential it could bring, I'm grateful for that alone beside giving me the best team member I could have in you," said Tayce meaningfully.

Both continued talking about the dayon in general, Lydia saw them and walked out worried that Lance might be finding the whole celebration, to much. Upon seeing that Tayce and he were just talking she casually and quietly announced that it was time for him to thank the guests for attending the Celebration of Passing. Lance nodded understandingly and walked ahead of Tayce and Lydia, back on into the celebration room. The room was roughly the size of a small Celebration Hall, big enough to hold medium sized functions. Lance like Waynard had done earlier, began asking for everyone's attention for the last time. They all stopped talking and turned their attention to him.

"Firstly, to all of you here, thank you for coming todayon, Father would have been pleased that so many of you had turned out to pay your last respects, thank you to Waynard, Lydia for your kind words at the ceremony, you too Tayce for your support, I know it's something Father would have enjoyed listening to, he would have been overwhelmed to see what so many people thought of him, in such an admiring way," said Lance with a nod.

"Well done, nice speech," said Tayce discretely at his side.

"Thanks!" he said glancing to her.

Some of the guests that had to leave, stopped to tell Lance to take things easy and take care, then walked on out of the room back to where they had come from. The remainder of the guests stayed and talked amongst themselves on many topics. Even though Jonathan had only been dead for two dayons, the discussion had turned to who might be his new replacement, for the council and the running of the vast sized base. Would it fall to Lance being his only son and heir? Who would it be? Adam and Aidan entered the Hall and crossed to the area where Lydia, Lance and Tayce were standing in discussion on the very subject. Lance deep down remembered his Father saying that all of Questa would be his some dayon, but did it mean that he would have to give up his duty on Amalthea, move back to the base, as the new replacement for his Father. He stood in thought for a minon, knowing that if anyone in his estimation was right for the job apart from himself, it was Lydia, she had good leadership skills, as she use to take care of affairs on Traun with Darius her coupling partner. She had done the same on their present surroundings until his Father died, been his right hand so to speak taking care of many of the arising matters, that had arisen. Adam came to a pause

"Ladies and Gentlemen, honoured guests, if I may ask for your attention once again, I know that it has been an extremely sad occasion for all of us todayon, but a couple of dayon ago when the other members of council found that General Largon was not going to survive this latest attack in his illness, it was put forth the choosing of a newly elected chief of Questa, it gives me great pleasure to announce that new chief here todayon and it is someone that General Largon would most sincerely approve of, I give you without further delay, Chief and councillor Lydia Traun, Questas new head of base," said Adam turning and beginning applause.

Lydia without further word fainted with the sudden shock of finding out it was her. Marc quickly caught her as she began to fall and helped her to a nearby seat. Lance quickly fetched a glassene of Plicetar, to revive her as thunderous applause erupted all around. Donaldo hurried to her side discretely checking that she was all right. After a few minons she regained both conciousness and her composure.

"Did I hear right, I'm the new replacement for Jonathan to run this base?" asked Lydia almost speechless at the very thought.

"That's right Mother, your the new leader and chief of Questa," confirmed Tayce pleased at the fact beside her.

"You deserve it Lydia, Father would be proud, and I for one give you my approval and good luck for the position," said Lance managing a smile through his sorrow, also glad that it wasn't him after all.

As everyone congratulated Lydia, Lance stood back and could in his minds eye, see his Father in the corner of the room smiling and nodding in total agreement of who had been chosen as his replacement. Lance was glad that Lydia had been chosen, as he liked his life amongst the stars, being a member of the Amalthean Quests team. Lydia after receiving all the congratulations sauntered back to

Lance, asking for a quiet word. He agreed. They walked together out of the room and onto the balcony. Tayce watched feeling overjoyed at what her Mother had become, wondering what her Father would think, it was truly something. Lydia paused out on the balcony expressing to Lance that just because she had taken his Father's place, it did not mean that he did not have a home to return to. Questa would always be his home and she would always be there for him, if he needed someone to confide in, because he would always be considered like the son she never had. Both Lance and Lydia hugged and he thanked her, with tears swelling in his brown eyes.

"Your one special lady Chief Traun, what you've said means a lot to me," he said breaking free.

"Your welcome," said Lydia with a motherly smile.

They returned to the reception noticing that most of the people that had been present for the announcement of the new leader had ferried on out. The cleaning Techs were already arriving to tidy and clean up the room after the celebration. They moved about with discretion. Lance noticed that they too were feeling the loss of the great Jonathan Largon and realised that they weren't probably the only section on the base to feel the same. Donaldo sauntered across to Lydia. Treketa followed. They were going back to the cruiser. Lydia thanked them for coming. Donaldo wished her luck, as the new chief, then began on out with Treketa to the entrance. Treketa paused turning.

"Are you coming Lance?" asked Treketa casually.

"It's okay. I'll come back with Tayce and Tom," he replied.

"All right, catch you later," she replied carrying on after Donaldo.

"Right Mother, I'll leave you with Adam here, to sort out your first orders as new chief of Questa and I'll see you before we leave tomorron," said Tayce bending giving her Mother a kiss on the cheek.

"I hope your first hourons aren't anything too hazardous in beginning your new duties," said Tom as he began away across the room.

"What would Darius say, first assistant to Jonathan and now running the base, he'd be proud that's what," said Marc kindly, then followed on behind Tayce and Tom.

Lydia watched all three team members head on back to the cruiser and Lance lagging behind, then Tayce turn and speak to him, that made him fall in with them. Adam prompted Lydia gently to accompany him, which she did, she walked on out heading to what was Jonathan's Officette, that was to be hers and would be known as her Officette and chambers. Adam and Lydia as they went, talked about how the base had been effected by Jonathan's sudden untimely death.

***

Next dayon on Questa, business was returning to near normal. Flights came and went as normal. Alien species travelled through the port on their way to somewhere else. Personnel began conducting business in the many purchasing centres around the City Square. But the flags that had hung in the square the dayon before, were still obvious and half mask, which they would remain, for the rest of the weekon in continuing respect to Jonathan Largons passing. Tayce walked off Amalthea with Tom and Lance. They briskly began walking along through the square on up to Lydia's new chambers, as her Mother said, she wanted to see her before they left Questa, to continue on with the Amalthean Quests voyage. They were greeted by people, that they had met the dayon before at the celebration as they went.

Lydia felt strange, as she sat at what was Jonathan's desk for the first time, it was hard to comprehend that she was now in charge of such a large headquarters base, as Questa. Adam smiled, as he caught her looking into nothingness in deep thought. He was going to make her adjustment as easy as he possibly could. He walked across the Officette Chambers carrying the Disc Chip on the Amalthean voyage, as requested. He handed it to her. The chambers doors opened and two men entered carrying another desk, they crossed and placed it to one side of the chambers. This was followed by Aidan, who under Lydia's orders had brought his personal belongings for his desk. She had decided that she wanted him in with her, so that they could freely and confidently discuss matters, enabling Adam to be involved as well. Aidan had been given promotion to First Officer to Lydia, whilst Adam would remain her immediate Personal Assistant, when visiting dignitaries would come to the base and assist her on council related matters, whilst Aidan would take care of the many problems that arose around Questa and consult her if needed. Tayce and Tom with Lance not far behind were the first to visit her in her new surroundings. As they crossed over to her, Lance remained to talk to Adam on things in general.

"Good mornet Mother, settling in already!" said Tayce noticing the two men leave, that had brought in the desk.

"Your early," said Lydia glad to see her just the same.

"Yes, we want to get under way, crime doesn't stop because we aren't out there, so what did you want to see us about?" enquired Tayce.

"I need you just to sign the new contract for your Amalthean Quests orientated voyage, for a further two yearons, that's all," replied Lydia casually.

Without further word, Tayce crossed to the imprint pad that Adam was holding, she picked up the imprint type utensil and signed on the screen to seal officially the contract with Questa and her voyage for another two yearons. Tom did the same to act as witness to Tayces indent.

"All signed, anything else you need us for before we leave you to settle in?" said Tayce giving Lydia her full attention.

"Lance I said yesteron that I wanted you to consider Questa still your home and your Father's residence will remain your home, despite I'll be in residence there, I want you to treat it as you always have done, until such time that you feel you want to do otherwise," she said with a kind motherly look on her beautiful features.

"Thank you, it means a lot to me, and you living there will give me comfort to know, that Father's residence is in good hands," he said pleased at the fact.

"We'll be like one big happy family Lance," said Tayce trying to cheer him up.

"Quite!" replied Lance, nodding amused at the fact.

Tayce glanced at her Wristlink time display, suggesting it was time they get going. Lydia walked with them to the outer Anteroom. Here she said her goodbyes and watched them leave. They walked away back down the corridor back to Amalthea. Lydia watched until everyone was gone from sight, then went back into her Officette Chambers to continue her new duty, as the new chief of Questa.

***

Jonathan Largon the founder of Questa was no more. Lance had lost his loving Father and true friend. Lydia was now chief over the whole of Questa. Something that a couple of monthons ago she would never had believed if someone had suggested it to her.

270

The Return of Vargon and Her Outlaws

Amalthea had been back in space on voyage course for three dayons. News that had materialised during this time was the kind that no one on board really wanted to hear, coming from Questa. Countess Vargon had surfaced in her usual style and already caused death and destruction in her wake, only this time she had brought into the open, her daughter, the one and only Sallen and this time around, she was aided by a bunch of outlaws. Several bases and vessels had already succumbed to the usual terrorizing tactics that the Countess was famous for. But for Tayce she had been looking forward to this moment and was more than ready to take on her arch enemy. She smiled to herself upon hearing the fact, Sallen was now part of the Countesses attack force, she guessed that some group, a bunch of ne'er-do-wells, had rescued Sallen from her set course, that she had been sent on after the last encounter with her. She wondered if the vessel she had been in had also been repaired. Now she was back with her Mother. Double trouble thought Tayce. No doubt she would probably have an ulterior motive in mind, as far as revenge went towards herself being on an unchangeable course, thought Tayce. Further reports stated that Sallen had rendezvoused with her Mother and she in turn had made a very appealing offer for her to join forces, form a large attack force to be reckoned with, their next subject was none other than the Amalthea and Tayce. Tayce raised her eyes not surprised by the fact when she received the information. What Vargon wasn't unaware of was the fact, that the Amalthea she had tried to destroy the last time, was the first Amalthean Cruiser, not the current new improved model, this one was far superior to it's predecessor.

Tayce as she sat on the bunk in the Life Ability Centre, began wondering what guise Vargon would try and attack her and the cruiser in this time? Would she use Sallen? Tom briskly entered the Centre, as the doors parted, he began that he had brought further news on Vargons resurface. Donaldo finished administering the injection, then stood waiting to hear what was the latest, as did Treketa.

271

"She has a battle cruiser this time around, also seems to have repaired the damage to her old Lair, though whether the battle cruiser belongs to her is, another thing, it could belong to the outlaws that she joined forces with," read Tom.

"I'm not interested, it doesn't matter what she's got, I'm ready for her," retorted Tayce unimpressed.

"No Tayce, it's too dangerous, she's not alone this time, she has Sallen and a group of outlaws," said Tom far from pleased at the fact, she was determined to take on Vargon on her own

"Who said I was going in alone, she doesn't scare me remember, I have just as much power source as she has and as I recall last time, I won," retorted Tayce.

"I hate to agree with Tom here, but he's right, it's dangerous and I suggest we all take her on together, when the time comes," suggested Donaldo, he could see Tom's point, if something went wrong, she could wind up dead.

"I'm depending on you to help me take on her outlaws Donaldo, leaving her to me," said Tayce heading towards the entrance doors, leaving Tom, Donaldo and Treketa stumped for words behind her.

Tom knew that no matter what they said Tayce was headstrong and what she decided to do, she'd do. He sighed shaking his head at her strong will, then followed on as she walked out the opening doors not looking back. Treketa and Donaldo exchanged raised eye glances, this was not going to be easy, Tayce was prepared to risk everything in order to end Countess Vargons life, once and for all. Treketa could understand Tom's concern, he loved Tayce and didn't want to lose her to the evil hands of Vargon, or the outlaws, at any cost. Donaldo shook his head, Tayce amazed him at times, how she danced in the face of danger. Treketa on the other hand even though she understood her brothers concern for Tayce, knew deep down that she could hold her own against the likes of Vargon and could see where she was coming from. She also knew that Tayce would not put the team or herself in danger deliberately it wasn't her style. She herself had a score to settle with Sallen for getting her kicked out of College Colony. Her last encounter was just the beginning of her revenge, sending Sallen on that one way trip.

Lance was back at his duty position in Organisation as Quests Research and Informations Officer. He had found that occupying his mind and immersing himself in his duty, would help him through the grieving process, even though at times it was hard to ignore the fact he would not be seeing his Father any more. He had no sooner seated himself and was immediately engrossed in keying away to search and probe the latest on the Countesses last moves, when he was suddenly distracted by a heated debate over the Countess of Tom and Tayce as they came up the corridor, something he found strange, as she and Tom were rarely at each other, in the way they seemed to be at present. They both soon entered Organisation, Tayce stopped at his position trying to calm herself.

Lance looked up at her meeting her furious look, he raised his eyes in jest, over what he'd just heard and silently whispered could he help? Tayce shook her head, asking for an update on what was happening. Tom joined Marc in the control seat and seemed less than impressed with Tayce, Marc glanced at him noticing his look of total angered impatience. It was something new to Tom the way Tayce was behaving, but it wasn't new to him. There was numerous times, he himself being aide to Darius Traun had witnessed Tayces stubborn attitude, the fact that if she set her mind to do something come what may, what the outcome might be, then she'd do it and there was nothing that was going to stop her, he'd been present when her Father had forbid her to do what she wanted, when it was considered dangerous. He'd lost count of how many times the Commodore had requested he find her and bring her before him, for disobeying orders. Lance began to recite the information that was rolling up on the screen before him.

"According to search probe information states the Countess, in the last two hourons alone, has destroyed no less than ten different kinds of vessel, wiping out quite a few people, whether they were innocent or not, what's more she's leading these attacks from a new improved domain."

"Up to her familiar tricks once more, no change there then!" said Tayce in a not to surprised tone.

"Certainly looks like it, I'll keep you up to date as things unfold, I'll see if I can search out anything on her battle cruiser she's suppose to be in command of, so that we can see what were up against," suggested Lance.

"Good idea, but be careful, I don't want her finding out the origin of search, us, not just yet, just in case she tries to catch us unaware, nothing would give her the greatest pleasure," said Tayce seriously.

"Don't worry I'll be discrete and protective, if I have to, she'll have a hard time tracking us," assured Lance.

Tayce began thinking what the kind of look the Countess would give if she knew that Lance was taking a walk around her computer systems, to gain the necessary knowledge in assisting herself and the team to know what they were up against. She smiled to herself, guessing that it wouldn't be a good one. She crossed to the Meeting Centre ordering Tom to join her, she wanted a quiet word. Marc kept looking ahead he was not going to be involved, but he found the whole thing somewhat amusing as Tom sighed and said under his breath "here we go again", as he left the seat. Midge said he was glad that he wasn't a human, at least he didn't have to endure human heated debates. Tom headed on into the Meeting Centre. The doors closed. Both Marc and Lance looked around their seats, in the direction of the clear vision doors of the Meeting Centre, then exchanged raised eye glances. It could clearly be seen that after a few minons, the heated debate was over. By what was taking place intimately. Both Lance and Marc smiled somewhat amused and went back to their duties.

Roughly three hourons later, when Lance had gained all the necessary information he needed and it had been discovered Vargon was in fact stationed at a new improved hideout/lair, which she had named Genuslan 2. Amalthea was on a set course to bring the cruiser into orbit of Genuslan 2. The battle cruiser that Vargon had been using had been her means to travel to her new base and had gone back to its own base, or suppose to have done according to research. Midge had managed to save the dayon, by stopping a feed back coming through from the Lair to Lances console during the probing in Vargons computer systems, it had nearly blew the whole on board computer system but he had quickly averted the power surge, as soon as the feed back came, Midge retaliated sending it back to where it had originated, which would cause trouble at the source.

"Thanks Midge, we nearly had it, they nearly broke the security link," said Lance much relieved.

"No problem, I quite enjoyed giving Vargon a taste of her own dirty tactics," said Midge light heartedly.

A while later it could be seen that Tayce and Tom had dissolved their differences and the air had calmed between them, over the outcome of Tayces decision over Vargon. No one would know what was said, only that they had both emerged from the Meeting Centre in a better frame of mind, than they had entered earlier. Midge announced discretely to Marc, that the storm clouds had passed! Meaning everything had returned to normal. Tayce began by ordering Marc, to take his duty break, she would take over. He stretched, as he got out of the control seat, as he had been seated for almost four hourons, without a Coffeen break. He headed off out of Organisation. Tom sat next to Tayce, in the Co-pilot seat.

"Your not going to believe this Tayce, but I'm getting the readings of a large object ahead and the readings are growing by the cencron," said Duncan suddenly over her shoulder.

"Anything on screen yet Lance?" requested Tayce.

"Information states it's a large battle cruiser and it's drifting, according to this, there doesn't seem to be any sign of life aboard," replied Lance keying in and retrieving the information he wanted.

"Put up our protection shield to maximum level AX-1 Midge, Now!" ordered Tayce in urgency.

"Raising protection shields to required level, it looks like the battle cruiser could be under some kind of computer operation and could be a decoy Tayce," replied Midge.

"This is the same battle cruiser that Vargons been using, but It's suppose to have left her, at her hideout and headed back to it's own planet, something isn't right here," said Lance

"Do you think that she would let it just drop her off and go away easily, because I don't," said Tayce knowing what Vargon was capable of and how Midge could be right.

"What happened to the crew, that's what I want to know?" asked Tom.

"I'm inclined to think that they joined forces and let her put their battle cruiser out here, as an elaborate decoy, which I'm not surprised at," said Midge.

Tayce sat back in thought, studying the drifting battle cruiser, waiting, prepared for the first move of action from Vargons domain. But nothing. Midge like Tayce was ready and waiting to act to block any unprovoked attack on the cruiser.

"Confirmation coming in from Questa, that our latest discovery before us, is to be treated as part of a Quest to find out what the Countess is up to, on Genuslan 2," said Midge.

Tayce listened, her mind still half on what kind of moves Vargon would make next with the battle cruiser towards them. But to her surprise without warning, it began to pull away from them, heading off. Lance stated as much over her shoulder, but added that he didn't know how it was being manoeuvred, as there were no sign of engine power, or life on board, that could make it leave their current orbit.

"Follow it Midge, but keep us at a safe distance, in case we need to pull away quickly, keep us on course for the hideout though, at any cost," ordered Tayce watching the sight before them through the sight port.

"You've got it," replied Midge undertaking Tayces request.

Amalthea followed on behind the battle cruiser, keeping at a safe orbital distance. Duncan at his position suddenly found that he was picking up a conversation between the Countess and her daughter Sallen, on the surface of Genuslan 2. He quickly turned informing Tayce. She immediately handed control to Tom leaving her seat walking over to listen to what was being discussed over the Miroceive. It could he heard that the Countess had somehow detected the Amalthean Cruiser and was discussing with her daughter. How she, Sallen would get the chance for revenge, for the unmentionable and unnecessary journey Tayce had sent her on, on their last encounter, after the annual awards ceremony. As Tayce listened further she could hear Sallen agreeing wholeheartedly to her Mother's suggestion and explaining various ways she could put Tayce through the worst kind of torture, she could imagine and Treketa. Tayce raised her eyes to Duncan at the mere threats that Sallen was making, he smiled and nodded, as he was also listening. They were both finding the whole scenario amusing. She knew that Treketa would more than be a match for Sallen, should she try something in revenge, because she hadn't finished with her yet either, regarding the College Colony incident. She knew that the next step was to put the investigative Quest into operation, prepare for arrival at Vargons new improved hideout. She removed the Miroceive and handed it back to Duncan.

"Thanks for the eavesdrop, very entertaining!" said Tayce amused.

"Quite, wasn't it?" said Duncan almost laughing.

"Midge block their scanners from finding our whereabouts, I don't want Vargon thinking that she holds all the aces in this game, I don't want them finding out we're nearby and that we are sneaking up on her, Sallen and her new outlaws," said Tayce.

"Already done, I put it into operation about half an hour on ago, when we first encountered this battle cruiser before us, I can't see why they are still able to detect us and track our every move," replied Midge.

"She's probably using some kind of device that breaks the law, remember she always likes to think she's a cut above anyone else in the unlawful stakes, she probably borrowed it from the outlaws she's currently running with, but if she thinks that's going to make a difference, using the latest technology to find me, she can think again, this cruiser has a few new surprises of her own," said Tayce with a hint of spitefulness in her voice.

"Quite!" said Lance in total agreement.

She continued on with the procedures for going down onto Genuslan 2. She crossed ordering Tom to place Amalthea in a risk-free protective orbit over the new improved hideout/lair. Tom agreed commencing the request. Tayce then began thinking about who she would take down to the planet surface, she wouldn't take everyone for the reason the battle cruiser may be playing dead and could be activated on Vargons command to attack and try and destroy the cruiser, at a cencrons notice, this Tayce was not prepared to take a chance on. Midge advised her that if Vargon was tracking them, maybe getting Amalthea to a protected Transpot distance would be wise, other than taking a Quest, just in case they needed to depart the planet surface at short notice and it would enable them to land in Vargons backyard, without being detected. Tayce could see where he was coming from, it was a good idea and wholeheartedly agreed.

***

Genuslan 2, Vargons improved domain, resembled an Army type camp environment, nothing interesting to describe about it. But it could be clearly seen, that it was a cover for something more deep below the familiar concretex and green vegetated surface. Something far more treacherous and the true identity of the Countess, namely technology that had come from an unknown source and the kind that was expected to form part of the Countesses new existence. She was the kind of woman that even though everything she stood for was classed as wrong and evil, she always expected the best out of her men and equipment, this now went for her daughter too.

"Mother, that Amalthean Cruiser is still in our orbit, what are you intending to do?" asked Sallen taking her eyes from the screen and the sight of Amalthea looking towards her Mother.

"At this precise moment nothing, let them carry on thinking that we haven't detected them, let them come, you want your chance for payback with both Traun and Stavard, well you'll get it if your patient, if it's one thing you learn in this Universe girl, all comes to those who lay plans and wait," Vargon replied evilly.

"I'm not with you Mother?" asked Sallen unsure of what Vargon was saying.

"No Sallen, you never are, listen, I've laid out my plan and Tayce Traun and her so called team will arrive unaware that I'm waiting for them," replied Vargon, not giving a damn at the fact.

"But what are you going to do to them?" persisted Sallen.

"Silence girl, wait and see, patience!" said Vargon getting fed up with Sallen's unnecessary persistence.

Sallen looked down at the grey floor, she felt that she had over stepped the mark. She did not probe any further, if it was one thing she had learned after a couple of powerful scolds from her Mother, was never to keep on persisting when needing answers. The Countess turned and abruptly ordered her to go and make sure that the troopers were in their positions, ready for the arrival of the Amaltheans. Sallen walked away like an obedient child, in her all in one black and red outfit, not looking back. The relationship between Vargon and Sallen was not a normal Mother daughter loving one. Vargon had always treated Sallen as something that she did not want, and considered her a mere accident, that should not have happened. She treated her no better than one of her outlaws, she ran with. Sallen had adjusted to a life of nothing more than doing what her Mother had so unlawfully wanted her to do, without protest. Hence what she had become had been down to the way in which she had been brought up. But on occasions, she had wondered what it would like to have normal law abiding parents. Her Father most of the time was away, so she rarely saw him and he like her Mother pretended she wasn't around, when he did come home, he just acknowledged the fact that she was doing well criminally.

**

The team for the Quest had been selected, it consisted of Marc, Tayce, Treketa, Duncan, Donaldo and Lance. They were all heading down to the Transpot Centre on Amalthea. Tayces Wristlink bleeped on her wrist. She raised it answering. Tom up in Organisation informed her in urgency, that the battle cruiser before them had suddenly sprang on alert status and in the last twenty minons Midge had picked up the Countesses life signs on board and they weren't there previously. Tayce upon this, ordered everyone back to Organisation Deck, the Quest was on hold to travel down to the new hideout. She began away in urgency, she had no intention of setting foot on Genuslan 2 with Vargon out in the Universe, obviously planning to ambush her the moment she set foot on the surface, with the Quest team. The Quest members ran back to Organisation keeping in time with Tayce ahead.

***

Outside in the Universe the most ugly looking battle cruiser, that anyone could ever imagine was in a stationary orbit. It sat looking dark and menacing, ready for action. Weapons were situated at every point of its is protruding points from the central round body. It was in orbit between Genuslan 2 and Amalthea and was ready to destroy Amalthea, at Vargons orders. Both vessels faced each other, at a distance, in an almost face off, in good against evil.

Tayce ran into Organisation to be greeted through sight port by the sight of the menacing battle cruiser facing them. Tom stood to his feet, coming round the control seat to meet her, glancing at the sight port as he did.

"You say she's over there right now, but twenty or so minons ago, she was detected by Duncan on the surface of Genuslan 2, she either has a clone, or some new form of our Transpot, are you absolutely sure it's her?" demanded Tayce, as the rest of the Quest team came to a pause behind her.

"Midge double checked the readings comparing them with previous readings of Vargon on the surface and believe me she's over there, like you say, she must have some kind of new Transpot," confirmed Tom.

"What's that evil bitch up to now, doesn't she know that this cruiser is an equal match for that battle cruiser, unlike our old one?" said Tayce, trying to make some kind of sense of it all.

"If you want my opinion, she's playing a game of what Earthon 2 people use to call, cat and mouse, only she's using you as the mouse, she's getting dangerous," said Marc.

"Let's let her think that she's calling all the shots, she won't have that hold over us for long, considering what I have planned for her and her so called daughter," said Tayce in thought.

"What are you going to do?" asked Tom seeing her in thought and staring out at the battle cruiser.

"Midge pinpoint the main power source on that battle cruiser, shut it down," ordered Tayce still staring blankly out at the cruiser before them.

Tom glanced at Marc in surprise. He just shook his head in awe. Without warning out from underneath the battle cruiser emerged Vargons new Fighter Troops, in sleek white Fightercron fighters. Midge confirmed their actions in urgency and announced he was raising protection shields. Tayce watched wondering just what this latest plan was, Vargon was unleashing. She tried to put herself for a moment in the evil woman's boots, to try and think what she would do to stop herself and the Amalthean members from coming close to the new hideout on Genuslan 2. Tayce as she thought along the lines of Vargons possible ideas, wondered what was so important to her on Genuslan 2, that needed protecting? She walked to the weapons console and paused for a few minons. It was time to let Vargon know just what this new version of the Amalthea One was capable of unleashing. Also, she wanted her team to fight in Quest Shuttle/fighters to show Vargon that she was just as much of a challenge, against the Fightercrons.

"Quest team to Quests, she wants to play dirty, let's show her we're an equal match, we'll meet on the surface when were through," ordered Tayce.

The Quest team turned and ran back out down the corridor, to head on down to the Flight Hanger Bay. Tom stood watching the Fightercrons get into an attack formation about a milon to the right of Amalthea. Then as Tayce headed on out the Organisation door, he silently said.

"I hope you know what your getting into."

He climbed back into the control seat and proceeded to watch what was unfolding throughout the sight port. Hoping to God that Tayce wouldn't try anything unnecessarily foolish, he wanted her back alive.

Countess Vargon on her battle cruiser laughed in her evil callous way, as she received an up to date report from one of her operatives, that they had lost all power in section 4 engines, all main engine power was inoperable. He could not see what was so funny, as they were now classed as sitting targets.

"Relax man, these are just feeble attempts by Tayce Traun to think that she can win, get men to that section now and redirect main power to our back up engines," ordered Vargon.

"Mother, our men on the surface are ready, your amused by something, what it is?" said Sallen walking to come beside her Mother in the middle of the deck, as she had just travelled up from the surface.

"Tayce Traun has made her first feeble attempt to stop me, you can join the men on the surface and get your chance to fight the Stavard girl, once and for all, while I take care of Tayce Traun," said Vargon

"Very well Mother, I look forward to taking Stavard on once and for all, I want to see the whites of her eyes when I put an end to her feeble little excuse for a life, once and for all," said Sallen with evil glee.

"Enjoy your fun, soon Stavards death will become a further achievement in your training," said Vargon.

For a moment Mother and daughter stood watching as the Fightercrons unleashed their immense firepower on the Amalthean Quest Shuttle/fighters, as they came into view from the Flight Hanger Bay entrance on Amalthea. The scene was one of immense battle, as exchange of firepower travelled back and forth between the Amalthea and the battle cruiser and exchange between the Fightercrons and the Amalthean Quests Shuttle/fighters. Without warning Vargon gasped for the sight she saw she could not believe. Tayce was heading straight for the battle cruiser, with another Quest, using continued extreme weapon fire.

Aboard the two Quests, Tayce glanced to Marc and ordered him to help her take the battle cruiser out before it gained full operational power. Marc even though he thought Tayces idea was mad did what she asked, he knew that with the right angle of fire, they could expertly send Vargon back to the surface of Genuslan 2. Round after round of Slazer fire flew, hitting the battle cruiser on all sides. Marc kept the Countess interested on his Quest, under shield. Whilst Tayce flew to the point where the main power for the Weapons was situated on the battle cruiser. With one single strike of high energy beam weapon fire, Tayce took out the whole of the Countesses Weaponry Operations, rendering the cruiser helpless. She flew back to join Marc who smiled triumphantly. And put up his hand to convey nice shot. Together they headed back to join the others, who had successfully taken out the fifty or so Fightercrons and were waiting safely to regroup.

"It's a good job you cut that weapon power, when you did, I thought I was going to end up as toast," said Marc over the Aircom as he had been taking quite a lot of weapon strikes.

"Midge watch the battle cruiser, when she nears the surface of Genuslan 2, give it every ounce of firepower Amalthea can achieve and destroy it," ordered Tayce over the Aircom.

"You've got it Tayce, Just like the old dayons, right?" replied Midge full of enthusiasm.

"Just like the old dayons Midge," replied Tayce laughing as she recalled many of the battles they encountered just as good as this one, single handed.

No sooner had the Quests team took their Quests towards the planet surface. The battle cruiser seemed to descend awkwardly ahead of them and begin to lose power as it went. Midge waited until it was in the sky over the Countesses Lair, then, unleashed immense firepower, hitting the battle cruiser head on. It changed to an illuminative burning red, glowing to extreme brilliance, then blew apart, sending debris and sparks far and wide, in a colourful array through out the sky, descending to the surface in debris, as far as the eye could see. Tayce turned to see the explosion and ordered the Quests to the surface quickly! Amalthea prepared for the possible shock wave and manoeuvred to a safe distance. It crossed Tayces mind suddenly had she managed to finally wipe the Countess and her evil daughter off the face of the Universe once and for all? But had she? Even though it would have been a nice thought, it just seemed to easy, she was dreaming.

"Do you reckon Vargon and Sallen went up with that battle cruiser?" asked Marc over the Aircom.

"No! It was way to easy for her, she's probably back on the surface by now," replied Tayce.

"Tayce we've got company in the form of Questa Security Patrol, coming up the rear," said Duncan over the Aircom.

Tayce glanced behind to see a Patrol Cruiser which covered a diameter of just under a milon and a half armed with every kind of weaponry source to stop trouble at a cencrons notice, if called for. Jan Barnford was aboard and in charge, he'd been personally requested by Lydia Traun to assist Tayce on this particular Quest. He had been warned by Lydia, that Tayce would not take kindly to him walking in and taking over, but that was too bad. He was there to make sure the new chiefs daughter and her team, did not get their heads blown off he thought. He announced his arrival over the Aircom to the point and no nonsense in his tone.

"Lieutenant Commander Traun this is Jan Barnford officer of Questa Security Patrol, I've been sent out here by Chief Traun to assist you in the apprehension of the Countess," he began in his usual gruff abruptness.

"Officer Barnford, we believe that the Countess escaped the attack on her battle cruiser and is now back on the surface of Genuslan 2, myself and my team are heading on down there now," replied Tayce.

"Let me congratulate you on the destruction of the battle cruiser, nice work, my team and myself will meet you down on the surface, Barnford, out," said Jan signing off.

Communications ceased Tayce gave word to the others, it was time to land. Her mind was on wondering just what it was, Vargon had to hide on the surface, that she did not want anyone finding out about, at any cost. Whatever it was, Questa Security Patrol had been brought in, she would be extra vigilant not to cooperate at any price if she didn't want found what was being protected.

Officer Barnford was in the process of briefing his patrol team of roughly forty or so officers, all highly trained in their field of bringing someone like the Countess down once and for all. He explained that Chief Traun had sent them out there to protect her daughter, at any cost. But their main priority was to capture Countess Vargon alive and quickly. They were required to work along side the Amalthean Quests team, blend in. He paced up and down. His men were stood to attention with their full interest on what their chief was saying. He continued that Countess Vargon had evaded being brought to justice before, this time she must not get the chance to try again. Also there was an accomplice in the form of the Countesses daughter, she was just as evil as her Mother and would do anything to avoid being caught, it was advised that they use extreme caution but the young woman had to be apprehended by whatever means available, at the time of coming face to face with her. Even stunning her if they had to. Both women where to be treated like any other worst kind of evading criminals. Jan dismissed his men knowing they had taken in what he had told them.

"I don't want anyone returning to be buried on Questa, because of their stupidity, so keep this in mind, these women especially if they turn on the charm, are not what they appear to be, is that understood, Got it, that's all," said Jan almost shouting, as his men began leaving ready dressed for the surface of Genuslan 2.

Jan glanced at his Wristcall time display, then briskly followed on behind his men, checking his gun was fully charged in case he needed to use it. He was the kind of man who gave his job and men one hundred percent, he liked nothing more than to be in the thick of the action. He approached his pilot and ordered him to be ready to depart when he requested him to do so. His pilot acknowledged. He was an average looking man in his late 30s early 40s the true military pilot type. Jan walked on out to the Transpot Area, closing the Slazer Hold, where one of his men had left it undone on route. He liked nothing more than to keep a tidy cruiser, as accidents could happen, when things were left undone and he'd seen some nasty ones in his time.

***

The Amalthean Quest team landed on the Genuslan 2 surface, bringing their Quest Shuttle/fighters down in a clearing, with easy walking distance to the entrance to Vargons hideout. Tayce ordered everyone to put the Quests into computer pilot mode, for easy retrieval. This would make the Quests go under a protection shield and leave the planet surface, for easy retrieval via Wristlink later. Everyone did as requested then took out their Slazers and began on behind Tayce, going through the thick green bushes and trees. The ground under foot was slippery and hard going. Tayce slipped, but was quickly steadied by Marc. Her Wristlink sounded it's tone, she raised it pressing the Commun button, pausing under the shelter of some trees in case Vargons ground team were aware they had arrived on the surface and were tracing them. Jan Barnfords voice came through. He was on the surface and trying to locate her.

"Ideal settings, very secluded wouldn't you agree?"

"Very! Far from ideal though, if your walking around here, humid, muddy under foot, need I say more?" replied Tayce in a sarcastic tone.

"We're not far from you, to your right, about a couple of yardons," replied Jan heading her way

"Be right with you," replied Tayce walking in the direction he was coming.

Tayce and the team carefully walked in the direction of Jan and his men, trying with difficulty not to slip and break something vital. Marc or Duncan grabbed Tayce when she slipped. Lance saved Treketa a couple of times. Finally after slipping and sliding for more than half an houron, the team rendezvoused with the Security Patrol Team and Officer Barnford. They all began discussing the plan of action. Jan explained that Vargon and her brat of a daughter were confirmed as being on the surface, by one of his officers, who had run a scan in the last houron and were underground in a type of colony.

"I knew it was too good to think possibly she'd saved us the job of apprehending her and perished aboard that battle cruiser," said Tayce in not to surprised tone.

"Officer Barnford, Sir, they are back on the surface, the Countess is ordering the men about ten to place more containers below ground," said an officer, who was watching via a pair of Vision Viewing glassene's.

Jan, Tayce and the teams on both sides walked into sheltered clearing, to watch the action in the enclosed area men were loading containers under the watchful eye of Vargon, ready to be taken below. Tayce wondered what was in them and was eager for a further look without further or thought, she began forward, but Jan grabbed her back in a rough manner, that made her glance up at him, shocked. She met his motionless grey eyes, that showed that he was not prepared to tolerate her foolish actions.

"You walk in there half in thought of what your doing and you'll get yourself killed, plus you'll blow our cover," he said down at her angrily.

"You forget Officer Barnford, I've had dealings with Countess Vargon before, I can more than hold my own against her, remember she destroyed my home world and I've come face to face with her monthons ago, when she lost in finishing me of then," retorted Tayce breaking free of Jan's stern grip on her upper arm.

"Just think of your actions Lieutenant Commander, that's all, I don't want to report to Chief Traun that you've been killed," he said to the point.

Tayce didn't like his attitude, what did he think he was nursing, a child! She found him somewhat abrupt and rude. Why had her Mother sent this officer and his team, didn't she think she could handle this Quest alone? She did not need this rule maker, breathing down her neck. He looked ahead ignoring her look of spite against him. He was sent there to do a job and that's what he intended to do, whether she liked it or not.

***

Countess Vargon glanced roughly to the area where the Amalthean Quest team and Jan and his men were watching. She looked about in true evil suspicion, having some idea that the teams were present, but couldn't prove it. Sallen glanced to her Mother, then in the direction that she was looking, spitefully. She wanted to head into the undergrowth with a team of men and flush the teams out her Mother suspected was in the vicinity, but her Mother had insisted she forget the idea, she did not want her shot, there was to much at stake and to be done to get the equipment in the containers below before nightfall.

"Hurry men, I want these containers below surface and in secure storage before nightfall," ordered Vargon callously, almost barking at the men struggling with the heavy dark green containers.

"Mother do you think the Amaltheans are here?" asked Sallen quietly to her Mother.

"I've no doubt they are and probably watching us right now, but whatever they are thinking of planning, they had better beware that I am more than a match for them," retorted Vargon, almost with a wicked smile.

"Do you think they'll play into our hands, I hope they do, I'm looking forward to putting an end to that bitch Stavard," said Sallen evilly excited at the prospect.

"Enough talk girl, come, let's go below, men continue what your doing, remember I want this lot stored within the next houron," said Vargon guiding her daughter roughly by the upper arm across the courtyard of dry mud, towards the entrance to underground.

Two tall strong looking humanoids in, brown leatherex uniform, stood on guard each side of the entrance as they approached, brandishing powerful looking hand cannon type weapons. The kind that looked like they could blow whoever, to the next realm, with one single shot. But this kind of weapon would be no surprise to Tayce, or the two teams, they knew that most of the weapons Vargon came by, were stolen. Sallen and the Countess were soon gone from the surface, leaving the entrance guarded and wide open for what the two teams in the nearby area had hoped would be easy access, to apprehend the Vargons by storming the entrance swiftly and quietly.

Tayce even though this was her Quest, realised that Jan Barnford as sharp as he was, was right in what he had done to stop her earlier, if she had stormed in to the enclosed area, it most certainly would have been the last thing she would have done and he was only protecting her interests. Jan glanced at her in a more mellow way, than when he stopped her abruptly earlier. He then looked back to the entrance of the underground hideout. All the men loading the containers onto a hover cart finished loading and began on the way below to store what was inside. The entrance was soon closed, by two heavy looking dark green doors sliding shut, but not before the two officers that had stood on guard had gone inside. Jan ordered his officer who was constantly scanning the area through the Vision Viewing glassenes, to check out the area for any infra red trip beams and scan in ground cams (cameras). The young dark haired officer flicked a small button on the Vision Viewing glassenes, then re-checked the whole of the surrounding area. Tayce looked to Jan in a questioning way.

"I'm not taking any chances Lieutenant Commander Traun," he said not looking down at her.

"You won't find me arguing with that knowing Vargon she no doubt has some kind of sophisticated protection to intruders like us," replied Tayce in total agreement.

Jan was somewhat amused even though he was trying to keep decorum at Tayces agreeing to his procedure. He glanced away, trying to breath through the moment of amusement, thinking this Tayce Traun was learning fast, that he was there to stop her getting killed, even if she did think he was mean. Jan's viewing officer confirmed after the scan, that there was a cross section of infra red trip beam alarms, in the area leading up to the entrance. He pointed and explained, how they ran around the outside fence area, also in a cross grid to the entrance. Jan gave an exasperated sigh. God when did this bitch Vargon ever give in. Another of Jan's skilled officers announced they could distort the signal enough to make it easy to cross and look as if an animal on the surface was causing the interference. Jan nodded in total agreement. A blonde well built officer stood to his feet, taking with him another officer, they both took distortion devices to interfere with the cross beam signal, setting them as they went. They were small devices, in the shape of square boxes, no bigger than what could be used as small trinket boxes, used in the twentieth century Earth times. Jan ordered for the hundred that had been brought to be used and placed where it would be most beneficial, then let him know when it was safe to move in. The young blonde officer gave an acknowledgement with his hand, heading away. Jan turned to Tayce and Marc, he began explaining what his two men would do, then they could get going. Tayce nodded as did Marc. Everyone waited silently. Without warning it started to rain, something that would put the whole Quest into dangerous mode, especially under foot. Jan gave an exasperated look, this was something they could do without. They all moved further in under the trees, to shelter until it was over.

***

Sallen Vargon below the surface laughed with evil delight, as one of her Mother's operatives had announced that the rain had arrived earlier than had been first stated and would not be going for the next few hourons. The Countess raised an eye in surprise at her daughter, she couldn't understand why she should find rain so funny.

"That should put a damper on the Amalthean team and Tayce Traun, should they be outside, but she and Treketa deserve it, it couldn't be falling heavier for me, I'd like to throw in some powerful lightening, it would save me the job of having to finish them off," said Sallen with hatred in her voice.

"Sallen do control yourself, your enjoying this a bit to much, when the time comes, if your not careful your over zealous attitude will be your downfall," said Vargon in a reprimanding way.

"You never allow me to have amusing thoughts, why?" shouted Sallen at the Countess.

"Enough! Sallen, I am in no mood for your pathetic behaviour, it's been a tough dayon," said the Countess turning on her daughter in a spiteful way.

Sallen looked away angry at her Mother, she was so bored. She wanted to take on the likes of Treketa Stavard and get the confrontation over and done with. Somehow right at that moment her Mother's offer, to join forces at the beginning was making her wish she hadn't accepted and she'd gone it alone. She wished she could just leave her Mother and head on outside, but she'd know that she'd left the hideout and would know doubt send a team to fetch her back and punish her, before she reached the surface. Looking back at her Mother the only comfort she had at that moment in time, was to know the likes of Treketa Stavard who she hoped was outside was suffering in the now treacherous weather condition, that was growing more powerful by the minon.

***

Outside Jan's men soon gave the all clear to proceed. The weather conditions were becoming horrendous, high winds, strong lashing rain which was making it near impossible to hear and see. Tayce began to wonder if Vargon somehow knew that they were on the surface and had conjured up the difficult conditions, just to be spiteful. The Amalthean team set their weapons on Jan's word, to the setting of kill/disintegrate. Tayce turned to the others and quickly advised them not to take any chances at all, when dealing with Vargon and Sallen.

"You shoot anything that's not the Countess and Sallen, we want to take them alive, but if you absolutely have to shoot one or the other, then you have permission to stun them, Treketa I know you have a vendetta against Sallen, but I want you to stun her, not kill her understand?" said Tayce in tone of command.

"Have you heard of these outlaws, Vargons currently running with, other than blowing their battle cruiser to oblivion," asked Jan watching his men.

"No nothing, only that Sallen was rescued by them and the Countess offered to have them join forces with her for this secretive project, that she seems eager to keep under wraps," replied Tayce.

Both found that the frosty atmosphere between the two of them had thawed and they were now working as leaders in unison with one thought in mind, to bring Vargon and her daughter to an abrupt stop. Jan was finding this Tayce Traun, daughter of the new chief of Questa, was something more than just a stickler for the rule book, which he had been lead to believe. Someone said she was like the ice maiden, but he considered her to be fair minded, but who didn't suffer fools gladly. He for one could see she was a damn fine leader and a very attractive one too. Which he liked. In time he could see them becoming good friends. Tayce was doing her own studying of this Jan Barnford without him realising it and could surmise that under the tough military leader appearance, was probably someone off duty who was a really nice man, who picked his friends with caution and quality, anyone that was lucky to be classed as his friend, would probably have a friend for life.

"Officer Barnford have you ever encountered the Countess before?" asked Tayce casually.

"No, but I've heard she blew your home world to hell and evaded being brought to justice, but she sounds like numerous greedy criminals I've encountered before, why do you ask?" he asked glancing to her.

"Be warned, she'll pull anything to avoid being apprehended, she's a powerful woman you could almost say she could be classed as a witch, whatever you do, don't fall foul of her coy acts," warned Tayce seriously.

"Thanks for the warning, I have heard rumours about her and was wondering if they were true or not, but you've just confirmed as much," he replied managing a slight appreciative smile.

"Your welcome, I just thought you should have some idea of what Vargon can do," replied Tayce.

As the team neared the fence, where the infra red distortion box's had been placed. Jan's men carefully guided the team on through into a clear area and on to the next box. Minon by minon both, the Amalthean Quest team and Jan's team, were gaining in reaching the entrance to the tunnel to below surface. Jan stayed with Tayce and Marc, whilst the rest of his men mingled in with the Quest team. No sooner had they reached the entrance and had managed to bypass Vargons entrance locking system. They began in as the doors drew apart. Inside the cavernous interior, everyone kept on alert on the look out for any sign of Vargons guards. The lighting was somewhat poor, it was hard to make out the journey ahead. Tayce held her Slazer poised ready to use if she had to. After walking stealthily for a while, they rounded a corner cautiously. Jan tapped Tayce lightly on the shoulder. She looked back at him, questioningly. He pointed to the first of the obvious outlaws that Vargon had teamed up with, he was lazily moving the supplies that had been brought down from the surface, to be secured under lock, when finished.

"So much for Vargons new outlaws, if your ready to go in, let's go," said Jan in a whisper.

"Ready," came back Tayce.

As both teams continued on into the central part of the new hideout, they were suddenly caught off guard by the onslaught of Vargons guards advancing, if by some magic. Tayce, Jan and Marc plus both teams quickly manoeuvred into position and began returning fire in full retaliation of the onslaught of weapon fire coming from Vargons side, suddenly what had become a quiet arrival, had blown into a full scale first wave of attack. Jan's men quickly began taking the outlaws out one by one, working with the Amalthean Quest team. Three of Vargons outlaws disintegrated on impact, at close range of weapon fire from Jan's officer, working along side Treketa. As more guards came forth, so Jan and his men, Tayce and her team fired on them taking them out, no sooner they made their appearance. Slowly the teams advanced into the central point of the hideout. The exchange of weapon fire was noisy and immense on both sides. Treketa and Lance ran behind some crates, with one of Jan's officers, to get a better aim at the advancing guards, advancing in their direction. Jan wondered how many more were coming, as there had been roughly forty or so already and he and his men had taken out a few of them. As Treketa figured the coast was safe enough to move in closer to back up Tayce, Jan and Marc, she moved out and realised that the move was one she shouldn't have made, as she ended up right in the path of a rather huge outlaw, that seemed to bear down on her and he was not the kind to be argued with. Treketa was almost frozen to the spot with shock. Duncan saw what was happening he wanted to help, but found he was once again pinned down by gun fire, as was Lance. The guard grabbed Treketa around the throat roughly and lifted her up off the ground. She struggled, raised her Slazer and fired right into the centre of his torso, making it count. He stared at her with dark alarm, then disintegrated, Treketa dropped back onto the concretex floor, landing on her rear, with a thud. She crawled to what she thought was safety, to gather her immediate thoughts together and found she was looking at a pair of black shiny boots. Abruptly she stopped, she had just crawled in the wrong direction, yet again. She felt a hand grab her hair and haul her up on her feet. Struggling she came face to face with none other than Sallen Vargon, who looked coldly and full of evil intent at her.

"Hello Stavard, nice to see you, I'm glad you've made it through the enemy barrier, it's a shame you've done so well, now it's time to face your destiny with my assistance and I'm going to enjoy this immensely," said Sallen in shear hateful anger, but softly spoken sarcasm.

"You bitch!" retaliated Treketa, lashing out in Sallen's hold.

"I wouldn't think of trying to fight me Stavard, you are no match for me, you know that, remember our encounter at College Colony, as I remember you were begging for mercy then and you will now," said Sallen finding Treketas actions no more than feeble.

Sallen held Treketa fast, as she was trying to attack her, with all her might. She raised her small hand held yet power gun and pointed it in Treketas face. Treketa knew that this was not the time to finish what was started at College Colony, she would bide her time, she would play along, because like Tayce had said, she wanted to take Sallen alive. Duncan and Lance tried with all their might to finish off taking out the latest onslaught of Vargons guards with a view to helping Treketa, but found it near impossible to try, as they had hoped. As Lance came out round a crate, he wondered what the equipment or whatever was concealed inside was going to be used for. In no time at all Lance, Duncan and Jans officer had surrounded Sallen, but they couldn't do anything because the way in which she had played it, she was using Treketa for a shield and as Tayce had firmly ordered them, she wanted Sallen taken alive, they had to play along. So they followed her waiting for her to make the wrong move, then they could stun her.

Jan, Tayce and Marc soon arrived at the main entrance into the Central Point of the hideout. Vargons new operations section, thought Tayce. As the entrance was sealed shut, so both Marc and Jan open fired on the door mechanism panel. The doors gave and slid back into the wall, each side. All three were met by another wall of more outlaws, that had doubled as operatives. Jans men quickly fell in and backed up Tayce, Marc and Jan in firepower. Before more operatives could leave their consoles and join in protecting their mistress, namely Vargon. Jans men rushed forth inside and aimed their guns, almost bearing down on the remaining operatives mid rise from their seats, quite prepared to kill if they had to.

"I wondered how long it would take you to come down from the surface, you've brought guests and he's quite handsome, isn't he?" said Vargon walking forth summoning Jan up interested.

Jan gave Vargon a cold uninterested look, that conveyed just what he was thinking, that she was no more than a poisonous pathetic woman. Sallen walked in with Treketa in front of her, with a gun aimed at Treketas head with Lance, Duncan and one of Jan's officers following in pursuit. Sallen walked to the centre of the large white chamber, turned and pushed Treketa before her Mother.

"Look what I found Mother, the one person I've been dying to meet," said Sallen keeping her gun aimed on Treketa.

So young woman, you thought you would out smart my daughter, wrong!" said Vargon and she struck Treketa across the face with force almost sending her to the ground.

Tayce fought back the strong urge to use her powers on Sallen and bring her to her knees in retaliation for her Mother's actions to Treketa, because she wanted to find out what Vargon was up to, this time around before Jan and his men took over the whole set up.

"Tell me Vargon, what's this all for, it's pretty elaborate even for you, hoping to build another empire?" asked Tayce sarcastically.

"So what if I am Traun?" replied Vargon coldly.

"We can't allow it this time, your under arrest by order of Questa Headquarters Base, for escaping during trial and you can come peacefully or be terminated here were you stand," spoke up Jan, in the true tone of security representation of Questa.

"Ha! You think your orders effect me man, you see I'm beyond Questa boundaries of being apprehended, so you've wasted your time, you have no rights here, so leave before I show you the kind of treatment I give to unwelcome visitors, that goes for you to Traun," replied Vargon.

But what she said fell on deaf ears, Jan was not the kind of man to be intimidated and as far as boundaries went, this woman had violated them more than once it meant nothing. The next move he made surprised Tayce and the Amalthean Quest team. He aimed his Slazer in a point blank aim at Vargon, setting it to stun, he ordered her abruptly to comply or die. The air was filled with deadly silence. Vargon looked at the gun and then Jan, she did not know if the gun was on stun, or disintegrate. Jan knew that he may be reprimanded himself for this actions, but when he'd thought about the many of innocent lives Vargon had taken, he didn't care, he was taking this bitch back to Questa either living or dead. Vargon began to walk away in thought. Tayce could sense that something of great proportion was about to come forth from her and did. She turned to face Jan with a deadly dark look in her eyes, she unleashed her power on him. Tayce without thought blocked her with her own powers, as the flaming ball of pure energy emitted from Vargons right hand Tayce dived and blocked it, with her own power, to Jans surprise. The gun he was holding went off and brought down ceiling above them.

"As usual Vargon you want to play power games, well play them with me," said Tayce in front of Jan and using her own energy, to reverse the Countesses sudden continuous power throws.

"Go ahead Traun, you will diminish long before me," retaliated Vargon.

Tayce laughed to herself, as she knew that Vargon was not aware that since they had last met, she had been trained by Empress Tricara to make her power strikes count. A battle of two forces commenced between Vargon and Tayce, each one unleashing what they felt towards the other. Jan was speechless that Tayce possessed such a power in the first place, he had to remember never to get on the wrong side of her, ever! Little by little for the first time and much to the delight of the rest of the Amalthean Quests team Tayce was winning against Vargon. Marc dropped back and walked from the central point of the hideout. Once out of sight he raised his Wristlink and contacted Midge on Amalthea, he wanted to find out, if in fact Vargon had been telling the truth about the boundary aspect.

"Midge check and see if this planet is out of Questa patrol space for apprehension, now please!"

"Checking now, what's happening down there?" asked Midge interested.

"Tayce is giving Vargon a lesson in powers, she won't forget," replied Marc.

Quite suddenly as he waited, he heard a piercing scream and it didn't sound like it had come from Tayce. He stayed out of the way, letting whatever was going on in the Central Point continue. Midge came back with the most interesting information.

"According to Questa scan of the universal area, Genuslan 2 is just inside the boundary for law enforcement but according to the Countesses charts, she is as usual making boundaries to fit her purpose," replied Midge.

"Thanks mate, I owe you one," said Marc signing off.

Marc knew they had got Vargon. As usual she had been bending the rules to fit her own gotten gains like Midge had said. Now they had something to call her bluff. He headed back into the Central Point to a sight that he was not expecting to see, Vargon under arrest by two of Jans officers, looking somewhat drained of life. She looked totally power drained. The operatives she had ruled, were all dead. As he glanced to Treketa so he was glad to see the sight he was seeing and that was, Sallen in a strong much enjoyed grip of Treketa and she was not prepared to let her go. She threw a pleased look in Marc's direction. Tayce was coming back to normality, from the powerful onslaught under the concerned and watchful eye of Donaldo.

"Officer Barnford should there be another occasion which I hope there won't be, think twice when going head to head with this bitch," said Tayce seriously looking to him, then at Vargon.

"Sorry I guess I didn't take in what you told me about her, but thank you, you saved my life, I won't forget it," said Jan grateful giving her smile.

"You might be interested to know, Vargon here has been moving the space boundaries, to suit her unlawful dealings," explained Marc.

"That doesn't surprise me, okay James take the daughter as well," ordered Jan to his officer now holding Sallen in a tight force field restraining grip.

"Yes sir, move!" ordered the young brown haired officer, taking Sallen, shoving her forth in a rough manner.

"I'm going to seal this place down, so that if she does the unmentionable and escapes, she won't be able to return and take up where she left off again," said Jan glancing around, as he stood with Tayce and Marc.

He left Marc and Tayce walking away to organise the explosives to be placed where they would do the most damage. He then sauntered on out into the outside cavernous tunnels. Sallen was led away struggling and protesting by two security officers. Treketa, as she passed Sallen in leaving the hideout, gave her a pleased spiteful look. Tayce caught up with Jan and enquired as to what would happen to Vargon this time around? He explained that she would be brought before the High Court, for Planetary Matters and before her Mother Chief Traun, where she would either decide to terminate her life, or send her to a confinement colony that she would not escape so easily from, as for Sallen, her future was uncertain. One thing was for sure she would be brought before trial for helping a criminal to escape hearing, even though it was her own Mother.

"What would be her penalty?" asked Tayce.

"They'll treat this as a first offence, despite what we think about it, she'll probably walk free unless your Mother has other ideas of what she wants done with her, she could send her to a mind correction colony where they will wipe her mind of evil thoughts and give her a new identity," explained Jan.

"If I know Mother, considering what Vargons done to us, she won't be able to contain her judgement over what punishment she'll unleash on her," said Tayce knowing whatever sentence Vargon was handed down, it would not repay what she did to her people of Traun, the innocent lives that were lost unnecessarily.

Jan suggested they get going, as all the explosives were set. The Amalthean Quest team and Jans officers began briskly walking back to the surface. Jan announced that he had discovered one thing, that was going on in the hideout when one of his men had questioned, one of the operatives before he was killed, that Vargon was planning to wipe out Questa Headquarters Base. Tayce gave a look of sheer shock, but she could believe it, considering what she did to Traun, her home world.

Once on the surface Jan shook hands with Tayce and Marc, expressing it had been a good success to the Quest in hand. then headed off to his vessel to leave the surface. Tayce began procedures to recall the Quests from space. In no time at all both teams had gone from the surface of Genuslan 2 leaving it to the detonation of the specially placed explosive devices.

The two teams made it off Genuslan 2 just in time, as the planet surface began to rock from the explosions going off below surface, so much so, it was becoming unstable. Trees up rooted and the destruction of the hideout began, hence the burial of Vargons material forever in dirt and fire. Tayce before heading back to Amalthea behind the team, paused outside in the Universe.

"This is one time you failed miserably Vargon," she said pleased at what had occurred

She watched the planet falling apart at the seams then put her Quest in forward motion and headed on behind everyone else back to the cruiser.

Blunder Over the Empress

Marc was in Organisation, he was working on Midge, as after the onslaught with the outlaws Vargon had teamed up with had fired on the cruiser, one of the shots had fried his on board temperature setting circuitry. One moment the team were dressing for Siberia, the next they were stripping off, as the temperature headed for the tropics. Marc had conversed with Jamie Balthansar back at Questa, on what to do and was trying in the somewhat difficult temperatures to restore normality. Tayce entered the deck, still feeling elated that she had almost killed Vargon in the power struggle. She crossed the deck with an up to date report from Lydia on Questa, over the decision of what was to happen to Vargon, after all. Marc upon seeing her approach slid out from under the console. He had to hear the latest and figured Midge wouldn't mind waiting just a bit longer to restore normal atmosphere. It had been almost a weekon since they had left Genuslan 2 behind in ruins. It was that time on board when duties that had been shelved for the Quest, had to be undertaken to keep the cruiser running smoothly. Tayce began reading the update, as the team members around her gave her their full attention. Countess Vargon much to their delight was on her way under a close guarded patrol team to a confinement colony where she would remain for the rest of her natural evil life. Marc gave a cheer then went back to repairing Midge. Tayce continued.

"Sallen because it's her first offence and the fact that most of her evil duties were thrust upon her by Vargon, is being sent to a Mind Correction Colony for a period of six monthons."

"Maybe she'll come back a much better person," replied Lance.

"She'll be a changed person, the life of crime Vargon forced on her to endure, will no longer exist I've heard of the mind wipe procedure, they programme your mind with a new existence, some say you come back with a new identity," explained Tayce.

"It's what she needs, a fresh start," spoke up Marc finishing his repair.

Midge broke the moment as he still had communication facility, by announcing that there was an incoming message. Tayce crossed to the control seat, ordering him to play it, when it had been fully received. After a few minons the Sight Screen flashed into life and Empress Tricara appeared.

"Tayce I'm on my way to rendezvous with you, I'd like you to escort me, to a seminar of importance which is to be held on the colony world of Trinott, I have clearance from your Mother, to ask you to do this for me, it's a planetary matters seminar, I need security protection, that I know and I can trust, I'll see you soon," said Tricara signing off.

"Why should she want us, surely Jan Barnford could have found someone trustworthy of escorting her," said Tayce, somewhat puzzled that the Empress had not asked Jan.

"Maybe there's more to it, she'll obviously tell you more when she arrives," spoke up Tom.

Tayce wondered if there was an ulterior motive behind the Empress wanting her and the team as chaperones? Was it a top secret meeting and still something left over from the dayons of Tristarcus that she felt she couldn't trust anyone finding out about, only herself? Was the reason for asking for her help also down to someone threatening her because of this meeting and she only felt safe by using the Amalthean Quests team? Whatever the reason, she would be there for Tricara, as she had always been there for her, whatever the situation and especially recently when she had helped with her power training. Tom looked up from his seat, he could see she was worried, he stood and walked to her side. He reached out and squeezed her upper arm reassuringly.

"You worry to much, it might not be anything to concern yourself about, wait and see," he discretely said in a whisper, then leaned in to kiss her gently on the cheek.

"I know I seem worried, but we don't know what's still lingering from her dayons of being on Tristarcus maybe there's an issue that has to be sorted by Tricara, she feels she can't divulge to much about, because it could be considered life threatening, she's a good person Tom and I'll do anything to protect her, she's done a lot of good things in this Universe and helped my parents and me in the past," said Tayce looking directly at him.

"I agree she's a good friend, all you can do is just wait and see, that's all," replied Tom in understanding soft tone.

Tayce nodded, then walking onto Lances position, to request he find everything he could on the colony world of Trinott. Lance nodded in agreement, getting straight on with the request. Tom sat back down in the Control seat in thought. He silently had to admit, that he was finding the fact of Tricara wanting to use the team instead of Questa Security somewhat strange. Because Questa Security were trained in situations to protect people like the Empress, at any cost, but maybe Tayce was right, there was a threat made against her over the unfinished business, regarding Tristarcus and she figured she could only trust someone she knew would protect her at this so called seminar and could sense trouble before it unfolded, also Tayce being gifted was something she was relying on in her being assisted. He silently didn't like this situation, it could get any of them killed, or injured, because of the very idea. But what Tayce decided, went, he would have to watch how everything unfolded and step in with his thoughts and warning advice, should he see trouble arising from what they were required to do.

***

Empress Tricara two hourons later, came along side in a Questa Private Launch. Tayce waited at the Docking Bay doors with Tom. The doors soon drew apart and Tricara walked aboard dressed in a close fitting silkene mauve long skirt suit. She looked truly breathtakingly regal. She looked at Tom upon coming to a stop and was reading his thoughts on why she was there, but quickly brushed them aside hugging Tayce. The young Private Launch courier handed Tom Tricara's holdall and silver attaché case, turning he headed back aboard the Private Launch, the Docking Bay doors closing behind him. Tricara began explaining why she had announced her ask for help, at such short notice, as they walked along the corridor.

"Firstly Tom I must apologise, I read your thoughts when I arrived, you have nothing to worry about getting any of this team or Tayce injured or killed, that's the last thing I intend to do, the reason I want all your help is, it all started after the destruction of Tristarcus, meetings and seminars that I would generally attend and were considered part of my every dayon existence, were suddenly ignoring my request to be there, I found that I was not being included in the guest lists of some of the most important ones, that would not have thought twice of not inviting me, because of who I am, they also made decisions behind my back, which they have no rights to do, I still hold the vote to have a say on behalf of Tristarcus, even though it's no longer in existence, I'm still classed, or should be classed as the sole leader," explained Tricara.

"You don't think it's just a genuine case of them thinking you perished along with your people of Tristarcus, after all, when Traun was destroyed no one knew I existed apart from Jonathan Largon and he had to search for Amalthea still being even in space?" asked Tayce carefully.

"No! At first I would have agreed with you, but I've been receiving threatening communications for me to stay away from any seminars and decline voting as once ruler of Tristarcus. If I valued my life, most of the threats were untraceable and the ones I did try to trace, they went into nothing," continued Tricara.

"Covered their path well then?" said Tom cutting in.

"Quite! Well this seminar on Trinott gives me the chance to find out just who is behind these threats," said Tricara.

"Don't you think it's dangerous to attend this seminar, if someone is determined to stop you, this could be the one they try to carry out that threat at, I for one do not want to lose you," said Tayce pausing in alarm at what Tricara was contemplating.

"And you won't, I will not be intimidated Tayce, you know this in the past, that's why I want your help, I'd like you to go with me take a team if you have too, I want to discover who this being is, who is carrying out the threats against me and if they see that I am not travelling alone they'll not attempt what they say they will and maybe we can catch them once and for all."

Tayce didn't like this idea, as far as she was concerned Tricara was deliberately placing her life in danger, just to prove that she was not going to be intimidated by a mere threat. They had to find a way to protect her from harm, considering she was determined to do. What she wanted to do. But what? Tom suggested they get under way for Trinott. Tayce nodded in agreement. He handed her Tricara's things, then hurried on ahead back up the steps to Level 1, whilst Tayce and Tricara walked onto Guests Quarters, where Lydia had stayed last time she had been on board.

***

A while later Marc entered the Organisation Deck having completed the final checks on Midges running repairs, he had made sure that the temperature was what it should be, for a comfortable living and working environment, instead of more like Siberia then the tropics. Everything checked out, much to both Marc's and the teams relief. Donaldo was concerned that the way the temperatures were going on board, that the team would catch a cold virus, that could prove fatal. Marc was glad, he didn't have to have Donaldo screaming in his right ear any more, on when was he going to get the temperature on board regulated. The course was set for Trinott colony/world. Duncan and Lance were in discussion on how they had to agree with Tayce, who was now, back in the Meeting Centre with the Empress, that it was madness for such a highly thought after and well respected woman, such as the Empress was, to contemplate putting her life in danger, just to prove the fact she was still alive and was not going to be intimidated over the fact, she still had the right to vote for her own planetary realm of Tristarcus, even though it wasn't there. Still it didn't matter what they thought, there would be no changing the Empresses mind. All they could do was attend the seminar, which was to prove interesting and protect her as best they could, from the person making the threats. Duncan's fingers keyed in a sequence to make sure that whoever had it in for the Empress, was not trailing them, waiting their chance.

"Where's Tom?" asked Marc curious.

"In with the Empress and Tayce," replied Lance running, checks for any unsuspecting trouble on their journey.

Marc on this sauntered up the three steps and entered in through the open doors. Tricara stood and turned delighted to see him as usual, both hugged in greeting. Marc had heard about what had been happening and the fact that she was prepared to put her life in danger, just to make a point. Upon parting he walked around the meeting table and casually perched on the edge.

"We're heading to Trinott for a seminar and exhibition on Planetary Needs and Spacial Requirements which includes a display on the latest weaponry and equipment, for medical and safety in space, I'm taking us all not only as a matter of interest, but as back up protection to Tricara here, it will also give you Marc a chance to see what's on offer, Midge will be in charge whilst we're on Trinott," said Tayce in the true tone of leader.

"I'm in total agreement with that," said Marc nodding.

"Maybe we can find something that could protect Tricara, like some kind of invisible portable force, so that should one of us not be near when this being decides to take a good shot at her, it will protect her," asked Tayce to Marc.

"What now, or at the seminar?" asked Marc.

"Now please," replied Tayce.

"Sure I think I can find something," said Marc thinking already on what he might be able to come up with.

He stood at the end of the meeting and casually walked on out tossing over in his mind, ideas of such a protection device, that could surround the Empress at a minons notice if called for. Tayce walked on out back into Organisation to find out what Lance had found out about Trinott, as not only had she suggested he keep an eye out for pirates during their journey, owing to the area of space they were journeying through, but to find a reference map of Trinott so that they could work out where the seminar was being held.

"Hows it coming Lance?" she said, leaning on the back of his chair.

"So far, no pirates you'll be glad to hear, I'm searching for the information on a chart of some description, I'll get back to you as soon as I find anything out of the ordinary, are you looking for anything in particular?" asked Lance, so it would help to know what he was looking for.

"Yes, escape routes, just in case this person who has been threatening Tricara makes an attempt at carrying out what they've threatened and makes a run for it afterwards," replied Tayce.

"Leave it with me," assured Lance getting on with the request.

Tayce returned to the middle of Organisation and came to a stop beside Tricara, she glanced at her powerful friend and could almost pick up on her thoughts of determination in the fact, no one, upon no one, was going to make her feel small regarding the threats, she'd had to date on her life. She turned her head to face Tayce and whisperingly said that it was rude to read another's thoughts, without knocking on the door so to speak! Meaning she should ask her first. Tayce smiled and apologised, together they stood watching the immediate

Universe ebb passed Amalthea. Both talked casually, as the journey progressed towards Trinott.

***

Trinott was along the lines of Questa Headquarters Base, in the fact that it was a living thriving colony in space. It's size was average, in comparable with universal planets, it came into a category of Neptune which is 30,775 milons in diameter. Trinott catered for all spacial entertainment and exhibition needs. The entertainment was considered totally breathtaking. Many space concerts were held there and the imagination was pure magic. People would come for milons around when a concert was in there. Hologram complexes were the biggest attraction, where anyone could live out their fantasy for a night, or longer stay of time. The hospitality motto was, 'we serve to please'. There was a vacation resort, totally under a glassene roof, for people from ships etc. to take a vacation at. Trinott was the kind of destination that remained open all yearon round. Part of the hospitality and staff on Trinott were young shapely females, in alluring costumes, that were known as Pleasure Queens. Everyone a stunning beauty and not above twenty-two yearons. Handsome males of roughly the same age dressed alluring costumes, that didn't leave much to the imagination were known as Pleasure Kings. Pleasure was their duty in any shape or form and a way of life. Their motto was to serve to the highest degree in pleasing guests. This was something Tayce was going to have to watch for, as far as her team were concerned. They were solely there for duty not pleasure and it would be quite easy for them to be persuaded to stray in the wrong direction, she'd be keeping an eye on them if not herself, then Marc and quickly remind them that they were there to serve the protection of the Empress, duty came first.

***

Marc roughly an houron later walked back into Organisation carrying a modified Wristlink. Tayce glanced at him and then to the Wristlink, wondering what was the reason for it, as she didn't see the fact that he had just worked what was termed a miracle in protection field stakes. He asked Tricara to raise her right wrist, so that he could place the Wristlink on. She did as requested, then Marc ordered her to step a bit away into free space and press the commun button twice. Tricara glanced to Tayce, then Marc uneasy. He smiled and assured her that everything was all right, to just try it. She did so and figured nothing had happened. Much to everyone's surprise and sudden horrified shock, Marc took a step back, drew his gun and fired in a stun setting directly at Tricara. She flinched and closed her eyes, feeling the shock that the others were wondering if Marc had lost his mind. The Slazer fire bounced off the invisible shield, that was surrounding her. Tayces sudden shock calmed, as she could see the point that he was making, even though it had been somewhat drastic in proving it worked. Tricara tried

298

to calm her heartbeat at the past moments of shock, over what had taken place. Then after a few moments everyone realised the reason behind Marc's madness, he wanted to show Tricara just what would happen, if the being that was making the threat against her, carried out their threat and how the modified Wristlink would protect her. Tricara smiled, she was glad Marc had made such a device that would be undetected to the naked eye, that would protect her. But by what Marc had just done it made her realise how easy it would be, if whoever was out to get her, shot at her the same way and without the protection, she would not live to tell the tale. She thanked Marc congratulating him on such a wonderful device. He just shrugged his shoulders, brushing what he had done aside, to him it was nothing. He informed her that all he wanted to do was see her protected. He also apologised if what he had suddenly done earlier in testing had freaked her out. But he just wanted to make a point. Marc was the kind of man who enjoyed making something out of the ordinary, technical wise, that stretched his imagination.

***

It was the middle of the night hourons aboard Amalthea. Every corridor and level was in dusk mode and all that could be heard was the sound of the cruisers engines, as it travelled on to Trinott. Midge was on night mode that meant he was in overall charge of the cruisers many functions, which was his normal mode during off duty hourons. The team were in a state of relaxed deep slumber. Tayce was peacefully curled up in Tom's arms, in their bunk sleeping blissfully unaware of what was about to unfold on board, in the next twenty or so minons.

They stepped aboard totally undetected by Midges on board scanner for intruders. They were dressed all in one drab jet black, from head to foot, as if they were wearing a tight body stocking. There were just two of them and they crept along in an alert manner, their forms were of humanoid shape, their faces were covered by matching masks, that were close fitting, over their heads, all that could be seen of the intruders faces, was the slits in the mask, for their eyes. Silently one intruder pointed to the door, thinking that according to their map it was the quarters where the Empress was suppose to be sleeping peacefully, unaware that in fact their map was wrong and in fact it was Treketa's quarters. One took out a large black bag almost the kind you could fit a body in. They entered Treketa's quarters silently, making sure that they did not make a sound for fear of trouble, if they woke who they thought was the Empress. But they did not enter the quarters through the normal way, they walked through the closed doors, like a blade cutting through paper. Once inside, they moved quickly. They moved through the living area on into the Repose Centre. Pausing by the bunk. They opened the large black bag and in the moments that followed, they would be moments that Treketa would remember for a long time to come. One of the intruders held her down, whilst the other produced an injection and quickly held it against the delicate skin on her neck, pressing the release key letting the contents enter her system. she slowly went under the influence of the drug. Soon she lost the fight to lash out and fight off the intruders. Her body went limp. Once she was rendered unconscious, they grabbed her up roughly into a sitting position and together they dropped the bag over her head bringing it down her body sealing her away into darkness, then one intruder flung her over his left shoulder. In a blinding purple flash with Treketa in their grasp unaware that they had got the wrong person, they vanished from the quarters and Cruiser Midge was still unaware that there had even been anyone aboard.

Tom didn't know why, but he found himself sitting bolt up right in his bunk, sweat glistening on his bare upper body. Was it a nightmare he thought. Suddenly something had woke him with a fright and was telling him that something had happened to Treketa. Tayce woke beside him, sitting up, looking at him concerned.

"Are you all right, what's wrong, tell me?" she asked in a true loving and caring tone.

"I don't know… It's Treketa. I don't know why but, something is wrong with her." On this Tom flew out of the bunk and headed for the entrance doors to their quarters, he grabbed his 'D'Gown on the way not waiting for Tayce, slipping it on, doing it up as he went in urgency.

"Tom wait, hold on! It might not be anything serious at all," said Tayce racing after him, hurrying to catch up in her silkene long length grey chemise.

She reached the outer living area entrance open doorway and stepped out into the corridor. Tom was at Treketa's quarters doors, banging for him to be let in and calling out her name in urgency, for her to open the doors. Tayce realised that the night before Treketa had locked her doors, when she had entered through them she had said she did not want to be disturbed till mornet.

"Tom stop it, you'll wake Tricara and the rest of the team, there is probably a simple explanation for her not answering, maybe she's taken a sleeping aid".said Tayce in urgent whisper.

"Midge this is Tom, get these damn doors open, now!" demanded Tom impatiently over his Wristlink.

"What's going on, what's happened, is there a problem?" asked Tricara coming from her Guest Quarters tying up her 'D' Gown.

As soon as the quarters doors were opened Tom raced inside and on into the Repose Centre. Nothing! Treketa was no where to be found, it was as if she had simply vanished. He turned back to face Tayce realising what he had was a premonition of Treketas sudden disappearance. But where had she gone and with whom? Tricara looked to Tayce, still unsure of what was happening.

"This is your fault Empress, they were probably looking for you, considering the threats you've been getting they probably thought Treketa was you," said Tom angrily at her.

"Tom that's enough, you have no proof, we don't know if it has anything to do with Tricara," said Tayce angry at his rudeness to her friend.

He sighed angrily and looked away in frustration worried beyond words what could have happened. Tricara felt uncomfortable and saddened, if Treketas disappearance had something to do with the threats she'd been receiving, she genuinely felt sorry for what had occurred.

"I know your angry Tom and I genuinely feel sorry, if this has anything to do with me, I have a feeling that somehow your right, it does!" began Tricara delicately feeling awful, that the intruders mistook Treketa for herself.

Tom turned back to face her, he stood at ease his arms folded far from pleased, ready to hear just what she meant by her words. Tayce looked to her friend also interested, considering the beings that had dragged Treketa away, had obviously been on board searching for her, in the first place. She couldn't understand why Midge had not picked them up as intruders.

"It would appear the people that have been threatening me have persisted in their determination to stop me attending this seminar on Trinott and found out somehow, that I'm travelling with you, they obviously boarded to take me and made the dreadful mistake of taking Treketa instead, I'm dreadfully sorry Tom, really I am," said Tricara apologetically.

By now the rest of the Amalthea team were now standing in the Quarters Level corridor, listening to what was going on, half awake and half asleep. Tayce glanced around to the others and decided that if Tricara could help in some way by identifying the boarders, they maybe able to track Treketa down before it was to late. Lance stepped up offering to forgo the rest of his nights sleep, if they wanted to get started on finding the kidnappers straight away. Tayce nodded, it was a good idea. Duncan suggested they count him in. It was settled. The team headed back to their quarters to get cleansed and changed into duty uniforms for the dayon ahead, even though it was going to be a long one. This thought Tayce was a true case of mistaken identity where Tricara was concerned, the beings that had done what they had, in kidnapping Treketa. Had to be a bunch of total idiots. Where were they going to start first, maybe pin pointing their abductors identity she thought which wasn't going to be easy. She walked on behind heading to get cleansed and changed.

Where Treketa had woken, it was dark and she couldn't see her hand in front of her face. Where was she? Wherever it was, it was cold. She felt a shiver run up her spine, but then again she was dressed in next to nothing, having been grabbed in nothing more than her night attire. She could hear engines in motion in the distance, they were obviously in transit, but where were they taking her? She could hardly turn around in this dark environment, it felt like they had locked her in some kind of cube like prison, it was obvious they didn't want her to escape easily and find her way back to Amalthea. She shuddered and was beginning to think the worst. Paranoia was beginning to give her all sorts of wrong thoughts and scenarios, that were playing out in her head. Was this her sticky end, but why? Quite suddenly she felt herself feeling frightened, for probably the first time in her galactic life. Were they going to kill her? Were they going to torture her before they did? Abruptly the sound of the distant engines stopped. Treketa braced herself for what would possibly happen next. She began telling herself, that she'd be all right, Tayce and Tom would find her before it was too late. She decided to keep telling herself this, it would keep her going for the time being. But as she tried, it was easier said than done. Without warning the entrance to her dark existence opened. Light blinded her for a few cencrons. She tried to focus and found herself staring into grey cold looking evil eyes and matching face of a tall thin man, who did not look too pleased to see it was her. She was hauled out of the darkened cramp surroundings, in a rough way and was brought to stand before the same evil man that had peered at her earlier.

"You idiots, who is this wretch?" he demanded coldly at the two masked beings, that had grabbed Treketa, thinking that she was in fact the Empress.

"Who you asked for sir, Empress Tricara," said one of the masked men, wondering why their leader was so cross with them and giving them a look to match.

"You total idiots, I don't know who she is, but that is not who I sent you after, this is not Empress Tricara you have the wrong woman, put her back where she was, until I can decide what to do with her," said the leader disgusted at his men

"Hold on, don't I get a say in this, before you shove me back in that box," protested Treketa.

"Go on," said the leader, not really interested to hear her.

"I'm Treketa Stavard from Amalthea One..." said Treketa, but was cut short.

The leader had heard enough, he had nor the time or patience to hear more he wasn't interested. He waved his hand in a gesture for his men to continue and Treketa was forced back inside her darkened surroundings and the door slammed shut behind her. What was she to do, she thought, as she heard the words of the leader outside discussing her. Would she ever see Tom and the team ever again? She felt lost and suddenly very alone.

***

Tayce was on Organisation Deck, thinking about Treketas possible whereabouts. Lance briskly entered the deck and headed straight for his Research Console, to start trying to trace any small sign, that something had been along side the cruiser in the last couple of hourons. Empress Tricara walked in also dressed and crossed to try and see if she could try and help Lance. Tom was dragged away by Tayce for a private word in the Meeting Centre. On route she ordered Midge to run a scan trace for anything out of the ordinary no matter how small, that may have been in their orbit in the last several hourons. Lance cut in and simply announced that he had it covered. Midge informed that he would assist Lance where he could. Tayce continued on into the Meeting Centre, letting the doors close behind her, once inside.

"Tom, Tricara feels bad about what happened, what these beings have done is not her fault and she is trying to help find Treketa, believe me it would be the last thing that she would want to see is Treketa hurt, or worse, she's not like that, it's totally the idiots fault that boarded and who got their bearings wrong and right now they are no doubt paying for it," said Tayce.

"So what are you saying?" asked Tom straight taking Tayces anger trying to control his own rising anger.

"I know Treketa means a lot to you, she does to all of us, but being nasty to Tricara, is not going to bring her back," said Tayce point blankly.

Tom looked away, he was now angry beyond words and figured that Tayce would take Tricara's side, but until he found Treketa, he was not going forgo the fact that the Empress had caused the whole situation to happen in the first place, if she had just travelled on to Trinott and left them out of the fact that someone was after her, Treketa would still be on board and safe.

"Tom I'm warning you, you may be my partner, but if you don't treat Tricara with respect and forget this matter happened, I'll pull rank on you, relieve you of duty and confine you to our quarters for a while to cool off, is that understood?" said Tayce without further word.

"All right, point taken, I'm sorry," he said realising he'd pushed her to far.

"It's not me that needs to hear it, it's Tricara when this is all over," said Tayce turning her back on him and walking towards the opening doors of the Meeting Centre, far from pleased.

"We've got it!" shouted Lance, triumphant from his duty position.

"That was quick, what did you do?" asked Tayce heading on out to Lances position and coming to lean on his high back chair.

"Tricara here gave me the times and dates that she had been receiving a certain communication threat, not to attend the seminar, I tracked through Questas Data Communications Log using my unique family code and traced it back to the source with Midges help and tracked our immediate orbit to find anything minute signal wise matching the message source that had happened in the last hourons and there it was, apparently these kidnappers are from our destination Trinott the threat involves a team of crooks, that Tricara here recognises the leader from, we found minute traces of them being aboard in the last hourons through the new intricate corridor scan," explained Lance.

"The leader is known by the name Robanna and is linked to your arch enemy Countess Vargon, but in what way, he never divulges, he's rather like an invisible source, but it is known that he wants Tristarcan rule, he's been trying for almost three yearons to take my place, when voting comes along, he's won so far, the only sight I've seen of him was a tall thin shape, one night when he managed to break through Palace security and enter my personal chambers, my guards apprehended him, he left with a threat that one dayon, he would make me pay for not wanting to follow and comply with his ruling, my assumption is, he's attempting that pay back now, before I attend this latest seminar," explained Tricara.

"So what your saying, he's the one that has Treketa right now and he thought he had you?" asked Tom.

"Yes!" replied Tricara.

"Why didn't Questa pick this up Lance?" asked Tayce.

"If I may Lance, I didn't want to worry Jonathan, so I never reported it and I figured that now Tristarcus has been destroyed, he would leave me alone and the threat would subside," continued Tricara.

"So right now he's on Trinott in whatever guise he likes to portray himself as?" asked Tayce.

"Right!" said Lance checking his source again.

"So the destination is Trinott, it would seem that we have a double Quest, protecting you Tricara and find a way to get Treketa back, because if the source is Trinott, that's where he'll have Treketa and will try to dump her, when he discovers she's not you and we're on his trail," said Marc thinking about it.

"I agree, let's get this cruiser to Trinott, like yesteron, time is not to be wasted, Midge forgo ordinary warp put us into Hyper Thrust Turbo speed and get us to Trinott as soon as possible," ordered Tayce.

"Going to Hyper Thrust Turbo speed now, arrival time just on two hourons," replied Midge.

Tayce stood looking out into the Universe in thought wondering what possible kind of moves this band of kidnapping criminals would make. Sometimes even though she was on the good side of the Universal law, it helped to put herself in the criminal way of thinking, so that it would help to get a better perspective on what could possibly happen with Treketa.

***

Treketa listened, She knew they had stopped somewhere, she'd felt the landing as they had touched down. But where? Once again she was hauled out of the cramped conditions and as soon as she stood in the light of the place she'd been dragged out into, she was once more injected with another concoction under protest by the tall thin figure of the evil man she'd come face to face with earlier. The drug hit her system with a blinding and powerful blow, just like it had done before. She crumpled in the hold of the two kidnappers that had taken her on Amalthea. They dragged her off the second class vessel towards a place where music and merriment filled the air. Namely Trinott.

***

Tayce watched the horizon, sipping her much needed Coffeen. Looking for the first sign of the colony/world of Trinott. Lance and Duncan at their duty positions in the last twenty minons had picked up communication of a vessel matching the same traces that Midge had found earlier, on board and trailing away from Amalthea which happened to be the origination for Tricara's threats, it was heading now towards the surface of Trinott. The communication consisted of the voice Tricara had heard numerous times before and matched the being who wanted to put an end to her. Tom headed off out of Organisation to go and get changed for the Quest, he wanted to be ready when they arrived. Marc decided to follow, he also could see that Tayce needed a hand in putting Tom right on the way he was treating Tricara and how he needed to treat her with more respect, his attitude was making the atmosphere very uncomfortable, to say the least. He quietly suggested to Tayce to leave Tom to him, he'd sort the problem, then ran on out of Organisation down the Level 1 corridor, to catch Tom up.

***

Just on two hourons lapsed. Amalthea came into orbit of the colony/world of Trinott. The team were ready and dressed in smart uniforms. Uniforms that would not raise suspicion, that they were not just attending the seminar with Tricara, the kind that would allow them to slip away and search for Treketa, as Midge had picked up Treketas life signs on the entertainment world, upon their arrival. It was decided that Tom would go with Tayce and Lance to find Treketa and the others would remain with Tricara, to make it look as if they were two separate groups, attending the seminar, for different research reasons. Lance and Duncan had been briefed about the alluring enticement of the Pleasure Queens and what would happen if they were found to be enticed by the shapely alluring beauties, by Tayce. They waited while the cruiser went into final docking clearance with Trinott Docking Port. Tom and Marc sauntered back into Organisation talking casually, Tom looked more happier, agreeing on a matter they had been discussing on the way up. Tom crossed to Tricara and to Tayces surprise apologised, he began that he understood she'd tried to put right what had happened in Treketa being taken instead of herself and he had been wrong in the way he had treated her, he was genuinely sorry. Tricara smiled and gently assured him that she understood the way he felt, Treketa was special to him. Tayce glanced at Marc, who in turn glanced back and winked affectionately. She on this had a feeling that Tom's sudden change in attitude towards the Empress, had something to do with him helping to put Tom right over Tricara.

"Final moments of docking Tayce," announced Midge informatively.

"Let's go, Tricara, you Duncan and Marc leave first, we'll follow on in fifteen minons, to avoid raising any idea that were together, as one team, I, Tom, Lance and Donaldo will leave after the fifteen minons are up, I don't want the band of kidnappers that have Treketa to realise, that we're from the same place as she is, if this was to happen they may try and kill her and we would be letting her down badly, I don't want that," expressed Tayce.

Everyone present nodded in total understanding, they then checked their Slazers. They knew that they were forbidden to use them on Trinott. It was a planetary rule, no weapons were to fired unnecessarily, but there wasn't any rules against wearing a weapon. The first part of the Amalthean Quests team walked on out the Organisation Deck with Tayce and her team following on behind, fifteen minons later. Midge immediately took overall charge of the cruisers functions, until they returned.

***

Treketa now found herself in an average sized room. It was something along the lines of a short stay living environment. She was all alone, sitting on a hard chair, equivalent of a dining chair. Her ankles were secured together with force field restraints. The doors opened behind her, in walked the same evil man she had encountered earlier. He was now dressed for the seminar in a burgundy all in one suit. He sauntered across and round in front of her, coming to a pause, he looked down at her in an evil uninterested way. Reaching down he put a callous broad hand around her delicate neck and pulled her up in front of him. Treketa felt awful from the drug wearing off. She had lost all hope of the team finding her. She looked frightened up into his cold calculating eyes and tried to fight against his strong grip on her, there was something in his eyes she didn't like the look off.

"I've checked what you've told me child, where your from, the leader of your team is a friend of the woman I'm after, Empress Tricara, sources tell me she's aboard your leaders vessel, now you'll tell me what I want to know otherwise what you've been through, will come to an unfortunate end for you," he said down at her.

"I'm not telling you anything, your that being that wants to kill the Empress aren't you, well your not getting anything out of me, so do what you have to," retorted Treketa she was frightened, but she was not prepared to let this barbarian think he could win.

"I'm Lord Robanna and Tristarcus is under my authorisation to rule, Empress Tricara is no longer the legal owner of the once said planet, when her empire fell, so did her ruling on decisions, she is now no more than useless, though she would like to think otherwise, I want to know her whereabouts, otherwise I will snap your pretty neck," he said in a near warning whisper down at her.

"I don't know where she is, so you might as well do what you set out to do," said Treketa refusing to budge on telling him what he wanted, even if it meant her losing her life.

He unexpectedly for Treketa dropped her back on the seat and bellowed at her, that she had one houron to rethink seriously of cooperating and telling him where the Empress was, otherwise he would turn her into a Pleasure Queen, solely for his undivided pleasure, when he so wished to pass those boring moments in space. He studied her young prettiness, and was suddenly finding her very appealing to the eye. He would also wipe from her mind any past of being a member of the Amalthean Quests team. With this he walked from the room letting the doors slide quietly with sound of gentle compressed air, behind him. Treketa sat silently. She rubbed her neck, why was it she thought, that every time a creep like Robanna grabbed her brutally, they did it around her neck. How much longer could she keep this pretence up to save the Empress, she thought? Where were Tayce and team. Voices could be heard outside the entrance to the room and she heard the word, 'Trinott' spoken. It all suddenly clicked in her mind, Trinott was where Empress Tricara was heading to for the seminar.

"I can't be on Trinott, that's impossible, what would a creep like Robanna want on a paradise world such as Trinott, other than to be here for the Empress, maybe help is a lot closer than I first thought and Tayce is here already, I have to do something," she said to herself in whispering thought.

She came to the conclusion, that she had to somehow try and find a way to contact the Amalthea. But how? Her feet were securely tied together with the force field restraints. She began looking around for the rooms communications facility for making contact with whoever in the outside Universe, there had to be one in there somewhere, unless Lord Robanna had already had it removed.

***

As soon as Tayce walked off the cruiser, she had a sharp premonitory feeling that someone she knew was in the vicinity and was in dire need of help. Where this person was, she couldn't explain, only that they were present on Trinott and the feeling was so strong, it was almost nauseating. Tricara suddenly flashed into her mind, she was contacting her with the same feeling, together they talked back and forth with their minds in a Telepathic link up.

"Do you think Treketa is here, let me concentrate, I'm more stronger than you, I might be able to clear the signal of the urgent source," said Tricara sounding helpful.

"Go ahead, this feeling is something I'm not enjoying," replied Tayce.

"Sorry, it's still unclear, it's as if something is blocking me," replied Tricara after a few cencrons.

"Don't worry, we'll start looking, we'll meet later at the seminar," replied Tayce breaking communications.

Tayce came back to the present to hear Tom saying if the kidnappers that had taken Treketa, had brought her to Trinott, then maybe they should start in the overstay area, were it would be a good place to hide out with someone.

Suddenly the moment Tom said about the overstay area, Tayce had a flash in her mind again only this time it featured Treketa, in capture, in a room. But again she couldn't pin point where. Lance as they exited fully onto Trinott found his sight was caught by a shady looking character who seemed to be watching all the females arrive. He was wearing hooded cloak type garment. He nudged Donaldo drawing his attention to where his attention, had been grabbed to. The shady character was still present and unbeknown to Lance had been one of the kidnappers that had taken Treketa, he'd been sent to watch for any sign that Empress Tricara was arriving by Lord Robanna, who knew that the Empress was still determined to attend the seminar. Lance decided to get Tayces attention. Tayce looked to where Lance was looking and saw how suspicious the shady character was acting. He glanced in her direction and seeing that he had been rumbled, turned on his heels and began running off at great speed, disappearing from sight. This immediately roused Tayce suspicion, they were on to finding where Treketa was. They quickly hurried after the male in a sprint, heading across the room in the direction of the fleeing suspected kidnapper. They pushed through mingling people arriving, it was near impossible to get a clear indication of which way the kidnapper had taken, then Tom caught sight of him, heading off after him. Tayce followed. Lance and Donaldo went in the opposite direction, hoping to find a way of cutting the kidnapper off. Tom gained on the escaping male and when he was in launching distance, he sprang and brought the kidnapper to the ground with a crash. He scrambled to his feet, bringing the kidnapper up roughly onto his feet, right in front of him, even though he was trying to break free in the process. Just up ahead of Tom was Robanna and he was holding a gun aimed directly at him.

"Release my assistant human, or I won't hesitate to shoot," said Robanna.

Tayce as she caught sight of what was unfolding before her, discretely reached for her gun in her side holster. She was aware of the gun rules on Trinott, but when a member of her team and her husband was about to die before her, she didn't care. Further up the corridor Tom was not releasing the being in his grasp, until he got some answers. Robanna had a feeling that Tom had something to do with the young woman Treketa, that he had in his hold and if he played his cards right, Tom could lead him to Empress Tricara, who he wanted in the first place.

"What is your business with my assistant, your not staff here?" demanded Robanna playing the moment to gain what he wanted.

"The names Lieutenant Commander Traun, you've got something that does not belong to you, namely one of my team, a female, I'd like her back," said Tayce realising that this was none other than Robanna, the man that had been threatening the life of Tricara.

"I have the woman you want, but I want something of you, Empress Tricara you know where she is, don't you, I will hand you back the woman you want, in exchange for the Empress," said Robanna giving Tayce a shear look of bribery.

He had to be joking thought Tayce, there was no way she was prepared to hand over Tricara to the likes of this evil bastard. Lance stepped up behind her as did Donaldo. Lance discretely whispered to Tayce maybe they should play this Robanna along, ask to see Treketa, if he claimed he had her. Tayce agreed, then put forth the idea.

"I'll give you the whereabouts of Empress Tricara, but first I want to see my team member."

Robanna realised that this Lieutenant Commander was not stupid, he stood in thought, he knew that in order to get what he was after he would have to comply with what Tayce wanted. He agreed, much to Tayces surprise, turning he began off to where Treketa was being held. Tom shoved the kidnapper ahead of him roughly and followed. Tayce with Donaldo and Lance followed on, at a safe distance with their hands on their Slazer weapons, ready to use at a cencrons notice, they did not trust Robanna he could change his mind at a moments notice and they would be prepared.

Treketa heard footsteps approaching and wondered how she was going to comply with what Robanna wanted without blowing the whereabouts of the Empress. As she had been trying to find the communications device without much luck, she jumped bit by bit, praying she would make it back to the chair, before Robanna burst into the room. She fell on to the chair, righting herself just in time. The suite doors opened behind her. Robanna entered, crossing to her. Treketa began, she couldn't do what he had asked.

"I've decided that I'm not telling you what you want, so you might as well do what you want to me," she began angrily.

"Silence! My plans for you have changed," he said, putting up his hand to stop her saying any more.

Much to her great relief in through the double doors walked Tayce, Tom, Lance and Donaldo. Tom smiled reassuringly down at her, silently telling her it was going to be all right.

"Before I hand over this woman, there is something I want to tell you about your precious Empress, she was a commoner, her Father was the original leader of the planet Tristarcus, he and I were friends, he let Tricara make decisions and because she despised me, she made preparations for a ruling to be put in place that on her Father's death bed I would never be allowed to return to the planet and take up commanding rule in her Father's place and take the power of the Tristarcan Crystal, she made her people turn against me, never to trust me, so I went ahead and decided that when the planet was destroyed, I would take back what was rightfully mine," Robanna explained.

"You said you'd kill her if she turned up here, why?" asked Tayce, she was not being taken in by Robannas words, she found them fabricating and untrue, she'd known Tricara all her life. But she was prepared to let this Robanea continue incriminating himself.

309

"Is that what she told you Lieutenant Commander?" said Robanna laughing.

"The threats were genuine, I traced them and they came from your men," spoke up Lance.

Robanna quickly realised he was losing ground, so reached out and grabbed Treketa, putting his gun to her neck.

"You give me the Empress, or I'll do what I set out to do with your crew person here, the choice is yours Lieutenant Commander..." he said coolly, Treketa firmly in his grasp.

Without warning the doors to the suite burst open and in ran six Trinott security guards. They nearly knocked Tom flying on entering so quickly. Behind them came the Empress herself. Tayce turned surprised to see her.

"No doubt this lying barbarian has been filling your mind Tayce with lies about me," she began staring at Robanna coldly.

"Lies! You know it to be the truth woman, you know that your Father handed command to me when he passed, it was you that poisoned your peoples minds against me, I am the real ruler of Tristarcus and I therefore have right to rule on decisions here," he said angrily back at Tricara.

"Your what Tayce here would class as a criminal Robanna and you know it, my Father banished you from Tristarcus because of the laws you tried to force through, one being that our peaceful planet should go to war and become a planet solely for fighting, you wanted the Tristarcan Crystal to use for your powerful advancement in evilness you so craved, these black clad beings that you now class as your assistants have no minds of their own because of what you did to them, they serve only you and what you command, they were once two of Tristarcans most prestigious officers, until you started enticing them with grand ideas and turned them into what they are now," said Tricara furious.

"What are your desired orders Empress?" asked the security chief, dressed in a smart green uniform.

"Make him release the girl, disarm him and take him away to do what you so wish to do with criminals such as him, I will contact you later with evidence to support that this man is a law breaker chief, to put him away for good, you might like to take his men too," said Tricara.

"Men do as the Empress here requests," ordered the security chief.

The guards surrounded Treketa and Robanna and gently set Treketa free. Robanna and his two assistants were led away under gun watch, their weapons primed ready to shoot, if any of them tried to escape. Once Treketa was free, she ran to the safety of Lance, who quickly put his arm around her and hugged her to him reassuringly. Tom felt somewhat peeved to find that Lance was the first person, she ran to for comfort, instead of him but just brushed it off.

"Don't think that you've seen the last of me Empress, this unfortunate halt in my plans is only a small blip but we'll meet again, that you can count on," said Robanna looking hard at Tricara as he paused on passing her.

Tricara gave a look of total and utter disgust at him, then looked away. Tayce walked over to her. As she was finishing her discussion with the security chief. Treketa felt glad to be back in the secure comfort of Lances arms. Glad that her ordeal was over.

"How come you knew where to find us?" asked Tayce curious to Tricara.

"Firstly you roused security suspicion by the way you ran after Robannas man, I had to explain the situation and the Chief fully understood, he also said, that he was surprised to see me, he thought like others of the seminar organisation team that I had perished along with my people on Tristarcus, as I had not attended the seminars in previous times, I explained what had been happening, he fully understood and wanted to bring Robanna to justice, as we talked I saw where you were in my mind and here I am."

"So they wanted you to attend the seminar after all, perhaps if we'd spoken to the person in charge they would have stopped all this unnecessary trouble for you and Treketa," said Tom stepping up.

"Yes, I am so sorry for all the trouble that has been caused, especially to Treketa, If I had known what I know now, I would not have let any of this happen, I'm sorry Treketa, that you had to endure this unfortunate treatment at the hands of Robanna," said Tricara walking over to her.

Upon Tricara coming to a pause before Treketa, she left Lances side and unexpectedly to everyone present slapped Tricara hard across the face in outright anger. Lance quickly grabbed Treketa back reprimanding her softly, but sternly. Tayce was far from pleased, but realised she would probably feel the same way if she had been through what Treketa had been through. After gaining her composure Tricara, held nothing against Treketa for such an act, she couldn't blame her. Donaldo moved Treketa away, he could see that she was in shock, because of her ordeal and he didn't want her stressed any further, than she was. Tayce stood talking with Tricara.

"How was the seminar, did it work out the way you felt it would?" asked Tayce trying to ignore what had happened, with Treketa and restore normality for Tricara.

"Tayce don't concern yourself, what Treketa did was a normal reaction, she's in shock for what she's endured and I probably would have lashed out the way she did too, being confronted by the person who had caused my unnecessary torture at the hands of that man, as for my seminar, there were lots of students who hold the gift of telepathic abilities, like yourself and I found it rather interesting to talk with them, I spoke to some of their teachers who helped them to adjust and fine tune their abilities and it gave me something to think about as far as projects go, I could help gifted children and students that find it hard to adjust in coming face to face with strange new powers, I was also thinking that I could become a teacher of gifted children and students on Questa, but that's something to think about in the future," said Tricara softly.

311

"Are we heading back to Amalthea now?" cut in Marc softly.

"Yes, if Tricara here is ready to leave," replied Tayce looking to her friend.

"It's up to you, wouldn't any of you like to take in the hospitality of Trinott before we go?" asked Tricara softly wondering.

"No, they would not, we have a voyage schedule to return to, we only came to Trinott to assist you Tricara and rescue Treketa here, maybe the next time we're passing through," said Tayce sounding like the true team leader, that she was, that didn't want her team going astray, by persuasive young attractive females.

Tricara nodded understandingly. The Amalthea team plus Empress Tricara, walked from the suite where Robanna had thought he could get away with his unlawful threat against the Empress, in finishing her off once and for all and trying to trade Treketa for Tricara unsuccessfully. Tom slipped a loving arm around Tayces shoulders and guided her on out. Once outside, he let the others walk on and halted Tayce gently, turning her to face him, he figured now that everything was sorted, he owed her an apology for his behaviour he lowered his head and kissed her full and strongly on the lips and drew her to him in a strong passionate way. By this Tayce could pick up he was saying sorry and she liked it, giving in to him. She put her arms around his neck in response. They stayed together in a long lingering embrace for a few minons, just enjoying each other. Quite suddenly and out of nowhere Tayce felt that this intimate moment between them was something that would be somewhat limited, that somehow she was going to lose him, in the foreseeable future. The notion made her stop responding to him and draw away. He looked down at her concerned, not knowing why she'd abruptly stopped.

"We should go," said Tayce turning to walk off.

"What is it?" asked Tom carefully, he could see she had something on her mind.

"I can't explain it, just tell me that you'll always be with me Tom," she replied looking back at his handsome features taking in the handsome man that she come to love deeply, tears almost welling in her eyes at the sadness she was unexpectedly feeling and for no reason that she could comprehend.

"Come here, I'm not going anywhere, what makes you feel I would leave you," he said walking to her.

Together they continued on up the corridor heading back to the cruiser before it departed leaving them on Trinott. They walked passed people enjoying the somewhat enticing way of life that was Trinott, the Pleasure Queens, making them feel the most amazing kind of alluring pleasure, on the way to their destined suites. Tom smiled to himself, as a male guest and a female Pleasure Queen passed in a lost embracing pleasure. Tayce nudged him, she picked up on his thoughts and they weren't duty based. As they went Tom found himself bothered by what Tayce had said, in him not leaving her, he would always be there for her. He wondered also if she knew something that he didn't, owing to the influence of her powers. But he was a great believer in the saying, never worry about tomorron, because tomorron would take care of itself.

***

Tayce and Tom arrived back on Amalthea and the doors closed behind them. On Tayces request Midge did a quick team check to make sure that everyone including Empress Tricara was back on board, then put into operation the procedure to depart the Entertainment Colony. As far as Tayce was concerned, it had been another successful Quest, everyone had won through in the end. Empress Tricara had been reinstated as ruler on decisions of her once home world Tristarcus and had been given back the right to share in planetary ideas and projects as once ruler of her home world. Treketa had been successfully found, much to everyone's relief, after her frightening ordeal unfortunate for her. She would probably remember what had happened for a long time to come. As far as the sudden premonition Tayce had felt back on Trinott, about losing Tom, She would have to wait and find out what the future held. Whether it would come true. She for one, against all odds, didn't want to think that it would.

Trouble on Trinott

After a couple of weekons Amalthea unexpected for the team was heading back to Trinott. It was by request of Lydia Traun, that the team attend a Space Exploration Equipment and Weaponry Exhibition. Tayce could not refuse to return, as her Mother was now her new chief and this returning journey was classed as her next Quest. She wasn't the only one to feel uneasy about the unplanned return journey to Trinott, Treketa also was feeling apprehensive, considering what she had suffered on the last visit. Tayce though had assured her that the chances of anything like it happening again was a million to one. Empress Tricara was along again for the interest in the exhibition and since her status to vote as once ruler of Tristarcus had been reinstated, she was going back to Trinot to check out a few things, regarding planetary exploration, for her own interest. To see how things had moved on from the dayons as once ruler of her home world.

"Trinott is in sight Tayce and closing," announced Midge over the on board announcement system.

Tayce and Tricara were seated in the on board Leisure Centre, with a cup of Coffeen, in discussion over Tayces abilities and especially the fact she had had the blinding notion the last time they had visited Trinott two weekons ago, she was going to lose Tom. Tricara didn't know what to say, she began that she had bad news but not regarding Tom. Something that she had not told her the moment she walked aboard. Robanna had escaped his escort to trial and Questa Security who he had been handed over to, were at that moment trying to track him down. Tayce gave Tricara a look of almost horror at the news.

"You mean he's back on the lose, why wasn't I told this, he nearly killed Treketa the last time," said Tayce furious, standing to her feet.

"Your Mother wanted you to take this Quest, the council were breathing down her neck in the fact that you hadn't done this kind of Quest your undertaking now, a councillor by the name of Barkin is making things difficult for your Mother, on the nature of this voyage, she asked me to break the news to you the moment I boarded, I'm sorry Tayce, I feel like you do knowing Robanea is out here somewhere," said Tricara standing and walking to Tayce.

"My biggest fear is he's going to show up at this exhibition and somehow he's the way I lose Tom, I don't know how, but I've this strong feeling, this is it for Tom," said Tayce turning to face Tricara calming herself.

"Don't concern yourself, the mind has a ways of playing tricks on situations especially for people like you and me, we get stronger feelings than anyone else in our sudden premonitions, Chief Barnfords men are the best in their field for hunting down criminals, you've nothing to fear as I see it," assured Tricara hugging her friend, though she wondered if Tayces premonition over Tom, would happen.

Marc entered the Leisure Centre, he paused upon seeing Tricara and Tayce in a moment of comfort. He sauntered over asking silently what was the a problem? Upon him reaching them, Tayce turned and quietly explained what Tricara had just divulged, that Robanna had escaped during transit to trial. Marc pulled a face that said it all and sighed impatiently, at the fact. He suggest he leave the matter with him, he would see what he could find out further. Tayce finished the last of her Coffeen, whilst Marc suggested to Tricara she tell him exactly what she knew. He guided her on out of the Leisure Centre. Tayce watched them go she could never understand it, but she always had seen a kind of deep admiration they had for each other and couldn't quite understand whether it was just true friendship, or something more meaningful. It was almost like the kind of loving relationship a Mother had with her son. But to her knowledge they were not related. But Tricara was certainly old enough to be Marc's Mother, if it were proven, somehow. Seeing the looming sight of Trinott approaching through the nearest sight port of the four, along the outside hull of the side of the cruiser, she quickly discarded her beaker in the waste incinerator, heading on out.

***

Amalthea went into the final docking procedures on approach to the Colony/ World of Trinott once again. Tom was waiting by the Docking Bay doors on Level 2. Tayce headed towards him, still with the feeling she was going to lose him suddenly, ever more stronger than before. She wished she could stop feeling the heart wrenching feeling. Tom explained as she came to a pause that Treketa and Lance had decided to remain on board to take care of the cruiser, it was their turn to take control duty, not that they minded. Tayce nodded understandingly, she knew that Treketa was feeling uneasy to be returning to Trinott so soon. Overhead suddenly Lance informed Tricara that a Questa aide called Daniel Mayford would be waiting to escort her during her visit to the Colony/World. Docking soon completed. The Docking Bay doors opened to reveal the walkway down into the Trinott Central reception area. The warm air and the sound of people and alien travellers down on Trinott came up the walkway in loud jovial noise. The Quest team consisting of Tom, Marc, Donaldo, Tayce, Duncan and Tricara walked forth down the walkway onto Trinott into the reception area. As informed, the moment they exited the walkway, the young Officer Daniel Mayford was waiting and walked forth introducing himself to firstly Marc, who to Tayces surprise because he was wearing a Questa uinform, asked for confirmation of his identification. The young pleasant faced officer, with blonde hair willingly obliged, taking out his ID, passing it to Marc. He nodded and handed it back to him. Daniel explained that he had been especially picked for this duty to Empress Tricara, by the Chief of Questa. He was one of Chief Barnfords special Security Escorts and was trained to take care of any untoward attack on the Empress, with the least of fuss, should it arise. With this Tayce watched as Tricara followed Daniel and left the teams side. She then placed her hand through Tom's arm, in case one of the Pleasure Queens thought he was available and together the Quest team began towards the Space Exploration and Weaponry Exhibition that was going to show the latest in every aspect of space wares, for space exploration and every dayon living in the present spacial time of 2417. Tayce tried to relax. Tom looked down at her, he was growing concerned that she didn't seem to be taking in the atmosphere, as if something was on her mind.

"Are you all right, you look far away about something?" he said softly and quietly down at her.

"I'm fine, it's just coming back to this place, brings back memories of what nearly happened when I thought Robanna was going to kill you in that corridor we were in, when we tracked that creep that ran off," she whisperingly replied, glancing around at the many mingling interested sightseers, seeing demonstrations of the latest gadgets. Upon everyone entering fully into the Exhibition Area, Tayce suggested they enjoy the many interesting demonstrations, but they were to meet up later for the revealing of the latest weapon that could benefit both Questa and Amalthea. The team all nodded, then walked off to look at what interested them most. Going different ways. Tom and Duncan noticed the new engineering and latest in computer systems. Tayce found herself standing alone and Tom heading away. She glanced around for something to try and occupy her nagging continuous uneasy thoughts of losing Tom it was driving her crazy. Donaldo's eye was caught by the medical stand and headed on over to see if there was anything he could consider for the cruiser.

"Excuse me, it's Lieutenant Commander Traun Isn't it?" said a male voice behind Tayce, so out of the blue it almost made her jump.

"Yes that's me, how do you know my name?" she asked turning unsure of who the voice belonged to, quickly coming face to face with a handsome man in his late 40's.

"Your somewhat of a legend in the galaxy, let me introduce myself, I'm the designer of the most up to date Slazer, that will I hope, benefit your team some dayon, I'm Cordec Parglen designer of the Pollomoss, which is the weapon that your seeing unveiled todayon, it's an honour to meet you," he said outstretching his hand for Tayce to shake in friendly manner.

"It's a pleasure to meet you too, it's good to see that technology is still being produced considering the cuts that are coming in, in funding on such projects, according to Questa Councillor Barkin, I'll look forward to hearing all about this Pollomoss weapon," replied Tayce shaking hands with Cordec.

"If you'll excuse me, I have to prepare for my speech," he said pleasantly and walked away.

Tayce glancing around noticed there was a strong presence of security. Trinotts own security officers were placed here and there, especially in the vicinity of the Pollomoss weapon. Tayce began to think maybe as there was such a strong presence of Security, had they been asked as more than just guests and that they were expecting trouble, like the Pollomoss to be stolen in some way? Was her notion of losing Tom wrapped up in the middle of this possible trouble, sometimes she hated her powers, especially when they made her see possible scenarios ahead, before anyone else could.

"There seems to be a lot of security here," said Tom discretely coming to her side.

"Yes I've noticed, I've just met the creator of the latest in weaponry design, for Questa, Cordec Parglen, he's the designer of the Pollomoss weapon, it seems that's why there's a strong presence of security here, because of the unveiling of the Pollomoss and I think they are expecting trouble.

"Ladies, Gentlemen and honoured Alien Guests, would you all gather next door for the unveiling of the latest in space technology and weaponry design," came the male voice of an announcer.

The Amalthean Quests team all gathered with the guests and slowly made their way into the next room. Six security officers fell in behind, heading to the outskirts of the room with their eyes on the crowd. Two closed the entrance doors. Tayce felt a sudden stabbing rush of unexpected panic, like she'd never felt before, ever. Something along the lines of sudden claustrophobia. It was obvious that whatever was going to happen to Tom was going to happen in their current surroundings, but even though the feeling was gut wrenching her mind would not let her see the proper picture, of how and who by. She fought to remain calm against the uneasy feeling and glanced around at the present guests focussing their attentions on the designer Cordec Parglen that was taking to the stand. Up on the stage on a white pillar, covered in a satinex white cover was the sleek shiny design of the Pollomoss Handgun. Cordec stopped to a loud and enthusiastic applause.

"Thank you for being here, many of you have come for pure interest, others have come to find out if this weapon the Pollomoss could be included in every dayon duty life, as you can see it's the normal size of a hand Slazer weapon, she's slim in design and lightweight, so both female and male members of crew or team can carry this little weapon quite comfortably, this is the prototype the first real model that will be available for Questa and Universal wide use within the next yearon, production is standing by to commence after todayons unveiling," announced Cordec.

"I bet it packs a mighty shot, small weapons like that, are generally very powerful," said Marc standing next to Duncan.

"Your right Commander Dayatso, this little weapon can disintegrate, an intense object like a wall, just by using the highest setting and when used as a weapon in battle, will disintegrate whoever it's aimed at, leaving no trace, they even existed, hence there's no bodies to clean up after a confrontation or battle," replied Cordec hearing Marc.

As the presentation continued Tayce glanced around and in the crowd her sight caught a couple of shifty looking guests, looking uneasy trying not to be noticed. They were discretely whispering back and forth and glancing around in a summoning way, around the room, particularly at the Pollomoss, as if they were planing something sinister. Tom taking his eyes from Cordec, looked in the direction to where Tayce was watching something with great interest. The being that she had been watching in particular suddenly looked back at her with unemotional dark eyes, then glanced away. Tom lightly nudged her discretely, asking her what she was glancing at? She informed him that she was interested in two characters acting suspicious. As she looked back, they had gone. The doors were seen closing to the room and security were acting as if there was nothing out of the ordinary occurring, but Tayce senses were telling her otherwise. What was she to do, make a complete fool of herself by telling security that she had suspicions, only to prove it was her mind playing tricks and that the wrongful looking characters were none other than, just travellers passing through and had left innocently. She didn't know what to do. The doors burst open as she thought the best plan of action, in walked two men. At first Tayce relaxed a bit, seeing that they were obviously designer techs and then were announced as such, by Cordec with him further saying that they had been responsible for putting the design before them together. One designer a thin knowledgeable looking man in his mid forties, the other young, like an assistant to the older one. They walked towards the stage. Tayce cursed silently as once more out of the blue she was feeling the stabbing in her head of the uncanny premonition, she just wished what was going to happen would materialise, so that her mind could leave her alone, before she was driven insane.

"Tom I feel something is wrong, I don't know what, but something is evolving here in this room," confided Tayce as Tom glanced to her again.

"Look I'll meet you outside if it's getting to much for whatever is bothering you, we can't just bring it to the attention of security on a whim, we'll be laughed at without any proof other than you just have some kind of notion something is going to happen," he whisperingly replied.

"All right, fine!" she replied in return whisper.

She sauntered out of the crowd and discretely walked from the Hall, her heart pounding in her chest, fit to burst. She could feel the blood rushing to her face. The sound of Cordecs designers answering questions from the gathered interested parties continuing behind her. The security guard nearest the entrance smiled a pleasant smile at her and stepped aside, as she walked out the doors into the outer exhibition area. Just as she had exited the Hall there came the unexpected sound of a female scream behind her, followed by the words of a woman in panic.

"That man has got a gun." Followed by the sound of further shouting and screaming. A panic situation was unfolding from within.

Tayce turned back towards the entrance doors in shear alarm, upon hearing what was materialising. She glanced around to see if there was another kind of weapon, that she could use to stop what was going on. But as she glanced to the stand where the Pollomoss second display weapon should be, it was missing. Slowly it was beginning to all knit together, the second weapon had to be in the hands of the man the woman had shouted about a few minons ago. This whole scenario was beginning to bring out into the open the lead up to her premonition, she had to do something and fast. She had to warn security somehow. She headed back to the entrance into the Hall where Tom and the others were. A sudden Slazer burst sounded from inside the Hall, as she approached the doors. Tayce flinched realising it had to be the second Pollomoss. She stepped onto the threshold in front of the entrance and as the doors opened, a rough and broad hand reached out and grabbed her inside, roughly. As she looked at the being it belonged to, she saw that it was the one of the pair of men in the audience earlier that had met her gaze, as she studied him and his accomplices, before they left unexpectedly but now had re-entered the Hall for trouble. He hauled her round in front of him, facing the audience of frightened guests now crouching down on the floor. As he raised the weapon, Tayce could see it was the second Pollomoss gun. Tom as Tayce glanced over to him was shielding the Empress in amongst the crouched frightened guests, along with Daniel Mayford on the floor. Marc as he was nearest, tried to reach Tayce. The accomplice of the two men nearest Marc, kicked him in the midriff sending him back onto the floor in winded agony. To the female cries of the female members of the audience

"Get down with the others," he commanded almost shoving his gun in Marc's face.

"Join them and don't look back, go!" said the leader of the two outlaws, pushing Tayce into the crowd.

Marc even though he'd been winded reached out grabbing Tayce to safety down beside him. He could feel that she was shaking from the shock of what happened, as he brought her into his protective hold.

"Who's in charge here," said the rough bearded looking leader, of the two scruffy looking obvious outlaws, as he fired off another shot from the Pollomoss in his grasp, for the fun of it, into mid air.

After another outburst of frightened female guests screaming, thinking that their end was not far off because these two gun happy outlaws would end up blowing them all to the next Universe, at the slightest touch of the weapons powerful Pollomoss setting, Cordec Parglen stepped forth.

"I am, this is my presentation and you sir are not welcome," said Cordec to the point, giving the leader holding his design a cold icy stare.

"Then I guess you're Cordec Parglen, great weapon sir, I congratulate you, you can now consider your gun tested," said the leader breaking into a callous laugh.

Without thought the leader turned the Pollomoss on the security guards and open fired taking out every guard to everyone's horror, with a spray of Slazer fire without a care, or thought of what he was doing. Tayce couldn't believe what she was witnessing, sure enough in her, one to one old dayon of travels with Midge she'd come across scenes that no lone female should witness, but not where she had seen innocent men doing their jobs, disintegrated from existence where they had stood.

"You can consider your design a success Cordec and it also proves to you what I am capable of, these people will remain here until you hand me the real Pollomoss, oh yes, I am aware that this is a display model, so the real one that is probably in your reach, I don't care where, I want it in seven hourons from now, otherwise there will be repercussions for all these people here, you can also arrange safe passage, once we have the weapon in question, you have been warned," stated the leader in a harsh callous tone, then the doors opened behind him and ten more men rushed in causing more chaos for the crowd, carrying weapons.

The Hall fell silent as everyone of the members of the audience wondered just what was about to happen. Cordec began, it was not up to him to just hand over the real Pollomoss, even though he knew that the display model was in fact the first real weapon of it's kind, he was just the designer of the gun, the rights had been sold to his design leader on Earthon 2. Tom glanced at Tayce in the shelter of Marc's arm, she felt him looking and looked back uneasy.

"Seven hourons Parglen, if all you people here cooperate during that time, you will be released to your vessels, if you cause any trouble during this time, then the person who is causing it will be dealt with," said the leader

"You haven't told us who you are?" said Tayce standing to her feet she didn't like this situation and she didn't like being threatened.

"Gardlen, Dayfor Gardlen you are?" he demanded striding forward and walking to where Tayce was.

He paused and looked at her darkly, with mean dark eyes of cruel intent, he could tell she was going to be the one that was going to cause trouble, but he liked the look of her and decided to play with her a while. Tayce looked back at him refusing to be intimidated.

"I'm Lieutenant Commander Traun and what your trying to do here, won't work, the main reception of this world are no doubt in talks with a security forces to rescue all of us and have a squad on their way right now," said Tayce plainly.

"Hey Gardlen look who we have over, here it's Empress Tricara," called one of Gardlens men, who looked like he hadn't shaved for a weekon.

Tayce turned to see the Empress in the grip of one of Gardlens men. Gardlen strode away from Tayce, over to where Tricara was. He upon reaching her pushed Tom back out the way, giving him a look that wanted Tom to challenge him, for pushing him. He grabbed Tricara in front of him, saying close to her right ear that Robanna sent his regards. She felt repulsed by his strong close presence and hated being in his hold. Tayce was feeling terrible at the strong onslaught of something happening rising inside of her, to much to bear, once again. To an overwhelming pitch.

"Seven hourons, that's a long time to waste, I could do with something of a distraction, how a bit of Empress to keep me company," he said eyeing her sexually interested.

Tricara had to swallow at the mere thought. It made her want to be sick. This barbarian before her made her cringe at the thought of what he had in mind, for seven hourons and she didn't like the thoughts she was reading. Anger rose inside of Tom, he was finding it impossible to control his patience, especially the way Gardlen seemed to be touching the Empress and what he had in mind for her, he considered him a real bastard. He had to act, do something fast there was no way he could allow Tricara to be Gardlens meat.

"Take your hands off her, she's not for the likes of you, you piece of space garbage," retorted Tom, lunging for Gardlen, his face angry and his eyes dark with fury, which Tayce had never seen before.

Gardlen didn't like the likes of someone trying to play hero. But this move Tom made, was the most stupid move he'd made to date. Gardlen before Tayce could act to stop it with her powers, as the thoughts she had been having all fell into place, put his Pollomoss into Tom's ribs and fired, without thought. Right before Tayces eyes Tom disappeared gone forever. Killed in the weapon fire of the Pollomoss. She gasped in shear horror her world as she knew it had gone right before her eyes. She felt like she wanted to drop to the floor from the shear shock of what had just happened. She felt her heart almost rip apart from the shear awesome sight she'd remember for the rest of her life and etched on her mind for some time to come. She forgot that she would be putting herself in the same danger as Tom and now that she had lost the man that meant the Universe to her, she sprang at Gardlen without a care and full of angered fury, at what he'd done. Marc quickly grabbed her back in split cencron. He found it near damned impossible to grab hold of her, as she was filled with such violent rage, she wanted to kill Gardlen with her bear hands. Marc tried to calm her, she was hysterical with gut wrenching pain and uncontrollable tears at losing Tom. Once Tayce was safely in his arms, he through a look that said it all at Gardlen, then tried to bring Tayce under control, soothing her strongly with words of comfort, which seemed to fall on deaf ears, she wanted to get Gardlen and she didn't care if she was killed in the process.

"Shut her up," said Gardlen at Marc turning the Pollomoss on Tayce ready to do just this if Marc couldn't, if there was something he couldn't stand, it was a hysterical out of control female.

"You've just killed her husband, you bastard?" said Marc angry fed up.

Tayce pushed away from Marc looking up at Gardlen with immense hatred in her eyes, she wanted time alone with him and the full use of her abilities she'd make him pay for what he'd done. Why she thought, why had her powers failed her, when she needed them to get rid of this murderer. Her normally beautiful features showed the shock and overwhelming hurt, that she was feeling, tears stained her delicate cheeks. Her whole life had suddenly plunged into the depths of darkened cold loneliness and despair in a split cencron, even though she had people around her trying to offer her support, she felt alone and if time had somehow stopped still right from the moment that Tom had disappeared. She'd lost her coupling partner and best friend who was a good member of team, just by one Slazer shot from. Gardlen. He showed no mercy as he looked back at her, unaffected by what had happened it meant nothing to him that she'd lost Tom, he was just another target. Tayce turned back to Marc's warm comforting arms, feeling warm and safe. He hugged her like a big brother comforting his sister, in a great time of need

***

On board Amalthea Lance Largon had problems of his own. He and Treketa had been watching what had happened and the shock had hit Treketa just as bad as it did Tayce, Tom was her brother, she was heartbroken. Lance held her in his arms trying to sooth her, as she broke her heart on his shoulder sobbing uncontrollably. Midge took control of the cruiser, but in his own way felt the pain that both his mistress and Treketa were going through. Tom Stavard had been an extraordinary member of the team and a good man. He recalled a memory of the first dayon, when he had arrived on the team and how he and Tayce had formed a very strong bond between them. He wanted to shoot this criminal Gardlen himself. Treketa broke away from Lance and ran off out of Organisation, she wanted to run and run to escape the pain of being torn apart inside no longer having her loving brother there for her as he always had been. Tears streamed down her face, as she ran. In Organisation Deck Lance knew that she wouldn't be thinking straight.

"Midge I've got to find her, there's no telling what she'll do in this state," said Lance.

"You go, I'll let you know if she attempts anything foolish and where she is on route," said Midge.

Lance ran out of Organisation Deck in urgency. He called out to Treketa, as he went, hoping she would hear him and stop. He headed straight for the Level Steps and as luck would have it, caught her up on the second flight down. He reached out and grabbed her arm, to stop her, which she did. She turned looking up into his warm dark brown eyes hurting like nothing else. She could see he understood her pain.

"Listen to me, you may be hurting right now, I've been there, I know what your going through, but think of Tayce, she saw what happened first hand, she's feeling pretty much like you, probably worse, come here," he said reaching out and pulling her into his warm reassuring arms.

"You're right, it's awful, I'm sorry," she replied in between sobs.

Lance guided her on to her quarters, suggesting she take time out, to reflect, he'd be in Organisation if she needed him. Treketa agreed. No sooner had Lance seen her to her quarters when he Wristlinked to Midge ordering him to watch Treketa, inform him the moment she needed him. Midge agreed. Lance headed back to Organisation thinking about Tom himself, he had always got on well with him and he realised that there was going to be a big gap in all their lives for some time to come. What had happened to Tom had him thinking about the last moments before his Father's death, he knew the kind of pain that Tayce had to be feeling at that moment. As soon as he reached Organisation, he took up his duty position.

"How is she Lance?" asked Midge as he sat down.

"Not good mate, like I said, keep an eye on her, if you know what I mean?" said Lance in thought he still wasn't sure that Treketa wouldn't try something foolish.

"Would you like me to attend to anything?" asked Midge helpfully.

"Get me Lydia Traun at Questa," said Lance wondering how he was going to break the news.

"Of course," said Midge obligingly.

Lydia soon appeared on Sight Screen and seeing Lance looking somewhat, as if something was badly wrong braced herself for the worst. And also ready to act to assist in anyway she could.

"My God Lance what's happened, what's the matter?" asked Lydia, growing concerned, that something had happened to Tayce.

"I've some bad news, devastating you could say you better brace yourself and sit down," said Lance solemnly

"Is it Tayce, what's happened, tell me?" replied Lydia softly, beginning to feel she was about to receive the worst on Tayce, as she was impulsive at the best of times with her actions.

"Its Tom. You know you sent us here to Trinott for the Exhibition, at the audience for the unveiling of the Pollomoss a band of outlaws raided the event and talk by Cordec Parglen, to cut a long story short, the leader of the outlaws, a character named Gardlen wanted to take Tricara for his pleasure time, Tom got in the way to protect Tricara, Gardlen shot him. There's no easy way to say this, he's dead Lydia," said Lance swallowing in saddened thought, of what had happened.

"No! I don't know what to say Lance, my God, what of Tayce, she must be devastated, where is she now?" asked Lydia shocked almost speechless, her heart almost stopping too, at hearing the news.

"Still on Trinott in the event from what I could see earlier, Marc was taking care of her," recalled Lance.

Lydia's mind began racing of what she should do. After a few minons of thought she suggested he leave the matter with her. He enquired what was she going to do? She explained that Jan Barnford and his team would be sent out, this was an urgent situation, before anyone else got killed on Trinott. Lance informed her that as far as he could make out Gardlen had killed all the security guards at the event, claiming he was giving a demonstration of what the Pollomoss could do. Lydia gave a disgusted look and shook her head at the fact, then she ceased communications, the screen going blank. Lance relaxed back in thought.

***

Back on Trinot at the Space Exploration and Weaponry Exhibition in the Hall, the chairs had been moved back against the wall and the guests were sitting down under gun watch from Gardlens men. Donaldo was concerned for the current state of Tayce, she looked full of emotional shock and drained in Marc's arms. Gardlen had pushed Tricara back to a seat near Marc. He no longer wanted her for his pleasure, after all he was there for the Pollomoss and to escape the present surroundings undeterred with the best weapon to carry on his lawbreaking actions, out in the Universe. Glancing at his wrist time illuminated display, he calculated that it was four hourons into the situation and Cordec Parglen had been allowed, to go ahead and arrange for the release of the weapon. He decided to allow thirty of the fifty or so hostages, to leave. The remaining hostages included the Amalthean Quests team which Gardlen had found out he had in his presence, upon checking who remained. He decided that he was going to use them, as his pass to freedom. If the officials did not play ball and allow him the real Pollomoss and safe passage off Trinott.

"You'll never get away with this, first murder and stealing the Pollomoss, it will be life for you at one of the prison colonies," said Tayce coming back to the present.

"Wasn't it enough to take out your husband Lieutenant Commander, let me tell you that's where your wrong by the time any kind of security force arrives, I shall be long gone, into the next realm, so shut up and sit down before I test this weapon out on you and you join your husband," he angrily retaliated, he figured she was now beginning to bore him.

The time on the hall square faced clock read 24:45 it was near to midnight hourons, how much longer would they have to endure this fiasco thought Duncan. He then glanced at Tayce concerned. Donaldo felt frustrated he wanted to get Tayce back to Amalthea, she didn't look right, quite strained and he didn't know how she was hanging in there, considering what had happened. He discretely leaned towards Duncan.

"What's the chance of taking them out," he put to Duncan, forgetting his medical ethics of taking a life.

"No chance, to many of them have their guns primed on us, I don't want to join Tom thanks," replied Duncan in near whisper.

The time ebbed away in the seven houron situation, that no one wanted to be in. Tayce felt tired and just wanted to get off their surroundings. Some of the guests that had been left behind, beside the Amaltheans had managed to grab what could only be described as uneasy sleep, waiting for the next outburst from Gardlen and his men. Marc glanced down at Tayce, he found it strange not to hear her and Tom whispering to each other plans that could possibly get them out of the current mess. He had to admit that he missed Tom he and Tom had had their differences, but they had become firm friends and Tom's sudden demise had left a gaping empty hole for them all. It would remain like it for some foreseeable time and the more he thought about it, he realised that he was now Tayces right hand man, not that he wouldn't want Tom to come back, he would. He glanced around the Hall. Women and men from other vessels, that had been at the gathering to hope to put orders in for the Pollomoss remained silent, thoughtful even, the situation was stupid beyond words, he thought. Cordec sat on a seat now on his own, he had done all he could to contact the person in charge of releasing the Pollomoss weapon in Gardlens hands, it was just a case of waiting for the permission to come through on his communications device, rather like a Wristlink. The two designers that had been with Cordec sat on adjacent seats. Marc found that his eyes were getting too heavy to stay awake, he like the others slowly drifted into sleep, not caring what was going to happen in the remaining hourons.

***

Next mornet the hostages were woken by the sound of the Pollomoss being fired. Tayce woke thinking that she had been sleeping with her head rested on Tom's shoulder and she said a soft good mornet to him. Marc's voice gently broke her sleepy pleasant thoughts, throwing her into a cold heartbreaking realisation Tom was gone. Tears welled into her eyes, she wanted to cry forever, she felt empty beyond words. Marc soothed her in an understanding way. Cordec was in the throes of being pushed towards the communication device in an uncaring way by Gardlen. Tayce felt her anger rise in her like never before and quite suddenly she decided that she'd had enough, she was damned if she was going to let the man that had killed the only man she had ever loved, walk free, even if she had to join Tom in the process, she stood to her feet. Marc was thrown into a blind panic on what Tayce was thinking of doing. He reached out, but missed her as she walked out of the group of hostages under everyone's questioning gaze. Tricara called to Marc in urgent whisper.

"What's she doing, she's crazy, she's not thinking straight?" said Tricara in panic.

"Being an idiot, I can't reach her, I hope to hell she knows what she's up to," replied Marc in whispered alarm.

"I want to talk with you Gardlen, I want to know how much longer your going to keep us all here in this situation, that you know you won't escape from, your seven hourons is up, according to my Wristlink time," said Tayce angrily.

"Not you again, woman your nothing but trouble," he replied walking down from the platform.

"I want answers, as do the rest of these people here, so?" said Tayce giving him a hateful glare.

Tayce stood her ground unafraid as Gardlen came towards her. He paused before her, trying to make her feel intimidated, but it wasn't happening, the way she was feeling. Over his shoulder, he ordered Cordec to continue finding out how much longer he had to wait before he could leave with what he'd come for. He then looked back at Tayce studying her with the same evil sexual intentions he used on Tricara. Without warning Tayces Wristlink bleeped. It was Midge informing her that Jan Barnford was on his way with a top security team. Gardlen grabbed Tayces wrist, with the sounding Wristlink and activated it to hear Midge announce that help was on it's way. This was something he did not want to hear. He gave Tayce a look that said it all He ripped the Wristlink from her wrist and dropped it to the floor stamping on it hard. Turning he ordered his men that trouble was coming, the plan had to be moved up a notch. Tayce glanced to Marc questioningly, he shook his head. Gardlen watched still in front of Tayce, as two of his officers walked to Cordec and bore down on him with their weapons primed. Cordec at this moment received communication that the permission to hand over the Pollomoss was in the final stages.

"How much longer do I have to wait, maybe I should start to shoot someone, someone of importance to get things moving," began Gardlen looking around the gathered group of hostages, for that very person.

"I'd like to see him try," whispered Marc, under his breath, his patience was now wearing thin.

Gardlen moved his grip from Tayces wrist, to her upper arm. Why she had no idea, perhaps he thought he was thinking of using her as his first target if things went wrong. She felt no emotion before him, only hatred. She knew that she could not use her powers on him, for reprise, his men would probably take her out or one of her team. She and the team were trapped. She knew though that she would only have to play along with this outlaw and his gang, just a bit longer. She hoped it wasn't long, because she could see his patience was wearing thin and he could kick off at any minon and start shooting.

***

Out in the Universe and fast approaching Trinott was Jan Barnford and his top priority Security Patrol Team of Questa. Lydia Traun had given him orders to head to Trinott and rescue Tayce and the team from an outlaw and his accomplices, trying to steal the Pollomoss and who was holding a lot of hostages in the process. Upon hearing Tayce was in danger, it touched a raw nerve for Jan, he and Tayce had a kind of respect for each other and he thought the Universe of her. He considered her a true gutsy woman and he liked her. He admired how she was trying to clean up the Universe, of criminals in the current crime ridden time that it had become. He stood briefing his team on how important it was to rescue the Amalthean Quests Team and Empress Tricara. To make sure the remaining hostages returned to their vessels safely. As for the outlaws and their leader. He wanted him and his band of accomplices arrested for trial. His men nodded in total agreement. They ferried out of the briefing and off to prepare to head into their mission of importance. He thought about Tayce in the current situation and had heard from Lance on Amalthea, she was doing her best to play Gardlen along, giving him time to get to Trinott. All he hoped was she didn't put herself in the line of extreme danger. Outlaws had a way of running out of patience and wasting woman like Tayce, just for the fun of it.

On another part of Trinott it was hard to imagine that the hostage situation was under way, on the west point of the world, everything looked normal, no one was aware as to what was happening, just a short jaunt away, they were laughing and enjoying the Paradise Holiday Resort, for what Trinott was known for.

The air was silent once more in the Hall. Gardlens men now had their weapons primed on the hostages. Tayce was back seated with Marc, minus her Wristlink. Gardlen was walking about in summoning thought of what move to make next. A sound sounded on the communication device, that Cordec had been using to ask permission to let the Pollomoss go. He answered it. Gardlen glanced motionless towards the designer who had been waiting. Cordec nodded. Gardlen did a triumphant cheer, he could get the hell off Trinott, then he turned asking what of his passage out? Cordec shook his head, this had not been granted. Without further thought he was beaten by the two men, nearest him for failing to get what Gardlen wanted. Tricara shook her head in disgust at the scene of the two rough men, taking turns to beat Cordec to a near unconscious state.

"Lieutenant Commander as your Amalthean cruiser is in orbit, I have decided to travel in style in leaving here, you wouldn't mind having us as guests for a while would you, we're well behaved, I promise," he said glancing to his men and smirking, then walking over to Tayce.

"You won't even get the chance to step one foot on Amalthea, my guidance computer would kill you the moment you tried, he's programmed to get rid of intruders like you," replied Tayce.

"Is that a fact, smart computer, if he's a good little computer, he will do as I instruct him to do, if he values the life of his crew," replied Gardlen his eyes turning cold.

Tayce could see that he had another handgun in his side hip holster and an idea was running through her head. One that she'd try, when she knew that Jan Barnford was coming close to their surroundings, she'd put into practice. There was no way she'd allow the likes of Dayfor Gardlen putting one foot on her cruiser, not if she could stop it. He backed away without suspicion and returned to his men laughing as they did.

***

In orbit of Trinott Jan's Patrol Cruiser had gone into a stationary orbit. Out from underneath came a group of armed fighters, taking up positions around the Departure Area, ready to open fire on the outlaws if they tried to escape with the Pollomoss. On board the Patrol Cruiser, the remaining officers of Jan's elite team were checking their handguns and making sure their protective suits were properly placed to avoid personal injury. Jan was dressed in full combat attire, he was taking part in the successful apprehension of these so called thieves and rescuing the hostages, including the Amalthean Quests team.

"Remember your briefing, apprehend the outlaws and the leader for questioning later and Trial, I don't want any casualties or deaths, to report on our side," pointed out Jan in ordering tone.

"Sir!" came the reply of his men, all at once.

"Right lets go," said Jan striding ahead of them, in a determined military way towards the Transpot Centre in urgency.

This duty ahead of Jans men was all in a dayons work, they had tackled loads of criminals in this kind of tricky situation before. They were considered elite, for their smooth actions in quickly bringing a situation to a successful completion, in quick time. This team were known as S.S.W.A.T (Space Special Weapons and

Tactics) team and Jan had only just been granted the status by Earthon 2 chief of the Earthon 2 equivalent to Jan's team because of a practice session, they had to perform to gain such recognition. They had passed with flying colours. Jan's pilot gave the all clear to move in. The men took to their positions in the Transpot. It activated and they de-materialised to the surface, into a near vicinity of the place of apprehension.

***

Back on Trinott, Gardlen had received word that a S.S.W.A.T. Team from Questa, was in orbit and upon him hearing this he was striding towards Tayce, he wanted his passage off his surroundings and Tayce was the one to give it to him, whether she liked it or not he didn't care. He grabbed her back onto her feet holding the real Pollomoss now in his grasp. Tayce pretended to struggle, as she had decided the plan she had was a good one. She had confided in near whisper with Marc and even though he thought it was risky, it was quite feasible.

"Let go of me Gardlen you've no where to run, if the S.S.W.A.T. Team are in orbit, by now they have surrounded this place and there is no where to go, give this up before it costs you your worthless life," said Tayce feeling a lot more brave, knowing Jan was on his way.

"Shut up woman before I kill you here and now, your cruisers where we're heading, now move," he said ushering her forward.

Tayce turned and went for his side weapon, before he had time to blink, she drew it and aimed it directly at him, the hatred she felt inside for him killing Tom showed in her normally beautiful sapphire eyes. Gardlen was wide eyed with shock, that she had moved so fast.

"Call off your men or I'll kill you where you stand, do it, don't think I won't hesitate to use this, I've never missed and it would give me the greatest pleasure," said Tayce pointing the small and powerful hand gun, directly in his face.

Gardlen even though he was an outlaw, valued his life and the way in which this female was conducting herself made him realise, that he did not dare argue with her, she looked like she would fill him full of Slazer power, over and over again, to let off the pent up hurt for killing her man. He turned his head doing what Tayce requested. At this precise moment Jan's men and Jan himself burst into the room guns primed ready for action.

"Drop all your weapons, this room is surrounded, Tayce don't shoot him!" said Jan his eyes wide with alert.

"Give me one good reason why I shouldn't?" said Tayce keeping the gun primed.

"You want be doing yourself any justice, men like him expect to die," replied Jan.

329

One by one some of Jan's officers took quick control of the situation and apprehended Gardlens men. The rest of the men quickly moved between the hostages, to check that everyone was unharmed. Jan strode towards Gardlen with another officer, who quickly placed him in force field restraints, to be lead away. Jan turned to see Tayce standing in a shocked dazed state, she was still holding the gun. He realised that she was in shock and had to calmly get her to let him have the weapon.

"Tayce it's all over, he's going to pay for what he's done, give me the gun," he said putting his hands on hers and gently prizing her slim fingers lose of the weapon

Slowly he managed to get her to give him the gun and couldn't understand why she was acting like she was. He could see that she had been to hell and back by her strained features. He hadn't heard from Lydia that Tom Stavard had been killed by Gardlen, his only orders were, that there was a situation on Trinott and he was required to rescue the Amalthean Quests team. Glancing around he couldn't see Tom. He looked towards Marc, who looked down solemnly.

"Where's Tom?" he asked quietly without thought, glancing around

"He's dead Jan, Gardlen killed him," said Tayce slowly, then met his eyes with a sorrowful look.

"What! I'm truly sorry Tayce really I am," he said shaking his head, not knowing what to say.

He did something that he rarely did, he gave Tayce a warm understanding and comforting hug. Tayce let him she felt exhausted, she'd used the last ounce of energy on preparing to shoot Gardlen. Jan over her shoulder ordered his men that had hold of Gardlens men, to move out, take them back to the Patrol Cruiser, then his other officers who were with the hostages, he ordered them to escort the people and aliens back to their vessels, so that they could get under way. Cordec staggered over fighting the pain of his attack, at the hands of Gardlens thugs, wondering about his design. Tayce broke Jan's hold and walked over to the weapon on the floor, picking it up, she turned and walked back to Cordec with it.

"I think this belongs to you," said Tayce slowly, seeing that he was in hell with the pain, but putting on a good face.

"Young woman you've shown amazing courage, Chief Traun will hear of this, I'm just sorry that your husband had to die," he announced in an understanding tone.

"Me too, but you played a good part also, it was wrong what they did to you," replied Tayce.

Marc walked across to her, he slipped a friendly arm around her shoulders. She wavered and everything had become to much, she collapsed. Seeing Tom being killed right before her eyes was something that she would take a long time to come to terms with and would no doubt see in her dreams for the foreseeable future. Marc scooped her up in his strong arms and carried her on out. Jan stopped behind making sure that the situation was under control, for a moment and met them at the entrance to the room.

"Is she going to be all right?" asked Jan to Marc discretely.

"It will take a long time to heal, what has happened, but I think she'll pull through," assured Marc.

"Tell her, if she needs anyone to talk to, or any help whatsoever other than Chief Traun at Questa, tell her to look me up, my door is always open," he offered in a true friendly manner.

"Thanks, she'll appreciate that, I'll tell her," replied Marc.

He continued on leaving. Leaving behind Jan and his officers to take reports from Cordec Parglen and his designers of what had happened. Tricara remained behind with Jan Barnford, she was going to return to Questa with him, but had advised Marc to watch over Tayce and be there should she need someone to confide in. She felt terrible in a way, thinking that somehow Tom's death was not just Gardlens fault, if she had foreseen what was going happen, she could have stopped Tom from taking it into his head to protect her. She wondered if Tayce would see it the same way, she'd have to wait and treat the moment as it came, should it arise. Donaldo ran on ahead briskly to get on board Amalthea, he wanted to get everything ready for treating both Tayce and Treketa. Duncan walked beside Marc, not believing what they had just witnessed. Daniel Mayfield remained with Jan Barnford, as he was one of Jan's men and he would have to make a full account of the situation, being a first hand witness.

***

Tayce two dayons later, was sitting in her quarters, still shell shocked at what had happened. She did not even want to think of commanding the cruiser, she felt that when Amalthea got back to Questa there would be no point in commanding the Amalthean Quests Team, without Tom by her side and she was considering giving the command over to Marc Dayatso. As far as she was concerned, Tom who had helped her form the team was gone, there didn't seem any point of continuing to bring criminals to deserved justice, when he had just been killed by one. The quarters entrance doors announcement system chimed.

"Come in," said Tayce sighing, she did not want to be disturbed.

The doors drew open and Lance walked in, he came to a pause in the middle of the living area. He looked at her studying her saddened look, she had to snap out of this hurt, he understood what was going on, but she hadn't strayed out of her current surrounding for two dayons since she'd arrived back on board. As her long time friend he felt it wasn't good, he was concerned for her welfare staring at four walls. They had known each other since they were young, he was not going to let her fall into the pit of total despair.

"Forgive me for being forward here, but what your doing isn't doing you or anyone on this team any good, we all understand where your coming, from

331

Treketa is working with Donaldo to try and keep her thoughts occupied, even though Dons beginning to wonder if he should carry a permanent container of disposable wipes for Treketas sudden floods, but she's trying and so should you, sitting here is just making the memories make you more ill and as your long time friend, I am not going back to duty until you come too, I couldn't believe it when Midge told me you were thinking of throwing it all in, handing over to Marc, because I know you can pull through this, you've come to far and done to much, to throw it all away, Tom wouldn't want you to and I'm not going to let you," he pointed out firmly.

"I can't, don't ask me to," she blurted at him, standing to her feet, she walked away.

"If you don't continue, there are a lot of people still out in this Universe that would love to know that, because your not out here, they can do whatever they like, like before, take Dion for instance, if he's alive somewhere, he'll be laughing up his sleeve at the thought you weren't going to be around, to put a stop to him again."

"I know where your coming from, but I need time, Marc can do just as good as job as me, he was Father's aide and he's been trained for command," said Tayce turning to face him.

"Just promise me that your not going to give up Amalthean Quests for good, okay, I understand you need time, but please don't remain in these quarters, this is your Cruiser Tayce, you can go anywhere, one more thing…"

Lance didn't get a chance to finish what he was saying, the Telelinkphone sounded on the small table top at the end of the soffette. Tayce crossed leaving Lance standing in the centre of the living area. She picked up the handset and was much relieved to find out that it was Lydia, but the news was not good. Lydia had told her the cuts had run deeper in council spending and she wanted to see her urgently at Questa, everyone and the cruiser were to head back. Tayce agreed, she had a feeling that her future was about to be decided for her and it had suddenly been taken out of her hands. Lance studied her interested, what was wrong he thought?

"Problem?" he asked curious.

"We're to head back to Questa," replied Tayce in thought.

"Maybe this is what you need, maybe whatever is waiting, is going to make you re-access your life, where you really want to go from here," said Lance calmly.

"Will you tell Marc, we need to head to Questa."

"No, you can tell him, we'll go together," he persisted.

He reached out grabbing her hand and guided her over to the entrance of the living area. As the doors opened he dragged her out into the corridor. He knew that he was probably crossing the line in ordering her around, being his leader and a rank higher than himself, but he didn't care, this was the only way to pull her back to where she would thank him some dayon. He was glad in a way, they had been summoned to Questa, this would give Tayce something to think about, other than the sadness of Tom's demise.

***

Amalthea One was on the way back to Questa minus Tom Stavard, after several monthons of rescuing crews and bringing criminals to justice, at a comfortable travelling speed. But the uncertainty of the Amalthean Quests was hanging in the balance. Lydia Traun had been asked by the Planetary Matters Council to have an audience with her daughter on Amaltheas future. But what was that future?

Ingram Content Group UK Ltd.
Milton Keynes UK
UKHW041853170723
425312UK00001B/71